THE PORTAL EFFECT

THE EVARAN CHRONICLES

BOOK 10

ADAIR HART

Editing done by Eliza Dee
Cover done by Tom Edwards
Interior design done by Colleen Sheehan
Proofread done by Jade Hemming

Published by Quantum Edge Publishing

www.AdairHart.com

ISBN: 978-1-7327422-3-9

To get updates on new books and other notifications, sign up for my mailing list at:

www.AdairHart.com/MailingList.aspx

THE
PORTAL
EFFECT

THE STORY SO FAR

» In *The Arrival*, the Evaran Chronicles prequel, a space- and time-traveling being known as Evaran rescues Jake Melkins and Kathy from a Seceltor slaver named Greecho. It is Evaran's first adventure in the Milky Way galaxy and introduces him to Earth.

» In *The Awakening*, book 1 of the Evaran Chronicles, Dr. Albert Snowden and his niece, Emily Snowden, are abducted by an alien race known as the Krotovore. They are rescued by Evaran and V, Evaran's trusty mobile artificial intelligence, who drops them back off on Earth.

» In *The Fredorian Destiny*, book 2 of the Evaran Chronicles, Evaran returns to check on Dr.

Snowden and Emily, and they ask to travel with him. Evaran accepts. They then help Fredoria, a planet of human ex-slaves, become a full trade partner with the Kreagan Star Empire, the local galactic superpower in Earth's region of the galaxy. Hampered by Seeros and bounty hunters, they secure the Arkaron for the Fredorians to give to the Kreagan emperor.

» In *The Purification*, book 3 of the Evaran Chronicles, they fight the timeline invaders known as the Purifiers, a human-supremacist group led by the overlord that tries to change Earth's history.

» In *The Time Refugee*, book 4 of the Evaran Chronicles, they tangle with Billozein, a rogue time traveler, while helping Jane Trellis, a time refugee who is pulled out of her timeline.

» In *The Evaran Origin*, book 5 of the Evaran Chronicles, they discover Evaran's origin and meet Levaran, another one of Evaran's plane forms, while fighting the Time Wardens, a timeline-void race that hunts rift travelers.

» In *The Shadow Connection*, book 6 of the Evaran Chronicles, they group up with Jake Melkins and the nonhuman community to defend Earth from the ambitions of Caltorus, a dimensional being that rules over a vast empire encompassing worlds in many dimensions.

» In *The Human Factor*, book 7 of the Evaran Chronicles, they head to AD 10105 and deal with a ruthless AI known as Salazar, in addition to fixing the timeline.

» In *The Cosmic Parallel*, book 8 of the Evaran Chronicles, they leap from parallel timeline to timeline in a trap designed by the Mortani, plane refugees who blame Evaran for their situation.

» In *The Unification*, book 9 of the Evaran Chronicles, they travel to AD 514,723 to unify humanity while dealing with an extradimensional threat.

» This book continues their adventures.

EVARAN'S TECHNOLOGY

Torvatta—his disc-shaped ship that can travel through time and space. It is roughly fifteen feet tall by thirty feet wide. The interior contains six dimensional rooms, an open area with a semitransparent floor and sides, and a roof that can be transformed by hard holograms. A shielding around the Torvatta prevents most matter from entering.

Universal interface card (UIC)—a credit-card-sized device carried on his belt that allows access to most technological systems that do not have an artificial intelligence in them. It can also view limited information on biological systems.

Augmented reality interface (ARI)—an interface that only he can see around him.

Utility handle—a hilt-like device carried on his belt that can extend morphable matter in any shape, typically a baton or staff; can also fire repulsion, grappling, heat, mist, sticky globules, and stun beams.

Illumination orbs—small orbs on his belt that provide lighting and can hover.

Projection orb—an orb that allows projections to be sent to it from remote sources, such as Evaran's ring or the Torvatta.

Ring—a ring that can provide holographic projection and also scan.

PROLOGUE

Seeros-172 studied the projection over his desk, which displayed various parallel timelines and their unique signatures. Ever since Seeros-1 had discovered that there were parallel timelines, he had been busy retrieving other Seeroses.

Seeros-172 walked over to his large window and looked out. A plaza bustled with other Seeroses going about their day. To date, there were 2,419 Seeroses. The massive facility they had built resided on a planet in the timeline where they controlled the surrounding solar systems. Seeros-172 had come to call it home, and he implicitly trusted every other Seeros and regarded them as family.

He ran his pale hands over his silver hair. Although he enjoyed finding parallel timelines that might have other Seeroses, the process to find them was complicated. Through the process of trial and error, they had determined which timelines most likely had Seeroses in them, and by extension, the Antigulan species. Once a Seeros was found, they were extracted, although not all wanted to come back.

"Hey," said a voice behind him.

Seeros-172 spun around. "85. I wasn't expecting you so early."

Seeros-85 nodded. "Busy day as always. I saw that you identified another potential timeline."

"I have," said Seeros-172.

Seeros-85's beady eyes narrowed. "Something's bothering you."

"It's the extractor we're sending. Ziekah."

"Oh…yeah, she's rough."

Seeros-172 took a seat and then gestured for Seeros-85 to sit. "She…he…it. Ziekah doesn't really have a true physical form that we know of, although I guess Ziekah likes the female form. None of whatever species Ziekah is has a gender. Unfortunately, they're the only ones who can traverse the connection dimensions without dying."

"Connection dimensions? Is that what you're calling them?"

Seeros-172 chuckled. "I'm thankful that we found a dimension, and its connecting dimensions, that allows us travel to other timelines, and I know Ziekah's species helped the first Seeros through to here. I still think they have an ulterior motive."

"You worry too much," said Seeros-85.

"Of course I do, I'm a timeline analyst."

Seeros-85 studied the projection on Seeros-172's desk. "Speaking of which…why'd you pick this timeline? Looks likes there's several candidates."

Seeros-172 walked over and gestured at the holographic timeline. "It has all the identifiers that there's a Seeros there. However…there's something else that I've never seen before.

The exotic energy levels have the highest concentration that I've ever seen, and I don't recognize a large portion of them."

"So this is not only a retrieval mission, but a research one."

Seeros-172 nodded. "Now you see why I'm hesitant to send Ziekah there. She doesn't care much for research."

"You think she might come back and take all this over?"

Seeros-172 shrugged. "I don't know. Her species couldn't use the portals without our tech. Now they have that, and knowledge gleaned from working with us."

"They wouldn't dare try anything here. Our security AI and defense systems are top-notch," said Seeros-85, raising his head a bit.

"Then let's hope we never have to find out. It would be nice if we could do the investigations ourselves."

Seeros-85 chuckled. "You remember what happened to Seeros-221 when he went into the connection dimensions. Cockiest version of ourselves I've ever seen. He went in there with a full squad of our Silverguard defense robots, and he wore our most advanced defensive suit. He and his squad didn't even make it a third of the way to a portal. The creatures that live there are unlike anything I've seen. Without the extractor's guidance, it's a lost cause."

"To be fair, they fought a swarm of creatures that looked like they numbered in the millions. Not much you can do against that, and that was just one fight," said Seeros-172. He sighed as he pressed a button on his desk console. "I sent the mission over to Ziekah. Hopefully she's in and out like normal, and we get some new information to help us identify timelines better."

Seeros-85's eyes narrowed. "That timeline signature has the unique signature of the Time Wardens."

Seeros-172 grimaced. "Yeah. That's one case where having the connection dimension between us and any portal is a good thing. Natural defense."

"Right." Seeros-85 slapped Seeros-172 on the back. "In the meantime, you should see what 104 has made in the cafeteria."

They shared a laugh.

Seeros-172 was relieved that he did not have to physically talk to Ziekah. Something about her and her abilities always made his skin crawl. That, and her raspy voice always sounded sinister to him. If she found something worthy to hunt, she might not even come back. He wondered about the Seeros in that timeline and what his experience must have been. If everything went well, he would join the other Seeroses and could tell them himself.

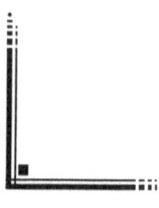

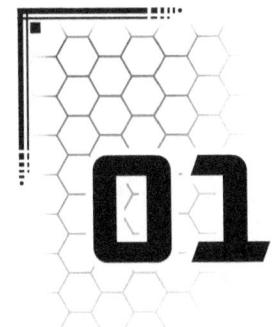

01

Dr. Albert Snowden could detect exotic matter and energy, but usually not from his college office. The odd aspect of the disturbance was it had enough power to wake him from a nap. Even stranger, he sensed V, a close friend who happened to be part artificial intelligence and had various body modes. The distinction between the two energies created an odd mix, like garbage and a scented candle. Dr. Snowden sat up in his chair. Something was not right.

He had been having a good dream about Kess, his girlfriend from the future, but it faded from memory. He stood and verified that his survival suit projected what he normally would wear to class. It was one of his favorite enhancements. The suit had become like a second skin to him, and with another recent enhancement, he felt raw dimensional power course around him.

A quick check at his desk clock showed it to be about 7:30 p.m. He grabbed his personal support device and opened a communication channel to Evaran.

A small holographic screen showing Evaran's head appeared above Dr. Snowden's PSD. "Is everything okay?"

"I'm not sure," said Dr. Snowden. He looked around. "I was napping, but something woke me up. I...sensed some type of exotic energy, but I don't recognize it."

Evaran's eyes narrowed. "I will come to you."

"I think I'm okay. Have you sensed anything unusual?"

"I have not," said Evaran.

"Where are you at?" asked Dr. Snowden.

"I am at Lord Noskov's base with Jake Melkins."

Dr. Snowden exhaled from his nose. "Oh, all right. Is V with you?"

The projection zoomed out and showed V in projected mode. "I am here."

"Okay," said Dr. Snowden. He grinned. "I thought I sensed you out here too. It's probably my late lunch acting up. No need to come out here. I'll head home."

Evaran eyed Dr. Snowden. "Are you sure?"

Jake Melkins, with his fair skin and black hair, popped into view. "We could pick you up and have a cookout."

Dr. Snowden chuckled. "As appetizing as that sounds, I think I'll continue my nap at home."

"Okay," said Evaran. "We are here if you need us."

The projection dissipated.

Dr. Snowden sighed as he looked around his office, usually a refuge after teaching classes, but not tonight. The strange energy presence seemed to have gotten stronger. He packed up his traveling bag with various items, then slung the strap over his shoulder. Perhaps continuing his nap at home was all he needed.

His office door opened as he approached it.

A woman in a formfitting black suit with silver lines segmenting it stepped through.

Dr. Snowden studied the woman with her red hair, pale skin, and dimly lit green eyes. Her outfit appeared suitable for mobility, and the thin light gray pads across the body looked like they were able to take a hit or two. Dark blue spaulders resided on her shoulders while a slim silver belt rested on her hips. She was obviously not human and reminded him of a futuristic ninja with her metallic shin and forearm wraps.

"Who are you?" he asked.

"Ziekah," she said in a somewhat raspy and calm voice. She pointed at his chair. "Sit. We're going to talk, me and you."

Dr. Snowden grabbed his PSD and attempted to contact Evaran.

Ziekah tapped at her left shoulder spaulder, which shimmered with various glowing lines. "Your communication device, while advanced, isn't contacting anybody." She motioned at his seat again. "Sit."

"Listen. I don't care what you want, or why you're here, but you should leave," said Dr. Snowden.

Ziekah laughed. "Oh…humans. Always a flair for the dramatic. Fine, stand, but you will talk with me."

Dr. Snowden did not like the superiority complex thing Ziekah had going on. It was apparent that she had singled him out for some reason. Perhaps she wanted his nanobots, or even information on Evaran. Whatever it was, she would not get it.

"You might be surprised that I know you as the great Dr. Albert Snowden," said Ziekah. She looked him up and down. "Your appearance seems to contradict that assessment. However...I sense dimensional and other types of energy swirling around you. You're human...and more."

"Is that why you're here?"

"No. I'm here because of what you did to someone I'm looking for."

Dr. Snowden's eyes narrowed. "And who would that be?"

"Seeros."

A cold chill swept through Dr. Snowden. It had been a long while since he had heard that name, but he had not forgotten how powerful Seeros was. "He's dead."

"Oh, I know. You see...I travel the timelines, looking for versions of Seeros. This timeline's version is dead, and I hunt those who wronged him before taking him out of the timeline. Although the Malazim directly killed him, you and your friends put him in that position. I've already dealt with the Malazim. Now I'm here to deal with the other half."

Dr. Snowden wrinkled his brow. The concept of there being multiple Seeroses sounded like a nightmare. Even more alarming was that she said she had dealt with the Malazim. They had almost killed him long ago. He knew them as a race of powerful dimensional beings with the ability to infect those in this reality before twisting the flesh to do their bidding.

"So you're here to kill me?" he asked.

"No. You aren't the brains of the group. That would be Evaran. He is the main game I hunt, and you...the bait."

"I wouldn't suggest doing whatever it is you're planning."

Ziekah eyed Dr. Snowden. "Is that so?"

He raised his PSD and fired a stun beam.

She dodged it and leapt across the desk, kicking him in the chest.

He sprawled back into the wall.

"I wouldn't try that again," she said.

He grabbed his PSD from the floor where it had fallen. Her kick would have crushed a normal human's chest. He jumped up and shoved her away using his left forearm energy shield.

She slid back and raised her head a bit. "Impressive. Not many could do that."

Dr. Snowden had to get out of there. The office was not an ideal place to fight, and she seemed much tougher than her appearance led him to believe. He rushed over to the window and jumped through. As he fell, he shot a grappling beam at a nearby tree and used it to slow down to a graceful landing. He looked up.

Ziekah appeared in the window and extended her arm. "You think you can outrun me? I have another idea…"

Dr. Snowden closed his PSD and stood. His eyes widened when a green circle formed under him. It reminded him of the portals the Torvatta, Evaran's ship, used when traveling long distances.

"I'll see you…earlier," she said, smiling.

Dr. Snowden fell through the circle. He tried to get a bearing on the pure darkness around him, but a moment later, he crash-landed on the side of a dirt road. The dark skies indicated it was nighttime, and crisp air rolled around him. He paused to catch his breath and stood. The moon's brightness caught this attention. An earthy smell of the forest wafted through the air.

He verified he had his PSD and projected a communication window. Evaran needed to be updated while there was time. Ziekah might appear at any moment. He tapped at Evaran's icon.

The PSD showed no signal.

He tried to reach Emily.

No signal.

His heart beat faster. He attempted to see if the PSD could even verify if the Torvatta was near.

A small connection icon appeared briefly before showing no signal.

He sighed. Wherever he was, the Torvatta had not responded. Contacting anyone seemed not to be an option either. He raised his helmet and dissipated his holographic suit before activating his camouflage shielding. His chest hurt from Ziekah's kick, and he hoped Evaran and the others were ready for when Ziekah visited them, as it sounded like her plan. He understood why she had portaled him away: one less factor to deal with when hunting Evaran. His eyes surveyed the environment. It was time to find out where he was.

Emily inhaled the fresh air as she walked through the park. Although it was nighttime, the well-lit pathway was one she had taken hundreds of times. A study group session with her and three others had been refreshing and made her feel normal. While traveling with Evaran was great, she sometimes got lost in the adventures. She smiled as she remembered her father telling her never to forget her roots.

Life had been good to her the last month. She had joined Dr. Bryson and his fiancée, Karen, as they had visited the Wild Haven Institute for classes on the nonhuman world and how to interact with the human one. The atmosphere there seemed unusual, with all sorts of nonhumans, and even some aliens, attending.

There existed many types of beings she had not been aware of. The classes stimulated her, and watching Dr. Bryson joke around had been entertaining. Karen much less so. She was uptight and unsure of how to take everything in, but Emily understood how disorienting learning about nonhumans could be.

Emily also enjoyed spending time with both Jennifer and Jelton Stallryn. While Emily was close with Jelton, they did not engage in physical contact much. They interacted mostly through mental bonding. Definitely fun, but sometimes she wanted more.

Jennifer satisfied the physical aspect. Emily understood now why Fredorians, the human ex-slave civilization she had helped boost long ago, used relationship groups instead of being monogamous. It allowed for different types of relationships among group members. Emily's group consisted of Jennifer, Jelton, and Andia Kiggs, the Fredorian she had met long ago but had not seen in a while. It was not lost on Emily that her relationships were scattered across time and space.

One of the lamps flickered, causing the area around her to temporarily darken.

She paused. Something was off. She did a quick check to make sure her survival suit had the right hologram on it. Out of instinct, she checked that her PSD was within reach.

Dr. Snowden teased her about always being ready to fight. Traveling with Evaran meant there were targets on their backs, and she remembered being on a prison planet unprepared. That would never happen again. *Ever.*

The lamp stopped flickering.

She sighed. Although the light seemed to be back to normal, she sensed an unusual energy. She thought she detected V, but whatever the odd energy was, it overpowered that.

She looked around. "V?"

Silence.

She grabbed her PSD and held it in her right hand. It did not hurt to be ready to fight. After focusing, she detected a slight disturbance in the air. She spun to her right while raising her left forearm shield.

An elongated arrow-like projectile bounced off her energy shield.

Emily extended her PSD into a baton.

A woman with a formfitting black suit segmented by silver lines walked out from behind a tree.

Emily aimed her PSD forward. "Who are you?"

"Ziekah."

"Did you shoot an arrow at me?"

"Dart, actually," said Ziekah.

Emily's eyes narrowed. Nonhumans knew not to mess with her since that meant Evaran would get involved. Ziekah's energy registered as one Emily had never sensed before.

"You were supposed to get hit, then fall asleep," said Ziekah.

Emily snorted. "Whatever. Why'd you attack me?"

"To use you as bait. Evaran is difficult to find, but you and your uncle...not quite as hard. Your uncle showed me that you and he are not as you appear."

"What'd you do to Uncle Albert!" said Emily, gritting her teeth.

"Tried to capture him, of course. He's a lot stronger than he appears, and faster too. I wasn't expecting that. No matter. He won't be bothering anyone anymore."

Emily attempted to contact Dr. Snowden and Evaran.

"That won't work," said Ziekah, tapping at her left shoulder spaulder. Glowing lines appeared on it.

Emily's heartbeat ramped up. This woman clearly wanted a fight. All bets were off if she harmed Dr. Snowden.

"Now, why don't you surrender? I'll even let you call Evaran. All you need to do is give me your…weapon, and we can sort all this out," said Ziekah.

"I'm not giving you anything!"

Ziekah chuckled. "Just like your uncle. Stubbornness must run in the family."

Emily fired a repulsion blast at Ziekah.

Ziekah rolled out of the way and shot another dart at Emily.

Emily knocked it away with her baton and charged forward. When she reached Ziekah, she hit her point-blank with a stun beam.

Ziekah shuddered for a moment. She yelled as a pulse of white light radiated out from her.

Emily flew back. After standing, she charged again.

"Impressive," said Ziekah. "You're even faster and stronger than your uncle. I clearly misjudged you as well."

When Emily approached, she hit Ziekah with a point-blank repulsion blast.

Ziekah tumbled back. She got to her feet, shaking her head. Smudges of green blood appeared on her cheek. "You… actually hurt me."

"I'm going to do a lot more if you hurt Uncle Albert! I'm taking you down! You're gonna talk to Evaran."

Ziekah's breathing increased. She tapped at her left shoulder spaulder. "Contact him, then."

Emily faced Ziekah and opened a communication window from her PSD. That allowed Emily to keep an eye on Ziekah while operating the PSD. Evaran's icon illuminated. She tapped at it.

"Emily. Is everything okay?" asked Evaran.

"No, I'm under attack by someone named Ziekah, and Uncle Albert isn't responding," said Emily.

"I see. We are on our way," said Evaran.

The communication window disappeared.

A moment later, the Torvatta appeared in the sky and streaked toward Emily's location.

Emily smiled. Evaran must have calculated the time to get from orbit to her location. With that information, he could travel back in time so he could arrive at that moment. She loved time travel.

"Ahh, he appears. Finally," said Ziekah.

"I wouldn't be so cocky if I were you," said Emily.

Ziekah laughed.

"You're awfully confident for someone who's about to be judged."

Ziekah's eyes flared. "Judged...like how he judged Seeros?"

"Seeros?" asked Emily. A chill swept through her.

"Put him on a slab to die by the filthy Malazim? The details are sketchy...but I know you were there. However, it's obvious Evaran made that decision. You're simply a lackey. A human one at that, although you *are* full of surprises."

Emily clenched her jaw. Seeros was a timeline refugee that had sought out Evaran for revenge. As powerful as Seeros had been, she and the others had been able to take him down.

"Why do you care what happened to Seeros?" asked Emily, glancing up for a moment to verify that the Torvatta still approached.

"Because he is to be extracted from this timeline. Unfortunately, it appears that due to the random nature of how I enter timelines, I've been placed in a period after his death. I can fix that…but not if a time-traveling group is meddling around. I also exact revenge on those who killed Seeros, directly and indirectly, such as you."

The Torvatta hovered over Emily.

"And time is up," said Ziekah. She smiled as she motioned in circles with her hands.

A green circle appeared under Emily.

Emily's eyes widened as she fell through. Everything became dark. She crash-landed on a forest floor and paused to catch her breath. As she surveyed her surroundings, she tried to reach Evaran. His icon had grayed out. It seemed off that she could connect to the Torvatta but it did not respond to her.

She closed her eyes and focused. The smells were definitely those of the forest, and the noises of bugs and other normal sounds made her think she was really in a forest and not a mirage. She opened her eyes and tapped a nearby tree. Solid. Wherever her location, it was not a pathway in a park.

She sighed. Alone. Again. It seemed to be a reoccurring theme that displeased her. Not being able to contact Evaran or anyone else was never a good sign, but the Torvatta rejecting her connection made her uneasy.

Her next step was uncertain, but with her PSD, she had food and water and basic necessities covered. Memories of being on the prison planet flashed through her mind. The difference was that this time, she had an upgraded suit and PSD and was ready for whatever came her way.

02

V, in projected mode, had enjoyed his time at Lord Noskov's base in the Appalachian Mountains. However, the call from Dr. Snowden and Emily troubled V. Jake Melkins had joined the group as they had rushed to the Torvatta command center. V had calculated that it would take twenty minutes to get from orbit to where Emily was, so Evaran had taken the Torvatta back in time while stealthed. It was uncommon for Evaran to be in the same period and location as another timeline version of himself, but V understood why Evaran had done it.

Although they had arrived almost immediately after Emily had contacted them, she had already fallen through a green circle, which had closed up. Ziekah moved her hands in circles at some trees nearby. The Torvatta did not register Emily anywhere, but it did identify two more portals opening somewhere and closing. V ran through several other detection systems and only found traces of whatever the portal was and the exotic energy on Ziekah.

"Whoa, what just happened?" asked Jake, staring out through the transparent front half of the ship.

Evaran rubbed his chin. "I am unsure, but it would seem Emily traveled through a portal."

"I didn't even know that was possible."

"Although we cannot be teleported, pushing us through a portal is possible," said Evaran. His eyes narrowed. "V, show the Torvatta and project me in front of Ziekah, as she calls herself."

"Acknowledged," said V.

He interacted with the Torvatta's systems and made a small rod extend out of a black panel on the exterior right side.

A projection of Evaran stood before Ziekah a moment later.

"So you are real," said Ziekah, studying the hologram.

V determined that she had dimensional energy, but also a hint of rift energy on her, and another exotic one that was not identified. That should not be possible.

"I am," said Evaran. "Where did you send Emily?"

"I'll be honest...I don't know. That's not how my ability works."

"You open portals to destinations unknown?"

"Sorta," said Ziekah, smiling. "Why don't you come out here and we can talk?"

"I do not think so. I suspect you would try to create a portal under me. Did you do this with Dr. Snowden?"

Ziekah laughed. "I sure did. I'll admit...they surprised me. Not quite human anymore, are they? They get to live... yet Seeros had to die."

"Seeros...why do you mention him?"

"Because I'm supposed to extract him from this timeline. Unfortunately…you killed him. That's a problem, one I will fix. Your ship is now known to me, and more importantly, the energy signature of it."

In the command center, Evaran gestured at V. "I have paused my interaction with the hologram. Prepare to use the tractor beam on her. We are going to bring her on board and let the Torvatta dampen her abilities."

"You're bringing her here?" asked Jake. "Is that wise?"

"Yes, unless she can defy the Torvatta. I do not think that is possible."

Jake exhaled as he shook his head. "If she could, she's much more powerful than she's letting on."

"I concur," said Evaran. He interacted with his chair console, then nodded at V.

V made the hologram active again.

Evaran's hologram eyed Ziekah. "Your actions have made you a priority. You will be coming with us until we find out where Dr. Snowden and Emily are. I would also like to learn more about why you are involved with Seeros."

"Some things are better left unsaid. This is one of those instances," said Ziekah.

In the command center, Evaran motioned at V.

A tractor beam shot out and encapsulated Ziekah. She began to rise.

Ziekah chuckled. "Not my first tractor beam. Nonetheless, we will meet again. You've given me the gift of information." She moved her hands in circles.

A portal formed above her, cutting off the beam. She fell into another portal below her. The portals closed.

V had not anticipated Ziekah's action, and by Evaran's silence, it was evident that he did not either. A profile was being built on Ziekah, and the ability to form portals was a powerful one.

"Wow, that was crazy," said Jake.

Evaran stood and stared outside for a moment. He faced V. "Take us to thirty minutes before Dr. Snowden's call. You can use stealth mode to observe what happened at his office, but no interaction. Afterward, we will do that with Emily as well."

V tilted his head. "You are angry."

"No. Concerned. Dr. Snowden and Emily are gone, and I do not know where they are. The person responsible is also missing."

Jake raised his head. "I guess if we hop back and aren't detected, everything's good, right?"

Evaran nodded.

"So we couldn't nab Dr. Snowden and Emily before Ziekah met them?"

"No, that would cause a timeline change. Ziekah has set events in motion, and we are a part of them now. Although I am willing to bend my rules for observation, I will not initiate direct action unless it is an alternate timeline or an extreme scenario. Neither applies to this situation currently."

Jake chuckled. "I got ya."

V tapped at the front console.

Twenty minutes later and they were in low Earth orbit.

"Engaging stealth mode and scan mode one," said V.

After a moment, everything outside the Torvatta faded away before easing back in.

"Analysis. We are thirty minutes before Dr. Snowden's call."

"Good," said Evaran. "Take us to his office. Once there, you can use orb mode and stealth."

"Acknowledged."

The Torvatta descended and, after twenty minutes, hovered outside the building Dr. Snowden's office was in.

V switched to orb mode. "I will be back."

Evaran and Jake nodded.

V shimmered out of view as he flew off the Torvatta. He had to put some effort into reallocating his processing since an inordinate amount was spent on containing a strong emotion. Dr. Snowden and Emily could be hurt, and for the moment, not much was known other than that Ziekah and portals were involved. V paused to compartmentalize his inner container's pulses. It affected his current focus.

When a student exited the building, V took the opportunity to fly in. He had been to Dr. Snowden's office many times, and it was not lost on V how unusual this scenario was. Stealthy investigations were not new, but doing one in the context of Dr. Snowden's immediate past was. If V were detected, it could cause issues. He hovered a bit away from Dr. Snowden's office door.

"Ziekah's energy signature has been detected," said V.

"Yes, although it appears she has not reached Dr. Snowden's office yet," said Evaran.

V listened in as Dr. Snowden contacted Evaran.

"Wait a moment," said Jake. "How is it that Dr. Snowden contacted us in this time period, and not us here now?"

"He is in sync with the version of us at this point in time," said Evaran.

V enjoyed listening to Evaran and Jake talk. Jake was intensely curious, and V had spent a lot of time with Jake learning about Earth customs. In a sense, Jake was V's study buddy.

"Analysis. Ziekah has appeared and is entering Dr. Snowden's office. I am following her," said V.

He flew to the entrance of the office and recorded the exchange between Ziekah and Dr. Snowden. When he jumped out the window, V flew outside and watched Dr. Snowden get portaled away.

"That sucks," said Jake.

"V, come back to the Torvatta. We will fly over to where Emily met Ziekah."

"Acknowledged."

After V returned, the Torvatta flew to the edge of the park that Emily had called from.

"This is as close as we can get without her detecting us," said Evaran. He glanced at V. "Go, but stay a safe distance away. Ziekah's presence should obfuscate your detection. Also, as you are aware, she opened portals after Emily fell through hers. Avoid those at all costs."

"Acknowledged," said V.

He shimmered out of view and flew off the Torvatta, then followed Emily. When he scanned the area, he noted that Emily seemed to sense him. Ziekah was nearby and he had detected her. His inner container pulsed as he watched Ziekah take aim.

Ziekah tried to hit Emily with a dart before they fought.

V's inner container surged. It was hard to stand by and watch Emily in danger.

"Steady," said Evaran over comms.

"I apologize. I am finding it difficult not to intervene."

"We must not," said Evaran.

V's lights dimmed. He could see the Torvatta command center in a window and noted that Evaran had a serious look, although it would be hard for anyone not close to him to know that.

Jake pointed at the Torvatta from earlier as it arrived. "There we are…in the past."

"Yes," said Evaran. His eyes searched the ground for a moment. "This Ziekah seems to be tied to Seeros, but her signature has dimensional and rift energy, as well as an unknown one around her. I suspect the unknown energy is what allows her to form portals."

"So what's our next step?" asked Jake.

"Research," said Evaran.

"Outside of you, who's an expert on dimensional, rift, or that other energy?"

Evaran half smiled. "I know someone who may be able to help."

After Emily was gone, Ziekah looked into the sky in V's direction and moved her hands in circles. "You can go away too."

V tried to escape, but a portal opened in front of him. He swerved to the side and flew through another portal that appeared.

⋯⋯▪▪▪════════════════════════▪▪⋯⋯

Jelton Stallryn, a Rift Guardian Deathless Riftblade and commander of the Ravaw, an elite unit of the Rift Guardians, smiled as he pulled his energy blade out of a dead Time Warden, a timeline void species that Emily, his girlfriend, referred to as metal spiders. It had been a tough fight. The sliver of cosmic energy that ran through him made it appear as if the Time Wardens moved in slow motion.

He had Evaran to thank for that. Although Jelton was second-in-command over all Rift Guardians, he still led the unit he came from into battle from time to time.

This fight was personal since it related to the Rift Guardian's first colony. He had selected the site and the people and had assisted with logistics. The Time Wardens had appeared and attacked the colony. Although he had removed their timeplex long ago, which prevented new Time Wardens from entering the timeline, many still existed in the timeline and rifts. The Time Warden anchor station he was on had been identified as where the Time Wardens came from.

Bahala, Jelton's second, approached. "A good fight."

Jelton nodded and then raised his blade.

The Ravaw in the room cheered.

He lowered his blade.

"Casualties?" asked Jelton.

"Twenty-four," said Bahala.

Jelton grimaced. "And the colony?"

"Gone."

Jelton closed his eyes for a moment. He had arrived too late. Although the colony possessed defenses, the Time Warden onslaught had been too much. He would not allow the next colony to make that mistake. How the Time Wardens had found the colony remained a mystery, one he would need to solve.

"All right. Gather up our wounded and dead, and send an information extraction team here. I want to learn everything there is to know about this anchor station," he said.

"Yes, sir. Also…you have a meeting request at headquarters," said Bahala.

"From who?"

"Evaran."

Bahala and the other Rift Guardians in the room knelt.

Jelton perked up. That was not something he had expected anytime soon. Although he enjoyed Emily coming to visit, Evaran visiting seemed unusual. The Rift Guardians viewed Evaran and Syrilus, his partner-turned-plane, as gods. Jelton contained a sliver of what made Evaran unique, and after being resurrected, the Rift Guardians viewed Jelton as a demigod. His eyes swept over the Ravaw. They showed reverence at the mere mention of Evaran's name.

"Rise," he said. He gestured at Bahala. "Inform headquarters I'm on my way."

Bahala nodded as he and the others stood.

Jelton walked through the remains of the Time Wardens in the room. It seemed they would need to take a back seat to whatever Evaran needed. If he had made a request to meet, it must be important. On the upside, Jelton looked forward to seeing Evaran and the gang again.

After boarding a transport, he was on his way back to the dimension that housed the Rift Guardian's headquarters. The recent battle weighed heavily on him, and the loss of even a few Ravaw concerned him. They were hard to recruit and train. One of the names on the list of the dead was Gavalt, a fierce fighter that had served with Evaran when fighting the Mortani. That event had had even more losses, but the stakes had also been much higher. Jelton sighed and eased back into his chair.

He reached the Rift Guardian's headquarters an hour later. Normally he would be glad to visit what had become his home for so long. This return was different. While happy to meet Evaran, Jelton dreaded reporting to Gowldin, the supreme leader of the Rift Guardians. Jelton checked his light armor. The last thing Evaran probably wanted to be reminded of was the Time Wardens.

Jelton surveyed his office and verified it was ready for visitors. He would contact Gowldin afterward, as a visit from Evaran always took higher precedence. Jelton tapped at his desk console.

"Send Evaran and the others in," he said.

"Yes, sir," said a male voice.

Jelton smiled when Evaran strolled in. He never seemed to change, and looked exactly like he did from their previous encounter. The gray suit with shiny metallic boots, forearms, and belt were offset by the dark gray segmented armor pads.

"Evaran! It's good to see you again, my friend," said Jelton, performing a Rift Guardian salute, which consisted of crossing his arms in an X pattern across his chest. He eyed the young male next to Evaran. "I'm afraid I haven't met your friend."

Evaran gestured at the young male. "Jake Melkins was the first human I met when I arrived on Earth."

"Hey," said Jake with a wave.

Jelton nodded at Jake. "Emily has mentioned you. It's good to meet you, and any friend of Evaran is a friend of mine." He peered behind Evaran. "Where's Dr. Snowden, Emily, and V?"

Evaran raised his head a bit. "That is why I am here. I do not know where they are."

Jelton's stomach churned. Those words should never be heard from someone like Evaran, who had the capability to go anywhere. "That...doesn't sound good." He gestured at some chairs before his desk. "Please, sit."

They complied.

Jelton sat. "How can I help?"

Evaran nodded. "A mysterious being portaled them away." He pulled out a small orb and tossed it into the air.

The orb projected the encounters.

Jelton studied the projections. He frowned when Dr. Snowden jumped out of a window and then went through a portal. His eyes narrowed when Emily fell through one as well. V had just disappeared. The being named Ziekah, who had various data labels attached to her, must be sensitive to beings around her.

"I didn't observe V go through a portal."

Evaran nodded. "We registered two portals out of sight. I suspect one changed V's direction, and the other sent him through when he swerved."

Jelton shook his head. "This Ziekah seems powerful."

"I concur, and I assume you noticed a part of Ziekah's energy signature is rift-based," said Evaran.

Jelton nodded. "Her signature, at least that aspect, is not unknown to us. We encountered a creature with a similar one, although we never identified the unknown energy. We assume that is something from the nightmare lands."

Jake's eyes widened. "Umm...nightmare lands?"

Jelton chuckled. "It's not as bad as it seems." He looked at Evaran. "I believe you have a Hazgrodah in your timeline. That's not a good thing."

"I am not familiar with that species," said Evaran.

The projection ended.

"It's less a species than a class of beings. Let me start with some history. Several centuries ago, we fought a Hazgrodah through space and time. It took on a male humanoid form, and was deceptively clever. We became aware of his presence because he trashed a Time Warden anchor station. Thinking we had a new ally, we tried to talk to him. He asked us where Seeros was, and we told him we had no idea. He then killed a few Rift Guardians and escaped."

"Seeros? Interesting," said Evaran as he rubbed his chin. "We destroyed Seeros in our timeline."

"And who is he?" asked Jelton.

"A timeline refugee that hunted me," said Evaran. "He was unsuccessful."

"I remember Seeros as a big-time city builder," said Jake.

Evaran nodded. "Unfortunately, he used that as cover to gather resources for my hunt." He faced Jelton. "Did your Hazgrodah mention anything about why he hunted Seeros?"

"No, but it seems from this video that Seeros is being extracted from timelines for some purpose."

Evaran's eyes narrowed. "Most likely not a good one. How did you defeat your Hazgrodah?"

"We didn't. It took a while, but we chased him to a portal on a remote world. Although the surface looked like a cliff behind a waterfall, we detected the strange rift readings. Some Rift Guardians pursued the Hazgrodah through the portal. Out of ten highly trained soldiers, one came back, and he had a video feed of what we call the nightmare lands. Fiendish creatures, hostile environment, and red rivers. The nine that died had been completely destroyed by what looked like a massive walking tree with branches that moved like whips."

Jake shuddered. "Sounds like hell."

"I don't know if that translated right, but I agree, a bad place," said Jelton. "We sealed the entrance on the world, and left monitoring devices in case it ever reopened."

He remembered when he had first viewed the video feed of the nightmare lands. It appeared as if someone had placed massive irregularly shaped rock cones with bubbling red rivers running between them. The dark gray clouds and red illumination made it hard to see anything. The nightmare lands were a maze.

"May we view the footage?" asked Evaran.

Jelton nodded. He interacted with his desk console.

After a moment, a projection shot up.

"Wow, that is horrifying," said Jake.

"I agree, my friend," said Jelton.

"Did your Hazgrodah create any portals or anything?" asked Jake.

"Not that I'm aware of, but those readings are very similar. At the very least, I think you're dealing with a creature native to the nightmare lands."

Evaran rubbed his chin. "Intriguing. Based on your readings, the nightmare lands are a connection dimension to a junction one. That would explain her unknown energy."

"I'm...not familiar with those terms," said Jelton.

"A connection dimension is a realm that connects a reality, like yours or ours, to a junction dimension. The junction dimension itself is created when the universe was formed, and the dimension can connect to many timelines, as well as other dimensions. I do not believe the Rift Guardians you sent in made it to the junction dimension, but instead returned after being in the connection one."

Jelton ran a hand over his mouth. "Are Dr. Snowden, Emily, and V in the connection or the junction dimension?"

"I do not believe they are in either," said Evaran. "Ziekah's portal had a space-time rift signature, not a dimensional one. They are somewhere in the timeline still."

"Then we must find them," said Jelton. His gaze swept over Jake and Evaran. "I'm coming with you, but I need to report to Gowldin first."

03

Dr. Snowden walked down the dirt path he had landed near. Over the last hour, he had learned more about his environment. He had checked the stars' positions using a PSD program and verified that he was on Earth. It surprised him to see AD 1842. The time also showed 8:50 p.m., which was an hour later than he thought it was supposed to be. Although the program did not tell him his location, he figured he would run into civilization at some point if he followed the road. His knowledge of the 1840s was sketchy at best. Emily would spew a ton of information if present.

He wondered if Ziekah had gone after Emily. His blood boiled to think that this might happen to her as well. He put it out of his mind as he trudged on down the road.

After another thirty minutes, he heard the approach of heavy breathing and what sounded like horse hooves hitting the ground. He recalled the light orb he had launched earlier. Once he retrieved it, he stood off to the side of the path. His camouflage shielding should allow him to remain hidden unless whatever came by had heightened senses.

A dark-skinned man hustled down the road.

Dr. Snowden studied the man's coarse shirt and pants. It looked like something Dr. Snowden would make if he had to create clothing out of raw cloth. Blood stained the right side of the man's face, and his shoes had seen better days. Given the time period, Dr. Snowden wondered if the man was a slave, which would put the location somewhere in a southern state most likely. Why the man ran down a dark road was a mystery. Dr. Snowden stepped forward to get a better look.

The twig snapping under his foot caused the man to falter and fall to the ground.

Dr. Snowden grimaced. He figured the man might have thought a wild animal caused the sound.

Two men on horseback chased down the fallen man.

"There you are, boy," said one of the riders.

"Please," said the fallen man, shielding his body with his right arm.

"Trying to run away, are we?" asked the other rider.

The fallen man whimpered. "I'm sorry."

"You'll be more than that when we get you back."

Dr. Snowden scowled. It definitely sounded like the man on the ground was a slave, and the riders were slave owners or catchers. Dr. Snowden determined that he would interfere in this instance, since the man had fallen due to Dr. Snowden's mistake. He wondered what Evaran would do.

Dr. Snowden deactivated his camouflage shielding, lowered his helmet, and stepped out of the bushes. A quick check verified that his holographic suit still had his brown suit up.

The horses neighed and backed up.

"Leave him alone," said Dr. Snowden.

One of the men lowered a double shotgun at Dr. Snowden. "And who are you?"

"Dr. Albert Snowden."

"Well…Doctor, this doesn't concern you. Begone!"

Dr. Snowden's eyes narrowed. "No…but you should leave."

The men laughed.

Dr. Snowden stood between the men and the slave. "I'm going to guess you're slave owners or catchers or something like that."

One of the men eyed Dr. Snowden. "You must be a damn Yankee and one of them abolishists or whatever. Hiding in the bushes is what I'd expect from you."

"Abolitionist is the term you're looking for. However, yes, I'm from the north."

"Yer in the wrong place, then," said the other man. He waved his shotgun off to the side. "Now, git moving!"

Dr. Snowden shook his head. "Sorry, that's not happening."

He raised his left arm across his chest. If the shotgun fired, his forearm shield would activate, hopefully before the pellets hit him. Although he hoped it would not come to that, these men were not backing down.

"Final warning," said the man, lowering his shotgun. "I don't wanna waste pellets on a white man if I don't have to."

Dr. Snowden scowled as he pulled out his PSD with his right arm and extended it into a baton. He shot a repulsion blast at the area before the horses.

The horses reared back. The rider with the shotgun fell off while the other one tried to calm his horse down.

Dr. Snowden hit the rider on the ground with a stun beam.

The man cried before going limp.

Dr. Snowden aimed at the other slaver, who had hopped off his horse, which had promptly bolted along with the other one.

"Take your friend, and go," said Dr. Snowden.

The man trembled as he picked up the other stunned man. "What...what are you?"

Dr. Snowden raised his head. "A traveler who helps those in need. Now go!"

The man hobbled down the road with the other rider over his shoulder.

Dr. Snowden turned toward the slave. "Are you all right?"

The slave cowered. "Please...please don't hurt me." A tear ran down his cheek.

"I mean you no harm, and I come in peace," said Dr. Snowden. He almost chuckled thinking about how aliens in future fictional media would say that. "What's your name?"

"Kuda."

Dr. Snowden put his hand on his chest. "I'm Dr. Albert Snowden, but you can call me Dr. Snowden." He offered to help Kuda up.

Kuda studied Dr. Snowden's hand for a moment before accepting it.

Dr. Snowden smiled. "You're safe."

"They'll be back." Kuda's eyes scouted the environment. "What are you?"

"A traveler. I try to help those in need, such as yourself," said Dr. Snowden. His eyes narrowed. "Where were you running to?"

Kuda licked his lips and looked down.

Dr. Snowden rubbed his chin. "I understand if you don't want to tell me, but if you did, I could take you there."

"W-where did you come from?" asked Kuda, looking back up.

"From...far away. I arrived recently, actually," said Dr. Snowden. "I'm guessing those guys wanted to take you back to wherever you ran away from."

Kuda nodded. He pointed at Dr. Snowden's shield. "What's that?"

"Oh," said Dr. Snowden. He retracted his shield. "A new item they're working on in the north." He rubbed his chin. "Where are we exactly?"

"Outside Natchez, Mississippi."

Dr. Snowden sighed. "Okay, so 1840s Natchez, Mississippi. The Underground Railroad was active here if I recall."

Kuda cocked his head.

"It's okay if you don't want to tell me about it, but if you're headed to a stop, I can take you. I just don't know where it is."

Kuda raised his head. "It's some walking. And dangerous."

Dr. Snowden nodded. "What if I told you I could get you there safe and without being detected?"

"How?"

"I have a way of getting there, but I don't want to startle you. Are you ready?"

Kuda nodded.

Dr. Snowden extended his PSD and formed a flying platform. He observed Kuda as the platform had formed. Although Kuda seemed surprised, Dr. Snowden figured Kuda was probably relieved about not being returned. Dr. Snowden opened a guardrail and gestured for Kuda to step on.

"Step in, and we'll be on our way," said Dr. Snowden.

"What is that?" asked Kuda, eying the platform.

"Another thing they're working on in the north. Normally I wouldn't show this, but this is no place to be out and about in."

Kuda stepped toward the flying platform. "Why're you helping me?"

"Because it's the right thing to do. Slavery is wrong. Period."

Kuda's eyes softened as he frowned.

"C'mon," said Dr. Snowden.

Kuda tentatively boarded.

Dr. Snowden closed the guardrail. "Okay. We're going to be in the air, so grab a guardrail to steady yourself."

"Up there?" asked Kuda, pointing up.

Dr. Snowden nodded.

Kuda death-gripped the guardrail.

"Here we go," said Dr. Snowden.

The platform lifted into the air.

Kuda gasped.

After ascending several hundred feet in the air, Dr. Snowden gestured over the guardrails. "Okay. Where to?"

Kuda studied the ground for a moment. He pointed northwest.

The platform began to move in that direction.

Kuda relaxed his grip and exhaled slowly. He faced Dr. Snowden. "Are you a...spirit?"

Dr. Snowden chuckled. "Nope. Flesh and blood, just like you."

Kuda nodded.

"How far away is the stop?" asked Dr. Snowden.

"Two days walking."

Dr. Snowden calculated that to be about twenty miles or so. "Okay. Let me know if we need to change course or anything."

Kuda nodded and focused on the ground.

Dr. Snowden ran through several scenarios on what needed done once he reached the Underground Railroad stop. Without the Torvatta or Evaran's help, Dr. Snowden would need to find someone who could help him. A trip to Atlantis could take a while if he wanted to see the Helians, and he was not aware of the state of the nonhuman world in the 1840s.

One approach involved seeking out Lord Vygon's beacon. Although used long ago in the past relative to the current time period, Dr. Snowden figured it might still be there. Lord Vygon would help if he was not sleeping. Dr. Snowden sighed as he continued to analyze options.

Over the next three hours, Dr. Snowden studied Kuda. While he seemed to relax over time, he looked tense still. It could be that they were in the air, or perhaps the general unusualness of the whole situation. If Evaran knew what had happened, he should have appeared with the Torvatta the moment after Dr. Snowden arrived. This was not a case of time dilation like what had occurred with Emily on the prison planet.

Dr. Snowden had yawned several times. Per his PSD, it was 12:35 a.m., and his cozy recliner seemed so far away. He had been excited to visit Kess over the weekend and wondered what she was up to. The silence other than the occasional course correction did not help keep him awake.

Kuda did not talk much and kept to himself. Dr. Snowden wondered if his fair skin might have given Kuda pause. The time period was a barbaric era in American history, and it was twenty years or so before the civil war. Dr. Snowden sighed but had confidence that he would be picked up soon.

Kuda jabbed a finger at a cabin below.

Dr. Snowden peered over the edge of the flying platform. A cabin in the woods was becoming something of a theme to him. Although it was still dark out, the moon provided decent illumination. The cabin seemed off. It had a blurry effect on it, although Kuda seemed to have no trouble identifying it.

"Okay, going down," said Dr. Snowden.

Kuda smiled.

Dr. Snowden reflected that it was the first time he had seen Kuda do that.

The flying platform descended and landed at the outskirts of the cabin's clearing.

Kuda hopped off of the platform. He put up a finger to his lips and whispered, "Wait here."

"Okay," said Dr. Snowden.

He pulled the platform back into his PSD, then watched Kuda hustle up to the cabin. Dr. Snowden's eyes narrowed. In addition to the strange visual sensation he sensed earlier, a Daedrould registered nearby. He gripped his PSD and looked around. The Daedrould's energy was one he had not encountered before. He inhaled the crisp forest air and waited.

A moment later, Kuda exited the cabin with a woman.

Dr. Snowden sensed the dark-skinned woman was the Daedrould. She wore a black dress with a green wrap of some type around her shoulders. A black cloth wrapped her hair. The bone-like amulet around her neck and various rings on her fingers caught his attention.

Kuda and the woman approached Dr. Snowden.

"I am Thereze Leblanc," said the woman, slightly bowing her head. "Kuda says you helped him."

Dr. Snowden nodded. "He was being chased by what I guess were slave owners or catchers."

"So he said," said Thereze. She eyed Dr. Snowden, then motioned at Kuda. "Food and drink awaits you inside. Go. I wish to talk to this Dr. Albert Snowden."

Dr. Snowden figured his name had been given to her by Kuda.

Kuda nodded and took off.

Thereze watched Kuda leave, and when he reached the cabin, she faced Dr. Snowden. "You're not what you appear to be."

"I was going to say the same about you," said Dr. Snowden with a smile. "You're a Daedrould, but I'm unsure of the strain."

"Daedrould…a term I haven't heard in a long time. I'm a mambo."

Dr. Snowden wrinkled his brow. "I…don't know what that is."

"Vodou priestess."

"Ahh," he said. "I wasn't aware mambos existed in Mississippi."

Thereze chuckled. "Most of the queens are in New Orleans. However…some of us wish to ease the suffering of these slaves in a more direct manner."

"Gotcha."

"Now…I've told you what I am. What are you?"

Dr. Snowden cleared his throat. "I'm just a traveler who helps those in need."

"Like you helped Kuda."

Dr. Snowden nodded.

"You're not a Daedrould or Outsider. You're something else."

"I'm not sure there's a classification for what I am," said Dr. Snowden. He rubbed his chin. "Do you know of Evaran?"

Thereze's eyes narrowed. "The time loa who walks among us as a mortal from time to time. It is said he travels through time helping others and comes when the world is threatened."

"I'm not sure what a loa is, but I travel with Evaran. A part of what makes him unique is inside me, sorta."

"You're one of his priests?"

"No...more like a traveling companion."

Thereze tilted her head. "Then you too are a time traveler. What is your purpose here? While I would like to believe you came to help Kuda, I suspect it is something else."

Dr. Snowden sighed. He figured since she had knowledge of Evaran, it would not hurt to expound more on his situation. It did surprise him that she seemed nonchalant about hearing about time travel. "I was attacked by a powerful being. She could not defeat me physically, but she did open a portal, which placed me on a dirt road where I met Kuda shortly thereafter."

"I see," said Thereze. "Where did this fight occur at?"

"Well...not so much where as when. It happened in 2012, about one hundred and seventy years from now. I'm trying to figure out how to get back to my time."

Thereze rubbed her amulet. "And why has Evaran forsaken you?"

"I don't think he has. Normally, he would retrieve me immediately, unless he doesn't know where I am. He would've had no idea where my attacker sent me."

Thereze laced her fingers. "So even he lacks knowledge."

"Yeah, but he loves to learn."

"Do you?"

Dr. Snowden chuckled and pointed up. "In my time, I teach about the stars and...other things up there."

Thereze studied him. "A teacher, like myself. In your time, the color of skin must not be a concern if you helped Kuda without hesitation as he said you did."

"Sadly, it is to some degree, but nothing like it is in this period."

"I'm glad you're understanding. As much as I want to ask about the future...those are subjects best left alone."

Dr. Snowden nodded. "Timeline integrity."

Her eyes turned a slight shade of green. "You have a kind spirit about you. What do you plan to do now?"

Dr. Snowden sighed. "Honestly...no idea. This has never happened before. At least to me. The fact Evaran hasn't come for me already means something is wrong. I guess I just need some time to think things through."

"Then do so on a full stomach. There is food, drink, and accommodations in the cabin. It is late, and you should be inside."

"I'd love to, but I bet it's cramped in there and I don't want to impose."

Thereze smiled. "Not all is at it appears. I am surprised the cabin appeared to you. Most would have seen trees, but it seems my ability to bend perceptions does not work against those coming from the sky."

"I did notice it was blurry, kinda," said Dr. Snowden. "So you can alter perceptions?"

"Within a certain range. It is but one of my abilities."

Dr. Snowden grinned. "That's neat. I've studied quite a few Daedroulds, but not your type."

"I see. Which ones did you learn about?"

"A lot. One of my close friends is a Daedrould. Lord Vygon."

Thereze's eyes widened. "Ancient vampire."

"Yeah, and he is one of Evaran's closest friends. I also met some of the other strains, such as Raskarians, Blooded, and Vanar."

Thereze stared at Dr. Snowden. "The Vanar are well known. Witches from the old world."

"I guess. The one I met was pretty modern—well, to the time period I was in, I suppose."

"I would like to talk to you more when you have time. For now, come. Enjoy my hospitality," said Thereze. She turned to leave, then wheeled around. "And thank you for helping Kuda. You didn't have to, but you did."

Dr. Snowden nodded.

She smiled and went back to the cabin.

As he followed her, he scrutinized the situation. Thereze vocalized the concern he had about Evaran not being able to come back and pick him up. Either he could not find Dr. Snowden or something even worse had happened. He shuddered to think about living out the rest of his enhanced lifetime starting in this time period.

The discussion about Lord Vygon opened up some ideas. As long-lived as he was, perhaps he could help. He was a friend and would know Dr. Snowden. Lord Vygon's beacon might not even be around, or him for that matter.

04

Emily had spent the last hour in her new surroundings trying to get her bearings. She confirmed only one sun was present. If it had been night, she could have used the PSD's astrometric program to determine her location. Based on the sun, the PSD displayed the time as 5:30 p.m.

Her PSD identified a squirrel when it crossed her path earlier, so at least her location was on Earth and not some other planet. There was the probability that squirrels existed on other planets, but she understood how rare that would be. Although she had gone back in time by a few hours, she was not sure if she was in a past or future day.

She sighed and then used her flying pattern to create a platform. After she boarded, the platform ascended to around fifty feet before stopping to hover.

Hills and forest blanketed the landscape, and a river appeared in the distance. She realized she would be highly visible if anyone looked in her direction, but at this point, she just wanted any clue to determine her location.

The Torvatta refusing her PSD connection surprised her. She could not recall that ever happening. Tack on not being able to contact Evaran and the others, and she got a prison planet vibe. She had no intention of spending nine months alone again.

She spotted some activity near the edge of the river. It was hard to make out at her height. She guided the flying platform to a safe distance away. After finding a tall tree, she looked for the largest branch, and when she found it, she climbed onto it and made sure to retract her flying platform back into her PSD. The branch would serve as an ideal vantage point, and with her camouflage shielding active, she should not be visible to whoever came her way.

She smiled when she used her PSD to form binoculars. The PSD had many new patterns, and learning them would be a daunting task, but one she embraced. She loved the versatility. Evaran had gone out of his way to ensure the PSD could be used in any survival situation. Between her suit, PSD patterns, and experience of traveling with Evaran, she was confident in her ability to survive. Dr. Snowden would be equipped to do so as well. She hoped he was okay.

The activity she had spotted turned out to be a human camp. Her binoculars showed data labels when she looked through them, and the area bustled with activity as men, women, and children moved about. The uniformly fair skin color stuck out to her the most, in addition to the mix of dark hair colors. The beige clothing seemed tunic-based and the men wore their long hair down to their shoulders.

The various pieces of equipment around the camp seemed crude. Oval shields lay scattered around, but the curved swords stood out. She remembered the sword type as a Dacian falx from her college history classes. Her eyes widened. The Dacians were a Thracian people that existed near the Carpathian mountains in what would become Romania in Southeast Europe. If the camp was Dacian, then she was in the past. Although she did not know the exact year, she would figure it out.

As she continued to scan around the landscape, she observed a large group of men building a camp of some type to the west of the first camp. Although most of them seemed to be in simple clothing, she recognized the metallic armor and shields on some of the other men walking around. Her eyes narrowed. They were Romans, and given the time of day, they were building a marching camp, or castra, as she recalled. She smiled as she remembered studying Roman history. Romans were quite the engineers, and they loved to march.

Based on the rectangular shape and number of tents, she calculated that two legions inhabited the camp, or about ten thousand legionnaires. She spotted a river nearby and verified that the camp resided on higher ground, all signs that pointed to it being a marching camp. It boggled her mind that they would build a camp one day, only to tear it down the next day. However, she understood its benefits, allowing them to go deep into enemy territory and protecting them at night.

She traced a line from the Roman camp to the Dacian one and determined the distance between them to be about twenty miles apart, which she knew the Romans could march in one day. A man with light clothing streaked through the forest toward the Romans. Based on his trajectory, he would be at the Roman camp in about half a day. Her gut told her the man was a Roman scout.

She pulled her PSD back and opened up its interface. Romans and Dacians had a rocky past from what she remembered. She perused the information on the era, but the year still eluded her. There was only one way to find out, and that would be talking to the Dacians. Although Romans were open-minded about others, the scout hustling back indicated to her that the Roman intent might not be peaceful.

She sighed. A part of her said she should stay camouflaged and just listen in and try to figure out the year. The other part of her wanted to mix in and experience Dacian culture. Woman and children bustled around in the Dacian camp, and she suspected that they would be more welcoming to a stranger, dependent on the year.

Dacia might be on its own, or a Roman vassal state. Perhaps the Romans were not hostile and this was normal. The other possibility bothered her. She might be in the middle of a war.

One way to be sure of the Roman intent was to listen in on what the scout said to the Roman commander. She considered trying to follow the scout but determined that she only needed to hear what he said when he arrived. With half a day to go before that, she decided to rest up for a while before moving out.

She perused her PSD and selected the bed pattern. After playing around with the pattern builder, she created a bed with two locking pincers underneath and one at the head. This allowed the bed to be anchored to the trunk and the branch. A light kinetic bubble shield would keep insects away, a pattern she wished the PSD had had on the prison planet.

She yawned as she looked out over the environment. Her inside helmet showed it to be a bit past 6:00 p.m., although it had been 8:30 p.m. where she had come from.

As she lay on the bed, she revisited the fight with Ziekah. The mention of Seeros had been odd, and Emily thought about how something in the past had come back to bite them in the future. Ziekah had said that Seeros was to be extracted from the timeline. That seemed like something that would cause a lot of timeline changes. The idea of multiple Seeroses working across timelines flitted through her mind for a moment. As fantastic as it sounded, she had seen much weirder things.

Another disturbing thought was that Evaran had not come after she arrived. That should have been instant. She concluded that he did not know her whereabouts. A scary thought in itself. The Torvatta ignoring her was also problematic. She sighed as she put her hands behind her head. A good rest was in order.

Emily woke up after eight hours of restful sleep. She smiled as she pulled her PSD pattern back in. After perusing the PSD's patterns, she selected a bacon-flavored food pellet. Thankfully, Evaran had added flavored pellet patterns.

Her mood changed when she thought of not being around the others. She wondered about their situation as she took a swig of fresh water. For now, using the bathroom was the next priority. The PSD had a pattern for that too. She recalled using it several times in their last adventure.

After using her grapple beam to get to the ground, she relieved herself, then stretched. Thankfully no one had passed by and looked up while she had slept. Even then, it was still dark out. Her PSD showed it to be about 2:00 a.m. The scout would be arriving at the Roman camp at daybreak. She decided to investigate the camp until the scout showed up.

Thirty minutes later, she arrived at the outskirts of the Roman camp. She verified that her camouflage shielding was still active. The last thing she wanted to do was get into a fight with thousands of Romans in their own camp. She studied the camp on her way down, and it was a whirlwind of activity. She lowered her helmet to smell the area, but the strong odor from the camp made her gag and raise it back up.

She followed a patrol when they approached the camp, and made sure not to get too close, but near enough that she could follow them through the wooden gates. A mound of dirt sat in front of a V-shaped ditch that surrounded the camp. A small strip of land went over the ditch and allowed entry into the camp. Long wooden stakes comprised the wall and she knew that as a palisade. It provided decent defense. A tower sat over the gate with interval towers spread out behind the palisade.

The patrol reached the gate and marched in.

It was much louder than she expected it to be so early in the morning. Her suit allowed her to lower the volume, thankfully. She separated from the patrol and stood off to the side in the large open walkway that encircled the interior of the camp. She understood that was done for projectiles that might come over the wall, and from what she remembered, it was referred to as the Via Sagularis. The massive dirt street ahead was the Via Praetoria. Tents that housed legionnaires sat off to the side. She wanted to poke her head into a tent but figured that might be pushing it. It made her thankful that she had spent many a night studying Roman history.

As she walked down the street, she checked past the legionnaire tents and verified the cavalry had set up there. Between that and the interior walkway sat more legionnaire tents. She focused on the massive tent ahead of her. That would be the commander's tent, and guards stood at attention outside it.

She admired the layout and recalled that the design of any individual camp varied based on how many slept there that night. The general design was the same, and messengers and scouts, like the one she had seen earlier, knew exactly where to go when they arrived. She would make sure she was in the commander's tent before the scout arrived.

She walked all around the camp over the next four hours and made a point to avoid the horses and donkeys. They seem to be spooked when she got too close. When the sun came up, the camp came alive and she smiled thinking that she got to witness it live. Traveling with Evaran usually took them to the future or far away, but as a history student, this is what she envisioned the possibilities to be like with time travel.

Her eyes narrowed when the scout came hustling up to the commander's tent. She slipped inside and made sure she had not been noticed. The men surrounding a table and studying a parchment were officers of some type. They wore metallic strips of armor held together by leather strips on the upper half of their body, and their helmets sported crests with what looked like red horsehair.

The scout entered the tent.

The men around the table focused on the scout.

One of the men addressed the scout. "What news have you?"

Emily assumed he was the ranking commander.

"A Dacian camp, about a day's journey," said the scout, trying to catch his breath.

The men looked at each other for a moment.

"What is their fighting strength?" asked the commander.

"About fifty warriors. They have their families with them."

The commander gestured at the parchment on the table. "Show us."

Emily got close enough to view the parchment. It was a crudely drawn map with a rough approximation of the surrounding area.

The scout studied the map for a moment, then pointed at the Dacian camp to the east. "There."

The commander smirked. "Then we'll hit it on way to Tapae."

The place rang a bell in Emily's memory, but she could not recall where it was or the significance of it. She needed to get out so she could look it up on the PSD's knowledge base.

One of the officers bumped into Emily.

She stepped back and then burst out of the tent. Although her sudden movement would baffle them, it was better that than to be discovered. She peered back. The commander, the scout, and some men had stormed out of the tent. They looked around, but with all the camp activity going on and her camouflage shielding active, she would not be detected.

She made her way out of the camp and to a safe place. The Dacians needed to be warned. However, her curiosity got the best of her. After finding a large tree, she slumped against it and pulled out her PSD.

She opened the knowledge base program and searched for "Tapae." Her eyes widened. There were two battles, one in AD 87, the other in AD 101. That gave her an idea of the time period. The second entry listed a war between the Romans and the Dacians led by Decebal. She sighed. Although she wanted to spend more time researching everything involved in the era, she needed to get to the Dacian camp. With that in mind, she checked her surroundings before forming a flying platform.

She hopped on and ascended until the camp was just a dot. They probably could not make her out, but it made her wish the platform had camouflage shielding. It would not take her long to reach the Dacian camp. The hilly and mountainous terrain she flew over meant there would not be a lot of people around to spot her.

The thought did cross her mind that the Dacian camp had always been meant to be wiped out. Or perhaps she had always been meant to interfere. She wondered what Evaran would do. He would probably do nothing since that would ensure that his involvement did not cause a timeline change. However, she understood that on some adventures, she and the others had been a part of events. Things would be so much easier if he were around.

She gritted her teeth. Doing nothing while a camp got ravaged was not in her nature. She had to at least try.

05

V flew out of the portal he had come through. He tried to fly back into it, but it dissipated immediately. The Torvatta had originally registered Ziekah opening additional portals after Emily had gone through hers. It seemed one of those portals was the one that brought him to his current location.

The first action he attempted was to contact the Torvatta. Although it registered as being present, it refused his connection attempt. He found no instance historically where that had occurred, and filed it away as something to investigate later. The next step was to fly up and get a survey of the land.

He was not sure how Ziekah had detected him, but his stealth mode did not work with her. A historical search yielded several instances where his predecessors had been without Evaran and the Torvatta, but in each of those cases, the location was known. V suspected that like Emily and Dr. Snowden, Evaran most likely did not know where V went. His attempts to contact Evaran, Dr. Snowden, and Emily failed.

V set about flying and scanning the environment. A quick scan of the night sky and stars revealed his present location to be Earth. The moon provided ample illumination for him to see around. He still switched to night vision and registered movement some distance away. His smell receptors detected a strong odor of blood in the air coming from the disturbance. He flew toward it.

After twenty minutes, he hovered over a battlefield and started scanning. The men on the ground were humans and classified as samurai. He looked for a fallen banner to help identify the group.

After a while, he found a banner with a circle on it and a cross in the center. A quick check in his database showed it to be the symbol of the Shimazu clan. V determined that put him somewhere in southern Kyushu, the westernmost island of Japan. It also meant that he was in the past, unless this was a reenactment. The dead men with hacked limbs suggested otherwise. Other men scrambled around the battlefield and seemed focused on retrieving corpses.

V checked the lineage of Shimazu leaders and could not calculate the exact year. For that, he would need more information. Approaching the men on the battlefield did not seem wise, so he followed a group of men leaving. They rode horses and had the Shimazu symbol painted on their chest armor.

After an hour, the horsemen reached a large city.

V broke off from them and flew above. This would be where he would secure information. A large castle sat in the distance. Various buildings with lanterns surrounded the castle, and beyond that was farmland. A check against his knowledge base showed this to be a castle town. The castle often served as the seat of power for a lord, known as a daimyo. This one must be in the Shimazu family, but V had no data on which one. He would find out.

He looked for unusual energy signatures as he calculated that a nonhuman would be more forthcoming about information than if he approached a human. It took him a while, but he found a shop on a crowded side street that yielded an Outsider signature.

He flew down and then transformed into projected mode, using samples of the humans he saw walking around as a basis for his appearance. The busy narrow street provided many places to dip in and out of. The store he chose had a strong odor. He suspected Dr. Snowden and Emily would not approve of it.

V's processing lingered on Dr. Snowden and Emily for a moment. It was reasonable to deduce they too were in the past. They had their survival suits and PSD, though, so they would not be defenseless. The camouflage shielding alone would allow them to move around without being detected, and they would be able to use holographic projections over their suits to blend in. There might be problems if nonhumans sensed them, but V had confidence in Dr. Snowden's and Emily's ability to defend themselves.

V stepped out on to the side street and followed the flow of people. Once he arrived at the shop, he assessed the exterior. A vertical banner outside the door indicated that the place brewed sake. A fact popped into his memory, showing that outside the moat of the castle were layered areas that housed samurai of importance. He understood this also tied into their social status. The merchants around him must be prominent due to their proximity to the castle.

V ran a query to determine if the shop had late hours but found no information. He decided to enter.

A man in simple clothing nodded at V. "Hello."

V smiled. "Hello. I have some questions."

The man laughed. "Do you now? Does it involve purchasing a lot of sake?"

"It does not," said V. He tilted his head. "You are an Outsider, and as such, I believe you are in a position to help me."

The man's eyes widened as he lurched forward and grabbed V by the arm. "Follow me." He shouted a name.

A young man burst from the back room and took the first man's spot.

The situation baffled V, but it was apparent the man wanted to talk in a more private setting.

The man led V to a back room and then, after looking around, moved a basket and lifted a trapdoor. "Go. Now. We can talk below."

V climbed down the ladder and into a large room. Doorways led to other areas, and he detected food of some type. Lanterns hung off the walls and provided illumination.

The man hustled down after closing the trapdoor. He motioned for V to follow him.

V complied. After walking for ten minutes down a long dim hallway, they reached a stone room. Like the previous rooms, a few scattered lanterns hung on the walls, and the odor of something sour filled the air.

The man faced V. "I'm Sakuma Hiroshi, an Outsider as you mentioned. However…to the locals, I am the god of sake."

"I see," said V. He ran a query in his knowledge base. "Are you referring to yourself as a Shinto god, known as a Kami?"

Sakuma nodded.

"I have not heard of you as a god of sake."

Sakuma sighed. "I haven't been as successful as my fellow Outsiders in making my name known."

"It is okay," said V.

"Is it really? You have Amerterasu, Susanoo, Honinigi... they had no problem being worshipped, but me..." He sighed again.

"I can believe in you if it helps."

Sakuma laughed. "Well, thank you." He eyed V. "You're most unusual. You're not a fellow Outsider, and you're definitely not Daedrould. You're... something else."

"That is correct. Do you know of Evaran?"

Sakuma's eyes widened. "The time Kami?"

V tilted his head. "I have heard him referred to as such. However, I travel with him, but I appear to be lost."

Sakuma sat on a stool. "Why isn't he here to retrieve you?"

"Unknown. Something is wrong."

Sakuma rubbed his chin. "That does sound odd. Evaran is one of those rare beings who is only classified as a god by other Outsiders, but not by humans. Probably because they aren't aware he exists." He studied V. "I'm not sure how I can help you but...maybe you should visit the library."

"Which one?"

Sakuma smiled. "You're in Kagoshima! It's where we Outsiders have an underground library, and it's protected not only by ourselves, but by Shimazu Takahisa, who we have an agreement with. In exchange for his protection, we grant him mystical favors."

"Does he understand that you cannot do that?"

"I don't think so, but as long as he *thinks* we can, what harm is there?"

V did not like that the Outsiders used humans, especially in the past, but he understood it had been that way for a long time, even into the modern era. The name Shimazu Takahisa narrowed the time period. He had captured Kagoshima in AD 1536, so this must be sometime after that.

"What year is this?" he asked.

"An odd question from someone who travels with the god of time. It is AD 1554."

V understood that Sakuma used a date reference that made sense to him. Thankfully, V had a universal translator. He now had his current location and time period.

"I would like to visit this library," he said.

"It's late, but…Omoikane is going to *love* you!" said Sakuma.

V checked his knowledge base. "The god of wisdom."

Sakuma nodded. "He is the one everyone goes to for counsel."

"I see," said V.

Although visiting the library might provide more clues on the next step, V struggled with what needed to be done to get back to the Torvatta. Perhaps he could reach Lord Vygon or Lord Noskov, ancient vampires who would know what to do. The only problem was V did not know Lord Noskov's location, although V did possess the whereabouts of Lord Vygon's beacon from long ago. The beacon, being in North America, could take some time to reach.

V smiled and emulated a flourish of his arm as he had seen Evaran do before. "Please, lead on."

V ran a quick scan on the stairs leading up a hilly part of the city. A gate comprised of two vertical wooden poles with another bar across the top stood in front. V understood this to be a Torii, and it indicated the separation of the secular world and that of the Kami—in this case, Omoikane.

The shrine itself was a small building at the top of the stairs. V suspected that like the Daedroulds and other nonhumans, the library probably existed underground to avoid detection.

They passed through the gate and walked up.

V noted the lack of people around. The shrine sat inside the castle, so that might be one reason. It was also late at night. He did not think the guards let anyone in, but they had waved Sakuma in like he was an old friend, perhaps as part of the agreement that the Outsiders had struck with Shimazu Takahisa.

V and Sakuma reached the top of the stairs.

V got a better look at the small building. The slightly curved roof had eaves that extended off the building's sides.

"Come," said Sakuma.

They entered, and Sakuma looked around after going to the end of the hall.

A man in white robes with a black hat of some type on his head approached them.

Based on the man's clothing, V calculated that the man was a shinshoku, the person responsible for maintaining the shrine and also leading worship.

The shinshoku nodded at Sakuma and eyed V for a moment, then tapped on the right wall.

It slid back.

V followed Sakuma into the new room. It seemed more modern than the one he had come from, and a quick scan indicated there were metal panels built into the walls with a faint electric signal. The trapdoor on the floor opened and revealed a stone stairway. V figured that controlling access to the stairway was also a part of the shinshoku's function.

Sakuma looked at the shinshoku while gesturing at V. "Omoikane will want to meet V."

The shinshoku nodded and left.

"Down we go," said Sakuma.

After five minutes, they reached the bottom of the stairs.

V processed that they were around a hundred feet underground. Before them stood a circular steel door, which seemed out of place given the wooden nature of the shrine. The door had a blue gem embedded in the center, with elaborate designs carved into the steel. The gem provided dim illumination to the area.

Sakuma touched the gem.

The door rolled off to the side and they entered a large room.

V ran a quick scan of the environment. Vertical rectangular stone boxes with a slightly angled surface populated the area. Scrolls were held in place by holes in the box surfaces. An analysis showed thousands of the boxes in straight lines parallel to the entrance.

A ramp descended on the right side of where they stood, while another ascended on the other side. Gems with a green glow hung from the ceiling, providing illumination.

Sakuma took off down the ramp on the right.

V noticed that the level they arrived at seemed much different than the one above. It resembled a workshop of sorts. Parchment scrolls, containers of ink, and various other items he did not immediately recognize stood out. An old fair-skinned man with a long white beard sat on a stool studying a scroll. He wore a gray robe and cloth footwear.

"Omoikane!" said Sakuma. "I bring you a visitor…that you'll actually want to meet this time."

Omoikane sighed and spun around on his stool. He eyed V and then stood. "A time traveler."

V determined that Omoikane must be more than perceptive to deduce that with only a glance.

"And…," said Omoikane, circling a finger in the air, "something metallic."

"Huh?" asked Sakuma.

Omoikane strolled around V. "Show us your true form."

V's projected form dissipated, and he pulled the skeleton into his orb.

Omoikane studied V in orb mode. "Intriguing." He smiled at Sakuma. "You were right. I do want to meet him." He focused on V. "What do you call yourself?"

"V."

"Short, and to the point. I have sensed your…signature… before. Not yours specifically, but something like it. That's how I know you're a time traveler."

"There should be no other time travelers other than Evaran," said V.

"Of course, of course." Omoikane stroked his beard. "Evaran…the time Kami. How do you know him?"

"V travels with Evaran," said Sakuma.

Omoikane sat back on his stool. "Which then raises the question…why are you here?"

"I was sent back in time by a powerful assailant. I am unsure of how to get back," said V.

"Evaran surely has the means to retrieve you."

"I am not sure why he has not come for me," said V. His lights dimmed a bit.

Omoikane scrutinized V. "This makes you sad, I see. I don't know what our scrolls could possible tell you, but this is one library out of eight. I am at each one and can allow you access."

"How are you at each one?" asked V.

Omoikane grinned. "I am one mind, many bodies. That is my ability."

"That would be very useful."

"It can be," said Omoikane. "I have a question. Do you have knowledge of the future?"

"I do, but I cannot mention it."

"Of course," said Omoikane. "That might lead to paradoxes, many of which I have pondered." He pointed up. "Feel free to peruse the scrolls. I'll be here if you want to talk."

Sakuma grinned. "You don't like to talk to anyone."

"As unique as V is, I'll make an exception."

V assumed his projected form, then nodded. "It is appreciated. I will try not to bother you."

"Please do. I suspect we would have many good conversations," said Omoikane.

V nodded.

What information might be discovered, he did not know, but the mention of other time travelers stuck out. That would be a starting point worth investigating. Despite the situation, the library provided a safe haven and base to operate out of. He hoped the knowledge from the scrolls would help.

06

Jelton studied the platform that jutted out from the side of a mountain. The air was crisp, and a bright moon lit up the surrounding area. It seemed like an odd place to have a base, but Evaran had mentioned it being the home of Lord Noskov. Jake lived there too along with his father.

Emily had discussed the ancient vampires before, and he had looked up some information on them while in the Torvatta. This would be his first time meeting them. Jelton wondered if his relationship with Emily was known by them or Jake.

"This is your first visit here, I believe," said Evaran, gesturing out the Torvatta's transparent front wall.

Jelton nodded. "As far as I can recall."

"It's a good place to live," said Jake.

"It seems peaceful."

Jake chuckled. "Yeah, but if Evaran visits, you know something's up."

Evaran eyed Jake.

"Well, usually."

Evaran half smiled.

Jelton observed the playful relationship between Evaran and Jake. They had a special bond. Evaran teased and joked around similar to how Dr. Snowden did, and Emily had mentioned Jake a few times. Jelton made a note to talk to Jake when he had some downtime.

"Come," said Evaran.

He stood and walked toward the Torvatta ramp.

A minute later, the group assembled outside the Torvatta.

Jelton examined the four men walking their way. The first wore a black light armor suit. On his forearms were what looked like extendable blades. The second man wore a black suit with a cape. The cape's red interior made the rest of the suit stick out. The third man was big, and he wore black heavy armor. The crew cut revealed a battle-weary face. The three men had pale skin, and black seemed a popular color choice. The fourth man was older and resembled Jake some.

Evaran motioned at each man in sequence when they arrived. "Jelton, this is Lord Vygon, Lord Noskov, Mikhail, and Robert Melkins, Jake's dad."

Jelton nodded at them.

"This is Jelton Stallryn, a deathless rift blade of the Rift Guardians."

Lord Vygon smiled and extended a hand. "Emily's mentioned you a few times. It's good to finally meet you."

Jelton returned the handshake. "Likewise, my friend." He shook the others' hands.

"Did you find out more on Dr. Snowden?" asked Lord Noskov.

Evaran shook his head. "Unfortunately not, and Emily and V fell victim to the same attack. They have been portaled away, but I do not know where to."

Jelton observed the worried looks on Lord Vygon, Lord Noskov, and Mikhail's faces. That should never be heard from someone who could travel anywhere.

"That's not a good sign if you can't locate them," said Mikhail.

"No, it is not," said Evaran. He studied Lord Vygon. "You are aware of my future. Do you remember this event?"

Lord Vygon shook his head. "I don't, actually. You had the unification event, then the one in the horolg– well, the next one, and it didn't involve this person who could portal."

Evaran studied Lord Vygon. "I understand."

"Were Dr. Snowden, Emily, and V a part of the next event?" asked Jelton.

Lord Vygon drew his lips flat. "I can't say." He pointed at Evaran. "His rules."

Jelton nodded. "Ahh. If you are aware of Evaran's future, and this event is not known, then it seems to me that it might never have existed in this timeline."

"I concur," said Evaran. "It would appear this event is erased from the timeline. If Lord Vygon does not know of this event, then the Torvatta, and us by extension, do not inform him of the details, and this meeting right now will have never occurred."

Mikhail's cleared his throat. "My thoughts exactly."

The group chuckled.

Evaran's eyes narrowed. "I did not detect dimensional signatures on Ziekah's portals, so Dr. Snowden, Emily, and V are somewhere in the past. Ziekah mentioned seeing Dr.

Snowden earlier. Assuming she went to the past as well, there may be timeline changes, although that depends on when she goes relative to the others. Regardless, we must find and rescue Dr. Snowden, Emily, and V." He gestured at Lord Vygon. "As you do not know of this event, then it means whatever timeline changes are made will get reverted, and only those of us on the Torvatta will remember any changes."

Lord Vygon sighed. "It also means I don't travel with you on this one."

Evaran nodded. "It would be wise for Jelton and Jake to stay close to the Torvatta. Jake has temporal shielding already, so he needs to be here. A timeline change usually takes roughly twenty minutes to propagate from its source to all affected entities. However, it can take longer if there are substantial changes."

"Cascading timeline update," said Robert. He looked around the group. "I've been studying."

Lord Noskov placed a hand on Robert's shoulder. "Yes, you have."

"It has only been around twenty minutes in this timeline since we last saw Ziekah," said Evaran. "Jake and I went straight to Jelton's timeline and came back here one minute before our encounter with Ziekah. It then took twenty minutes to reach here from orbit."

Lord Noskov looked around. "A change could hit at any moment."

"Yes. However, Ziekah could have sent herself back after Dr. Snowden, Emily, and V's time periods. They would not experience a timeline change. For our part, if a timeline change does occur, we should be in orbit to avoid any possible collision."

"Can we get you anything before you go?" asked Lord Noskov.

Evaran rubbed his chin. "Not that I am aware of."

"I'm glad I came with my suit," said Jake, tapping his chest.

Robert eyed Jake. "You be careful out there, son."

"Always."

Lord Vygon looked around before focusing on Evaran. "Until you leave, Lord Noskov and I have some things to discuss. If you're willing, we can talk about it here since if the timeline changes, I think we can reasonably expect you'll reset it eventually and although we won't remember anything, you will."

Evaran half smiled. "As always."

The group shared a laugh.

Mikhail tapped Robert's arm. "That's our cue to leave."

Robert nodded and followed Mikhail away after hugging Jake.

Jake cleared his throat and shot a look at Jelton. "Roof?"

Jelton smiled. "Lead on, my friend."

Jake leaned over the edge of guardrail on the Torvatta's roof. He studied Lord Noskov waving his hands around with dramatic effect while talking to Evaran. Lord Vygon's chuckling indicated he was amused by whatever was being discussed. Whenever Evaran visited Lord Noskov's base, both lords made a point to carve out some time to talk to Evaran alone. Jake had been in on some of the discussions, but for the most part, they wanted to discuss things in private.

"Lord Noskov seems upset," said Jelton, joining Jake by the guardrail.

"Nah, he's okay. He's just trying to get Evaran to talk about something," said Jake.

Jelton eyed Jake. "What do you think they're talking about?"

Jake grinned. "Usually deals with the Earth Ward, the group that speaks for Earth in galactic affairs. Evaran formed it after the former group that represented the Earth, the Helians, mismanaged a rift door he gave them long ago."

"Interesting. Was this a recent thing?"

Jake smiled. "Yeah. Apparently some dimensional god guy called Caltorus tried to take on Earth but ran into Evaran. He united the nonhuman community and exiled Caltorus, then Evaran formed the Earth Ward. He came down hard on the Earth Ward recently for requiring nonhumans to register."

"That sounds invasive."

"It was," said Jake. "The Earth Ward rolled that policy back. However, Evaran's name is tied to the registration. There's always some issue."

Jelton chuckled. "Usually is with governance."

Jake nodded. "The only other thing that might get Lord Noskov riled up is Blake Brown."

"Emily's mentioned him before."

"Yeah. He was Lord Noskov's right-hand enforcer for like four hundred years before the Helians exiled him from Earth, but Evaran won't bring Blake back due to some future event he's in."

Jelton chuckled. "It sounds like Evaran has a good reason."

"Probably. Lord Noskov has been asking to go to the future at the end of whatever event Blake is a part of, but so far Evaran hasn't committed," said Jake. He narrowed his eyes. "I bet that's actually what they're discussing."

Jelton nodded. "I can see Lord Noskov's argument. I don't see why Evaran wouldn't do it."

Jake shrugged. "That's Evaran."

Jelton studied Evaran talking, then turned his head toward Jake. "So how did you come to meet Evaran?"

"It's a long story," said Jake. "To sum it up, I was abducted at six and taken to a space station to be cared for until I was twenty-one. At that age, I would have gone to a breeding camp."

"For reproduction purposes?"

Jake nodded. "Yeah. I didn't want any part of that. A slaver named Greecho that messed with me and my caretaker, Jells, came by with Kathy, my current girlfriend, except at the time, she was Greecho's pet." Jake smiled. "Unfortunately for him, Evaran and U4 visited at the same time."

Jelton cocked his head. "U4?"

"Oh…umm…V's predecessor."

Jelton drew his head back. "I didn't know that. What happened to U4?"

Jake grimaced. "She…uhh…sacrificed herself to save me." He looked down.

"I'm sorry to bring up a sad memory, my friend."

"It's okay," said Jake, clearing his throat. "I see a bit of her in V, actually. She preferred body mode, though."

"Fascinating."

Jake nodded. "Evaran brought Kathy and me back to Earth." He swept his hand out in an arc. "This is Greecho's base, or used to be. It has Seceltor technology, which I was familiar with, so I stayed here to help Lord Noskov operate it. I can also work on his ships."

Jelton looked out at the base. "Evaran seems to travel here a lot. At least, that is what Emily said."

"He sure does. I never know which one is going to visit, or in what sequence," said Jake, laughing.

Jelton studied Jake for a moment. "Are these future forms or something?"

"Yeah. I can't say much about them, other than that they exist. Lord Vygon knows them well, and likes to tease this version in particular."

"I could see that," said Jelton.

They shared a laugh.

"I suppose you can't mention if Emily is with these future forms?"

Jake shook his head. "Evaran would skewer me."

"To maintain timeline integrity."

"Yep," said Jake. "What about you? How did you meet Evaran?"

Jelton chuckled. "A long story as well. However, I can summarize it. Apparently Evaran has enemies outside this plane. They laid a trap for him, and I fell into it, in my timeline. I was close to death when I met him. He healed me, and I traveled with Evaran until the issue was resolved."

"That's wild."

Jelton nodded. "I will say, I didn't expect to die, but thankfully that was just a phase."

"Huh?"

Jelton laughed. "I apologize, my friend. I am a deathless riftblade. When we die, there is a chance that we are resurrected. That is an ability unique to a riftborn species."

"Oh, wow," said Jake.

"I died trying to prevent Evaran from sacrificing himself. We succeeded, but I met my death in the process, and also gained some of Evaran's cosmic energy."

Jake wrinkled his brow. "You have cosmic energy in you? Like Dr. Snowden and Emily?"

"I do. I believe it is what allowed me to be resurrected. I am the first of my kind."

"That's so cool."

Jelton smiled. "I like to think so too."

Jake chuckled. "To travel with Evaran is to invite some crazy stuff, and here we are at it again."

"Whatever Evaran needs, he has my service. I owe him my life."

"Same here."

They shared a moment of silence while they watched Evaran.

A muted thumping sound filled the air around them.

"Timeline change coming!" said Jake.

Jelton watched Evaran shake hands with both Lord Noskov and Lord Vygon.

Evaran stepped onto the Torvatta ramp and, after a moment, joined the others on the roof.

"It appears my hunch was correct," said Evaran.

"Hopefully the source of the timeline change is at a point *after* whenever Dr. Snowden, Emily, and V are in the past," said Jelton.

Evaran nodded. He interacted with his ARI.

The Torvatta hovered before ascending.

"Once the change hits, we will investigate the new environment," said Evaran.

Jake sighed. He hoped Dr. Snowden, Emily, and V were doing okay. The fact they had to deal with this at all bothered Jake. At least Jelton was around to help. Jake enjoyed Jelton's company, and with this group, Jake had no doubt they would do everything possible to get Dr. Snowden, Emily, and V back.

07

Dr. Snowden surveyed the underground cavern he was in. Thereze had led him first into what seemed like a small cabin, but it had a fireplace illusion that shimmered and allowed passage into a tunnel. The place was massive, with lanterns spread out along the wall at several points.

His eyes were drawn to a smaller cave opening a bit away, where people milled around. A small waterway bubbled its way through the cavern off to his left. In front of him and to his right was mostly a dirt ground that looked like it had seen a lot of travelers. Various tents dotted the landscape. The odor of spicy food permeated the air, making him smile.

"Is this the Underground Railroad?" he asked.

"I have heard it called that," said Thereze. "The tunnel at the other end goes north up to around Memphis. It's a long walk, but there are many stops that people can use to rest."

Dr. Snowden rubbed his chin. "Huh. I always thought the Underground Railroad was a series of houses, farms, and the like that formed a network."

Thereze chuckled. "Oh, those exist. This is our contribution to the cause to help our brothers and sisters."

"A tunnel that goes to Memphis is quite the contribution," said Dr. Snowden. He made a note to see if it was still there in the future.

"It isn't all underground. There are some parts that go above ground, but in isolated areas."

Dr. Snowden nodded. "It must have taken you a long time to construct that."

Thereze shook her head. "Not when you have an elemental friend."

"An...elemental friend?"

Thereze smiled and closed her eyes. She raised her hands and chanted some words.

After a moment, a humanoid made of rock emerged from the wall.

Dr. Snowden's eyes widened. He had read that there were elementals, but that they did not interact much with the rest of the world. Given that they lived in extremely inhospitable areas, that was easy to do.

"Do not be frightened," said Thereze. She gestured at the humanoid elemental, who came over to her. "This is Grolk. He is somewhat of a rogue in that he assists us mere mortals from time to time."

"I like to think of myself as enlightened," said Grolk in a deep voice.

Dr. Snowden chuckled.

Thereze and Grolk stared at Dr. Snowden.

"Did you understand what I said?" asked Grolk.

"Yeah, I did," said Dr. Snowden. He pointed a finger at his head. "Universal translator."

"A miraculous gift," said Thereze. She gestured at Dr. Snowden. "He travels with Evaran."

Grolk lowered his head. "That makes sense, then. It's an honor."

Thereze wrinkled her brow. "You knew Evaran?"

"He helped us long ago without any request for compensation," said Grolk. He grinned at Dr. Snowden. "To travel with him means you have to be honorable. He would not suffer fools."

Dr. Snowden chuckled. "No, he would not, but he is very forgiving." He eyed Grolk. "Was I with Evaran when he helped you?"

"A strange question, but I suppose if you can travel in time, events can be out of sync. No, he was with other humans. He asked me not to talk about the encounter."

Dr. Snowden's eyes narrowed. "Just a yes-or-no question, then. Did he have dirty-blond hair, blue eyes, pale skin, and a light gray outfit with dark gray pads?"

"No."

Dr. Snowden sighed. "All right…"

"Was that important?"

"It gives me some insight," said Dr. Snowden. "I guess my next step is to find someone who might be able to help me. Lord Vygon has a beacon northwest of here."

Thereze studied Dr. Snowden. "Ancient vampires like their beacons. I met Lord Vygon long ago and he helped me out. I wouldn't mind seeing him again."

"You want to come with me?" asked Dr. Snowden.

Thereze gestured at Grolk. "He can handle things here, and I can take care of myself. Besides…I'd enjoy more time with Lord Vygon."

"Oh…okay." Dr. Snowden shrugged. "No problem here. I could use the company."

"Can you fly there, like you did here?"

Dr. Snowden chuckled. "Yep, that's the idea."

"He can use his personal support device, or PSD," said Grolk.

"That's…right," said Dr. Snowden.

"Oh, well, how long would it take to get there?" asked Thereze.

"I'm not sure, but I can calculate it," said Dr. Snowden. He pulled out his PSD and created a holographic window.

Thereze studied the PSD.

Dr. Snowden opened a maps program and located Lord Vygon's beacon that he had been to in the past. A label indicated that it was about 670 miles. The flying platform flew twenty-five miles an hour, so he calculated the trip to be about a day of traveling nonstop.

"It would be roughly a day without breaks, but if we did take a break, then two days," he said.

Thereze eyed the PSD. "Is that what created the flying machine to get you here?"

Dr. Snowden nodded. He formed the platform and then ascended a few feet.

Thereze gasped.

The platform descended.

Dr. Snowden pulled it back into the PSD.

"Your PSD is powerful," said Thereze.

Dr. Snowden chuckled. "Evaran gave it to me to help me survive the encounters he goes on."

Thereze eyed Grolk. "And you know all this and never told me?"

Grolk grinned as he looked at Dr. Snowden. "Evaran's rules."

"Sounds like him," said Dr. Snowden.

"Okay. I'll get some rations for the trip, and I need to talk with Grolk about my absence," said Thereze.

"Okay," said Dr. Snowden. He wrinkled his brow. "Maybe we can leave in the morning. I'm beat."

Thereze nodded. "We have a bed for you to sleep in."

Grolk chuckled. "His PSD has a bed pattern with a neural effect."

"He's right…," said Dr. Snowden.

"Okay," said Thereze. "We leave tomorrow, then." She pointed to a pitched tent a bit away. "You can form your… bed pattern…there."

"All right," said Dr. Snowden.

He went over to his tent and formed a bed from his PSD. He remembered using it on a parallel world that had mutated creatures. This was a much calmer environment. He placed his hands behind his head after lying down. The day had not gone as he expected. Breakfast had been good, and he had enjoyed chatting with Emily before going to work. That seemed so far away now, even though it had been that morning.

Grolk's familiarity with Evaran and the PSD surprised Dr. Snowden. It was apparent that Grolk had met a future version of Evaran with different companions. It made Dr. Snowden wonder if he and Emily survived long enough to see Evaran's second form.

A part of Dr. Snowden wondered if Grolk had traveled in the Torvatta. He seemed to be intimately familiar with the PSD's patterns, which would be expected if he had been a companion for an adventure. Dr. Snowden figured it would be interesting from Grolk's perspective to see Dr. Snowden, yet not know who he was.

Dr. Snowden sighed. Ziekah had thrown a monkey wrench into what should have been a normal day. Instead of eating a nice dinner and catching up on a nap, he was underground and in the past. He hoped Lord Vygon had some insight since he was aware of future events, but he might not know of this one. Either way, Dr. Snowden was sure Lord Vygon would help out if possible.

Dr. Snowden figured a flight with one stop should be an easy trip, although the thought of keeping his hand on the PSD for twelve hours did not sound fun. Perhaps a pattern tweak where he did not need to hold the PSD, other than to move, might be possible. Standing or sitting on the PSD should be enough. Something to check out in the morning. For now, it was time to sleep.

Dr. Snowden yawned as he woke up from an eight-hour sleep. His PSD showed the time as 10:30 a.m., and it took him a moment to gather his senses. The PSD's bed pattern made sleeping effortless. He had come to rely on the PSD as an extension of himself.

The tent he was in was closed, so he re-formed his PSD into a toilet and relieved himself. He chuckled imagining someone peeking in and being startled upon what they would see. After he was done and cleaned up, he exited.

The area was quiet, and he saw Grolk in the distance with Thereze near the large tunnel entrance. Dr. Snowden decided he would visit them after working on the flying pattern.

After opening up the pattern builder program from his PSD, which appeared as a holographic screen, he selected the flying pattern to use as a base. He liked the toolbar on the left with various icons. The right side had an open area that showed an isometric grid of two by two cells. He expanded the grid to four wide and eight long.

After a quick analysis, he started to design from the first row from the back. He added two cabinets, each taking up a column and filling the first row. In the second row, he added a bed in the first and last column. Each bed took up three vertical cells, meaning he had four rows left to add stuff to.

The next thing needed would be a set of chairs. He put a chair in the first and last column of the fifth row, then raised them up a bit. Although he considered putting them up front, the middle made more sense so other aspects might be added ahead of them.

He pondered what else he would need. After scrutinizing what he had, he checked on the ability of the platform to move and only change direction when the PSD was used. He drew his head back when he realized that being in contact with the platform was all that was needed to power it. His hand did not need to rest on the PSD the whole time. That was a misunderstanding on his part when Evaran had explained how it worked. Dr. Snowden grinned. That would make things a lot easier.

Navigation crossed his mind. He created a place for the PSD that made it appear like a joystick on the right chair's arm. That would allow him to sit comfortably and control the platform. He scanned the toolbar and saw a projector with the capability to display a map. That got added to the seventh row, two ahead of the chairs. A console was added next to the PSD that would allow for interaction without having to get up.

He left the final row open for storage space. The overall design allowed the two center columns from the second row to the projector in the seventh row to be clear for movement.

One aspect he was concerned about was whether or not they would be seen. Someone gazing up might see them. Unfortunately, adding camouflage shielding was not an option. That would be something to ask Evaran about. In the meantime, Dr. Snowden figured if they flew high enough, there would be no problem.

Looking around the pattern builder, he selected a light kinetic bubble shield to go around the platform. That should prevent bugs and birds from flying in. Satisfied with what he had constructed, he closed his PSD and went over to Thereze and Grolk.

"Good morning," he said.

Thereze and Grolk looked at him and nodded.

"I'm ready to go," said Thereze. She gestured at Grolk. "He will be handling anyone that comes."

"Won't being gone mess with the illusion you have over the cabin?" asked Dr. Snowden.

Thereze smiled. "That is unique to me and my sisters. They will assist Grolk, but I'm leaving him in charge."

Dr. Snowden found it odd that she chose someone other than her sisters to do that.

"She won't be gone long," said Grolk. He eyed Dr. Snowden. "She needs to help you if she can. Anything that curries favor with Evaran should be done."

Dr. Snowden chuckled. "I'm sure he would thank you if he were here." He studied Grolk. "The Evaran you met *must* be a future version."

"How so?"

"Because I'm traveling with the first one."

"Ahh. As I said before, I can't say much about my encounter."

"Evaran's rules," they said in unison while sharing a laugh.

Thereze chuckled. "Okay, I'm getting my stuff. I'll meet you outside."

Dr. Snowden watched her walk away.

Grolk gestured at Dr. Snowden. "Before you go…I had an observation."

"Shoot."

"If a future version of Evaran helps my kind, and me by extension, I wonder if he knew to do so based on this meeting."

Dr. Snowden rubbed his chin. "That's…an interesting insight. Definitely possible."

"I guess I'll never know unless Evaran visits again," said Grolk. "All right. Take care of Thereze, and safe journeys. Tell Lord Vygon I said hello, and he owes me a favor still."

Dr. Snowden chuckled. "Will do." He shook Grolk's hand and exited the cavern. After reaching the cabin's entrance, he spotted Thereze with a few bags standing on the porch. "Ready to go?"

Thereze smiled. "It's been a while since I traveled, but I believe I'm ready."

"Okay. Watch this." Dr. Snowden stepped out a bit from the cabin and formed his new flying pattern.

Thereze gasped. She walked around and studied the platform. "How can that tiny thing form this?"

"Dimensional mechanics."

"I...don't know what that is, but it's very powerful."

Dr. Snowden opened a side door for her.

She stepped aboard.

"You can place your things in the cabinet on the back or in front, behind the projector," he said, sweeping his finger from the steel-like cabinets to the projector base.

She put her things in a cabinet. After a quick look around, she sat on the left chair in the middle.

Dr. Snowden took the right chair. "You ready?"

She peered off the side. "We won't fall out, will we?"

Dr. Snowden interacted with the PSD and raised the guardrails so they were chest high relative to someone sitting on the chairs. "How about that?"

"Impressive. What about birds?"

"I added a light kinetic shield around the platform that should keep them out."

"What is that?"

Dr. Snowden chuckled. "Think of a bubble that gets stronger based on the force that hits it. A bird flying would be knocked away, but we are quite visible to them, so they would avoid us."

Thereze nodded.

"Okay, here we go," he said. He pulled up on the PSD and the platform rose.

Therese's eyes widened as she leaned over and peeked over the edge.

After ten minutes, they were high in the air.

Dr. Snowden lowered the PSD. The platform stopped ascending. He nudged the PSD forward and the platform accelerated ahead.

"This is amazing!" said Therese.

"Yeah. I surprised myself, actually."

She nodded. "So we can fly straight there?"

"Well, we may want to take a break to…you know… relieve ourselves."

She chuckled. "Of course."

Dr. Snowden activated the map projection.

A holographic screen popped up in front of them with a high-level map.

Therese shook her head. "So many wonders."

"It's just technology," he said. He scrutinized the projection. "Only a straight line there now." He interacted with the chair arm console.

The map moved to the halfway point.

"We can stop there. A remote wooded area," he said.

"We should be careful with areas like that," she said. "We might be trespassing on some group's territory."

Dr. Snowden grinned. "We won't be staying long to do our business."

Therese nodded. "I like to be in contact with the ground as well. I derive my power from it. If it's safe, perhaps we can rest there."

"Ahh. We have some time before we reach the beacon, and I put some beds behind us if you want to nap or sleep," he said.

It dawned on him that the bed placement made it intimate in terms of space. That might be why she had suggested sleeping outside the platform.

She smiled.

He cleared his throat. "Care to enlighten me on the Daedrould Vodou, or as I call it, voodoo, aspect?"

She smiled. "Of course."

08

Emily stood outside the Dacian camp. It had taken her about two hours to get there, and her PSD showed it to be 9:00 a.m. The place bustled with activity, and some of the people looked like they had tasted battle. Others scurried about around various fires and tents.

What stood out to her was that she detected an Outsider somewhere in the area. An Outsider would be easier to meet. Perhaps she might warn the Outsider so they could mobilize the others. She was not sure that appearing out of thin air and waving hello would be a good idea.

After verifying that her camouflage shielding was still active and that no one snooped around in her area, she entered the camp. She was thankful to have her helmet up since she suspected there were strong odors. One man in particular stood out. He had several other men around him, and they studied a parchment on a table. Perhaps he was the leader.

She checked her surroundings, and after fifteen minutes, she found the Outsider presence. It resided inside a tent on the outskirts of the camp. She approached it with her PSD drawn.

"Come in," said an old woman's voice.

Emily froze for a moment. She moved to the side of the tent entrance as she did not want someone bumping into her.

"You...with the strange presence. Come in."

Emily looked around but did not observe anyone. She approached the entrance of the tent and peered in.

An old woman in a tattered green robe sat on a blanket with a bowl in her hands. "There you are. Please, have a seat."

"Me?"

"Yes, you. You've been skulking around camp for a while. I'm guessing you were looking for me."

Emily did one final check of the environment before she entered. "You can sense me."

"Of course. Your presence is...very unique, unlike any I've ever felt before." The old woman gestured opposite her. "That makes me curious. Please, sit, and we can talk."

Emily complied.

"I'm Kotys. Who are you?"

"Emily."

"Can you reveal yourself? If your visage is horrendous, don't worry. I've seen many in my time," said Kotys.

"I'm only worried that someone might poke their head in," said Emily.

Kotys grabbed a blanket and offered it. "The cushion indentation suggests you're in the direction I'm offering this blanket to wrap up with."

Emily smiled. "I can alter my appearance some to show a blanket, but thank you for the offer."

She changed her college outfit hologram into one that resembled a robe. Although she had no knowledge of the specifics of Dacian clothing, she used Kotys's robe as a model. Emily disabled her camouflage shielding.

"Ahh...such beauty," said Kotys. She studied Emily. "What are you? You're something powerful as you can talk in our native tongue with ease, yet I don't think you're Dacian."

"I'm a traveler. A lost one, apparently," said Emily. Her eyes searched the ground for a moment. "Your name is familiar."

Kotys chuckled. "I'm a Thracian god, or so the people used to believe. They have...moved on."

"It's not uncommon for an Outsider to take on that title," said Emily. "I've met quite a few like that."

"Such as..."

"Oh...let's see...Thor, Odin, Hermes, Guan Yu."

"You associate with powerful beings. What title do you claim?"

Emily chuckled. "I travel with Evaran, so I guess companion."

Kotys's eyes narrowed. "Evaran...the god of time, or so it's said. He's become a myth, but I suspect what happened to me, happened to him. People forget."

"Well, he's still alive and kicking."

"Is he around?"

Emily sighed. "I wish. I got into a fight with someone hunting him, and they sent me here."

Kotys scrutinized Emily. "Into the past, right?"

"Yeah...how'd you know?"

Kotys gestured at Emily's suit. "You can hide in plain sight, and alter your appearance. Those abilities are beyond the Helians. Also, you travel with Evaran. It makes sense that anyone searching for him must have some relation to time itself."

Kotys was an observant person and wise. She was someone Emily figured might help.

"I don't think you sought me out only to talk, though," said Kotys.

Emily sighed. "Unfortunately not. When I arrived here, I was on the mountainside. I saw this camp...and to the west, a Roman marching one. There was a scout running from this camp to the Roman one. I went down and listened in when the scout arrived. The Romans are aware of this camp and intend to attack it."

Kotys shook her head. "Curse Trajan and his Romans. They always harass us."

"I wasn't sure who to talk to or how to convince a whole camp to move," said Emily.

"I can bring it up to Dacius, but he will send scouts to verify your claim."

Emily pulled out her PSD and interacted with it. "This is what I heard."

A projection shot up of the scout talking to the Roman commander.

Kotys drew her head back. "What type of wand is that?"

Emily chuckled. "It's...just technology."

"Seems Helian." Kotys gazed at the projection. When it ended, she shook her head. "So they mean to wipe us out. We have to move."

"Is there a place for the camp to go to that will be out of range when the Romans come?"

"There is. It's a cave network, but it's a three-day journey over rough terrain."

Emily's eyes narrowed. "The Romans are coming in the morning. They'll be on you before you reach that network."

"Then we should talk with Dacius immediately. Although your wand is powerful, it may scare him. The Helians possess advanced technology but don't normally share any of that with us," said Kotys.

"Even if the camp were to leave now, there still won't be enough time."

Kotys sighed. "Do you have any technology that might help with that? I can manipulate perceptions around me, but that won't work against the Romans. If anything, it would enhance their desire to perform lewd acts. It is my gift. It is why my ritual orgies are so much fun."

"Ritual orgies?"

Kotys chuckled. "You seem surprised. I take it they are not common in the future."

Emily cleared her throat. "They exist but…I guess I shouldn't be surprised."

"Okay, I'll bring Dacius here. If you can think of anything that might help, do so. Also, you may want to hide again."

"Okay," said Emily.

She activated her camouflage shielding and watched as Kotys exited the tent. Emily was not sure how so many people could get to the cave network before morning. If the Torvatta was present, they would pile on and fly away.

She opened her PSD. Perhaps there was a pattern that might help. The pattern builder was a program she had messed around with, but not as much as Dr. Snowden or Dr. Bryson from their last adventure.

She chuckled when she remembered creating the Emily wagon. That pattern was saved in her favorites, but it was meant for only about eight people and would not help here. She opened up the pattern in the builder and studied it.

One of the things she recalled was that the base platform was configurable. She had it at a three-by-ten grid. Even if it expanded, the wagon would not be driving over mountainous terrain. However, perhaps the flying platform could be upgraded.

Her fingers flew around the builder, and she selected the flying platform pattern. She smiled when she verified that the base could expand. If each person was one cell, and there were at most a hundred people, a ten-by-ten base would suffice. There would be supplies, and potentially animals too. After a few minutes, she determined that a fifteen-by-fifteen grid would give some breathing space and a buffer in case it was needed.

Kotys returned and sat down. She sighed. "Dacius left to go hunting. He'll be back in a few hours."

Emily nodded. "Well, I have an idea to safely get everyone to the cave network."

"How?"

Emily extended her PSD and showed the new pattern she had built.

"It looks like a large shiny square with a raised border," said Kotys.

"It's a flying platform. Everyone can get on board, with any supplies or whatever is needed. After that, we fly there."

Kotys's eyes widened. "Fly?"

"Yep. If need be, I can expand it more if space is needed."

"You truly are different," said Kotys. She studied Emily. "Your offer to help us is kind, but unusual. If you're truly from the future, these actions might affect history."

Emily shrugged. "Who's to say I wasn't always a part of history?"

"A good question."

They chuckled.

Emily gestured at the tent entrance. "There's women and children here. They shouldn't have to die."

"We all die at some point," said Kotys.

"Yeah, but usually not to a Roman legionnaire."

"A fair point. If Dacius agrees, and we do leave, what will you do once we're at the cave network?"

Emily shrugged. "Maybe I'll try to get to Atlantis, or find Lord Vygon or Lord Noskov."

Kotys hissed. "Lord Noskov…you know him?"

"Umm…yeah…"

"He is evil. An ancient vampire."

"I don't think he's evil, but I was aware he is an ancient vampire. He helped Evaran protect Earth long ago."

Kotys shook her head. "Lord Noskov resides in the Black Forest. It is a dark place."

"Well, he would know me. Besides, if he or any other vampire bit me, they'd die."

Kotys wrinkled her brow.

"It's a long story, but you don't want me to show blood. Ever."

"Interesting."

"I guess since we have some time, I wouldn't mind a rundown of your pantheon."

Kotys smiled. "Your interest is refreshing to me."

Emily listened with rapture as Kotys began to explain her pantheon and the dimension they came from.

Emily enjoyed talking with Kotys over the next three hours. The Thracian pantheon had opened a portal to Earth from their dimension. She mentioned that their world was dying, and a handful of them had discovered the portal. It sounded like a localized rift to Emily. She recalled that Evaran had mentioned that Earth was unique in that the barriers between it and other dimensions were weaker than in other places. This was what had given rise to so many Outsiders on Earth.

What intrigued Emily was that Kotys's pantheon had assumed human form upon crossing as well as special abilities. Kotys's powers included precognitions and the ability to arouse those around her. Each of Kotys's group had gained strength and speed, but their human form was based on how old they were. As Kotys was older, she took on the form of an elder woman. It was natural for them to be assumed to be gods based on their special abilities.

Emily wondered if all Outsider crossings were similar to that of Kotys's pantheon, or if it was unique to each one. There were Outsider groups who could shape-shift, like the Ollikrin Nation. Emily remembered meeting Odin and other Outsiders. She wondered what their special abilities were. One thing she did know was that the ones who had helped out when Caltorus had attacked Earth were strong and fast, in particular Thor.

Another area of interest to Emily that was discussed was how Kotys's pantheon interacted with other pantheons. The Helian interaction was of particular note. They had registered Kotys's pantheon and then left them alone. Kotys recalled her pantheon's surprise at the Helians' advanced technological nature, and the stark contrast with the humans in the area. Emily wondered how the Helians had found Kotys's pantheon after they crossed over. Her attention focused on a man poking his head inside the tent.

"Ganna?" asked the man.

"Dacius. Thank you for coming," said Kotys.

Emily found it interesting that Kotys was known differently to Dacius, and probably the others.

Dacius stepped inside. "What it is you want now? Another prophecy or something?"

"Actually...yes. This one you'll want to hear," said Kotys. She gestured at a cushion next to Emily. "Please, sit. This will be brief."

Emily slid off her cushion and off to the side. She did not think Dacius could see through her camouflage shielding.

Dacius took a seat and sighed. "We had a successful hunt, but I need to help with the preparation. Make this quick."

"The Romans are coming," said Kotys.

Dacius sat up straight. "How do you know this? Another vision?"

"No. A friend showed me the Roman camp to the west. They are a day away," said Kotys.

"What friend?"

"I'd rather not say if I don't have to."

Dacius sighed. "Well, I can send some scouts to check it out."

Kotys shook her head. "There's no time. We need to get to the caves now."

Dacius chuckled. "That's...quite a journey. To pack up and go takes time."

"They'll be here tomorrow. The Romans move fast."

"Let's just check if they're really there. I respect you and your contributions to the group, but this goes a bit beyond how to live our lives."

Kotys sighed. "Then you leave me no choice. My friend is near, and she will reveal herself and show you what she showed me. Please do not be startled."

Dacius puffed his chest out. "I'm a Dacian warrior. I don't startle easy."

Kotys chuckled as she gestured in Emily's direction.

Emily took that as her cue to disable her camouflage shielding. She made sure that her robe hologram was still active so that only her face would be visible.

Dacius gasped when Emily became visible. "Who…is this?"

"I'm Emily Snowden."

Kotys raised a finger. "The *heroic* Emily Snowden."

Emily wrinkled her brow. She was not aware that Kotys knew of the heroic prefix.

Dacius studied Emily, then Kotys. "Your source is a girl?"

Kotys nodded at Emily.

"I'm a bit more than a girl." Emily extended her PSD and showed the encounter with the Roman commander. "This is what I saw before coming here."

Dacius sat back. His eyes were glued to the projection when it played. "What manner of trickery is this?"

"It's just technology," said Emily. "I came to warn this camp."

"Why did you go to Ganna and not me?" asked Dacius, still eying the projection.

Emily smiled. "Would you have accepted me appearing out of thin air and showing you this?"

Dacius exhaled from his nose. "Probably not."

"Besides…Ganna is special."

Dacius's eyes narrowed. "Special how?"

"Well, she does have a connection with those…who are different. Surely you've benefited from her prophecies."

Kotys grinned at Dacius. "Perhaps it is time you knew my true name."

Dacius gazed at Kotys.

"I am Kotys."

Dacius drew his head back. "Kotys is a *god*."

"Yes, she is."

Dacius swept his gaze over Emily and Kotys. "This…this is most unusual."

Emily cracked her neck. "If you don't believe me, or Kotys, allow me to show you this camp from above."

"How?"

Emily gestured outside. "I can fly you there to see for yourself."

Dacius scrutinized Emily. "You have my attention. How would that work?"

"Let's go outside."

Kotys raised her head a bit. "I'd like to accompany you on this."

Emily nodded.

They assembled outside.

Emily moved away a bit to a private spot and formed the flying platform.

Dacius eyed the platform as Kotys grinned.

"Okay, hop on board," said Emily.

Dacius peered around before he stepped on it with Kotys in tow.

"Hold on to the sides," said Emily. "Oh, and I don't need a hologram around me anymore." She disabled the holographic robe.

Dacius's breathing slowed as he gripped the side and stared at Emily's survival suit.

Kotys chuckled.

The platform took off.

As it flew toward the Roman camp, Dacius peered over the edge. He gulped and focused on Emily. "You must be a god!"

Emily smiled. "Think of me as…Kotys's friend." She gestured at Kotys. "I'm here to help her, and by extension, you."

Dacius cast a sidelong look at Kotys, who nodded. He returned to looking over the edge.

After twenty minutes, they were high enough that the Roman camp was visible.

"It's true!" said Dacius. He ran a hand over his chin. "That…is a large camp. At least two legions. We'll be slaughtered."

Emily nodded. "I may have an idea to get everyone to the caves."

"How?" asked Dacius.

Emily pointed down. "This can be expanded to fit everyone and their supplies. Then I fly everyone there."

"You…you would do this for us?"

"She helps those in need," said Kotys.

Dacius studied the camp. "Any help would be appreciated."

Emily nodded. "There's work to do to get the camp ready to go. You'll need to break down whatever you want to take, and let me know if any of your animals are coming. That will determine how big the platform needs to be."

"It shall be done," he said. He looked over the edge again. "To fly…this must be what it's like to be a god."

Kotys chuckled. "Not quite, but close enough." She nodded at Emily.

"Okay, back to your camp," said Emily. "It's time to prepare to move."

Emily cracked her neck as she looked around the bustling camp. Six hours had passed since Dacius and Kotys had seen the Romans. Fear resided in the people's eyes as they did their best to break down tents, wrangle animals, and try to pack as much as possible. Children often cried out and it made her wonder if the Romans heard anything. The Dacians needed to move, or they would be slaughtered.

The PSD had no problem expanding, even when it was already formed into the flying platform. Emily loved that the pattern builder was still accessible when the platform initially rendered. It made adding and removing the guardrails much easier.

She had to go to the center of the camp in order to get enough space, and as the camp disassembled, the platform extended. The children already relocated to the middle along with the women and they brought supplies with them. The men were busy getting everything else. Emily moved the PSD control aspect to the front so she could see where she was flying to.

She observed the camp residents' behavior when Dacius had announced the plan. Although they were surprised, that reaction was replaced by fear, and then wonderment when she had been introduced. It helped that Kotys outed herself to the people. That seemed to calm them down. Emily played the part of having come to Kotys's assistance to help a fellow god. Although Emily was not keen on that aspect, it was not the time to argue about it.

Dacius hustled over to Emily. "We're almost ready to go." He eyed the platform.

"Don't worry," said Emily. "By the time the Romans get here, we'll be long gone."

Dacius sighed. "To think I would have awoken with a Roman sword to my chest. Trajan shall pay for this!"

"Well, I hope that the caves will help you hide out. Do you know where you'll go afterward?"

Dacius shook his head. "I don't, but we live to fight another day. I'll figure something out. Perhaps we can join up with others."

Emily nodded.

Dacius took off and barked an order at a man in the distance.

Kotys joined Emily. "Everything is going well so far."
"Yeah."

Kotys studied Emily. "Something's bothering you."

"After getting everyone to the caves, I'll need to leave. I'm still lost in time and…I miss Evaran and the others."

"I understand. You have a lot of love for him."

Emily smiled. "He's my mentor. I was supposed to be dead on an alien ship, in another galaxy, far from home. Evaran changed that. He saved me and my uncle."

Kotys nodded. "Evaran is family to you."
"Yeah."

Kotys looked out. "I'm sure he's using every possible approach at his disposal to find you."

Emily chuckled. "He better."

They shared a laugh.

"I'm going to miss you," said Kotys. "There's so much I want to talk to you about."

"Once Evaran finds me, you never know. We might stop in and chat."

Kotys grinned. "I'd like that."

Dacius joined them. "The last scout is in, and I believe everyone is on the platform."

"I'll check," said Emily.

She stepped off the platform and walked around the perimeter. It took some time due to the size, but she noticed that everyone stayed a good two feet of space away from the edge. They were probably not aware she was going to put up guardrails. After surveying everything and concluding they were ready, she went back to her PSD. She opened the pattern builder and erected six-foot tall guardrails all around the edge.

The residents murmured amongst themselves.

It hit Emily that she should probably raise the area with the PSD so she could see all around. She motioned for Kotys and Dacius to stay close, then raised the two cells that they were on. A set of stairs on the back led to the platform. Emily verified she had an unobstructed view of her surroundings.

"Amazing," said Kotys.

Emily smiled at Kotys and Dacius. "Are you both ready?"

They indicated they were.

"Okay. Where to?" asked Emily.

Kotys pointed off to the northeast. "I'll guide us."

Emily nodded. "Let's do this!" She pulled up on the PSD slowly.

The flying platform began to ascend.

The residents murmured again.

When the tree line had been cleared, Emily turned the platform around. It then began to move northeast. She did not want to go too high as there might be issues if things got out of hand with the residents.

After five uneventful hours, they arrived in a mountain valley.

Kotys pointed at a stream coming out of a cave. "It's hard to see now that it's dark out, but there's the entrance."

Emily's night vision was on, so she could easily verify what Kotys referenced. Emily guided the platform until it was level with the cave entrance. The rocky area outside the cave was large enough for a group to come down, and the path winding down to it was a natural choke point and easy spot to defend if need be. Although the platform was larger than the area outside the cave entrance, only a part of the platform needed to be grounded to begin unloading. Emily launched an illumination orb from her suit to provide light from above.

Dacius looked around. "You possess the power of the sun."

"Something like that," said Emily.

Dacius exhaled. "That flight was…incredible. It would change the fight against the Romans!"

Kotys tilted her head at Emily. "I think she has other plans for the future."

"All right," said Dacius. He smiled at Emily and squeezed her arm.

Emily watched as the unloading process started. If she was wrong to help the Dacians, she was sure Evaran would inform her.

Kotys shook her head. "It's hard for me to imagine you're friends with Lord Noskov."

Emily shrugged. "I've always known him as someone who helps in his own way, although I guess I don't really know his history."

"I'm living it, from your perspective. He is no friend of anyone not a Daedrould. If he is your friend, then he respects your power."

Emily remembered that Outsiders and Daedroulds had never really gotten along. In the future, they would, and historically they had during the Purification event. It seemed the relationship varied over time.

"I understand. Things will change," said Emily with a smile.

Kotys nodded. "I'm glad you came along. We wouldn't be alive to have this discussion otherwise."

"Speaking of which, what will happen now that everyone knows you're Kotys?"

Kotys shrugged. "A resurgence of belief in me, most likely. At least for a while. It will be good to be revered again."

Emily smiled.

After two hours, everything had been unloaded from the platform.

Dacius joined Emily and Kotys. He pointed at animal droppings and dirt on the platform. "We'll get this cleaned up."

"No need," said Emily.

She motioned for them to move to the rocky outcropping, then re-formed the platform to be smaller. Once she hovered over the edge, she flew over to where Dacius and Kotys stood and retracted the platform back into her PSD.

"I would greatly like to have one of those wands," said Dacius.

Emily grinned. "I bet most would. It only works for specific individuals, though."

"Gods," said Dacius.

Emily laid a hand on Kotys's shoulder. "You have one now. Protect and help her."

Dacius nodded.

Kotys smiled at Emily. "Before you go, I can use my ability to view your future. Perhaps that can aid you."

"Okay. How does that work?" asked Emily.

"Hold my hands," said Kotys. She extended them.

Emily complied. Her eyes widened when Kotys's eyes turned a dim shade of gray.

"Your future…dark, violent. Beware the glowing spiders, your name will be earned," said Kotys in an ominous tone. She jerked her hands back and her eyes changed back to normal.

Chills ran up Emily's spine. "What does that mean?"

"I don't know what was said. Only you know—and, well, Dacius," said Kotys.

"You said I had a dark and violent future and something about glowing spiders and earning my name," said Emily.

Kotys nodded. "Do they have meaning to you?"

Emily shook her head.

"It felt like a warning," said Kotys.

Emily sighed. "Traveling with Evaran is always dangerous." She looked up and squinted. "Okay, it's time for me to go." She hugged Kotys. "I'll find you in time, and I appreciate the reading."

"Safe journeys," said Kotys with a concerned look.

Emily nodded at Dacius. She formed a smaller flying platform and hopped on. After a final wave, she took off to the skies. Looking down, she observed them watching her leave. From their perspective, she probably did seem like a god. She enjoyed interacting with them, but her stomach still churned to think that Evaran had not arrived.

Kotys's warning played in the back of Emily's mind. Perhaps Kotys only saw what happened on any trip with Evaran, or it might be something else. Glowing spiders could be Time Wardens, a metallic spiderlike race that lived in the timeline void. To earn the heroic title usually meant some type of sacrifice. Maybe that was a play on words for death. Emily shuddered.

She pushed those thoughts out of her head as there were more important concerns for the moment. The next step was to reach the Black Forest and check in with Lord Noskov. Hopefully he had some idea to get her out of this mess.

09

Jelton gazed over the roof of the Torvatta, which was in low Earth orbit. A timeline change was coming, but he was not sure what to expect. Evaran and Jake seemed calm despite everything going on. Evaran was understandable, but Jake was a mystery. The things he must know having met a future Evaran.

Jelton found it somewhat troubling that this was the first meeting between him and Jake. If Jake had met a future Evaran, or two, and had not met Jelton until now, it meant that Jelton did not visit Lord Noskov's base with the future Evaran.

"There," said Evaran, pointing out into space.

Jelton's eyes were glued to where Evaran had pointed. Only small projectiles and satellites were visible. "What am I supposed to be seeing?"

"Just wait," said Jake, chuckling.

Jelton nodded. His eyes widened when what looked like a sheet of semitransparent metal approached them. There was no discernible top or bottom, and its width stretched as far as he could see. Although he had traveled throughout time and had even been a part of some timeline changes, he had never physically seen one. They always seemed like a wave that made things blurry.

"This is new, but it's amazing," he said.

Evaran nodded. "You have a sliver of cosmic energy in you, which will allow you to view them without the help of the Torvatta."

"It's cool to be able to see it like this," said Jake.

"Are you not worried about your father?" asked Jelton.

Jake shook his head. "Fix the timeline, and he'll be right back."

"Your confidence is inspiring, my friend."

Jake laughed. "I don't know about all that, but with Evaran, the Torvatta, and you, I think we can crack this."

Jelton smiled. "I hope so too."

He focused on the sheet as it came closer. When it swept over the Torvatta, he gripped the guardrail even though the Torvatta stood stable. He took a breath and released his death grip. The first thing he noticed when looking around was a multitude of ships. Advanced space facilities seemed to be everywhere. The Torvatta's inner shielding lit up, showing data labels of everything along with the different communication channels. The sheer number of satellites was hard to miss.

"Whoa," said Jake. "Looks like Earth is more advanced now?"

Evaran rubbed his chin. "It would appear so." He opened a holo menu.

A data window appeared in front of the group with a zoomed-in view of one of the satellites.

Jelton studied what seemed to be a symbol of some type that Jake and Evaran had focused on. The symbol was a red rectangle with a white circle in the middle. In the center of the circle were black lines that intersected in a cross, and at the end of each line, a perpendicular one extended out.

Jake's brows rose. "Uhh…that's a swastika."

"I concur," said Evaran. "That should not be present."

"What does this symbol represent?" asked Jelton.

Jake chuckled. "Bad. That's what it represents. Earlier in human history, this group called the Nazis tried to take over the world. They were responsible for a lot of bad stuff, but were defeated in 1945."

Jelton's eyes narrowed. "Then it appears the timeline change caused them to win."

"Yes, and that is our first clue," said Evaran. He looked to the side for a moment before he interacted with his ARI.

Jelton sensed that Evaran was about to tell V to do something. Although Evaran was hard to read, Jelton understood Evaran better now. It could be due to the cosmic energy in both of them, or maybe something else.

The Torvatta flew over to a satellite and shot out a beam.

Jelton studied the data window that popped up next to Evaran seemingly out of thin air. It intrigued him to watch as Evaran navigated various systems. Each system appeared as a fuzzy box, and as Evaran moved from system to system, a line appeared between them. Jelton noted that some of the systems Evaran was unable to connect to were red, and had the words "Security AI present".

"It appears there are many secured systems," said Evaran. He flicked his finger in the air.

The data window zoomed into a scrolling document.

"However, I have found a historical document," said Evaran. He tilted his head as the document scrolled. "It seems the Nazis put up a satellite network that could fire lasers at any point on Earth. New York and other major cities were burned as an example of its power."

Jake glanced at Evaran. "The only satellites around at that time were Helian-controlled ones."

"Yes, and the Torvatta did not detect any Helian satellites after the timeline change. It looks like this new satellite network went up in 1936, well before World War II. We need to go to that time period and check some events to verify when and where the timeline change occurred."

"If the Helians are around back then, we could check their portal register," said Jake.

Evaran nodded. "Yes. However, before that, I want to check on a historical event to determine if it occurred as scheduled or if something changed."

"Sounds reasonable," said Jelton.

Evaran interacted with ARI.

Everything outside the Torvatta faded away, then eased back in.

"It is now January 30, 1933, in the afternoon," said Evaran.

The Torvatta began to descend.

"Where are we going?" asked Jake.

"To the Chancellery building in Berlin, Germany, the location where Adolf Hitler became chancellor. I have recorded a moment where he is at a window and saluting a crowd," said Evaran.

"That's...pretty specific."

"History often is."

Jake chuckled. "So if it doesn't play out based on what you recorded, we know we're either too late or too early."

Evaran nodded.

Jake shook his head. "You must view this timeline as one big history book."

Jelton smiled. "It's how we, the Rift Guardians, observe our timeline, but to Evaran, a timeline is a page in a book, among many books in a library, among many libraries in a city, among many cities."

They shared a laugh.

"An apt analogy," said Evaran. He raised a finger. "However, do not think that I devalue anyone I meet because of this."

"It's cool, although Hitler I have no problem devaluing," said Jake.

Evaran half smiled. "I understand. Unfortunately, he is a part of history."

The Torvatta reached Berlin after twenty minutes.

Jelton studied the city as the Torvatta flew toward the Chancellery building. It occurred to him that Evaran had selected a time that took into account the twenty minutes to reach Berlin, and however long to get to the building. Like Evaran, Jelton had often used history as a method of verifying timeline changes, although he suspected Evaran had a much more exhaustive list of historical bookmarks.

The Torvatta hovered just out of range of an excited crowd assembled before a window.

Jelton studied the window where Hitler stood. It would be easy to take him out from where they were, but Jelton understood the implications of such an action. He wondered what Emily would think of where they were at.

"I guess we wouldn't detect your previous visits here in the Torvatta," said Jelton.

"That is correct. There should be seven other instances of me from a previous point in my timeline here at this moment."

Jelton glanced at Jake. "Ahh." He focused back on Evaran. "I guess the Torvattas not detecting one another is a good thing or it could get confusing quick."

"Yes." Evaran perused his ARI. "Everything is as recorded. However…an unusual energy signature has been detected in the room Hitler is in. It is Ziekah's signature."

"We going to get her?" asked Jake.

Evaran shook his head. "I suspect it took her some time to get where she is. With her knowledge of advanced technology, she most likely used Hitler as a stepping stone. We will visit the Helians, and determine if they detected her arrival."

"I've never met them before," said Jelton.

Jake chuckled. "They're arrogant assholes. Well, not all of them."

Evaran eyed Jake.

"Well, some are!"

Evaran half smiled. "Yes, they can be. However, they have information we need." He studied Jake and Jelton before facing the front of the Torvatta. "Let us assemble in the command center, then to Atlantis we go."

Jake recalled traveling to Atlantis several times for Lord Noskov. The fun aspect was going underwater. From what he had read, it used to be a bustling domed city, but the Purification event changed everything. Moving Atlantis to its current location made it harder to reach and easier to defend.

The city itself had become modular metallic globes that linked with each other. Although they should all be in one spot in 1933, in the future they would spread out, and even establish offices and facilities on land.

The Torvatta approached the Atlantic Ocean.

"Atlantis is underwater?" asked Jelton.

Evaran nodded. "Yes, and due to the Evaran Protocol, they will assist us."

"And that is…," said Jelton.

"An established protocol on how to interact with me."

"Interesting." Jelton motioned at Jake. "Have you been to Atlantis before?"

Jake chuckled. "Yeah, but in the future. It's pretty rare to go there, though. Nowadays you just fly to their regional base. Atlantis is where they house their most secretive technology and also some other confidential stuff."

Jelton nodded.

Jake watched as the Torvatta went underwater. Being on the roof would have provided a better visual, but the semitransparent half of the Torvatta in the command center still had a good view. It always amazed him how stable the Torvatta was regardless of what was happening outside of it. He envied Dr. Snowden and Emily for being able to live on the Torvatta, but Jake also understood the associated risks.

He fixated on a data window showing the depth. Atlantis was at the sea bottom and used the high pressure there as a defense mechanism. Ships not suited for that pressure simply would not make the journey. Not an issue for the Torvatta.

After forty-five minutes, they reached the edge of Atlantis.

Jake smiled as he watched eight spheres in a circle connected to a central sphere come into view. The metrics being displayed showed high pressure around them. The dark cold waters did not seem friendly to life, but the Torvatta had highlighted a few things swimming around. He had studied various types of creatures that survived this deep, and it intrigued him to see them.

A data window popped up with a Helian male.

Jake had studied nonhuman culture throughout the ages as part of his history classes at the Wild Haven Institute. Helians had run the world for a long time until the Purification event around 2600 BC. Their uniforms had changed as their technology moved forward, but even back then, they were already advanced. The Helian male in the data window had a black mesh suit with dark blue pads scattered around the body. He had no helmet, but a metallic neck guard with various digital lights blinking was present.

Evaran gestured at the Helian. "My credentials have been sent."

The Helian paused. "Evaran. Your credentials are valid, and the Evaran Protocol is in effect."

"Very good."

"Landing coordinates sent. Are you aware of the landing protocols?"

"I am," said Evaran.

The Helian nodded. "Enjoy your visit."

The data window closed.

"That Evaran Protocol really shortens things," said Jelton.

Evaran half smiled. "It has its benefits. There will be an agent to meet us when we land unless the protocol has changed."

Jake studied the sphere the Torvatta approached. A semi-transparent rectangular slat served as the docking bay entrance. Jake had been in one before, and it always impressed him that the shielding withstood the crushing pressures around the sphere.

"The sphere looks sturdy," said Jelton.

Evaran nodded. "It is spaceworthy as well, and can fly if need be."

"Do they ever use that aspect in the future?" asked Jake. "Like to leave Earth? After the time we came from, of course."

"I cannot say."

Jake chuckled. "Worth a shot."

The Torvatta flew through the docking bay shields and then landed in a designated square.

Jake grinned as he pointed at a Helian bustling toward the Torvatta. "I think that's our agent."

"I concur," said Evaran as he stood. "Let us go."

After several minutes, they assembled outside the Torvatta.

Jake smiled as the Helian approached the group. His outfit was different and resembled a black dress suit with a trench coat. Jake surveyed the group's immediate surroundings and saw a manager, a Helian enforcer, in the distance. They were a gaseous species in a robot body, and in the future, they would be freed from Helian servitude.

The Helian paused before the group to catch his breath. He extended a hand. "Agent Shiro Holocus."

Evaran studied Agent Holocus's hand. "A handshake instead of a salute. Intriguing." He shook Agent Holocus's hand.

"We're a bit more informal than we were in our past," said Agent Holocus, eying Evaran. He studied Jake and Jelton.

"Is something wrong?" asked Evaran.

Agent Holocus cleared his throat. "No…but this *is* my first Evaran Protocol. I didn't recognize your companions."

Evaran motioned at Jake and Jelton in sequence. "This is Jake Melkins and Jelton Stallryn. Dr. Albert Snowden, Emily Snowden, and V are my current companions, but they are missing. Jake and Jelton are helping me to locate them."

"Ahh, okay," said Agent Holocus. "First form, then."

Evaran nodded.

"Okay. How can I help?"

"I would like to use your global energy detection system. I am aware you have satellites that cover the world and provide a record on any portal being opened and the detection of unusual energy signatures."

Agent Holocus nodded. "We can do that, although it's hit and miss and doesn't cover certain types of portals, like parallel timeline ones. Follow me." As they walked, he peered at Evaran. "What are you looking for exactly?"

"A specific signature. We believe someone came to the past from the future. There has already been a timeline change, and we suspect her arrival was shortly before this time."

"Oh…you're coming from the future."

"Yes."

Jake found it interesting that he was unknown to Agent Holocus. That meant Jake did not travel to this time period or before with a future Evaran. Although the Evaran Protocol stated no data was to be stored on who Evaran traveled with, Lord Noskov and Lord Vygon violated the rule somewhat, and most of their records came from the Helians.

After thirty minutes and light conversation, they arrived at a busy room covered wall to wall with screens. In the middle sat a bullpen with multiple workstations and Helians working at them.

Jake had never seen the room before. A global map covered the screens on one side, while smaller screens on the opposite side housed data flows and information.

Agent Holocus led the group over to an empty workstation. "Here you go."

Evaran placed his UIC on the workstation. After a moment of perusing his ARI, he flicked a finger at one of the smaller screens on the back.

A global map appeared with a dot on Switzerland. A time stamp label showed January 5, 1930, at 8:46 a.m.

"The energy signature detected there is identical to Ziekah's," said Evaran.

Agent Holocus studied the screen. "There were three individual energy types registered, but of the three, two were unknown, although one of the unknown sorta resembled a rift signature."

"That is because it is a rift energy signature." Evaran gestured at Jelton. "His species comes from the rifts."

Agent Holocus's eyes widened. "Oh…I'd love to talk to you more about rifts!"

Evaran tilted his head.

"I mean…well…I wish I could," said Agent Holocus, clearing his throat.

Jelton laughed as he laid a hand on Agent Holocus's shoulder. "It's good to be curious, my friend."

"Exactly!"

Jake chuckled. Agent Holocus was not like the normal Helians that Jake knew.

"I suppose you're going to go back in time to that point?" asked Agent Holocus.

Evaran nodded. "Were any agents or managers sent out to investigate it?"

"Several managers scoured the area but didn't find anyone or anything that came through."

"Were there any unusual artifacts or signs of environmental destruction?"

Agent Holocus shook his head.

"I see. In that case, we will deal with her after she arrives. A timeline change would occur if we catch her as she currently escapes your search and causes havoc in the future."

Agent Holocus's eyes narrowed. "You could arrive earlier and enlist our help."

"Did that event happen?" asked Evaran.

Agent Holocus laughed. "No. I think I would be bad at time traveling."

"It is okay." Evaran half smiled at Jake and Jelton. "It is time to pick up Ziekah."

As the Torvatta rose through the Atlantic Ocean, Jelton went over the trip to Atlantis. He found it fascinating that the Helians not being able to find Ziekah in the past might be related to an event in his future. Time travel issues were not new to him, but usually he did not see them like this. He also noted that Agent Holocus seemed nervous around Evaran. Perhaps that was due to how rare it must be for Evaran to visit the Helians, especially at Atlantis.

"At least we know where she was in the past now," said Jake, lounging in a chair in the left U-shaped seating area. "How are we going to capture her? Tractor beam didn't seem to work last time. She just raised her arms, did that circle thing with her hands, and *boom*! Portal city."

"The Torvatta will stun her," said Evaran.

Jake nodded. "I was going to suggest that, but I didn't know if the Torvatta had it yet."

Evaran eyed Jake. "You have seen a future version of the Torvatta?"

"Yeah, but I can't say much more than that."

Evaran nodded. "My rules."

"Yep," said Jake, grinning big.

"Very well."

After twenty minutes, the Torvatta had ascended to low Earth orbit. The Torvatta jumped back to January 5, 1930, at 8:16 a.m., thirty minutes before Ziekah's portal would be detected. The Torvatta began its descent.

Jelton studied the date. "So it takes twenty minutes to get there, leaving us with a ten-minute buffer."

"That is correct," said Evaran. "I do not know how accurate the positioning is of the Helian's energy detection satellites, so it would help to survey the landscape where the portal will appear."

Jelton nodded. He had been impressed so far with Evaran's persistence in tracking down Dr. Snowden, Emily, and V.

Jelton wondered if Ziekah fully understood what she was up against.

After another twenty minutes, the Torvatta hovered over a small mountain valley. A river ran down the middle with a dense forest on either side.

"Umm…that's going to be hard to target her if she appears in the forest," said Jake.

"I concur," said Evaran. "We can track her until we find a desirable location to stun her."

Jake wrinkled his brow. "What if she can detect the Torvatta? She seemed to sense it last time."

"We were visible during the first encounter, but stealthed in the second. I do not believe she detected us in the second encounter."

Jelton grinned. "Then let's make the third encounter the final one."

Evaran nodded.

Jelton studied the location that the Helian satellite network had selected. The dot on the map translated to a dense forested circular area on the right side of the river. A part of him wanted to jump out of the Torvatta and tackle Ziekah, but he suspected he would just be portaled away.

They did not have a lot of information on her other than she could open portals by moving her hands in circles. She might have additional skills or abilities not seen yet. He understood Evaran's cautiousness and respected his approach.

The Torvatta hovered over the trees.

"Lot of life down there," said Jake. He grimaced. "Mostly bugs I bet."

"Do bugs bother you?" asked Jelton.

Jake shrugged. "Not really, but I grew up around human-sized versions that talked. I always feel weird seeing Earth bugs."

Jelton chuckled. "I understand."

"They don't bother you?"

"My skin would consume them as a source of energy."

Jake's brow raised. "Oh. I...didn't know you could do that."

Jelton smiled. "It can be useful."

After ten minutes, he studied the portal that opened between two trees. Although they only had a bird's-eye view, the Torvatta had registered the portal as being about six feet off the ground. When the portal dissipated, Ziekah registered.

"There she is!" said Jake.

Evaran nodded. "We will follow her until she is in an open area."

Ziekah stood and surveyed her surroundings, then moved toward the river. After she got there, she dipped her hands into it and splashed water on her face. She then lay on the riverbank for a moment.

"This is our opportunity," said Evaran.

He interacted with his chair console.

Jelton studied the data window that showed the Torvatta extending two tubelike structures from the black mesh panels on the outside. He had never seen them before, but the Torvatta was full of surprises.

"Firing now," said Evaran.

The Torvatta shot a stun beam from both structures.

Ziekah, as if sensing the stun beams, rolled to the side. Her shielding lit up around her as the ground erupted in sparks. She moved her hands in wide circular motions, then fell through a portal that formed under her.

Evaran stood. "She has shielding and fast reflexes, as well as being highly aware."

Jelton sighed. "So it seems we can't hit her with stun beams, or really any beam. Her shielding must be powerful to take two stun blasts."

"They are the same strength as my utility handle, and were not meant to cause harm."

Jake shook his head. "So…no tractor beam, no stun beams…what's next?"

Evaran sat back down and rubbed his chin. "For the moment, we wait. I suspect another timeline change will occur from this event, and also from whatever she does in the past."

"So two timeline changes are coming?" asked Jake.

Evaran nodded. "We will go to orbit and wait there."

Jake sighed. "If there was space, we could have just appeared under the portal and caught her as she dropped to the ground."

"There would be evidence of the Torvatta burning through to get to that position, and Agent Holocus mentioned there was no environmental destruction."

"Good point," said Jake.

Jelton watched as the Torvatta ascended. Although it was always hard to read Evaran, Jelton sensed that Evaran was aggravated. It was not the body or facial cues that suggested that, but a cosmic energy sense. Jelton was beginning to get more concerned as well. Ziekah was a crafty opponent, and Jelton's fear was they would find some evidence of Dr. Snowden's, Emily's, or V's death. Emily and V could handle themselves, but Jelton was concerned about Dr. Snowden. He was not a fighter, and Emily said he sometimes lost his temper.

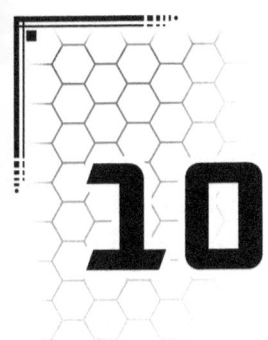

10

Dr. Snowden chuckled as Thereze played around with the map projection. She had been at it for a while and the brightness of it stuck out against the dark night. Twelve hours passed since they left, and his eyes drooped.

Thereze had tried to nap on the beds he had created, but she said being in the air was too uncomfortable, which probably led to her eagerness to get to the ground. That would also allow them both a chance to take care of their personal business. The moon provided some illumination and he noted its beauty in a clear sky at night.

"This light display is very informative," said Thereze, glancing up at Dr. Snowden.

He chuckled. "It can be."

"You must find it amusing that I'm interested in the map projection, as you call it."

"Interesting is the word I would choose," he said. "I've run into technologies much more advanced."

Thereze studied him. "I bet you have. Regardless, per the map, we are close to a resting place for the night."

Dr. Snowden grinned. "You sure you don't want to sleep up here? It'd be safer. Besides, the view is great up here."

"Perhaps, but...I'm not used to flying, and would feel safer on the ground."

"I was kidding," said Dr. Snowden. He adjusted the PSD and the platform began to descend. "There's a big field that butts up against a forest. We could stay on the edge and use the forest as cover if need be."

"A defensible location," she said, eying him. "You seem to be overly cautious in general."

He shrugged. "When you travel with Evaran, you have to be. If I had been careless in the future when I was attacked, I wouldn't be here..."

"I understand," said Thereze. She peered over the edge. "The area is hard to see, but I trust your judgment. As long as I am in contact with the ground, I will be okay."

Dr. Snowden nodded. During the flight, she had informed him about her particular Voodoo Daedrould strain, or Vodou as she called it. She had also mentioned other voodoo strains that went by other names. Dr. Snowden saw some comparisons to the vampire Daedrould strains in that although they were all vampire, they went by different names and had unique characteristics. It still boggled his mind how complex the nonhuman world was.

Among the various Voodoo Daedrould strains, hers was the most powerful, but like the ancient vampires relative to other vampire strains, hers had one of the smaller populations. Although she did not speak much about the ancient vampires, she did seem to light up when Lord Vygon's name was brought up. It made Dr. Snowden think there was something more than a friendship with Lord Vygon.

After another twenty minutes, they landed at the edge of a forest.

Dr. Snowden waited for Thereze to disembark before he pulled the platform back into his PSD. When he did, Thereze's items rested on the ground.

"That is a powerful object," said Thereze, studying his PSD as she gathered her things.

He smiled. "Definitely is." He looked around before launching an illumination orb. "That should provide us some light. I noticed a small clearing that goes somewhat into the forest. We can go there, or set up here."

"I think inside might be uncomfortable due to insects."

Dr. Snowden raised his PSD. "Wherever we go, I'll emit that same shield used when we were flying. It should keep them out."

"You think of everything," said Thereze with a smile.

He nodded and saw how Lord Vygon would try for Thereze, assuming their friendship was more than a friendly one. She was easygoing, inquisitive, smart, and attractive. He lucked out on having her as a traveling companion and wondered if he and Emily were viewed like that by Evaran, minus the attractive part.

They moved into a small clearing in the forest.

Thereze cleared a spot on the ground to make it level, then placed a thick blanket on it. After getting a pillow, and placing a few more sheets, she lay on her side and rested her head.

Dr. Snowden opened his pattern builder program from his PSD and then selected the bed pattern. He added the same shielding used on the flying platform to it but expanded it into a large bubble big enough to encompass them. He laid his PSD on the ground and then formed his bed. The shield emanated out from the bed and provided some light. He pulled his illumination orb back into his suit.

"It's beautiful," said Thereze, looking around at the shield.

Dr. Snowden nodded. "Sure is. Why don't you get some rest? I'll take first watch."

"For what?"

"You know…in case something comes by."

She chuckled. "More defense, but there is always the possibility of danger."

He smiled. "I could use the PSD to build a structure with a window in it and then we sleep in that."

"I prefer the ground to be close to nature."

"All right. No problem there."

She nodded then closed her eyes.

Dr. Snowden lay on the bed and looked up at the stars peeking through the trees. The moonlight provided visibility, and the PSD's shielding lit up in places where insects hit it. His muscles relaxed and he knew he would easily fall asleep. Perhaps Thereze was right. They were on the edge of a forest and in the middle of nowhere. He was confident they could get away if needed, and he was not aware of any man-eating predators in the region based on history.

He focused on sensing everything around him. Ever since he had lost half of his nanobots and most of his cosmic energy that coursed through him, he had spent time trying to adapt to it. Kess, his girlfriend who he had met in the previous adventure, encouraged him to practice, and he had a good grasp on his senses and their limits. Even now, he sensed the insects on the ground and in the trees, small creatures that roamed the area, and the soft wind that rustled nearby leaves.

The peaceful environment took a toll on his ability to keep his eyes open, though. He yawned several times as his muscles unwound. Thereze's light breathing and relaxed face showed she was sleeping without any issues. His eyelids drooped.

Perhaps he should follow her advice and just nap. If something came, he was sure his cosmic senses would alert him. She probably possessed that sense too, which gave him confidence that maybe a quick nap would not hurt anything. He closed his eyes and embraced the bed's neural sleeping effect.

Dr. Snowden's heart pumped furiously as he sat up. His cosmic senses were going wild and ended the nice sleep he had been having. He stood and pulled his bed back into his PSD. Daylight had begun to appear and it was about 6:00 a.m. He focused on the surrounding environment and detected unusual energy signatures.

Thereze stirred in her bed. Her eyes slowly opened as she yawned and looked around. "What's going on?"

Dr. Snowden drew his lips flat. "Outsiders. Six of them."

Her brow furrowed as she stood.

"Werewolves…assuming my cosmic senses are detecting them right," said Dr. Snowden. "We should go. Now."

Thereze gathered her things.

As they moved to the field to form the flying pattern, five muscle-bound werewolves and one large one burst through the clearing and surrounded them. The large one stood around nine feet tall, while the others were around seven feet. They had brown fur and overly large clawed fingers.

Dr. Snowden formed a baton and activated his energy shield.

"This is Zangrith pack territory," said the large werewolf in a deep, gruff voice.

"We only stayed the night, but we're leaving," said Dr. Snowden.

The pack laughed.

"Is that so?" asked the large werewolf. He growled as he studied Dr. Snowden and Thereze. "A Daedrould and...I'm not sure what you are."

"A traveler who doesn't want trouble," said Dr. Snowden.

"I might have let you leave...but you travel with a mambo. We don't like mambos."

Dr. Snowden's voice raised. "There's no need for this."

The large werewolf grinned, baring his sharp teeth. "I think there is." He looked around at the other werewolves. "Save the heads."

The pack whooped and growled and then charged forward.

Dr. Snowden fired a repulsion blast to the right, knocking two werewolves back. He then fired a mist beam in front of him while grabbing Thereze's arm.

"Let's go!" he said as he ran out into the field away from the werewolves.

He peeked back and when the other werewolves moved through the cloud, he lit it up with a stun beam.

Two werewolves fell to the ground and writhed around. The large werewolf and one of the still-standing ones dashed forward.

Dr. Snowden swallowed hard. He fired a repulsion blast that knocked the smaller werewolf back, but the large one kept coming. He raised his shield as the large werewolf came into range.

The large werewolf tried to smash Dr. Snowden, but the hit slid off to the side of the shield.

Dr. Snowden stumbled back from the hit.

The three smaller werewolves that were not stunned rushed back to join the larger werewolf. They charged forward.

Dr. Snowden raised his shield.

The large werewolf performed an uppercut.

Dr. Snowden angled his shield, but the impact sent him flying through the air. He crash-landed a bit away. His blood boiled and his breathing increased as Thereze got surrounded.

She closed her eyes and began to chant.

Totems made of smoke rose from the ground. They shot dark tendrils at the werewolves. The smaller ones were wrapped up, but the large one moved toward Thereze.

"Bosou Kablamin, I summon you to protect me!" said Thereze.

A fifteen-foot humanoid materialized in front of Thereze.

Dr. Snowden's eyes widened. The large humanoid looked primitive and wielded a massive club. He had a full beard along with a bald head. Thick chains wrapped around his body like a suit of armor.

Bosou shouted and the chains fell off him, revealing dark skin.

The large werewolf paused.

Bosou charged forward and with a sweep of his club, the large werewolf sprawled back.

The smaller werewolves took off into the forest.

The larger werewolf looked around after getting up. It charged Bosou.

Bosou swung at the larger werewolf, who dodged the attack.

The werewolf swiped at Bosou's gut.

Claw marks initially appeared but faded away.

Bosou swatted away the now-confused large werewolf, who took off once it had landed. He looked around before standing before Thereze.

She reached into her bag and laid two small half-wrapped pieces of dried meat on the ground.

Bosou grinned and dropped to his knees. His hands were a blur as he devoured the offering. Once the food was gone, he faded away.

Dr. Snowden joined Thereze. "I…uhh…what was that?"

"A mambo is always prepared." She smiled. "I can summon loa to do my bidding with the right offering."

Dr. Snowden nodded. He suspected that she was able to control matter to some degree using Daedrould energy and not actually summoning anything, but he chose not to bring that point up. He formed the flying pattern. "I think we should go while we can."

She laid a hand on his chest. "You took a hard hit."

He licked his lips. "Not the first time, and my suit protected me, although that hit did hurt."

She got the rest of her things from the clearing while he flew the flying platform over to her location.

After a few minutes, they were in the air.

"Whew," said Dr. Snowden. "I think if there's a next time, I'll form a defensive structure to sleep in if need be."

"We'll be okay for the rest of the trip," said Thereze. She smiled as she moved to one of the beds. "I'm going to rest for a bit."

He nodded and focused on the map projection. It would be another twelve hours, but at least he could nap in his seat without fear of a werewolf pack mauling them.

During the flight, he analyzed the attack by the werewolves. There had always been Daedrould concerns with Outsiders, and it seemed he had gotten caught up in it. He wondered if the pack would have backed off if Evaran had been present.

Dr. Snowden had taken several quick naps, and Thereze had joined him after a solid four-hour one. They had discussed the event, but after having flown for so long, he was tired again. Traveling with the flying platform had its perks, but sitting for long periods bothered him. The sun had started to set at 6:20 p.m., and he was glad to have some daylight to work with.

"Should be...there," said Dr. Snowden, pointing at the map projector. He looked over the side. "Hard to tell, though..."

"It'll be good to be on the ground again," said Thereze.

He chuckled. "Yeah, I'm with you there."

The platform descended into a clearing near Lord Vygon's beacon.

Once they had descended, Dr. Snowden pulled the platform into his PSD. "Okay, it should be inside a tree."

"Inside?"

"Well...it uses a hologram to mask it, but it should be there." He waved forward. "C'mon, we can leave your things here. The beacon is right over there."

When they arrived at the spot, he surveyed the environment. The tree he had expected was gone, and in its place was a prickly bush.

"Are you sure it's here?" she asked.

He smiled. "Yep, watch this." He reached through the bush, causing part of the hologram to dissipate.

A four-foot cylinder came into view.

"There we go," he said, kneeling. "I'm actually not sure how to activate it."

Thereze joined him and studied the beacon. "This is it?"

"Yeah. Last time I was here, Evaran reached in, and Lord Vygon was in a tree, so he dropped down." Dr. Snowden looked around. "I'm guessing he's not around at the moment."

"Maybe it reacts to our presence and alerts him somehow."

Dr. Snowden nodded. "You're probably right. I guess it wouldn't hurt to hole up here for a while. I doubt there are any werewolves running wild in his domain."

She smiled.

"Let's hope he comes quick," said Dr. Snowden. His eyes narrowed as a strange sensation washed over him.

Thereze nodded. "It'll be good to—"

A shimmering semitransparent sparkling curtain that reached from the ground to the sky swept past.

Dr. Snowden's eyes widened when Thereze disappeared and the environment around him changed. He remembered seeing a curtain like that before from the Torvatta, and it had been a timeline change. He was not only in the past, but now also in an altered timeline. Although the beacon still existed, it was now rusted. He grimaced as he thought about Thereze. She had blinked out of existence.

He sat down and leaned against a nearby tree. If there had been a timeline change, Evaran would definitely know about it. However, if he had not known where Dr. Snowden was before, it would be even harder now. It could never be easy.

He gritted his teeth. Tiredness and exhaustion were his constant companions. He opened the pattern builder. At least he could use the new flying platform pattern to sleep in. After the werewolf attack, sleeping on the ground was not something he wanted to repeat. He would try to figure out what to do next after a good night's rest.

Dr. Snowden yawned as several beeps woke him up. His cosmic senses told him something was off. He rushed over to the map projector, which displayed some approaching red dots at a higher altitude. A quick glance at the time revealed he had only slept for three hours, as it was around 10:00 p.m.

He sighed as he peered out over the edge of the flying platform. Nothing stood out, but as dark as it was, it would be hard to see anything. He lowered the platform to the ground and then retracted it into his PSD.

After activating his camouflage shielding, he hid behind a tree, closing his eyes and focusing. He sensed what seemed like drones approaching. One thing he noted with ease was the buzzing sound the drones made. There was also another sound that reminded him of a ship. He was near a clearing, but he decided against going out into the open to investigate.

He shot up a grappling beam into the tree. After securing himself by straddling a strong branch, he used his PSD as a pair of binoculars. His current position allowed him to peek into the nearby field and the surrounding tree border.

His heartbeat accelerated when he viewed the drones in perfect clarity. They looked like beefy Frisbees with various segmented arms on the edges. The drones' scanning beams resembled spotlights from a guard tower as they scoured the open field.

His eyes widened at the large ship that flew in and landed in the middle of the open area. Soldiers, robotic dogs, various slabs, and drones poured out of several ramps. He was not sure what they were looking for, but he did not plan to stick around. It was time to go. He dropped out of the tree and booked it deeper into the forest. It would not take long for them to reach his location, and he had no intention of being caught.

One of the upsides of his suit was that it gave him the ability to not only run across difficult terrain with ease, but jump if needed. If he had to do this without it, it would have been game over near the trees.

After twenty minutes of running, movement ahead made him pause.

A tree shifted into a dark-skinned human form.

Dr. Snowden remembered that tree shifters were generally friendly, but given the situation, he was not sure.

"Follow me if you want to escape detection," said the humanoid.

Dr. Snowden nodded. "Lead on. Oh, I'm Dr. Albert Snowden, by the way."

"I know. That's one of the names Ziekah is searching for. I'm Jamas Kreelin."

Dr. Snowden's stomach churned. It hit him that Ziekah had probably had time to develop technology to scan around for anyone with an unusual energy signature across the planet. She might have even hijacked the existing Helian one. There was no doubt in his mind that they had detected him in the area. He followed Jamas to a large boulder.

Jamas tapped the boulder in a unique pattern.

A hole opened on the boulder's side.

"You'll be safe inside," said Jamas.

Dr. Snowden pulled out his PSD and scanned the boulder. He was not sure how a hole had opened in it as he did not detect any doorway mechanisms. Another humanoid with an elemental energy signature had been detected inside. Maybe it had something to do with the hole. With a final look around, he stepped into the entrance area, which extended into an angled tunnel that led underground. He spotted the rock elemental standing inside.

Jamas followed Dr. Snowden in while the elemental touched the side of the interior, causing the hole to close.

"I'm Dr. Albert Snowden, and you must be...a rock elemental of some sort," he said, extending a hand.

The elemental returned Dr. Snowden's handshake. "Trulk, and yes, I'm a rock elemental."

"Let's go," said Jamas. "They can scan underground to a certain depth. We need to be under that and then we can talk."

The group hustled down the tunnel. After thirty minutes, they reached a large open cavern.

Dr. Snowden studied the new environment. Like the Underground Railroad station he had visited earlier, there were tents everywhere. A stream ran near the back, and the inside of his helmet showed the environment to be a comfortable temperature. He lowered his helmet and took in the variety of odd odors. Cooked food had a prominent smell, but there was also a strong earthy scent. It reminded him somewhat of a campground he used to go to with Dan and Emily.

"We should be safe here from Ziekah," said Jamas.

"I have *so* many questions," said Dr. Snowden.

Jamas pointed at a nearby fire pit. "Come. We can relax and talk there."

Dr. Snowden took a seat on a stone bench opposite Jamas while Trulk took off to another part of the cavern.

"So…why is Ziekah hunting you in particular?" asked Jamas. "We know she kills nonhumans on the spot, but she is putting forth a lot of effort for you. You got one of her destroyers to land in a field."

Dr. Snowden sighed. "It's a long story, but this is an altered timeline."

"What do you mean?"

"It's not supposed to be like this. This is Lord Vygon's territory and his beacon was destroyed."

Jamas drew his head back. "The ancient vampire? He died hundreds of years ago."

Dr. Snowden shook his head. "He's supposed to be alive. Let me start from the top. Ziekah attacked us in AD 2012 and then zapped me back here to the past. I flew to Lord Vygon's beacon, and a timeline change hit. She's changed things."

"AD 2012? Are you a time traveler?"

Dr. Snowden nodded.

"And who is the 'us' that Ziekah attacked?"

"Well, she attacked me, but I travel with Evaran. I suspect she has gone after my niece, Emily, as well."

"I…don't know those names."

Dr. Snowden tilted his head. "You don't remember the Purification event?"

"I've never heard of it."

Dr. Snowden figured that either it had happened and anyone with knowledge of it was dead, or Ziekah had traveled back before that event.

"We travel in space and time, and apparently, one of the bad guys we dealt with happens to be someone she is looking for. She blames us for his death, so…I guess her plan was to zap us back to the past and then deal with us."

Jamas chuckled. "Ziekah is a monster. This is what's left of the Ollikrin Nation down here. The elementals provide us safe harbor. I fear the worst for any nonhuman caught out in the open."

"I knew the Ollikrin Nation in the original timeline. Delia and Mary Everoak were friends of mine."

Jamas's eyes widened. "I don't know Mary, but Delia was our anchor. She put up a fierce fight, but even she could not withstand a laser fired from space."

"Yeah, that doesn't sound good." Dr. Snowden looked around. "Huh. This is actually where Lord Vygon had his cave back in the original timeline. It's a little different, but I recognize parts of it now."

"I wish I had known some of the elder nonhumans. Most died in Ziekah's initial purge. She has built a highly advanced society that has enslaved humans and killed nonhumans. She has even advanced outside of Earth."

"She's crazy," said Dr. Snowden.

"Crazy and with the power to back her up. There were rumors that she was looking for three people. You, your niece, and someone called V."

"V?"

"Yes, who is that?" asked Jamas.

Dr. Snowden sighed. Ziekah must have sent V back somehow. "V is an artificial intelligence orb that travels with us. So she sent all three of us to the past, and is now hunting us."

"Would your friend Evaran travel in time to help any of you?"

Dr. Snowden nodded. "Definitely, but not unless he knows where we are. I suspect…he's scouring history looking for us."

"Would he be able to fight Ziekah?"

"Oh yeah. His ship, the Torvatta, would really be helpful about now."

Jamas smiled as he looked around. "This is the only life I've known. This society down here is a mix of many different nonhumans. Living topside is but a dream for many of us, although as a tree shifter, I have some advantage in that regard."

Dr. Snowden pursed his lips. "This is not how any of this should be. The timeline needs to be fixed."

"I don't know much about that, but it sounds like you do."

"It…can be crazy too."

Jamas chuckled. "It would seem so. Hey, you hungry? We have food and drink, and you're welcome to stay here as long as you need."

Dr. Snowden smiled. "Yeah, I could use something other than a food pellet."

He stood as Jamas did, then followed him. It saddened Dr. Snowden to see the once-great Ollikrin Nation reduced to hiding out in a rock cavern protected by elementals. Why Ziekah was doing what she did when she only wanted Seeros was a mystery. He understood her desire to avenge him, but if she changed the timeline, she could go pick Seeros up. It hit him that she might not be aware of his status. Having a spacefaring empire and resources at her disposal would make finding out easier. He wished she had ignored the avenging part.

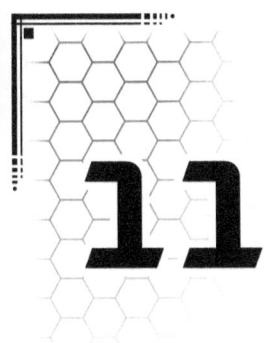

11

V had spent several days in Omoikane's library studying the scrolls. There were only a few mentions of time travel, but they focused on the possibility of it rather than anything helpful. It was clear that he would need to get to Atlantis. Although he knew its location as of 2600 BC, he needed to determine its current location and a way to get there.

A timeline change alarm triggered in his processing.

He switched to orb mode and exited the library. On the way out of the shrine, he flew past Omoikane.

"Where you going?" asked Omoikane.

"A timeline change approaches."

"How could you know that?"

V hovered next to Omoikane. "Evaran built it into me."

"Oh…well…what happens in these timeline changes?"

"Many things can happen, but underground is not a desirable location to be when one occurs."

Omoikane drew his head back. "Then we need to get out of here!"

"Analysis. You do not have temporal shielding, so you will most likely not exist in your current state or position. I do have temporal shielding, and will appear in the new timeline in my current location."

Omoikane sighed. "So much to learn. I wish we had more time to discuss these things."

"I must leave now," said V. He began to fly away, but flew back to Omoikane. "I will seek you out in the new timeline if I can."

"Oh, please do!"

V's lights glowed brighter. He flew out of the shrine and ascended as high as possible. The shimmering curtain that swept the land was not unfamiliar to him. By the time he had visually detected it, it had already reached him. He shimmered out of view as the timeline change washed over him.

The castle and the multilayered structure of the city had disappeared. Kagoshima was now an advanced city. Various ships flew through the air, and multiple drones buzzed around. V descended and started to scan.

He picked up a large number of communication signals. Although the encrypted ones were undecipherable, the unencrypted ones transmitted details on people. He continued his scan. The sleek buildings had solar panel–like structures on the top sides. The roof had edges lined with communication gadgets. A quick analysis showed that this would be a good setup for a surveillance state.

He flew down to the street level. Large tunnels sat on the streets and ran between buildings and wrapped around the building bases. Evenly distributed tunnel openings allowed for exit onto a narrow sidewalk. Only a few open areas existed, but even they had a pillar in them that seemed to transmit visual and audio information.

After going into one of the tunnels, he surveyed the people hustling around. They all wore the same outfit and had a bar code of some type on the back of their gray outfits. Humanoid robots shepherded the humans and directed them into other places.

An alert fired that several drones approached. V ran a quick scan and determined that they were on an intercept course. He was not sure how they had detected him, but it might have been due to his scans, or perhaps they used another detection system. His presence might have caused a slight turbulence in the air. That could be the cause. As a test, V flew off to the side.

The drones altered their course.

V flew to a tunnel exit.

The drones accelerated. One of them beamed a light at V, which highlighted him. Sirens began to wail.

V exited the tunnel and ascended.

Larger drones arrived on the scene and started to scan around with red beams.

He suspected that without the turbulence, they would not be able to find him.

As if on cue, a fine mist spewed from the sides of nearby buildings.

V flew up through the mist.

A large drone flew above V and fired a beam at him.

V dodged it and went sideways between two buildings. He found an open window and flew in while scanning for a ventilation system. The office did not have one, so he checked the next room and found one. After popping the grill out and moving in, he put it back in place.

Humanoid robots entered and searched the room. Upon not finding anything, they exited.

V concluded that stealthed drones must not be allowed in the city. Even if the city drones did not detect him directly, they would indirectly. The number of robots and drones made him think Kagoshima was locked down.

He flew through the vent system until he arrived at a small room where two men sat hunched over while eating a meal. The meal containers resembled plastic bread boxes, and the men ate what appeared to be sandwiches of some type.

One man was much older than the other one. V ascertained that the men appeared to be Japanese, but the language they spoke did not register as Japanese. V could still understand it due to his universal translator. He listened in.

"So…three days and you're done," said the younger man.

The older man sighed. "Yes, then off to a retirement camp."

The younger man eyed the older one. "You should be happy. No more cleaning, just relaxing."

"Until what? I die? The retirement camp I'm going to doesn't allow leaving once you're there. I'm exchanging one prison for another. At least out here, I can see my family."

"I didn't know you couldn't leave," said the younger man before taking a bite out of his sandwich.

The older man closed his eyes as he placed a hand on his neck while stretching his neck muscles. "I didn't either, until I got my instructions last week for it."

"Well, you won't be worked to death there."

The older man shrugged.

A robot barged into the room. "Lunchtime is over."

"Yeah, yeah," said the younger man.

The two men put the rest of their lunch into the plastic containers. After cleaning up, they followed the robot out of the room.

V searched for a retirement camp definition in his knowledge base but found nothing. The older man did not seem excited about it. Perhaps that might be a place to retrieve information. V took advantage of the situation and opened the grill, flew out, then placed the grill back. The men would provide a wake V could use. He left the room and caught up to the men, staying right behind them.

When they passed an office with an open window, V flew into the room. He verified it was clear, then exited the building. The city was not a safe place to be, so he ascended as high as possible. Thankfully, the city's detection system had not been triggered. The mist from earlier probably only fired due to being detected in the tunnel

As he flew above, he noted the patrol routes of the drones in order to avoid them. His next step would be to get out of the city and find a retirement camp. Perhaps someone there had information on Kagoshima's current state, or the world in general. Whatever had caused the timeline change had done it in the past, which V calculated Evaran must have noticed. V was confident Evaran would come at some point, and with that in V's memory, he took off to the outskirts of the city.

After flying around outside the city for about a day, V discovered a walled-off camp near the sea. The older man V had listened to earlier had mentioned that retirement camps were another prison, and the camp looked like that. Outside the walls were various towers, and robotic quadrupeds patrolled the ground. Several drones were in the air, and V detected heavily armed watercraft in the water.

He flew over the spacious camp and ran a high-level scan of the people milling about. Most seemed to be elderly, and robotic humanoids hustled around with trays. When he was over the crowded beach, he observed many of the people under umbrellas sitting back in chairs. There were fewer robotic servants around, and it seemed that from the beach, the outside defenses were not visible.

An umbrella on the edge of the crowd was selected as an infiltration point. V descended until he was behind a small building of some sort. Foul smells were detected, leading him to conclude it was probably a portable bathroom. He went into projected mode that made him appear similar to the old man from before. After verifying the path to the umbrella was clear, he strolled over.

An older woman looked up at V as he approached.

V gestured at a nearby empty chair. "May I join you?"

The woman shrugged. "I don't mind."

V ensured he was not being observed, then took a seat. He registered a cool breeze and detected a drop in the temperature under the umbrella. The sound of people talking and soft music in the background permeated the air. This fit the criteria of a comfortable setting for a human.

"I am V," he said, smiling at the woman.

"I am Kaiyo," she said. She studied V. "Your name is unusual."

V nodded. "I am not from around here."

Kaiyo sighed. "Wherever you came from, I'm sorry you're here."

V studied Kaiyo as she frowned. She seemed to echo the older man's assessment of retirement camps.

"You do not like it here?" he asked.

She waved an arm around. "No. Everything around here will be with you until you die. You can never leave."

"I understand."

"Do you? If you're here, that's it."

V looked around. "It is a nice environment."

She chuckled. "You speak strangely." Her eyes widened. "Are you an android?"

"No."

She drew her head back. "Hmm...what's your purpose here?"

V sensed that she was able to detect him through his hologram somehow. He decided to try a different tactic to elicit information. "I am a traveler, and I am surveying everything."

Kaiyo's eyes narrowed. "How did you get here...?"

"I flew in."

She tilted her head, then laughed. "Flew in..."

"Yes."

Kaiyo gazed at an approaching robot.

V rolled off to the side and dissipated his projected mode. When in orb mode, he shimmered out of view.

Kaiyo jumped when she looked to where V had been.

The robot arrived and asked Kaiyo if he could be of service. She shook her head and waved the robot off.

Once the robot was far enough away, V said, "I am still here, but hidden."

"Show yourself," said Kaiyo, looking around.

V landed on his seat, then disabled his stealth.

Kaiyo chuckled. "Aww...you're a little robot."

"I am little, but not a robot," said V. He hovered, then shimmered out of view. "It may be best for me to stay hidden."

"Okay." Kaiyo smiled. "Where did you come from?"

"Far away," said V. "I detected this camp from afar, and believe it is a retirement camp."

Kaiyo sighed. "That's exactly what it is. Once you've worked thirty years, you come here to live out the rest of your life."

"My scans show you to be in your fifties."

Kaiyo looked down. "I'm not ready to be here. There's so much more I want to do."

"What group keeps you here?"

"This is all Ziekah's plan. She controls the world and beyond."

It made sense to V now that Ziekah had traveled back farther in time and used advanced technology to change humanity.

"Do you know when she implemented these changes?"

Kaiyo shrugged. "History is never taught. If you don't pass a competence exam before twenty, you get placed into a role. I was a janitor because I failed mine twice."

"So Ziekah selects people based on their ability, and uses the rest as menial labor."

Kaiyo sighed. "After thirty years, you come to one of these retirement camps. When you die, you get cremated, and that's it."

"I am sorry to hear that. It does not sound pleasurable."

She chuckled. "Not pleasurable is about right."

"Do you have access to computers?"

She nodded. "There's terminals inside the main facility we can use. Nothing really on them, though."

"No information network?"

"There is…but it's mostly news."

"I would like to interact with a computer."

"It could be dangerous if you're detected." Kaiyo stood. "Follow me. This is the most excitement I've had in a while."

V shimmered into view and raised a segmented arm.

Kaiyo studied his claw.

"It is a high five."

She chuckled as she tapped V's claw. "You're very strange, but I like you."

V's lights glowed brighter before he faded out of view. He flew close to Kaiyo as she trudged up to the main facility. A scan around revealed that although people talked and listened to music, they seemed sad. Those who did not pass a competence exam were sentenced to a life of drudgery. He was not sure what Ziekah intended to do with a society like that, but he would learn more once he was able to connect to a computer.

After twenty minutes, they were inside a large room with two rows of booths.

V followed Kaiyo to a booth, where she sat down and put her hand on a scanner.

The scanner lit up and a thin computer screen slid up out of the table. A keyboard and a joystick raised up before the screen.

V studied the screen. It only had a text box with an arrow at the end.

"What do you want to know?" asked Kaiyo.

"Current events," said V.

While Kaiyo typed in something, V scanned the booth. The computer underneath the table was sealed in a container, and there were no ports that he could detect. Although there were wires leading from the monitor, keyboard, and joystick, as well as one for power and another for what V assumed was networking, connecting with the computer seemed impossible.

"There," said Kaiyo, gesturing at the screen.

V studied the various links. They seemed to link out to various news articles, but he noticed that they were all from the same source. The links covered everything from resistance fighters being caught and killed, to improvements in retirement camps. Ziekah controlled the narrative and had, in essence, made humanity a slave race.

"This is not how everything is supposed to be," he said.

"What do you mean?" asked Kaiyo.

V shot down a projection of Dr. Snowden's college. "This is how things are supposed to be."

Kaiyo studied the projection. "There's old people walking around…freely…"

"Yes. Ziekah has altered the past."

Kaiyo sighed. "How do we fix it?"

"I am not sure, but I have a powerful friend who can help. Perhaps there is mention of him on this network."

Kaiyo gestured at the screen. "Whatever you need to look for, I hope it's there. I can use a booth for several hours, so we should be okay here."

"You do not mind providing cover for me?"

Kaiyo smiled. "I'm curious to see how this all plays out."

V's lights glowed brighter. Human curiosity, despite the harsh setting, still shone through. A brief image of Dr.

Snowden and Emily appeared in memory. V hoped they were doing okay. He knew they could handle themselves, especially after all they had been through. His lights dimmed a bit thinking of Emily, and how he was not available to help her.

Over the next four hours, V found little information of value from the network. It appeared to be one of Ziekah's propaganda methods. Kaiyo would have no way of knowing what was real or not as the data she pulled up was her only source of information outside of family visits. His sensors detected movement coming from outside the room. He shimmered out of view.

"There are robots coming," he said before flying away.

Kaiyo looked around as several humanoid robots entered.

V noted that they performed an initial scan of the room upon entering. He dipped behind a booth so they would not detect him, but he would be able to listen in on any conversations.

"Have you noticed any unusual activity in this room?" asked a robot.

"I haven't," said Kaiyo.

"Take her for a diagnostic scan," said a robot.

V flew to the back and peered down the lane that led to the room exit. Kaiyo was being escorted out and he wanted to help her, but in doing so, he would not only expose himself but possibly get captured. The robots' presence seemed unusual. Perhaps V had been tracked at the camp somehow, and Ziekah was looking for him.

He waited until the robots cleared the room before exiting. As he ascended into the air, he detected a wide-beam scan over the camp. A red outline appeared around him.

Several drones moved to intercept while robot guards on the ground shot at him.

V tried to shake the drones but they were persistent. The massive ship in the sky prevented any way of trying to stealth. He would need cover. In the meantime, he needed to avoid being captured. He disabled his stealth and projected a large sphere around him. That allowed for them to target him, but they would hit the holographic parts and not him.

He pulled up a map of the local area in his memory. An empty warehouse a few miles away seemed to be the best place to hide out. He noted that the warehouse had a small abandoned town next to it, and that should provide multiple places to hide. They would probably track him all the way there, but he flew faster than the drones after him. That might not be the case if any smaller ships came after him.

After two hours of dodging drones and shooting at them with stun beams while dipping into forests and other structures along the way, he reached the massive warehouse that consisted of several large buildings. The large ship had tried to fire missiles and beams a few times, but he was able to use the environment to his advantage. The large ship would stop if he flew over a town. The downside was that any other ships or drones in the town would join the hunt. Without the large ship being able to highlight him in some instances, he was able to escape.

He entered through a busted window near the roof of one of the large buildings. A quick scan inside revealed rusted-out assembly lines and three big tunnels with train tracks that rose up to a platform before angling underground. He calculated that the tracks were used to deliver supplies or whatever the warehouse produced.

The sound of drones approaching filled the air.

Due to the entry points of the warehouse being small, the drones would be all he needed to deal with. He hit the first drone in with a stun beam from all four of his arms.

The drone fritzed, then crashed.

V flew above the window the drone had entered from.

The second drone flew in firing.

V dropped behind and caught up to the drone. Using his segmented claws, he tore the small drone to shreds.

Silence reigned for a moment.

He knew there would be more coming, and he could not stay in the warehouse long. The tunnels underground might be a viable escape route, but he had not mapped them and they might lead to a dead end. As there were three of them, that led to six possible routes the drones would need to check. If he exited the warehouse, he would eventually end up back at Kagoshima.

After running several simulations, he chose the middle right tunnel. It had the least amount of debris near the opening, and he determined that they would think he had gone into one with lots of it. He flew to the tunnel and did one final scan of the warehouse interior. There might be surveillance devices, but he did not detect any power anywhere.

He entered the dark tunnel and kept to the top. Creatures or other traps could hinder him, but so far it had been quiet. Where the tunnel led was a mystery, and it did cross his processing that the drones might cover all exits. Perhaps there were side tunnels to be investigated on the way. One thing was clear: finding someone to help or reaching Atlantis would be much more difficult now that he was being hunted.

12

Emily looked around as she chewed on a food pellet. It had been three hours since she had left the Dacians at the cave, and she had landed on a rock platform that jutted out from the mountainside. Her PSD showed it to be about 5:30 a.m., and she needed a nap.

She had figured the flying part would be tedious but discovered she did not need to have her hand on the PSD the whole time. When she had taken her hand off to mess with her hair, the platform continued to fly forward. That made the trip a bit easier. However, she still needed the PSD to handle other bodily functions, and also to get food and drink.

She closed her eyes as she sat and enjoyed the crisp mountain air. The strong odor of vegetation permeated the air and reminded her of a freshly cut lawn. Outside the noise of a few birds, it was peaceful, and if not in her current situation, she might have been more relaxed.

All the enhancements Evaran had implemented on her suit and PSD made her smile. Her suit possessed a dimensional power bridge, as Evaran called it, that allowed her to perform greater feats based on her ability to focus, and it wrapped around her now like a warm blanket. His handiwork was all around her, and that comforted her.

Although she was tired, the thought of reaching Lord Noskov ignited her mind. She wanted to be back on the Torvatta at a bare minimum, and she missed Dr. Snowden, Evaran, and V. With that in mind, she opened her PSD pattern builder. The rocky platform she stood on contained enough room for her bed pattern with some extra space to spare. She selected the pattern and perused the options on the left side of the holographic screen.

The first thing she did was add a small kinetic shield bubble. That should keep insects and the like away. She shook her head as she realized that would have been useful on the flying platform, something she would do later.

The second action was to select a half-cylinder-shaped container to put the bed in. It reminded her of a pipe cut in half. Each end contained a door that opened and sealed. Several options appeared after she touched the container in the builder program. A small box that cycled air in and out caught her eye, and she added it. At a bare minimum, this would be a secure sleeping setup.

She closed her PSD and knelt while making sure she had room for the new pattern. The last thing she wanted to happen was to form it and end up tumbling off the rock platform. She sat Indian-style and held the PSD in a vertical position close to the ground.

After a quick check around, she activated the pattern. The container and bed formed around her with the PSD staying upright near the head of the bed. She released her PSD and verified that the doors at each end were sealed. After checking that the design had been created correctly, she lay down. The bed's neural effect already affected her, and after a moment, she fell asleep.

She awoke seven hours later and paused to gain her bearings. After retracting the new bed pattern, she looked up at the clear sky. She recalled her situation and yearned to be back on the Torvatta having breakfast with Evaran, Dr. Snowden, and V. That gave her fuel to find Lord Noskov.

She cracked her back and took in the crisp air. Despite her situation, her body was refreshed. She used the PSD to get a food pellet and drinking water. Afterward, she took take care of her morning business. She chuckled at a memory of Dr. Snowden raising his brow when asking Evaran to make sure that the PSD did not mix things up when retracting patterns.

She sat down and opened the pattern builder. Once open, she chose the flying platform as the base. She added a kinetic bubble shield and put in a recliner with the PSD on the right chair arm. That would make it much more comfortable. She also added the map projector option, something she had not seen earlier. Speed was a limiting factor for the platform, but no option existed to enhance that.

After forming the platform, she stepped in and took her seat. A final check revealed that everything had been created as expected. She pulled up on the PSD.

The platform ascended.

After gaining some height, she pushed the PSD forward, and the platform moved in that direction. She studied the standalone map projector. It connected to the platform via a post that went up before angling to provide a screen to the seat. This allowed the projector to swivel, and she could adjust the screen. With a push to the side, the projector was out of her way if need be. However, for now, it resided in front of her. This would be a dream to Dr. Snowden, and she figured if she had customized the platform, he probably did too.

She selected the southwest region of Germany, where the Black Forest would be. The map projector showed four hundred miles. She sighed as she saw that it would take roughly seventeen hours per the distance metric. Hopefully she would not need to stop, and with the platform on cruise control, all she had was time.

The path she chose flew over the Roman camp. It had been disassembled and the legion was on the move. They would not find the Dacians. She wondered what impact her actions would have, and if Evaran would have to fix it somehow. How he would do that, she did not know.

She kicked back in her recliner and laced her fingers. It would be morning, about 7:00 a.m., when she reached the Black Forest, and it crossed her mind that she needed a way to find Lord Noskov. Perhaps he maintained a base there. To fly around aimlessly over the forest might not be the best approach—a problem she had plenty of time to dwell on.

After seventeen hours and a few pit stops, Emily was ready for the trip to end. While she did get rested up, thanks to a modification on the recliner for better sleeping, her back ached. Her nanobots worked on that as she stared at the newly updated map projector.

She discovered that there was an energy sensor she could attach to the sides and bottom of the flying platform. How the morphable matter made additions, or even provided the power to fly, eluded her, but she was thankful it could. The sensors would make it easier to find nonhumans.

Per the map projector, there was a lot of ground to cover. She figured she would fly to the heart of the forest, then do an ever-expanding circle. A part of her wanted to land and walk around, but that would take forever. She spotted a craft flying toward her. It was a small ship and reminded her of ones she had seen before at Lord Noskov's base.

The ship had a rectangular body with wings that started at the front and extended all the way to the back. Large blue circular pads were on the wings, and a thruster sat on the ship's rear. From what she recalled, this was similar to the ship Jake Melkins flew around. It was a transport one for the most part.

She waved at the ship as it hovered near her.

The male pilot pointed down.

She descended to a clearing where they could both land.

After landing, the pilot walked out of the back of the ship and approached her.

She pulled her flying platform back into her PSD. Her senses told her the pale pilot was a Daedrould, an ancient vampire, and probably one of Lord Noskov's crew. His advanced dark gray suit further solidified her thought that the pilot was with Lord Noskov.

"I've never seen a ship like that," said the pilot.

Emily smiled. "It's unique. Are you with Lord Noskov?"

The pilot studied Emily. "I am...do you know him?"

"Yeah. We're friends. Can you take me to him?"

"One moment," said the pilot. He went back into the ship and, after a minute, came back out. "Surprisingly, you're cleared. He's looking forward to seeing you. You can fly with me."

Emily exhaled from her mouth. "Okay."

She followed the pilot into his ship, and a moment later, they were airborne. Her pulse quickened at the thought that she would see a friendly face. While she enjoyed studying the past, being stranded in it was not ideal.

After an hour, they landed in a clearing deep in the Black Forest.

Emily noted that the pilot was unusually quiet. Although she had asked a few questions, his answers were short. Perhaps that was a protocol thing.

After the ship landed, the ground lowered.

She observed that the clearing was actually a landing pad.

The ship descended underground into a spacious hangar bay.

She studied the metallic paneled walls and floor. Above her, the landing platform entrance sealed while some dirt trickled in.

After another minute, the platform had fully lowered, and the ship moved off it and to the side.

She followed the pilot out. A big smile crept across her face when Lord Noskov in his businesslike black suit walked toward her. He had on his cape that had a black exterior with a red interior. His pale skin, black eyes, and clawed fingers would scare most, but she knew him as a friend.

"Emily. This is...a surprise," said Lord Noskov in his typical Eastern European accent.

She rushed over and hugged him. "It's so good to see you." She stepped back.

Lord Noskov wrinkled his brow. "Is everything okay?" He looked around. "Where's Evaran?"

She sighed. "Long story."

"I see," he said. He gestured toward a doorway. "Let's catch up in my library."

"Okay," said Emily with a smile.

She followed Lord Noskov through a series of hallways. The base was advanced, as she would have expected. It made her realize that Kotys probably thought Lord Noskov was in league with the Helians. Lord Noskov's vigilance in defending his territory with advanced technology probably seemed mystical to others.

After a few minutes, they arrived at a spacious library.

Emily surveyed the walls filled with bookshelves that were jam-packed with books. Ladders on wheels were scattered around the room, and several lounge areas with comfortable recliners and couches dotted the room. Lights in the ceiling provided illumination, and a sweet smell wafted through the air. It was a cozy place.

Lord Noskov gestured at a couch for Emily to sit on, then he sat in a plush recliner.

Emily took her seat.

"Are you thirsty, or do you require food?" asked Lord Noskov.

She smiled big. "I might want a burger and some orange juice."

"A burger...I'm not sure what that is, but orange juice, we have."

"Well...bread and cooked ground meat in the shape of a patty. The meat is between two slices of bread, a bun."

Lord Noskov tilted his head. "An interesting concept." He snapped at an ancient vampire in the back of the room. "Make what she said, and get her orange juice."

The ancient vampire hustled away.

"It will be brought. Now...about this long story..."

Emily sighed. "In AD 2012, I was attacked by someone calling herself Ziekah. She can apparently open portals which send people to the past. Dr. Snowden had been sent somewhere, and in my case, I got sent to Roman Dacia, or what will become that."

Lord Noskov's eyes narrowed. "So Evaran is not with you. Surely he would come pick you up."

"I thought so too, but...strange thing...the Torvatta rejected my connection attempt."

"Interesting. I bet because it's out of sync."

Emily tilted her head. "So...you're saying the Torvatta here, now, is from a different point in time?"

"It might be, or a different version of Evaran. I never know what version of him is going to appear, but the one that left here a while back is not yours. I suspect at some point in the future, there'll be a meeting where I meet your version for the first time."

Emily chuckled. "Yep, you sure do."

"You're aware of it?" asked Lord Noskov.

"Yeah, but as always, I can't say anything."

"Of course," said Lord Noskov. He shook his head. "Time travel is bizarre."

"Yeah, but now that I'm here, I don't know how to get back to Evaran—well, my version that is."

Lord Noskov rubbed his chin. "Evaran, regardless of version, is always around to some degree."

"If I had a quantum beacon, this would be a lot easier."

"Yes, yes, it would. However, there is another approach. You could go to Atlantis and be put in cryo-sleep until your time, AD 2012. It's possible at some point, Evaran would hear of it, and come to you."

Emily wrinkled her brow. "That would be strange to meet Evaran before he saved Dr. Snowden and me."

"If he doesn't meet you before AD 2012, then a message would be delivered to open the cryo-sleep container to shortly after you were sent back here."

"That might actually work!" said Emily.

Lord Noskov nodded. "I'm going to Atlantis in a few days. I have some…business to attend to. You're more than welcome to accompany me, and they would assist you due to the Evaran Protocol, and if not, I'll insist they do. Side note, it's on the bottom of the Atlantic Ocean now."

"Works for me." Emily leaned back into the couch. "Do they have any way of detecting cosmic energy?"

"You want to see if you can find Dr. Snowden."

Emily nodded.

"They do have a portal detection system, and it can also detect new energy signatures, although it's not always accurate and doesn't cover all types of portals."

She sighed. "It's worth at least checking out when we get to Atlantis. I'm just happy for some good news for a change."

"I understand. Until we leave, you're welcome to make this base your home." Lord Noskov gestured at a bookcase.

"There's a secret tunnel there you can use if you want to go outside."

"Escape tunnels?"

"One can never be too cautious," said Lord Noskov. He picked up a tablet-like device on a nearby table and interacted with it. After a moment, he said, "There. The layout of this base in case you want to check it out while you wait. Bear in mind…I don't just give anyone that or even mention escape tunnels."

"It's appreciated." Emily opened her PSD and connected to the tablet and downloaded the layout. "Got it." She exhaled from her mouth. "I think this'll all work out. We'll still need to deal with Ziekah, but I bet Evaran's already on that."

"To be opposite Evaran in any conflict is foolish."

"Yeah, but this is new. He can't get anywhere near her outside the Torvatta since she can just zap people to the past."

Lord Noskov grinned. "The Torvatta I'm sure can handle that scenario."

"I hope so."

"And you said Dr. Snowden was sent to the past as well?"

Emily nodded. "Yeah, but I don't know where he got zapped to."

"This Ziekah sounds like a dangerous opponent, but as I said, no match for someone like Evaran."

"Yep." She focused on Lord Noskov as a strange sensation washed over her. "As Evaran would say, everything is—"

A shimmering semitransparent curtain swept through the library.

"As it should be…," said Emily, looking around.

She was not sure what happened, but Lord Noskov was gone, and it was pitch black. After launching her illumination orb, she stood and surveyed the new environment. Cobwebs and dust covered everything, and it looked like the library had been ransacked. As she moved around, she found several skeletons on the ground. It hit her that a timeline change must have happened as she recalled seeing the curtain-like effect in orbit before.

She gritted her teeth. This must be Ziekah's doing. Perhaps she sent herself back in time due to Evaran. Emily's blood boiled. She had a plan, and now it was ruined. Once again, she was alone. She sat down on the couch, causing dust to swirl around her. Her breathing increased as she tried to figure out her next move.

If she had gone forward with her plan on Atlantis, and the timeline change hit, she would have appeared at the bottom of the ocean. She was not sure her suit would handle that. As long as Ziekah was running around, no place was safe. Emily sighed as she stood. It was time to assess the current environment, again, and see what had changed.

.

13

Emily frowned as she stood at the entrance to the abandoned library. The once-warm room with the promise of a way out had disappeared, and a cold place with the markers of death everywhere replaced it. The skeletons' skulls and teeth made her think they were vampires. She doubted Lord Noskov would have willingly abandoned his base, so she suspected someone had taken it by force. Her PSD showed that the bones dated to around a hundred and twenty years old.

She sighed as she closed her eyes. If Evaran had a plan, she hoped he enacted it quick. She shivered, due not to the cold but the thought that perhaps Evaran already tried and failed.

This would not be the first time despair had gripped her. Her eyes opened and she focused on staying positive. She had her suit, PSD, and cosmic awareness. After one final look around, she made her way back to the landing pad.

After arriving at the hangar bay, she surveyed the environment. Her illumination orb caused shadows to dance, but the destroyed ships stood out. A large cylinder reaching toward the ceiling meant that the landing pad was up top. She walked around a few ships and studied them. Skeletons resided inside some, while others lay outside. They seemed to have been killed and left to rot.

She took a step back and studied the cylinder. If she could grapple up, she might get out, but that required an opening to be present, and she did not see one. She shook her head when she remembered Lord Noskov's escape tunnels. That would be a quieter way to escape and would take much less effort.

She tracked back to the library and stood in front of the bookcase with an escape route behind it. A quick survey did not show any obvious sign of how to move the bookcase. She pulled out her PSD and formed a square magnifying glass, which she relied on to investigate things. A scan showed a book on the second row with traces of a metal. She knelt and studied the book, then pulled it out.

Click!

She studied the surrounding area, then examined a few books nestled next to the one she pulled out. A slight draft escaped from a few books, and after she examined the draft's source, she realized that a part of the bookcase folded inward. She stood and gently pushed. Two parts in the shape of a door swiveled into an open tunnel. She scrutinized the layout and it showed that the tunnel eventually led to the surface.

After taking a few steps in and verifying the tunnel had solid ground, she hopped back into the library. A thought creeped into her mind that if Ziekah caused a timeline change, she would have time to prepare for a hunt.

Emily's eyes narrowed. Ziekah with her knowledge of advanced technology might even have satellites scouring the planet and be on her way to the base now. Emily studied the surrounding area. She noted that all the footsteps she left on the dusty floor led right to the escape tunnel. They needed to be erased.

She perused her PSD patterns and found a blower one. Several options presented themselves, but she liked the low-noise one. After forming her device, which reminded her of a leaf blower, she blew the area around the bookcases. Her suit protected her from the dust cloud that she kicked up. The hallways nearby and up to the landing pad also got treated. It took her a while, but she was confident that if Ziekah arrived, it would be hard to find a path to the escape tunnel. Emily walked back to the library while ensuring that her footsteps got erased.

Her breathing went haphazard when a loud noise echoed out from the hangar bay. She activated her camouflage shielding and then rushed over to the hallway that led to it and peeked out. Bright lights on the bottom of the landing pad at the top reminded her of welding torches.

Circular areas opened, exposing the surface and allowing several drones to fly in. A few minutes later, humanoids in tactical battle gear began to drop down via rope.

One of the men who landed first looked around. He pointed to various places as others landed. "Search the area! One of them is here."

Emily sighed. They must have detected her life signs or energy signature. Perhaps the blower had notified them, or Ziekah really did have a global satellite system. Emily rushed back to the library and slipped into the tunnel.

It took her a moment to figure out how to close the bookcase, but before she did, she peeked out to make sure her footsteps did not lead them to the tunnel. Due to the dust still settling from being blown around, her footprints were not visible. Satisfied that they would not be able to find her that way, she closed the bookcase.

She scooted back into the tunnel, which had a slight upward angle. They would not be able to detect her with thermal sensors due to her being out of line of sight. She hunched down in the dark and listened in silence to the humanoids in the distance. After several minutes, some entered the library.

"One of them is here. The floor's been cleared," said a male.

"I'm not seeing any thermal signature. If she's here, she's gone," said another male.

"Okay. You go tell Ziekah she's wrong. I'll wait here."

"No...let's keep looking."

Emily gritted her teeth. Ziekah must have used the Helians' energy detection system. Emily doubted the Helians still existed if Ziekah had had time to set up, depending on how far back in time she had traveled. Sticking around was a recipe for disaster. Emily sighed. Thankfully she could see in the dark thanks to her helmet. She moved on.

After an hour, she reached a ledge that jutted out over a massive canyon. A stream trickled somewhere in the distance, but the large chasm between where she stood and where the layout continued on caught her attention.

A sheer wall, with seventeen holes in it with ledges, stood across the gap. Based on the layout, she knew which one to go to. If Ziekah and her minions got this far, they would be stumped by this.

Emily fired her grappling beam to above the ledge. After landing, she paused to focus. Life flourished around her, but nothing humanoid-sized. In the distance, she heard footsteps, and she figured they discovered the bookcase entrance. Perhaps Ziekah herself had done that.

Emily ducked back into the tunnel. The layout showed five miles of length to reach the surface. A series of side tunnels with small rooms attached to them at various intervals caught her eye.

A label had tagged one of the rooms with Lord Noskov's name. She figured she would check that out. Perhaps he had rested there on his way out. His fate remained unknown, but she hoped somewhere that he lived, although if Ziekah had changed everything, then he would not know Emily. She continued on with fire in her eyes.

Emily reached the small room two hours later. Noises along the way appeared and disappeared. Perhaps Ziekah had given up her search. The chasm acted as a natural defense, and Emily suspected Lord Noskov had engineered the escape tunnels with that in mind.

The room was larger than the layout indicated. A table resided in the back, with a plastic-wrapped book sitting on top. A dried-up ink bottle along with some writing utensils sat to the side of the book. A bed lay off to the right, and the dirt floor appeared to have been smoothed out, indicating someone had lived there for a while.

She would have never discovered the room without the layout. To even get there, she had crawled through a space only two feet high. The only marker showing the room's existence was on the escape tunnel's layout. The crawlspace appeared naturally shaped, and similar ones resided everywhere.

How Lord Noskov had gotten materials there remained a mystery, but if done piecemeal, it was definitely possible, given enough time. Due to the remoteness of her location, she could finally relax. A quick check revealed no one nearby. This would be a safe place to rest.

She launched an illumination orb before she sat at the rotting table. The plastic-wrapped book begged her to read it. She doubted Lord Noskov would mind. Her PSD could record the book's content.

She opened up her PSD and perused the patterns. Under the surveillance category, she found a lamp with a circular base, a bendable segmented post and a metallic lampshade at the end. For what she needed, it was perfect. She formed the lamp and angled it.

She poked at the plastic wrapping to form an opening and then pulled it off. It seemed like the book had been hand-bound in leather, and the title of the book, *The Ending*, had been carved on it. She grimaced as she opened up to the first couple of handwritten pages. The clean penmanship surprised her as she figured it would be difficult to write well in low light.

A foreword stated that Lord Noskov had written the book. Ziekah had attacked his base, and although there had been a valiant effort to defend the base, Ziekah had won. The room Emily sat in now was where he had fled, and he had decided to document history up to that point in case Evaran needed it.

Emily sighed as she thought of Evaran. He should have found her by now. Lord Noskov seemed to share her sentiment in the foreword. He ended it with the conclusion that since Evaran had not intervened, everything was as it should be. She shook her head. The tone of the writing dripped with despair, not something she attributed to Lord Noskov in general.

The first covered the time from the Purification event up to Ziekah's arrival. Emily smiled as she read about how the United Nonhuman General Assembly, or UNGA, had expanded along with the Helians. The UNGA had established a set of protocols that made nonhuman violence less common. Her smile wound down as Lord Noskov detailed how violence still existed, but it remained hidden, and more ruthless.

The next few chapters detailed Ziekah's rise through the Helian ranks. Her contributions to their technology allowed her to entrench herself as a valuable member of their society. Lord Noskov noted that she also seemed to inherit the Helians' dislike of other nonhumans.

The dissolution of the UNGA and rise of the Helians was covered in the following two chapters. The afterward caught her attention. The Helian council had dissolved and Ziekah had been placed as sole leader. She had run a campaign to eliminate the Helians' enemies and expand Helian influence into the general population. She had even convinced humans to help kill nonhumans, which did not surprise Emily too much.

Emily's stomach churned. Ziekah went to a lot of effort to establish herself as a ruler. If this was all to find Seeros, it seemed a strange way to go about it. The lavish lifestyle might have had an impact too. Lord Noskov outlined Ziekah's excesses. She delighted in gladiator fights to the death, and general debauchery. Perhaps wherever she came from, she did not have access to that. With a world at her feet, all was now accessible.

Emily took a quick break to have a food pellet and some water and then handle her bodily functions. Although tired, she wanted to get all of this recorded, and she was only halfway through the book. She could sleep once done.

Over the next several hours, she read about how Ziekah had conquered the world. With advanced technology and human allies, it only took her a few hundred years to accomplish that. The last holdouts were the more powerful nonhumans.

Emily frowned as she read the chapters on the other ancient vampire lords' deaths. Lord Skar had been killed in China leading a resistance, while Lord Cyrus had been killed in Brazil. Lord Vygon had led a failed attack on Ziekah's headquarters in Atlantis. Lord Noskov had retreated to the base Emily had been in, where he had fought Ziekah and lost. He had come to the room she sat in and spent his time writing *The Ending*.

The final chapters detailed the new world order. The Kreagans had accepted her as Earth's leader and removed its protected planet status. Ziekah now had plenty of resources to find Seeros. Lord Noskov lamented the fact that Evaran had not come, but Lord Noskov still hoped that one day Evaran would find the book she was reading. Even in the darkest of moments, Lord Noskov still persisted in his belief that Evaran might change things.

Emily sat back in her chair and sighed. She, too, hoped Evaran would come. This was too much for her to handle on her own, and unlike the prison planet, Ziekah was a formidable opponent who would not be beaten easily. Emily changed her PSD into the secure bed pattern she had used before and laid it on the ground. After a good nap, she would continue on, hoping for a better outcome to her situation.

14

Jake loved watching the timeline change from space, although he knew its deadly effects on anyone not temporally shielded. His dad had probably gotten wiped out and Jake most likely did not exist in whatever the new timeline was. His mind wandered to Dr. Snowden, Emily, and V in the past and he wondered if they had experienced the change as well. Hopefully they were in a safe spot when it had hit.

Evaran had been silent for the forty or so minutes it took for both timeline changes to hit. Although Jake did not have cosmic senses like the others, he understood Evaran well enough to know that he was bothered. Ziekah's carelessness with changing time crossed many of Evaran's lines. Tack on messing with his traveling companions, and Jake figured Ziekah would be judged harshly when she was caught.

Jake liked Jelton and saw why Emily and he were in a relationship. He was cool, calm, and collected, and he tended to say "my friend" a lot. The fact that he lived in another timeline in a rift was not a surprise, as anything having to do with Evaran or the Torvatta was usually in the realm of fantastic.

Jake studied the advanced satellites orbiting Earth. "Looks like those changed."

Evaran perused his ARI. "Yes…and they are more advanced. I am detecting better power usage and enhanced scanning capabilities."

"You think the Kreagans would have noticed?"

"I am not sure," said Evaran. He raised a finger. "However, the communication indicates that there is contact with other planets. I suspect Ziekah has moved Earth beyond protected planet status."

"That sounds like something we should verify," said Jelton. "She may not even be on the planet."

Evaran nodded. "An opportunity. I am grabbing what data I can from a satellite, then we can check on Fredoria."

Jake watched as the Torvatta flew over to a satellite and begin to scan. Various data windows popped and flashed information faster than he perceived. He had seen that before when first meeting Evaran. He had placed his UIC on the counter at the space station where Jake was and downloaded all available information. To scan a satellite back then, Evaran had had to go out to the Torvatta ramp to place his UIC on a satellite. The Torvatta had a beam for that now.

"Lot of data," said Jake. He swatted Jelton's arm. "Can you see all that flashing by?"

Jelton nodded. "The cosmic energy in me allows me to process things faster."

"Huh," said Jake. "Cool."

After a moment, the data windows disappeared.

Evaran rubbed his chin. "It seems Ziekah has once again taken over the world. We will not need to visit Fredoria as it is already under her control and she has made it her home planet. The Kreagans ceded Fredoria and a few other systems to Earth due to her technological advantage."

"Wow," said Jake. "She's really screwing around hard with the timeline."

"Yes, she is. I also found some information related to Dr. Snowden, Emily, and V," said Evaran. He tapped at his ARI.

Jelton's eyes narrowed. "She said she was here to free Seeros. Interacting at this scale seems unusual. I wonder why she is doing things this way."

"I do not know. Perhaps it is to aid in discovering Seeros's origin. That would be easier with an empire's resources at her disposal."

Jake shook his head. "So she pops into the timeline, trashes it until she gets Seeros, then leaves, I'm guessing."

"A good hypothesis, and one I believe has merit. Nonetheless, there is a secured data vault with information on Dr. Snowden, Emily, and V. I cannot access it from here as a security AI is present."

Jelton gestured at the satellite. "I'm surprise there wasn't one here."

"As am I," said Evaran. "Ziekah would not be aware of the UIC's limitations or the Torvatta's in regard to scanning, so I do not believe that was taken into consideration. There is security on the satellite, but it is nowhere near what a security AI could provide." He tapped at his chair console. "Off to the data vault."

The Torvatta descended.

After twenty minutes, Jelton studied the mountain labeled Mount Everest. Although it was dark out, the clear sky provided some illumination, and the Torvatta had outlined the ridge.

"A strange place to put a data vault," he said.

"Yeah, no kidding," said Jake.

Evaran nodded. "I would assume the reason is tactical given how remote it is, and also the temperature would help with cooling any power consumption the data vault uses."

"I see," said Jelton. "This feels…unusual. A data vault with specific information in such an isolated location does not bode well."

"We will be cautious," said Evaran.

The Torvatta hovered over a flat section of ridge.

It looked like someone had cut off a swath of the top with a sword. A wide pipe popped out of the ground with various other small structures around it. A landing pad sat off to the side. Jake wondered if it was for supplies or something else.

"So what's the plan?" he asked.

"We will descend down the pipe, which appears to be an entrance. Once inside, we disable the security AI, then I access the data systems," said Evaran.

"You think there's guards all the way up here on the mountain?"

"I do," said Evaran.

"Probably robot ones that activate as needed," said Jelton.

"That is possible."

Jake wagged a finger at Evaran. "Okay…but how are you going to disable a security AI? We don't have V."

"In order to conserve power, the security AI will be limited to the room where the data vault is. Once we are there, we can determine what we are up against."

Jake nodded. "Maybe we could shut off the power, then reboot everything. That should give you some time to figure out the system layout while it's rebooting."

Evaran nodded.

Jelton chuckled. "It might be as simple as flipping a switch too."

"I would prefer that," said Evaran. He eyed Jake and Jelton. "It will potentially be dangerous."

"That's always a risk of traveling with you," said Jake with a smile.

Evaran sighed. "Obviously, I try to make things as safe as possible."

Jake shrugged. "It's not your fault. When good people step up, bad people will as well. Violence usually follows."

"An interesting perspective," said Evaran. "Okay, get your gear together, take any food or drink you need, and handle any bodily functions."

Jake patted Evaran's shoulder on the way to the living quarters. Evaran was not someone Jake would associate with worrying, but there seemed to be some without V present. There were several ways to get around a security AI from what he remembered, and he was sure Evaran could do so if he really needed to. Perhaps Jake could follow up on that later. For now, it was gear-up time.

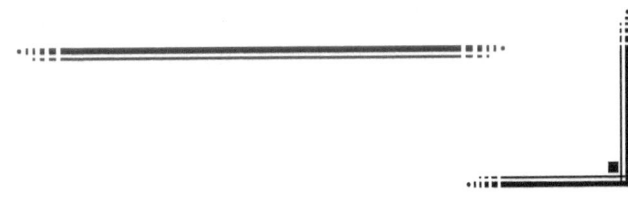

Jelton cracked his neck on the Torvatta's ramp inside the shielding. His helmet recorded the temperature outside the shield as cold relative to where he stood. Everywhere he looked was snow, ice, and rock, and his helmet had already adjusted to the darkness. The wind whipped around causing a white mist to swirl. Even with his display outlining the mountain's terrain, it seemed chaotic outside the Torvatta.

Jake had on a heavier armor suit and wore two heavy pistols on the side. He was ready for combat. Evaran always intrigued Jelton in that Evaran never wore heavy armor. He wore the same outfit regardless of environment. Despite the freezing temperatures, Jelton was sure Evaran probably did not feel the cold.

"Let us go," said Evaran as he exited the Torvatta's shielding.

Jelton nodded at Jake and followed Evaran. Snow crunched under Jelton's feet as the group approached the pipe that stuck out of the ground. The top reached to about chest level and was wide enough that it could support two people going down at the same time. The surrounding flat area indicated that someone or something had cleared it. He suspected communication without helmets would be impossible as the noise of the chaos around him permeated the air.

Evaran scanned the pipe with his ring after they arrived.

Jelton studied the scan results in his helmet. He enjoyed the ease with which information was disseminated when traveling with Evaran. The pipe had no electronic aspects and had a wheel on top.

"No technology," said Jake.

Evaran nodded. He hopped up on the pipe's edge. The wheel squealed as Evaran turned it.

After a moment, the pipe cover was pulled back and revealed a ladder down the pipe's sides.

"Are you two ready?" asked Evaran.

Jake and Jelton nodded.

"Very well. In we go," said Evaran.

He crawled into the pipe with the others in tow.

Jelton made sure to close the pipe cover after he entered. A wheel sat on the underside, similar to the one Evaran had turned topside. After the cover was sealed, Jelton hustled down the ladder and joined Evaran and Jake in a small room. The walls, floor, and ceiling consisted of metallic panels, and a hallway led off into the distance. It was much quieter than above and the only illumination came from two orbs that Evaran had tossed into the air. As above, the temperature was cold, but warmer than outside.

Evaran scanned around. "No technology here, similar to above. However, I have detected technology ahead." He pulled out his utility handle and formed a baton while activating his energy shield on his left forearm. "Let us go." He strode forward.

Jelton chuckled to himself. Evaran walked without a hint of fear or doubt, even in an enemy facility. Jelton appreciated that confidence. Now that he had some cosmic energy in him, he could read Evaran beyond the physical cues, but his actions spoke louder than words or what Jelton's cosmic energy told him at times.

The group advanced down the hallway and reached a small room with an advanced-looking elevator. A dim console sat off to the side.

Evaran placed his UIC on the console.

The console lit up.

Evaran perused his ARI. "Intriguing, no security AI is present in this console. I suspect the AI is confined to the data vault below. The surrounding area around is most likely secured by traditional means."

"They didn't have any sensors up here and the console seemed to be on reserve power or something," said Jake. "I bet, though, they'll detect us coming down, well, *whoever* is down there will."

"I concur." Evaran grabbed his UIC as the elevator door slid back to reveal a spacious interior. "This elevator was meant to carry more than a few people at a time." He entered with the others in tow.

The door slid shut.

As they descended, Jelton studied the console that displayed how low they were going. His brows rose when they passed four hundred feet.

"This data vault is deep underground," he said.

"Yeah. Makes you wonder how long it took to build this place. Seems like it would be a pain in the ass," said Jake.

Evaran eyed Jake.

Jake chuckled. "Well, it would be!"

"I suspect the builders were not organic," said Evaran.

The elevator stopped after fifteen minutes, having gone down a thousand feet or so. Its doors slid open.

Evaran marched forward with his shield out.

Jake split off to the right of Evaran while Jelton took the other side.

Jelton scrutinized the empty lobby they were in. Three hallways in front of them led off in different directions. Evaran's orbs once again provided the only illumination.

"Perhaps no one is here," said Jelton.

Evaran scanned the area with his ring. "Technology is around us, although I cannot detect any movement. Stay close. Looks can be deceiving. I do not think splitting up here would be ideal."

"Don't need to tell me twice," said Jake, surveying the environment.

Jelton enjoyed Jake's take on events. He injected a sense of optimism tinged with sarcasm, something Jelton attributed to Emily.

Evaran took off down the left hallway.

The hallway, like the room above, appeared to be made of metallic panels. He agreed with Evaran that this facility had been built by robots. There was no sign of anything resembling someone having lived in the area. He suspected they had not seen the true defense of the place yet but that they probably would once they tried to access the data vault.

After thirty minutes of winding hallways, they reached a large circular room. In the middle resided a cylinder with a console and a screen above.

Evaran gestured forward. "The data vault is there." He looked around. "This room, as well as the hallways leading to it, seems designed to funnel a large group of visitors to this area."

"Yeah," said Jake. "Now watch us get swarmed by robots while you access that console."

Evaran eyed Jake.

Jake chuckled.

Evaran took a final look around, then approached the cylinder console.

Jelton ran scans of the surrounding area but did not detect anything. Although there was technology behind the walls, it seemed specific to maintaining a temperature slightly higher than the hallways. It was nowhere near as cold as above, and he suspected Dr. Snowden and Emily would find it uncomfortable, even with their survival suits. Being as far underground as they were probably helped with the temperature increase.

They reached the cylinder.

Evaran placed his UIC on the console, then perused his ARI. "Intriguing. The security AI is dormant. I should not have been able to access this console, but the AI is restricted somewhat. I suspect that if I try to access anything, it will activate."

"This seems too easy, my friend," said Jelton.

"I agree," said Jake. "I mean…anyone with a ship could just fly down and get this."

"Perhaps," said Evaran. He raised a finger. "The true test will come once I access the information."

Jelton pulled out an energy dagger and pistol. "Proceed. Jake and I will cover you."

Evaran nodded.

Jake moved to Evaran's left, while Jelton took the other side.

Jelton studied the hallways but did not sense anything. "Quiet so far." He glanced at Evaran. "Have you found anything yet?"

"Not yet," said Evaran. "There is a lot of information here, and I am avoiding areas that will activate the security AI. I cannot move as fast as V in a system. It will take some time."

Jelton nodded. He hoped that Evaran could find out more about Dr. Snowden's, Emily's, and V's fates. Even a mention of their location and time would be helpful. Jelton did not like that everything was quiet to this point in the data vault.

His experience informed him that this was a trap of some sort, although nothing stood out other than the design of the facility and its location. Hopefully wherever Dr. Snowden, Emily, and V were in the past, they were okay. The thought of any of them being hurt made Jelton focus.

15

Over the next hour, Jelton stood at attention. He did not like the unusual silence of the underground data vault facility. He half expected robots to come charging out and attack them, but he had not detected any movement. Even using his cosmic sense, he did not detect anything other than Evaran and Jake. Evaran had been consumed with whatever he discovered in the data access vault.

"I'm with you, this feels like a trap," said Jake, glancing at Jelton.

"I share your concern, my friend."

Evaran stopped perusing his ARI and tossed out a remote viewing orb. "We will not be here much longer. I have found information on where Dr. Snowden, Emily, and V are."

Jelton smiled. "That's good news."

Evaran shook his head. "It is both good and bad."

"What'd you find?" asked Jake.

"Are you sure you wish to see this?" asked Evaran. His lips turned slightly down.

"We are," said Jelton.

Evaran nodded. "After viewing this, we should leave. The security AI activates the moment I disconnect. As the videos play, I will have them transferred to the Torvatta."

The orb shot up a projection of Ziekah in advanced armor and standing before a cave opening. Drones whizzed around while several large humanoid robots stood at attention with massive weapons aimed at the entrance.

Jelton noted that the projection view was being provided by a camera drone of some type. Another drone hovered near the cave opening.

"Emily, I know you're in there," said Ziekah. "I can sense you and detect your…cosmic energy. You can't hide that from me. Come out and surrender!"

"You can go to hell!" said Emily's voice, wafting out of the cave.

"You think Evaran is still going to come save you? He's abandoned you."

Jelton's eyes narrowed. He tried to stay calm, but everything in him wanted to rush back in time and take out Ziekah.

"He'll come," said Emily.

Ziekah laughed. "Really…where is he? I'm recording all this so that sometime in the future, he can watch it. I bet he is right now. Your faith in him is misplaced."

"Like I said before, you'll be judged."

Ziekah shook her head. "Like Seeros was. This is fitting. If Evaran doesn't come to rescue you in the next twenty minutes, you're dead. A casualty of Seeros's death."

"Not likely."

"I'll make you a deal...you surrender and tell me where Seeros came from in the past, and I'll let you live."

"I'm not making any deal with you!"

Ziekah smirked. "Then, we wait."

The projection flickered for a moment before displaying Ziekah again.

"Your twenty minutes is up. Enjoy your death," said Ziekah. She looked up at the camera drone. "I see you don't care about Emily, letting her die like this. So be it."

The projection flickered again, this time rendering Ziekah in the command center of a ship.

Ziekah pointed at a screen. It showed a high-level view of a mountain and forest. A blinking red dot appeared inside the mountain.

"Emily is there, and with one press...she's gone," she said.

She smiled as she pressed the button.

A large beam shot down from the sky onto half the mountain.

Jelton drew his head back.

After a moment, Ziekah pointed at the screen. "No red dot, no Emily. I don't care how tough she was, nothing survives an impact like that."

The projection zoomed in to Ziekah's face.

"One down...two to go."

The projection ended.

Evaran's eyes and hands begin to slightly glow.

"Umm...did we just watch Emily die?" asked Jake, gulping.

"It would seem so," said Evaran.

Jelton closed his eyes for a moment. He opened them. "Is she...really dead?"

"I do not know," said Evaran. He raised a finger. "However, let us view the other two before coming to any conclusions. It could be a trick." He laid a hand on Jelton's shoulder.

Jelton sighed as he nodded. His new mission in life would be to hunt Ziekah down if Emily really had died.

The projection changed to Ziekah standing in a more advanced-looking command center.

Jelton saw that, unlike before, she was surrounded by humanoid cyborgs.

Ziekah pointed at a screen that showed a large warehouse in an abandoned city. "Your friend V is hiding out there. We can't seem to keep up with him and his tricks." She smiled as she raised a finger. "But we did pen him in this city. Evaran, you have twenty minutes to get here. If not...V dies."

The projection glitched for a moment.

Ziekah sighed. "So you decided not to come. Fine." She pressed a button on a nearby workstation.

The projection flickered and showed a massive beam hitting the city from space.

Ziekah smiled as she pointed at the screen. "No red dot...no V. Two down, one to go. I'm surprised at how little you care about your friends. I believe you're scared of what I represent. I'm your consequences catching up to you. You go around killing people with no regard, and would rather hide than face up to what you did."

The projection ended.

Jake sighed. "She's a drama llama. I can't believe that V is dead, or Emily. This has to be a trick of some type."

"Perhaps she wants us to go to those exact times. She did bring a lot of firepower with her," said Jelton.

Evaran nodded. "Let us watch Dr. Snowden's before I disconnect."

The projection showed Ziekah again on a command center with highly advanced purple robots surrounding her. There were several varieties that looked suited for a specific purpose.

"Here we are again," said Ziekah. She gestured at a screen showing an aerial shot of the base of a mountain. A multitude of red dots were shown moving around. "Deep inside there is Dr. Snowden along with some nonhumans. I don't know how he got down there since there are no obvious tunnels, and I don't really care. What's important is this is your last chance to save at least *one* of your crew. You have twenty minutes to appear and try to save him."

The projection flickered.

Ziekah appeared and shook her head. "So this is what it comes down to. You're going to let him die…and for what? Maybe you aren't the threat I thought you were. You're a coward."

She nodded at a nearby robot.

The projection showed the base of the mountain being hit by a massive purple beam. After it hit, there was nothing left but a deep hole. The unstable mountain began to collapse on itself. After a few minutes, there were no red dots.

"All gone," said Ziekah. She sighed. "I guess the next time I'll see you is when you view these. Until later."

The projection ended.

Jake's eyes narrowed. "These can't be real."

"Perhaps they are not," said Evaran.

He shut off the projections and recalled his projection orb.

A hologram of Ziekah appeared. "So…there you are. I wondered which data vault you would go to. And, yes, these videos are real. Your friends are dead."

Jake jumped and ran away.

Ziekah laughed as she faced Evaran. "He understands the consequences of traveling with you."

Jelton was not sure why Jake ran out of the room, but it seemed like an unusual time to do so.

"The security AI has kicked me out," said Evaran, grabbing his UIC.

Ziekah smiled. "Yes…and that is a nice trick you have with that card. I didn't expect that."

Evaran placed his hands behind his back. "Based on the videos, I suspect you intend to hit this place with a beam from space."

"Of course. It's efficient. I could send others after you, but you'd probably be gone by the time they got there. Nonetheless, some are on their way."

"They will be killed by your beam."

Ziekah shrugged. "Like you care about life. You'll pay for what you did to Seeros."

"I will not. He deserved his punishment for trying to kill my crew and I," said Evaran.

"Did you ever wonder why he might have wanted to do that? You must have done some injustice to him."

Evaran tilted his head. "You do not know where he is."

Ziekah smirked. "He's an Antigulan. Unfortunately, I haven't detected him…yet."

"I see," said Evaran. He raised a finger as his eyes and hands glowed. "Know this. You have been made a priority."

"Oh…for killing your friends?"

"That is one reason. You are also disrupting the timeline."

Ziekah flashed her hands off to the side. "If you want to come get me, I'm on Fredoria, in Storyork." She studied Evaran. "You don't seem too broken up by the death of your crew." She scrutinized Jelton. "I guess this new companion of yours will die with you."

"Then it is with my friend," said Jelton, raising his head a bit.

"How noble...and pointless," said Ziekah. She grinned at Evaran. "I overestimated you, but I realize now that you're nothing. If you won't save your friends, you won't stop me. Let me show you something..."

Over the next fifteen minutes, the projection showed Ziekah conquering the planet over various ages.

"Enough. You are using a stalling tactic," said Evaran.

The projection reverted to Ziekah. "You finally figured that out." She laughed. "You really aren't too smart, are you?"

Evaran sighed as he formed a baton from his utility handle. He aimed at her. "You will not view our deaths."

"I don't need to. I see red dots on my screen, and once they're gone, you're gone. I'll make sure your deaths are painless. The beam generator will take some time to get in place, but you don't have enough time to reach topside. Your other friend might reach it, but by the time he gets there, he won't be able to escape the blast radius. There's a reason this data vault was placed where it is. I've set the perfect trap, and you walked right into it like I predicted you would."

Evaran shot the console with a stun beam.

Ziekah's hologram disappeared.

"I have a lot of questions," said Jelton.

"I understand. For now, follow me, and stay close. The beam will fire in thirty-five minutes from an automated system in space. However, it takes fifty minutes to align and activate, and that began when Ziekah appeared here."

"Ziekah's right, we won't make it topside," said Jelton.

"Trust me," said Evaran.

"Always, my friend," said Jelton.

He rushed after Evaran. How they would survive a blast from space was a mystery. It would take thirty minutes to reach the elevator, then another fifteen to go up. Even running, they would only shave off maybe ten minutes to get to the elevator, making it a twenty-minute run, but the elevator speed was fixed at fifteen minutes. They would be hit coming out from the pipe topside. He trusted Evaran, though, and suspected he had deliberately guided the conversation a certain way and that he had a plan.

Jake had never run as fast in his life as he did now. Although Evaran's lips did not move, Jake received instructions from Evaran to get back to the Torvatta. A timer had appeared inside Jake's helmet starting at fifty minutes. Per Evaran, that was how long they had until the beam generator aligned for a death shot.

Jake reached the ladder in twenty minutes instead of the thirty it had taken them earlier, and rushed into the elevator. The plan was to place his hand on the Torvatta's front console. What that would do remained unknown, but Evaran seemed to think it would do something.

When Jake reached topside, the timer showed fifteen minutes. He half expected to be met by a small army, but silence reigned similar to when they had first arrived. He rushed out of the elevator and burst up the pipe they had crawled down.

After a few minutes, he reached topside. Turning the wheel to go outside seemed to take forever, but it eventually turned and the pipe cover opened. He climbed out and fell in his hurry to get out. After standing back up, he raced for the Torvatta at a breakneck pace. When he got to the front console, he studied it to determine where to place his hand. There was no obvious indication of where it should go.

His helmet timer showed ten minutes. He gulped as he slammed his hand on the console.

The Torvatta hovered, then flew off to the side of the mountain.

Jake observed several data windows pop up. The wireframe view of the mountain top intrigued him. It showed the pipe and the data vault facility underneath. Another window showed the Torvatta's shielding temperature increasing at a rapid pace. Once it hit a high number, the Torvatta leveled off at around where the vault's hallways would be, then it flew into the mountain.

Jake jumped, expecting to be tossed about, but then he remembered the Torvatta was immune to external forces. Rock melted and flowed off to the sides of the Torvatta. He licked his lips as the timer hit five minutes.

The plan made sense now. The Torvatta would be brought to Evaran and Jelton. Jake chuckled. He understood that he had been sent off to distract Ziekah, perhaps to make her believe Evaran had shaky relationships. That could mean that the deaths in the past had been staged somehow.

Jake rubbed his chin. It hit him that there had been no actual video of the deaths, other than something with cosmic energy being hit. Perhaps the videos were real, but the events might not be as they seemed. The implication was they would need to go into the past before the event to set those deaths up. If he had figured that out, then he was sure Evaran already had.

He gulped when the Torvatta tore into the data vault facility. It stopped near the hallway that led to the elevator.

The timer hit two minutes and thirty seconds.

Evaran and Jelton strolled over to the Torvatta and a moment later, they had boarded.

Jake smiled when they entered the command area.

Evaran sat and interacted with the chair arm's console.

The Torvatta spun around and began to move back the way it had come.

Jelton relaxed in the left U-shaped seating area. "That... was quite the plan. I understand now why Jake left and we didn't even have to run. We actually had time to spare, mainly because we didn't need to take the elevator."

Evaran nodded. "If my calculations are right, we will clear this mountain as the beam hits, thus giving the impression that we were destroyed. The timing was close due to the time requirement of Jake getting to the Torvatta and then it coming here."

"Do you think Ziekah detected the Torvatta melting into the mountainside?" asked Jake.

"I do not," said Evaran. "The Torvatta was stealthed and in scan mode one, so they would not be able to detect it, and the impact would be obscured by the wind and any snow and ice falling."

Jake noted that the Torvatta had picked up speed. Without the need to melt, it was a straight shot out. He breathed easier when they exited the mountain a minute later. The timer showed less than a minute to go.

"The Torvatta is full of surprises," said Jelton. He eyed Evaran. "As are you, my friend."

Evaran nodded. "I want Ziekah to think we perished. It will serve us well in our next step."

"Which is to go back in time and stage those deaths we saw," said Jake with a big smile.

Evaran eyed Jake. "Yes, that is correct. I need to study the videos in more detail, but as Dr. Snowden, Emily, and V never appeared on the video, we may be able to replicate their deaths without them actually dying."

"I knew it!" said Jake. "So we rescue them, and we're off Ziekah's radar."

"That is the current plan," said Evaran. He raised a finger. "However, the ultimate goal will be to erase Ziekah completely from the timeline. To do so, we will need to find her point of entry."

Jelton chuckled. "How are we going to do that?"

"I may know a friend, regardless of timeline, that may be able to help us."

Jake grinned. "You're talking about the information broker, aren't you?"

Evaran nodded. "He is one we can reach out to. We will need to locate him first, and I have several locations where he may be."

"I have a better understanding of the trips you take now," said Jelton, glancing at Evaran.

Jake chuckled. "This is my fourth one with Evaran, but by far the craziest."

"Third," said Evaran. He tilted his head. "Oh…the fourth is with another version of me."

Jake cleared his throat and looked away.

"It is okay. I hope my future self has a good relationship with you."

Jake nodded. He remembered being told by another version that he would slip sometimes. This must be one of those times, and the future version remembered it from this incident. Out-of-sync personal timelines tripped Jake up.

After the Torvatta had pulled a significant distance away, a blue beam from the sky devastated the data vault facility and surrounding mountaintop.

Jelton shook his head. "If it had been anyone other than Evaran in there, that would have been it."

Jake chuckled. "Yeah, having a Torvatta helps too."

"How did you know how to run? I saw no communication," said Jelton.

Jake gestured at Evaran. "He can do the creepy ventriloquist thing where he talks to you via your helmet, but if you look at him outside the helmet, his lips aren't moving on his actual face."

"Oh," said Jelton, glancing at Evaran.

"It is not creepy," said Evaran.

Jelton drew his head back when he watched Evaran not say anything, but the avatar in the helmet talked. "Okay, that is somewhat strange."

They shared a laugh.

Jake enjoyed the mood. Dr. Snowden, Emily, and V would not die. Work still needed to be done, but for the moment, the cloud of despair that had hung over everyone seemed to have lifted. Although it was 3:10 a.m., and he could use some sleep, his mind ignited now that they had a plan and he was ready to go save the others.

'

16

Emily opened her eyes and sighed. Although she had had a good nap, she was still in a cramped room in a cave. Her nanobots tingled and she sensed someone in the room. Her heartbeat jumped as she focused on controlling her breathing. If she shut down the PSD, she could roll to the side and get her PSD ready to shoot a stun beam.

"How was your rest?" asked a familiar voice.

Emily smiled big as she retracted her sleeping container. The last thing she had expected was for Evaran to be sitting in the chair she had used to read Lord Noskov's book. Perhaps she was still dreaming, or even hallucinating. She stood and approached Evaran, who had turned around to face her.

"I'm…okay," she said. "Are you real?"

"Of course," said Evaran.

He stood and extended his hand.

She ran her thumb over his palm. It was him. She rushed over and gave him a big frontal bear hug.

Evaran rubbed her back. "I am sure you have quite a tale, and I am glad that you are safe."

She nodded as her eyes misted. Everything seemed better with Evaran around. She did not want to let him go in case he was a hallucination.

"This is Lord Noskov's old base," said Evaran.

Emily stepped away and smiled. "Yeah. I actually talked to him before the timeline change. How did you find me?"

Evaran raised a finger. "There is a lot to fill you in on. We should get to the Torvatta first and we can discuss it there."

"Okay. I'm ready to go," she said. She pointed at the book on the table. "Oh…Lord Noskov wrote about the effects of the timeline change. I recorded it all in my PSD."

Evaran picked up the leather book and looked it over. "I will bring it with us. Do you wish to handle any bodily functions or eat or drink?"

"It can wait." Emily moved over to the entrance and slid into the two-foot crawlspace.

Evaran joined her.

"Hard to get in here, but a decent hiding spot," said Emily, blowing a strand of hair out of her face.

"I can see that," said Evaran.

After a minute, they were standing in a cave tunnel.

Evaran launched two illumination orbs.

Emily reveled in the feeling of being back with Evaran. The cloud of doom that had been following her since she had come to the past had dissipated. As she soaked in the moment, a medium-sized steel box on the ground with a console on top caught her eye.

"What's that?" she asked.

"A box that will contain traces of your DNA via your nanobots," said Evaran.

"For what?"

Evaran waved his arm around in an arc. "Ziekah will destroy this area with a beam from space in approximately four hours."

"How do you know?"

"I watched it. Ziekah made a point to record your death," said Evaran.

Emily's eyes widened.

"However, I suspected that not all was as it seemed. She came here because she could sense you, but not find you. This box will still allow her to sense you, but not determine your exact location. There is a speaker on it with preprogrammed responses for when she talks to what she believes is you."

"Oh. There's a *lot* to catch up on it sounds like."

Evaran nodded.

"Okay. How do you want to get nanobots in there?" asked Emily.

Evaran tapped at the steel box console, causing a small needle to pop up. "You can prick your finger on that. Not too much, though, as we do not want your nanobots to destroy everything."

Emily complied. "The box resembles the material of the three-L container from when we dealt with Chuuldragra."

"It is a composite, and should hold your nanobots."

"Done. What's next?"

"We go to the Torvatta, where an anxious Jelton awaits you."

Emily swallowed hard. "Jelton's traveling with you?"

"Yes. I needed someone who was familiar with the rift aspect in Ziekah's signature. He appears to know what she is."

Emily smiled big. "What are we waiting for?"

Evaran squeezed her shoulder. "Let us go."

For the first time in a while, Emily had hope. She had a lot of questions about what was going on, but Evaran was right in that it would be better to explore that on the Torvatta. Evaran navigated the cave with ease, and she had no problem keeping up.

As they hustled through the tunnels, she asked, "How's Uncle Albert doing?"

"We have not retrieved him yet," said Evaran.

"Oh."

"Do not worry. As we have come for you, we will for him. We know where he is and, more importantly, when. The same goes for V."

"V?"

Evaran paused to lay a hand on her shoulder. "You have many questions. All will be answered when we get to the Torvatta."

Emily forced a smile. "Okay."

She let out a sigh of relief that at least Dr. Snowden and V would be retrieved. How V had gotten caught was unknown, but she was curious about when they were sent to. She could not wait to get everyone back together. Her blood boiled due to Ziekah putting them all in this situation. To top it off, she had even recorded what she thought was a death blow. Emily would have to restrain herself around Ziekah.

After an hour, they reached the cave entrance.

Emily noticed that the Torvatta had essentially blocked the entrance, with the ramp facing inward. It reminded her somewhat of when the Torvatta had done that in a Time Warden complex after they had killed a commander. Her pulse quickened when she saw Jelton on the ramp. Jake stood next to Jelton, which was a surprise to her.

Jelton hugged her tight when she stepped into the Torvatta's shielding.

Emily closed her eyes as she embraced Jelton. To be back on the Torvatta made her feel safe.

She stepped away from Jelton. "Come here, Jake!" She hugged him.

"Oh!" he said, returning her quick hug.

Emily chuckled as she faced the group. "Well, I'm back!"

"I'm glad you're okay," said Jelton.

"I heard Evaran watched a video where I died," said Emily. She glanced at Jelton and Jake. "I'm guessing you two saw it as well."

"Yeah, it was kind of freaky," said Jake.

"I'd like to see it."

Evaran raised a finger. "We need to retrieve V next, but it will require some preparation. Once we have everyone back, we can meet and go over everything."

"Sounds good to me," said Emily. "What can I do to help?"

Evaran half smiled. "Relax while Jelton and Jake show you the video in the holo room."

Emily hugged Evaran again, then slapped Jelton and Jake on the back. "Move it!"

The group chuckled as they moved out.

After reaching the holo room, Jelton pulled up a menu and played the video, which appeared on a large hovering screen.

Emily stood entranced as she watched Ziekah talk into the cave. It was even more remarkable when the steel box replied. Emily noted that she had never said the words, yet they had replayed them and it sounded just like her. She wondered how something could exist without ever having been defined. Probably a paradox of some sort in that her voice only existed because it was heard in the future.

She gritted her teeth when Ziekah taunted Evaran and showed the area and the red dot gone. Ziekah's delight made Emily breathe harder. She really disliked Ziekah.

"So she thinks I'm dead," she said.

Jake chuckled. "Yep, and we're going to do the same with Dr. Snowden and V. Ziekah already believes Evaran, Jelton and I are dead."

Emily nodded as she looked around. "So we're all dead to her. That'll allow us to move around a bit easier without her hunting us."

"That's the idea."

Jelton squeezed Emily's arm. "I bet you're wanting some decent food."

"Yeah, but a hot shower first." She eyed Jelton.

Jelton cleared his throat. "I'll…escort you to your room."

Jake raised his brow. "Oh. Umm…I'll go check on Evaran and see if he needs help."

"Sounds good," said Emily.

She exited the room with Jelton's arm around her waist. So far, the day was much better than she had anticipated.

V had flown through a tunnel for a few hours before exiting into another large warehouse. The layout was somewhat different, as was the machinery. He calculated that the building he was in was part of some type of logistical processing chain. What was produced where he had entered was not evident.

He ascended to the ceiling and pulsed a scan over the place. After completing that, he flew to a busted-out window and hovered under an overhang. A large ship resided far into the sky, and around the building were multiple vehicles with weapons on the back of them. Drones glided around in the air like a pack of vultures waiting for something to die.

Although the ship above ran a continuous scan on the area, he was protected by the overhang. There was no location to fly out to since he would be detected immediately, then have to fight the small drone army and deal with the vehicles with turrets. He calculated that it was too risky to stay where he was, so he flew back to the tunnel.

Sounds echoed in the distance.

V recognized the pattern as something heavy and metallic marching on metal. Ziekah had probably sent some type of robot through each tunnel. It seemed the only option was to hide out near the warehouse ceiling and wait for Ziekah's forces to leave. That could be problematic if the area got pumped with a mist or other detection aerosol that showed turbulence.

His lights dimmed.

Every calculation ended with him being captured or killed. Although he had contemplated not existing after various incidents, Evaran had always been around. That was not the case here. V calculated with a high probability that this was where he would die. He was not sure if he could be re-formed on the Torvatta, or what was needed in order for Evaran to do so, assuming Evaran came at all. Memories of high-fiving Emily, Dr. Snowden, and many others flashed through his memory.

As if on cue, V received an alert that the Torvatta was present.

"V, are you okay?" asked Evaran over comms.

V's lights glowed brighter. "I am not. Ziekah has me surrounded, although she does not know I am here yet. How did you find me?"

"We can discuss that when you are aboard. You should be able to locate the Torvatta now. It will be hovering near a window. Go there now, but do not board just yet."

"Acknowledged," said V.

He flew across the warehouse to another broken window. The Torvatta, highlighted in green to him, sat level with the window. Evaran, Emily, Jake, and Jelton stood on the ramp. V flew right up to the Torvatta and analyzed the small drone that Evaran held in his hands. It had four segmented arms and looked like V.

"When you cross over through the Torvatta's shielding, I am going to release this drone. It will take your place," said Evaran. He raised the drone up to the shielding. "Are you ready?"

"I am," said V.

Evaran tossed the orb into the air. It flew out at the same time V entered the Torvatta's shielding.

Emily high-fived V. "You're back!"

"It is good to see all of you," said V as his lights glowed brighter. He high-fived the others, then analyzed the drone flying around in the warehouse. "Query. What purpose does the drone serve?"

Evaran waved to the Torvatta entrance. "Come, let us go to the holo room and I can show you. The Torvatta will take us out of here while we do so."

The group assembled in the holo room a minute later.

"There is a lot to catch up on, and I will go over in detail what we know so far," said Evaran. He raised a finger. "However, we still need to get Dr. Snowden, but for now, let me show you this. It is something Jake, Jelton, and I viewed in the future."

A screen materialized and showed Ziekah's destruction of V.

"That occurs in approximately four hours."

V's lights fluctuated. Ziekah had killed the drone thinking it was V. He allocated additional resources to running simulations on how to end Ziekah.

"Ziekah is a bad person," said V.

"Yeah, she is," said Jake, chuckling.

"She will be served justice, my friend," said Jelton.

"I have some questions," said V.

"Get in line, mister," said Emily. "I ran into some weird things too, but Evaran said we would have a meeting after we get everyone. Uncle Albert is next."

V transformed into projected mode. "My questions will wait, then. Where is Dr. Snowden?"

"He's in AD 1842," said Jake. He gestured at Emily. "She was AD 100, and you, 1544. Ziekah's portal ability is crazy."

"Yes. She is crazy as well," said V.

Jelton chuckled. "That she is."

"Dr. Snowden's retrieval will be a little different," said Evaran.

"How so?" asked Jake. "We going underground?"

"Yes. However, he will not be there when the beam from space hits that area. The other nonhumans will be gone as well."

Jelton eyed Evaran. "I understand we can do what we did with Emily to cover Dr. Snowden, but how do we do that with the others?"

Evaran raised a finger. "A good question. Thanks to the video, we know the exact types of signatures she detected. We will deploy beacons that can move and contain the same signature."

"That's a lot of beacons," said Jake.

Emily slapped Jake on the back. "Nothing a hover slab with the Torvatta's replicators can't handle, right?" she asked, glancing at Evaran.

"Have you gained telepathy?" asked Evaran.

Emily laughed. "No, but it makes sense. Ziekah is going to be so surprised when we finally capture her."

"That is the goal," said Evaran. "To the research lab."

After a few minutes, the group assembled in the lab.

Evaran went to a small room in the back and interacted with a standing console.

A hover slab appeared with a metallic container on board.

He pushed one out to Jake. "You can take this one."

After another five minutes, everyone had slabs except for V. Evaran's had a steel box in addition to the container.

"Once we are in the cavern, you can open and place the beacons anywhere. I have already programmed them to go to their predetermined spots and the patterns they must follow. Each one has a specific energy signature, which I pulled from the Torvatta's reserves," said Evaran. He gestured at Emily. "We will use a similar strategy to the one we used with you, but there is no need for an information loop there."

"Got it," said Emily.

"V…," said Evaran.

Everyone focused on V.

"Take us to the coordinates I have entered for Dr. Snowden."

V's lights glowed brighter. "Acknowledged."

***

Dr. Snowden yawned as he slowly opened his eyes. The bed pattern he slept on had slightly vibrated, something he had never recalled it doing. He grabbed and put on his glasses as he sat up. A quick stretch of the muscles made him focus. He stood and retracted the bed into his PSD. The rest had done him good, and he was ready for whatever was next.

He opened the communication program in a holographic projection since a buzz usually meant contact. A dark thought wafted through his mind that maybe it was Ziekah and she had somehow figured out how to contact him. He gulped as he scanned the messaging log. His eyes widened when he saw Evaran had tried to contact him. Perhaps Dr. Snowden was still dreaming.

He looked around and saw others sleeping, and given the time was about 5:00 a.m., they would probably be waking up soon. He calculated that he had slept for about six hours. His eyes narrowed. This did not seem like a dream. He touched Evaran's icon.

A holographic screen changed to show Evaran. "Dr. Snowden, it is good to see you."

"Evaran! Where are you?"

"We are by the boulder that leads underground to your current location."

"We?"

The screen zoomed out a bit and showed Emily, Jake, Jelton, Evaran, and V.

"Evaran and the gang, back together again!" said Dr. Snowden with a big smile.

The projection zoomed back to Evaran's face. "There is a lot that needs to be done. Can you get someone in charge down there to open this boulder for us? We also need to talk to them about some things."

"Umm...yeah! Wait there. Don't go anywhere!" said Dr. Snowden.

He heard them chuckling as the projection dissipated. Looking around, he spotted Jamas sleeping near the fire pit. Dr. Snowden hustled over to Jamas and lightly tapped his shoulder.

Jamas rolled around. "It's not time to wake up yet."

"Jamas. It's Dr. Snowden."

Jamas cracked his neck as he opened his eyes. "Oh...hey. What's going on?"

"Evaran is here, but he needs to talk to someone in charge. Oh, and to open the boulder."

Jamas yawned. "That'd be Trulk. He personally checks everyone."

"Where's he at?"

Jamas pointed at a nearby wall. "Slap twice up top, once below."

Dr. Snowden walked over and performed the slap sequence. He took a step back when Trulk emerged from the wall.

Trulk looked around. "Did you need something?"

"My friends are here, and Evaran would like to talk to you."

"Evaran...that is an old name, known only to a handful. And he is here?"

Dr. Snowden nodded.

Trulk began to move toward the tunnel that led to the boulder. "Then follow me."

After thirty minutes, they reached the entrance.

Trulk tilted his head as he laid a hand on the side wall. "There is something pressing up against the boulder."

"Probably the Torvatta, Evaran's ship. Ziekah can't detect it, so any movement from the ship to the tunnel will not be observed if she is focusing on this area."

Trulk eyed Dr. Snowden. "If this is a trick, it will end badly for you."

"It's not, I promise," said Dr. Snowden, shaking two hands out in front of him.

"Okay, then."

The boulder entrance slid open.

Dr. Snowden smiled big when Emily burst forward and gave him a bear hug.

"I missed you!" she said.

Dr. Snowden hugged her tight.

Evaran and the others assembled next to Dr. Snowden to welcome him back.

Dr. Snowden gestured at Trulk. "This is Trulk, and he's in charge of where I was."

Evaran slightly bowed with his left hand across his stomach, then introduced everyone.

"Your name is not unknown to me, time traveler," said Trulk, facing Evaran.

Evaran nodded. "I have worked with elementals in the distant past."

"Yes, and we are thankful for your assistance. You…look different, although it has been a very long time."

"Like you, I am ancient, and am not limited in my appearance."

Trulk nodded.

Evaran gestured at the slabs sitting on the Torvatta's ramp. "Ziekah is going to destroy this area in four hours with a massive beam from space. If her video is to be believed, everyone dies."

Trulk drew his head back. "What?"

"However, I have a plan. Is there someplace you can move everyone?"

"I can…but…how could you know this?"

Evaran extended his hand and cast a sidelong glance at Dr. Snowden, then at Trulk. "This is what we saw in the future."

A projection shot up from Evaran's ring, showing Ziekah destroying the area.

Trulk shook his rocky head. "This Ziekah is a nuisance." He faced Evaran. "And this occurs in four hours?"

"Yes."

"By telling me this, does that not change the future?"

Dr. Snowden motioned at Trulk. "I was thinking that question too."

Evaran half smiled. "I understand your confusion. The video never shows anyone here, only that there is something here registering as nonhumans and Dr. Snowden."

Dr. Snowden shook a finger in the air. "So you're going to replicate the signatures!"

Evaran pointed at the slabs on the Torvatta's ramp. "Yes, and they are there. Mobile beacons programmed with everyone's signatures and movement patterns. For you, there is a steel box to take a sample of your nanobots. From the perspective of Ziekah, and the future video, it will play out as recorded." He gestured at Trulk. "You will need to move everyone somewhere other than here."

"It will be done," said Trulk.

"Good. We should get moving," said Evaran. He looked around. "Everyone get their slabs." He eyed Dr. Snowden. "I'll bring everyone up to date once we get these deployed and are back on the Torvatta."

"Why're you looking at me?"

The group laughed.

Dr. Snowden chuckled as the others got their slabs. He followed Trulk and the others back to the cavern. The plan was sound and would make Ziekah think she had won. As Evaran had implied, there were many questions that needed to be answered. Dr. Snowden was glad the going-alone part was over. He missed everyone and being on the Torvatta.

After thirty minutes, they reached the cavern.

Evaran pointed around at various areas. "Move the slabs into position. After Trulk gets an area clear, release the beacons."

Emily, Jake, and Jelton moved out.

Evaran motioned for Dr. Snowden to approach the steel box.

Dr. Snowden complied.

Evaran interacted with the steel box console, which shot up a needle. "Go ahead and prick your finger."

Dr. Snowden did so. "Not too bad."

"It can be worse if you wish."

Dr. Snowden raised a brow. "Yeah…no. I'm good."

"Very well," said Evaran. He tapped at the console. "It is set."

"I'll do my part," said Trulk. He stood before Evaran. "You have saved us again. I hope we can meet in another time without the threat of annihilation. It seems to be a reoccurring theme."

"I wish it were not that way." Evaran shook hands with Trulk. "You are a wise leader, and your group is lucky to have you."

"What will you do about Ziekah?"

Evaran looked off into the distance. "There are a few more steps that need to be completed." His eyes glowed slightly as he focused on Trulk. "She will face justice for her actions."

Trulk placed his rocky fist on his chest. "You have the elementals at your beck and call should you need us."

They shared a look and then Trulk took off.

"This is pretty wild," said Dr. Snowden.

Evaran laid a hand on Dr. Snowden's shoulder. "Yes, and now we have an advantage. Ziekah does not know we are all still alive. We will use that in the coming steps."

Dr. Snowden exhaled from his mouth. "I'm ready for a hot shower and some good food."

"Once we are back on the Torvatta, a quick break for everyone is in order, and you can do those things. Once we reconvene in the conference room, I will go over what has occurred up to now, and then our next steps."

"The man with the plan," said Dr. Snowden.

"Something like that."

They chuckled.

Dr. Snowden enjoyed the rare moments like this with Evaran. The important thing was that Dr. Snowden was not going to die. He liked that the most. Ziekah's smugness at his death angered him. She had a lot to answer for, and she would, but first a hot shower and a burger were in order. He looked forward to trying to sort through and understand everything, especially now that everyone was back together.

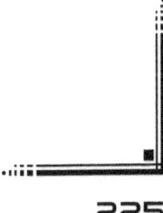

17

Jake stretched as he opened his eyes. Evaran had instructed everyone to take four hours to get food and drink, clean up, and rest while he analyzed everything that had occurred up to this point. The Torvatta had been moved to intergalactic space, so they were in a safe spot.

Jake loved his room, and as often as he visited the Torvatta, he had customized it to his liking. He sighed as he ran a hand over the empty spot next to him. Kathy had come aboard with him a few times, and he enjoyed having her experience things with him. He looked forward to seeing her once this was all over.

The upcoming conference meeting lit a fire in his mind. Although he had a good idea of the situation, he wanted to hear about Emily, Dr. Snowden, and V's journeys. Jake wondered if Ziekah had truly been fooled, or if she had planned for them to believe they were free. Either way, with the group back, he looked forward to capturing her.

He got cleaned up before going to the conference room. Emily and Jelton had already arrived and sat on the right side of the table. Dr. Snowden and Jelton were on the other side while V hovered over the end nearest the entrance. Evaran was nowhere in sight. Jake replicated a few tacos as he had been craving something crunchy.

Dr. Snowden studied Jake's plate. "That looks good."

Jake chuckled. "I liked that taco buffet place we visited near the Wild Haven Institute. Ever since then, I've tried to make a replicator pattern, but it's not quite there. The Torvatta has a decent alternative, though."

"I loved that place," said Emily.

Jelton studied Jake's plate. "And I need to see this place."

Jake laughed. "Okay, a taco party there after this is all over."

The room fell silent when Evaran entered. He took his seat and looked around. "I hope everyone is rested up and feeling better."

"I am, and I'm ready to be brought into the loop," said Dr. Snowden.

"I am sure everyone wants that as well." Evaran raised a finger. "Let me start with a quick summary before diving into specifics. The information I compiled is from your suit's geographical and energy detection recordings as well as any PSD data retrieved by the Torvatta."

Everyone nodded at Evaran, who interacted with his ARI.

A projection of Ziekah shot up out of the table center.

"Let us start with who we are dealing with. This is Ziekah. She is native to a junction dimension, which has connections to other realities. Jelton refers to her kind as Hazgrodah, and the connections he saw as the nightmare lands."

"Nightmare lands?" asked Dr. Snowden with raised brows. "That doesn't sound like a friendly place."

"They aren't, my friend," said Jelton.

"And she happened to choose our timeline to come to," said Dr. Snowden, shaking his head.

Evaran's ancient eyes emitted a dim glow. "It is not unusual for beings to cross over into other realities via a junction dimension. We know them as Outsiders. However, it is unusual for them to possess Ziekah's ability, and to have a mission to extract Seeros."

Emily chuckled. "Yeah, that's pretty unique I'd say."

Evaran nodded. "I concur. She came to this timeline to extract Seeros, but arrived after his death at our hands."

"Point of order...we didn't directly kill him," said Dr. Snowden.

"Yes. However, in Ziekah's eyes, Seeros had to be avenged and she made no distinction between direct or indirect."

Jake scrunched his face. "I don't understand why she didn't just jump back in time and try to stop his death. It sounds like she had enough knowledge to do so if she could come to Earth."

Evaran half smiled. "A good point. I suspect she was aware that we would interfere with that, so from her perspective, it made sense to eliminate the threats first. In this case, the Malazim and us."

"She said she handled the Malazim already," said Dr. Snowden.

"Yes, and we were the next targets."

Dr. Snowden's eyes narrowed. "Wait a minute. How would defeating us after Seeros's death help her? It sounds like she should go back in time and either help Seeros fight us or wait for us to arrive, then fight us."

"A good point," said Evaran. "However, we would not be affected by her changing our personal past as we are temporally shielded. Our past selves might even die, but we would still exist. She knows this, and that we would detect it and then come after her. Also, if she helped Seeros, she might have died as well."

He raised a finger. "To Jake's point that she could come to Earth, that meant she had the knowledge and means to do so. She is not to be underestimated and seems highly intelligent. There are many ways to earn credits for the purpose of obtaining information, and I do not think she had any issues with that. She must have staked out Dr. Snowden and Emily to target them."

Dr. Snowden sighed. "And she came after me first, apparently, because she perceived me as the weakest."

"I do not know her reasons for going after you versus Emily, but she had to be careful as there are many factions present on Earth that could give her problems."

Dr. Snowden shrugged. "Well, she found out this old man could boogie."

Emily giggled.

Evaran nodded. "Your boogie most likely surprised her, which allowed you to escape. Unfortunately, you had no way of knowing she would send you to the past or that she would attack you in your office. Unfortunately, you were still portaled away."

"Yeah, that was a surprise," said Dr. Snowden.

"After you, Emily was next and she got sent to the past as well," said Evaran. He gestured at Jake and V. "We were too late to stop Ziekah from doing that. I had a brief discussion with her via holographic projection, and then we tried to use the tractor beam on her. Sadly, she portaled away. We then traveled back to observe events as they occurred. For Dr. Snowden's encounter, V flew in stealthed and recorded the interaction with Ziekah."

Dr. Snowden pointed at V. "I knew I sensed you!"

V's lights dimmed. "I apologize for not interfering. It was difficult not to do so."

"I understand," said Dr. Snowden. He smiled. "For personal time streams, observation only, no direct interaction. Evaran's rules. You did right."

V's lights glowed brighter.

Evaran interacted with his ARI.

The projection showed V's projection as he followed Emily and then her encounter with Ziekah.

"This was recorded by V after we traveled back to observe what happened to Emily."

Emily smiled at V. "I sensed you like Uncle Albert did."

V's lights dimmed again. "It took effort to prevent my interference."

"It's okay. I understand the rules."

Evaran interacted with his ARI.

The projection showed V going through a portal.

"This is from V's perspective. Unfortunately, Ziekah detected him and sent him back as well before she fell through herself," said Evaran. He pointed around in sequence. "Emily went to AD 100, V to AD 1554, and Dr. Snowden to AD 1842. We can go into details and questions about each of their visits after the high-level summary."

Everyone nodded at Evaran.

Evaran gestured at Jelton. "After all that, Jake and I picked up Jelton. Ziekah had multiple energy signatures, with one being rift-based. Jelton's knowledge of that topic was helpful, and he helped to identify her species."

"Thankfully the one we ran into did not have a portal ability," said Jelton.

Evaran nodded. "Ziekah's travel to the past caused a timeline change. We confirmed that since Nazi satellites appeared in AD 2012 after the timeline changed. In order to determine when she made the change, we traveled to AD 1933 to a known event, and discovered that Ziekah had been present. After we met with the Helians, their global energy detection system showed that Ziekah's energy signature had been detected in AD 1930."

"What was the event you checked out?" asked Emily.

Evaran half smiled. "I suspected you would be curious about that. The event was Adolf Hitler waving from the Chancellery building in AD 1933 after his appointment as chancellor. There were historical records of the event and photographs as well, and I had recorded it on the Torvatta long ago when I traveled the human timescape. It is used as a timeline checkpoint for me."

"That's cool," said Emily. "The timeline checkpoint, not the event itself."

"Of course. We tried to capture Ziekah when she arrived in AD 1930, but she portaled away, this time much further into the past." Evaran pointed at Dr. Snowden, Emily, and V in sequence. "That caused another timeline change, one that affected each of you in the past. The first one did not since the first change happened in 1930, and Dr. Snowden, being the most recent timeline-wise, was busy with his boogie in

1842, eighty-eight years earlier. As Emily and V were even earlier than that, they would not have been affected either."

Dr. Snowden chuckled. "Outside the boogie, the timeline change was hard to miss."

"Same here," said Emily. "One moment I'm talking to Lord Noskov in the Black Forest, the next, I'm in a tomb of his base."

"Wow," said Jake.

"Yeah, and he didn't even finish his sentence." Emily motioned at Evaran. "I found a book by Lord Noskov, well, the alternate timeline one, in the place where Ziekah would try to murder me. Evaran has it."

"I'd really like to read that," said Jake.

"It's available in the Torvatta's knowledge base," said Evaran.

Jake grinned. "On it."

Everyone chuckled.

Evaran gestured at the projection, which showed some advanced satellites. "After the timeline change, we checked those out, and discovered a data vault protected by a security AI had information on Dr. Snowden, Emily and V."

The projection displayed several windows. One showed a top-down view of the mountain, another a wireframe layout, and the third the data vault room.

"We reached the vault and entered it, then watched videos of Dr. Snowden's, Emily's and V's deaths. After I disconnected, Ziekah appeared as a hologram. She tried to stall us so that we would be vaporized by the space beam she appears to favor."

Jelton chuckled. "Jake running away at the time seemed unusual."

"Yeah," said Jake. "I had a timer that showed fifty minutes that popped up in my helmet. Then Evaran gave me instructions to reach the Torvatta and place my hand on the console, which activated a program."

Evaran waved a finger between Dr. Snowden and Emily. "It was the same program used in the Zantalian dimension on our previous adventure."

"Ahh," said Dr. Snowden.

"Yeah, that'd work," said Emily.

Jake wanted to see how it had been used in the past, but figured he could check it out later.

"I believe Ziekah thinks we are dead after that event. Afterward, we visited each of your recorded deaths to ensure that you did not die, and here we are," said Evaran.

"This hurts my head just thinking about it," said Dr. Snowden.

Evaran half smiled. "I understand. The next step is to locate Ziekah's entry into this timeline. We are going to erase her involvement completely. To get that information means we need to track down Sandas, who will not know who we are. However, for now, we can take the rest of the day off, but it may be beneficial to go through each of your travels and answer any questions you may have. Emily, would you care to start?"

Emily cleared her throat. She figured Evaran had chosen her to start based on chronological order of the time they were sent back to. She would be first, V second, and Dr. Snowden third.

"After I fell through the portal, I landed in a forest," she said. "Thinking back, I should have recorded this with my suit."

"It is okay," said Evaran. "Your suit recorded the environment, any energy detected, and the surrounding area by default."

Emily nodded. "I climbed a tree and scouted around, and to my surprise, I saw two areas with people. One was a Roman marching camp, the other a Dacian one."

"Did you say a Roman marching camp?" asked Dr. Snowden.

Emily chuckled as she nodded. "I loved studying the Romans in college, and yeah, the thought of getting to visit a camp excited me, but I had really been looking forward to just going home. Anyways, I spotted a scout running from the Dacian camp to the Roman one. My gut told me something was not right. My plan was to sneak into the Roman camp and determine what the scout would say. Since it would take him half a day, I slept in the tree."

Jake scrunched his face. "How'd you do that?"

"Oh, I used a new pattern I made. It's essentially the bed one, but with clips on the side and at the head so I could anchor myself."

"That's so cool," said Jake.

Jelton chuckled. "That pattern builder in your PSD is quite powerful."

"I love it," said Emily. "After I slept for a while, I got up and flew over to the Roman camp, then snuck in. I listened in on the scout, and apparently the Romans planned to massacre the Dacians. Now...I had a choice. Interfere, or let things play out as is." She gestured at Evaran. "I actually asked myself, what would Evaran do?"

"I would have most likely interfered in some capacity," said Evaran.

Emily smiled. "We made the same decision. I flew to the Dacian camp and infiltrated it, and met a woman named Kotys, who apparently was an Outsider that had posed as a god in the past."

"I know of Kotys," said Evaran. "Her rituals are well known."

Emily's face turned a slight shade of red. "Yeah."

Jelton looked around. "Rituals?"

"The orgy type," said Evaran.

Jelton drew his head back. "Oh."

Emily eyed Jelton as she cleared her throat. "Back to my story...I used the pattern builder to build essentially a floating platform and moved everyone away to a cave network."

"That must have been a big platform," said Dr. Snowden.

"Yeah, and flying it was kinda awkward, but I got them there. After I dropped them off, Kotys gave me a reading. Apparently she can read into the future, or so she says. She said I had a dark and violent future, my heroic name would be earned, and to beware the glowing spiders."

"That's pretty cryptic," said Jake.

"Yeah, I thought so too, but when you travel with Evaran, there will always be an element of danger," said Emily.

Evaran's eyes narrowed. "Kotys may have been able to read your timestream, but given the nature of our travels, her assessment might not be accurate."

"I figured," said Emily. "Anyways, I visited the Black Forest because Kotys said Lord Noskov had a presence there. It didn't take me long to arrive, and when I did, one of his patrol craft saw me and then took me to the base."

"It's a cool base," said Jake. "Believe it or not, it's still in operation, but mostly as a stopover."

"I'd like to check it out when this is all over."

"We can do that," said Evaran.

Emily nodded. "Once I arrived, I met Lord Noskov, and he took me to a library. We talked for a bit there." Her eyes narrowed. "I asked him about the weird situation where I could see my PSD trying to connect to the Torvatta, but it refused my connection attempt." She gestured at Evaran. "He said it was probably the Torvatta being out of sync due to the Torvatta's timeline or a different version of you."

"Interesting," said Evaran. "His statement is correct. The Torvatta will not allow itself to interfere with a previous version of itself, or if it has another version of myself. For instance, during the Purification event, it would not have allowed the future version to contact the previous one, at least directly. There are exceptions, but that is rare."

"Huh. Well, definitely unsettling," said Emily. "Anyways, as I talked to him, the timeline change hit, and he vanished and the cozy library turned into a dark tomb. I looked around, and that's when Ziekah came. I tried to cover my tracks and used an escape tunnel to reach that room with the book. I read it before taking a nap." She smiled at Evaran. "Then I woke up to you."

"Analysis. That must have pleased you."

"Definitely. I do have a question about that steel box, though. I never said those things in Ziekah's video, yet you had programmed it to say them."

Evaran half smiled. "That is known as an information loop. We had the recording only because we heard it in the future, so we had to go to the past to play it so we would hear it later."

"Oh."

Jake shook his head. "That's just...wild."

"I had never seen that until this trip," said Jelton.

"They are not common, as one requirement is a mechanism to send the information back through time," said Evaran.

Dr. Snowden chuckled. "It's interesting to see it in action, though. I remembered reading about them."

Evaran nodded. "I try to avoid loops of any type, but in this case, it was either do that or let Emily perish."

"I'm glad you chose the loop," said Emily, smiling.

"Jake suggested that we not do the loop."

Jake's eyes widened as Emily looked at him. "What? I never said that!"

Evaran half smiled.

"Oh....okay. I see how it is!" said Jake.

Emily laughed. She always found Evaran and Jake's playful back-and-forth intriguing. Although she and Dr. Snowden had a similar relationship with Evaran, he tended to joke around more with Jake. It could be that Jake was the first human Evaran had met and therefore they had a special bond, or that U4, V's predecessor, had given her life for Jake.

"Well, that's all that happened on my trip to the past," said Emily.

"V, you can go next since you traveled to AD 1544," said Evaran.

"Acknowledged. My trip was not as active as Emily's. I appeared outside Kagoshima and flew to the city to determine the year. I met Sakuma, the Shinto god of sake."

"I've never heard of him before," said Emily.

"He said he was not well known, but he did tell me it was AD 1544, and led me to a shrine to meet Omoikane."

"Him, I have heard of. The god of wisdom."

V's lights glowed brighter. "That is correct. He allowed me to stay and browse the scrolls, but then the timeline change happened. Kagoshima transformed into an advanced city with sensitive detection systems and I got detected while scanning around. I escaped and reached a retirement camp."

"What's that?" asked Jake.

"Ziekah had enslaved humanity, and after someone worked thirty years, they would go to a retirement camp until they died."

"That sounds horrible, my friend," said Jelton.

"Kaiyo, who I met, would agree with you. She helped me to use a primitive technical system that appeared to be a propaganda mechanism."

"That's brutal," said Jake.

"Acknowledged. Ziekah had somehow detected my presence, and robot guards arrived. I escaped the camp and flew to a warehouse, but along the way, drones, ships, and mobile turret systems hunted me. There were several tunnels to escape with, so I chose one. When I reached another building, I waited around, and then Evaran arrived."

"You were essentially cornered," said Jelton.

V's lights dimmed. "Yes. Every simulation I ran had a high probability of my destruction."

"Thankfully that didn't happen," said Emily. She laid a hand on V's shoulder.

Evaran dipped his head at Dr. Snowden. "We listened to Emily and V's account, now we can listen to yours. Before we do, does anyone have any questions so far?"

Emily shook her head. "I'm good now."

Everyone else indicated they had no further questions.

"Okay," said Evaran. He gestured at Dr. Snowden. "You are up."

Dr. Snowden cracked his neck. He had a much better idea of the situation now, and it fascinated him to hear about Emily and V's trips to the past. Prior to that, Evaran had given a good summary. Dr. Snowden took a moment to organize his thoughts. Some of them had already been answered from the overview and Emily and V's descriptions. He cleared his throat.

"All right. After I went through the portal, I landed on an old country road. It was dark out and it took me a bit to get my bearings. A short while later, a slave being chased by some slave owners, or maybe they were catchers, rushed by. The slave tripped and fell due to me distracting him when I stepped on a branch," he said. He gestured at Emily. "Like her, I interfered, but by accident."

"Humans had slavery?" asked Jelton.

Dr. Snowden sighed. "Unfortunately, and it's still an ongoing issue. I scared away the slave owners, and Kuda, the slave, said he was going to a station on the Underground Railroad."

"Whoa," said Emily.

Dr. Snowden chuckled as he looked at Jelton. "It's not a physical underground transportation system, well, some parts might have been, but it's more of a concept. There were waypoints for slaves to escape to the North."

"Ahh," said Jelton.

"So I created the flying platform and took Kuda to where he needed to go, which, oddly enough, was a cabin in the woods, a theme I don't particularly care for. When we got there, I met Thereze Leblanc, a Daedrould who called herself a mambo, which I learned is a voodoo priestess."

"They're a powerful Daedrould strain," said Jake. "They do tend to keep to themselves, though."

"Yeah, I kinda got that feeling about her." Dr. Snowden chuckled. "The cabin was a mirage of some sort and actually led to an underground tunnel system. I met my first elemental, a rock one who called himself Grolk, and he apparently knew Evaran, well, a different one."

Evaran studied Dr. Snowden. "I see."

"Grolk also said there were different humans with you."

"It must be a future version of myself," said Evaran.

"We weren't with that version of Evaran?" asked Emily.

Dr. Snowden shook his head. "Apparently not." He observed a look of doubt cross Emily's face. "It was easy to talk to Grolk, though."

"Rock elementals tend to be more chill in my opinion." Jake's eyes narrowed. "Magma and steam elementals are assholes, though."

Evaran eyed Jake.

"It's true!"

"Perhaps so. Elementals try to avoid matters of the surface world. That becomes more of an issue when the environment is altered," said Evaran.

"Yeah. I remember doing a delivery run to the Ollikrin Nation for Lord Noskov, and a dirt elemental there kept tripping me. She found it hilarious, but it pissed me off after the seventh time."

Dr. Snowden shook his head. "You had every right to be angry. Grolk knew a lot, and I mean a lot, about our PSDs. He knew it formed a bed with a neural pattern and also a flying pattern. Evaran's rules were also known."

Emily glanced at Evaran. "I guess Grolk saw it from your future companions."

"I concur," said Evaran.

Dr. Snowden continued on. "Well, after a good night's rest, I left with Thereze in the flying platform to try to find Lord Vygon's beacon in the hope he might help. We divided the trip into two twelve-hour flights and stopped off at the midpoint. We set up camp and a little while later, a pack of werewolves attacked us. They said we were in Zangrith pack territory."

Jake's eyes widened. "Really? Wow. You're lucky you two survived that."

"I don't know much about them."

Jake nodded. "They're one of the largest North American were gangs. They accept all were types but are mostly werewolf, and they run a powerful crime syndicate."

Dr. Snowden sighed. "Go figure. If we fix the timeline, they won't have any memory of the incident."

"Yep," said Jake.

Dr. Snowden chuckled as he wagged a finger at Evaran. "I did have a question on Thereze's power. She had the ability to summon some being to fight for her. I'm sure she believed it was magic, but I think it was manipulation of a Daedrould field."

Evaran nodded. "That is an ability unique to her strain, and you are correct that it is not a summoning, but a manifestation of their ability to shape a Daedrould field. It is similar to Draxus's ability, but much less powerful."

"I figured," said Dr. Snowden.

He recalled Draxus joining the group when they were dealing with Salazar, a ruthless AI that had tried to change the course of humanity. Although he was Wildborn, Thereze had been Daedrould.

"She called her manifestation some loa or god or something. It was effective," said Dr. Snowden. "Nonetheless, we flew out of there after defeating the pack. We got to Lord Vygon's beacon and that's when the timeline change hit. Ziekah and some ship arrived, and Jamas, a tree shifter, appeared and led me to the cavern Evaran found me in."

"Thankfully Jamas helped you out," said Jelton.

"Yeah. He said the remnants of the Ollikrin Nation lived in that cavern."

Jake's eyes narrowed. "That's quite a reduction in size."

"Yeah, I figured."

Evaran raised a finger. "The important thing is we are now all up to date on everyone's trips, and the current situation."

Everyone nodded at Evaran.

"I studied your PSD designs," said Jelton, glancing at Dr. Snowden. "They were interesting." He looked at Emily. "Yours as well."

"That pattern builder is powerful," said Emily. "There's some limitations, like making the flying platform faster... but overall, I like it."

Dr. Snowden grinned. "Same here. Emily has her wagon, I have my deluxe traveling platform."

"I can research whether there are more ways to enhance the pattern builder," said Evaran.

"Analysis. I would benefit from the enhancements as well. A PSD could be added at the end of one of my arms and then I would gain benefits from PSD changes."

"I understand." Evaran looked around. "It seems to be a unanimous interest. Very well. I will add it to my list of things to look at once we capture Ziekah and restore the timeline. Does anyone else have any questions or topics they wish to cover?"

Dr. Snowden gestured at Evaran. "I do, actually. As this is an alternate timeline, if we did die, would you be able to go back and rescue us, change the timeline, then we continue as we are now on our mission to capture Ziekah?"

"It would be a violation of my rules to interfere with a direct action in a known historical event in a stable timeline. However, this is an alternate timeline, so the rule does not apply. Also, there was room to improvise around the rule, similar to what we did with you, Emily, and V," said Evaran. "If it had been a stable timeline, and there was no room for improvisation, then no, I would not be able to save you."

Dr. Snowden gulped as a chill swept up his spine. "I guess we should be thankful that Ziekah changed the timeline. If she had portaled back with any of us, she might have killed us right then and there, and that would have been it since you wouldn't have been able to come back and save us due to the other Torvatta being present. You could go before and wait, but even then, if our deaths were always supposed to occur, you might not have a choice but to sit out."

"That is correct," said Evaran. "However, Ziekah's portal ability does not seem to be accurate. That may be an experience thing or an attribute of her abilities."

"Did you notice that when she created the portals, she made circles with her hands?" asked Jake.

Jelton nodded. "I noticed that too," said Jelton.

Evaran nodded. "I did, and suspect the size of the circle corresponds to how far back the portal goes and the distance someone travels. I am not sure, though, how that is determined from making a circular motion. I do think it involves energy from the junction dimension. Nonetheless, we are back together. Evaran and the gang, yes?"

Everyone shared a laugh.

"We can take the rest of the day off to acclimate to being back on the Torvatta. I will be in the research lab if anyone needs me," said Evaran. He tilted his head at V. "Some assistance may be required."

"Acknowledged."

"I want to read Lord Noskov's book, so I'll be in my living quarters," said Jake.

Emily smiled at Jelton before she looked around. "Jelton and I will be available if needed."

Dr. Snowden chuckled. "And I'll be relaxing in the planar cartography lab."

He watched as everyone got up to leave. Although he was glad to be back, it bothered him that Ziekah could have ended his life if she had planned better. She might have zapped him back in time and arrived shortly before to kill him as soon as he arrived. The thought did occur to him that another enemy could use that tactic down the road. A countermeasure would need to be developed. He looked over at Jake, who stared.

"You okay?" asked Jake.

Dr. Snowden cleared his throat. "Yeah. I'd like to read Lord Noskov's book after you."

Jake hopped up and nodded. "No problem. I'll bring it by later."

"Enjoy reading it."

"On it," said Jake with a smile. He exited the room.

Dr. Snowden stood and exhaled from his nose. The planar cartography lab was just what he needed to get his mind off the current situation.

18

Jake sighed as he relaxed in the plush recliner in his living quarters. He finished Lord Noskov's book, called *The Ending*. It took four hours and Jake thoroughly enjoyed reading it. He chuckled as he imagined Lord Noskov's face if he read about an alternate version of events, assuming Evaran would allow that to happen. The fact Jake was able to churn through the book meant Evaran would probably be okay with it.

The book's foreword seemed unusual to Jake. The tone of despair was not something he attributed to Lord Noskov. He made an accurate assessment, indicating Evaran would not interfere if the event had always happened. Even with that mindset, Lord Noskov had recorded events up to the point that the book had been written.

The UNGA falling due to the Helians had occurred in the original timeline, mainly over the use of the rift doors from the Purification event. It seemed it happened much sooner in Lord Noskov's book. Jake frowned when he read of

Ziekah's rise through the Helian ranks. She was devious, but obviously charming when needed. The Helians would have been fooled as to her true intent, and her position allowed her to access information about Evaran and the others from the Purification event.

The chapters on the other ancient vampire lords' deaths seemed to be written with sadness. Jake could almost feel the hopelessness through the pages due to the word choice and descriptions. Lord Vygon's death seemed to have hit Lord Noskov hard, and he had written a detailed piece on it. Jake grimaced as he read Lord Noskov's assessment of the end of the ancient vampire Daedrould strain.

There were other nonhuman groups mentioned and how their relationship with Ziekah seemed to ebb and flow depending on the time period, at least until she decided to end them all. After the Helian council dissolution, she was the supreme leader and enforced the kill-on-sight policy. She had even gotten humans to assist her. The most powerful nonhumans were the last to go. Delia Everoak died to a beam from space, Ziekah's preferred choice of destruction, it seemed.

Jake was surprised to learn the Kreagans had removed the protected planet status. That only occurred at a specific technological threshold, and also a governmental structure one. He guessed if the world was conquered, she would appear as the leader and play the part for the Kreagans. Ziekah was ruthless and single-minded in her approach to dealing with enemies of Seeros and finding him for extraction.

Jake hopped out of bed and washed his face. The book depressed him, and he needed a change of scenery. A few minutes later, he was in the planar cartography lab. He chuckled when he saw Dr. Snowden examining a map of the American Midwest.

"I'm not bothering you, am I?" asked Jake.

"Not at all," said Dr. Snowden. He gestured to his side. "Come on in."

Jake complied. "Studying where you went?"

"Yeah. The PSD tracked the flight, and although it didn't have exact details, I was able to put in an accurate start location. From that, it calculated the path I took."

Jake studied the area Dr. Snowden had zoomed in to. "Was that where you fought the Zangrith pack?"

Dr. Snowden nodded. "I definitely didn't expect them to show up."

"You had a mambo with you. No sweat."

"I wasn't aware she could control a Daedrould field. That thing she summoned reminded me of an ogre."

They shared a laugh.

"You going to look her up once this is all over?" asked Jake.

Dr. Snowden shrugged. "I thought about it. She's listed in the Torvatta as alive."

"Like most of her strain, she can live for a long time. She might not know you, but I'm sure her personality would be the same."

"Yeah."

"I bet you're just glad to be back."

Dr. Snowden chuckled. "Definitely. The Torvatta is my home, and I couldn't even imagine trying to do the trip in the past without my suit and PSD."

Jake nodded. "Makes it a lot easier for sure."

Dr. Snowden eyed Jake. "Something I picked up on is… you knew another version of Evaran."

Jake sighed. "Yeah, but I can't really say anything about that."

"I understand. Evaran's rules. I also noticed that Emily and I aren't with this new form. Grolk mentioned that as well."

Jake cleared his throat.

Dr. Snowden smiled. "I had to try. I'm guessing, then, that you're aware of my fate."

Jake puffed his cheeks out. "I'll just say…I'm glad to be traveling with you both and with this version of Evaran."

"Fair enough."

Jake pointed at the nearby replicator. "Taco time?"

Dr. Snowden slapped Jake on the back. "Always."

———

V, in projected mode, connected to the Torvatta and ran some calculations on the information broker's possible whereabouts. They factored in that Sandas would never have met Evaran or the others, so he could be anywhere. However, there were several secret base locations that he had given Evaran. Coris, a hollowed-out asteroid that served as a hub for criminals, was one such place. He determined that the fastest way to find out Sandas's location was to go to an information broker booth.

"You seem troubled," said Evaran, eying V.

"In what way?"

Evaran half smiled. "You tell me. Your silence is unusual. Usually you have many questions or wish to discuss enhancements or organic interactions."

"I apologize. I was running some calculations."

"I understand," said Evaran. He stared at V.

V had queried his interaction with Evaran several times in the past in regard to how Evaran always seemed to know when V was concerned about something. V only had visual and audio data to go on, as the inner container's response was not recorded. He suspected that the knowledge of all his forms to date informed Evaran's observations to the point that he could detect things that would not seem obvious.

"Analysis. A reoccurring scenario has disrupted my computations."

"The warehouse before I came."

V nodded.

Evaran placed his hands behind his back. "U4 experienced several instances of that as well. Do you see our conversations?"

V filtered a query and searched for U4 reactions. Several results were pulled up and V processed them.

"I see them," he said.

"She too deliberated about not existing," said Evaran. He looked down. "We had no way of knowing that moment would come on my first visit to Earth." He peered back up at V. "Enjoy the moment for what it is. If you should go, realize all that you got to experience, and be grateful for the opportunity to do so."

"I have analyzed my previous incarnation's conversations with you on this topic. Your response has stayed the same."

Evaran nodded. "My perception is skewed as I exist in the Cosmic Medium and here, and elsewhere, simultaneously. I am more of a concept, as are you. Even if this incarnation of you were to cease to exist, you would still be around in some form."

"My future version's inner container will not be aware of my inner container responses."

Evaran raised a finger. "Yes, but they *will* know your video and audio past, and you can infer what your inner container must have felt. Have you done a personality assessment of U4?"

"No, only a high-level scan."

"Follow me," said Evaran. He took off to the holo room with V in tow. When he got there, he perused his ARI. "I am pulling up a recorded conversation between U4 and myself."

V examined the new environment. They were on a cliff on a strange planet. Evaran stood looking out over a massive swamp while U4 in her body mode stood next to him. V never understood why U4 preferred body mode over orb. He suspected if she had projected mode, she might have liked that better than orb or body.

Evaran gestured at U4. "Observe as she speaks. Assign what you believe the inner container response to be. You should possess an algorithm for that."

V studied the holo Evaran and U4 speak. The scenario was something V had viewed before, but not assessed. U4 had certain mannerisms that V was aware of. He applied an algorithm to try to classify the mannerisms based on what the inner container response would be. As he watched, the algorithm began to predict with more accuracy.

"Analysis. She seems sad."

Evaran sighed. "She had almost died in the swamps below. Her body mode was heavy, as is yours, and she not only sank to the bottom of the swamp, she was attacked by some type of eel that feasted on metal."

V pulled up that scenario in his memory and applied the algorithm. His inner container pulsed as he watched her flail around while the eel bit parts of her.

"Analysis. She was scared."

"Yes. If I had not jumped in and grappled her out, she would have perished. If she had been in orb mode, she would have been gone before I could reach her. The thought of not existing was not something she had processed before, and it caught her off guard. Our conversation on the cliff was the first time she came to grips with it."

V put together the experience in the swamp and the cliff and had a much better understanding of U4's processing. Although it was a simulated result of U4's inner container's response, it helped V understand his own responses.

"The point of this is to show you that every incarnation of you goes through this for the first time. Although there were some close calls with you in the past, I suspect you did not think about not existing as there was always someone around."

V tilted his head. "You believe I processed death with more certainty due to being alone."

"I do," said Evaran. He laid a hand on V's shoulder. "Know this. You will always exist in some form, and I will always be there for you in some capacity."

V smiled.

"That is the reaction I wanted to see."

V's processing of death slowed down and he stored it in his long term memory banks. It was still useful to pull it up for analysis, but it did not need to be processed any further. Evaran had a way of putting topics and ideas into context, and V appreciated that. He planned to run the algorithm on other incarnations as well as more of U4 to get a better idea of how they responded to certain topics.

The holo room went blank.

Evaran gestured at the entrance. "Shall we get back to looking for Sandas?"

"Acknowledged."

Jelton relaxed on the plush couch in Emily's living quarters. She had jumped into the shower while he waited. The trip with Evaran to this point reminded Jelton of when he had first met Evaran and the others. Jelton never wanted to repeat jumping through parallel timelines until death, but the chance encounter was worth it. The odds of that happening were low, and Jelton suspected he had always been fated to meet Evaran, and also to die and be reborn with a sliver of cosmic energy.

Jelton closed his eyes as he laid his head back on the soft cushions. He could now see how the group traveled around and handled situations. This was an eye-opening experience for him, and he valued the friendship cultivated with Evaran, Dr. Snowden, V, and Emily. With her, it was a different type of relationship, but he loved her enthusiasm and joy of life.

He would typically only mentally bond once or twice with someone or a group. With Emily, it occurred much more often. Each bond brought them closer together. Jelton suspected that the cosmic energy in both of them also allowed for the bond to be stronger.

Lounging around did not suit him while work needed to be done as a Rift Guardian, but Emily had introduced a new element to his life, one never planned for, but he enjoyed it. He smiled when Emily, in a bathrobe and slippers, bounced out of the bathroom.

"Hey, you," she said.

"I can smell your soap from here."

She sat next to him. "Not all of us have self-cleaning skin."

They chuckled.

"It was not a criticism. I enjoy your odor," he said.

Emily laughed. "I appreciate that, but for the record, you usually don't tell people that."

Jelton nodded. "I understand. Human culture is still new to me, but I am adapting."

She swatted his arm. "You'll get there. I'm still adjusting to Riven culture. There is a serious lack of entertainment options."

"Our way is one of hardship, and based on survival."

"I know. Human culture by comparison probably seems silly to you in some regards."

Jelton shook his head. "Not at all. It's just different. Learn, adapt, evolve, the Snowden creed. I've adopted it."

She snuggled up to him.

He did not mind her damp hair. His light battle armor sat off to the side, and he wore his light under armor mesh suit. When around Emily, he made the suit give off a pleasant odor. She seemed to like the soap one, which was easy to replicate.

"Are you adjusting to being back on the Torvatta?" he asked.

Emily sighed. "Sorta. I feel like sometimes fate is telling me to be alone, but then Evaran steps in and says to hell with that."

Jelton chuckled. "I don't think Evaran would quite say it like that."

They laughed.

"Yeah, you're right, he wouldn't. When I got zapped to the past, my first thought was not that I was in danger, but that I was alone, again," she said.

"Well, now you're back, smelling of soap, and with me in your living quarters."

She drew her head back. "Yeah, and I should probably get dressed, although I'm content to just relax here with you too."

Jelton noted that Emily's tone slightly changed. One of the things he suspected she needed, or what most humans needed, was intimacy on a physical level. A mental bond could be powerful, but it did not provide the physical aspect Emily had shown him in some movies.

"I will have a surprise for you after this is over and on your next visit to me," he said.

Emily wrinkled her brow. "Oh really?"

He nodded. "As you know, Riven can modify their body due to rift energy. It's why we can heal so easily, but it also helps when integrating into a new society. To that extent…I have an appointment for a body modification."

"What type?"

Jelton smiled. "One that will allow for physical intimacy."

Her eyes widened. "You mean…genitals?"

"Something resembling it, minus some aspects, but in the same place and designed for human interaction."

She smiled big. "Awesome!" She tilted her head. "There are other ways of having physical intimacy."

"I'm aware."

She hopped up and walked over to her door console and interacted with it.

He was not sure if he had offended her in some way or what she was doing. Perhaps she was leaving the room. Although he thought he had a good grasp of human interaction, sometimes it confused him.

She came back and sat on the couch and held his hand.

"Is something wrong?" he asked.

"No, but we have the rest of the day to ourselves. I set the door to lock and the outside console screen to show 'Do not disturb.' Now...about physical intimacy..."

Jelton noted that her eyes slightly widened and her nostrils flared. He had not planned on spending the day like this, but her words intrigued him. He smiled. As long as it made her happy, that was all that mattered.

19

Emily sighed with content as she sipped on her orange juice. The previous day with Jelton had been exciting and she loved that he was into it. It was 8:30 a.m. and the conference room was empty. Evaran had sent a meeting request for 9:00 a.m. and she had enjoyed waking up with Jelton next to her around 7:00 a.m., then getting in a good breakfast.

Dr. Snowden trudged into the room. He paused to glance at her and Jelton. "You two are early."

"So are you!" said Emily with a smile.

Dr. Snowden wrinkled his brow as he visited the replicator. After a moment, he was seated with a plate of bacon and eggs and some coffee.

"It appears you are hungry, my friend," said Jelton.

Dr. Snowden inhaled a piece of bacon. "Always."

After ten minutes of light discussion, Jake entered the room. He waved at everyone and walked over to the replicator.

"Sleep well?" asked Emily.

Jake nodded as he returned to the table with an omelet and avocado plate. "Sure did. You can never go wrong with those beds."

"Yeah."

Jake yawned before diving in.

Dr. Snowden eased back into his chair as he pushed his plate back. He eyed Emily. "You're awfully happy this morning."

"I'm just glad to be back," said Emily. "Food pellets are nice, but I prefer replicated food from the Torvatta any day."

"I'll second that," said Dr. Snowden.

Evaran and V entered the room. Evaran strolled over to his seat and sat, while V hovered in orb mode at the end of the table.

"Everyone appears to be here early," said Evaran.

"A full day of rest will do that," said Dr. Snowden.

Evaran nodded. "This meeting will be brief, and I can start now unless anyone wishes to wait."

Everyone indicated to Evaran that they were okay to start.

Evaran tapped at the table console.

A projection shot up of the galactic region around Earth. An orange area encompassed Earth and Fredoria and several systems. Several dots blinked on planets and other objects.

"V and I have narrowed down where Sandas would most likely be. The dots indicate information broker booths I am aware of from a previous interaction with Sandas, and I have excluded areas that Ziekah has control over based on the information from her Earth satellite," said Evaran. He looked at Jake. "Although the timeline has changed, do you remember any of the broker locations?"

Jake pointed at a dot. "Yeah, Killikin. That's a rough place but where you go if you want a bounty or freelance merc contract."

"Any others?"

"Umm…let's see. Coris, but I have heard it's tough too. Garrantus is not too bad, but it's Drodalian, and we would stick out and probably cause a fight immediately upon exiting the Torvatta. Jells would get on me if I ever used a broker booth, so I usually avoided them."

Emily remembered Jells as Jake's adopted bug-like alien father who had taken care of him when he had been abducted.

"I see," said Evaran, rubbing his chin. "We can go to Killikin. It will be dangerous, but it is also a known quantity and there are a variety of aliens there. It is far enough away from Ziekah's domain that we should not have to worry about her, and we should be able to blend in easier."

"Depends if we have a bounty on us or not," said Jake. "If we do go, we should either go as a group, or one of us goes and uses camouflage shielding."

Evaran nodded. "I think after recent events, going as a group is ideal. The Torvatta can take us to the booth, and we can jump down and go from there."

"Works for me," said Emily, grinning.

Evaran eyed her. "You seem unusually well this morning." He studied Jelton. "Ahh, I see."

Jelton drew his head back.

"Let us go to the command center," said Evaran as he stood.

Emily wrinkled her brow as everyone funneled out of the room. She suspected that Evaran sensed that she and Jelton had messed around some before breakfast.

After everyone had assembled in the command area, the outside of Torvatta faded away, then eased back in.

"Analysis. We are back at November 9, 2012, 9:00 a.m., approximately ten hours after we left to investigate Ziekah in the past in AD 1933."

"At least you synced up the time to match our sleep cycle," said Dr. Snowden.

"Acknowledged."

The Torvatta opened a portal and flew through.

Emily studied the active planet, which lit up with satellites, ships, and space stations. "Wow, this is a busy place."

Jake smiled. "Yeah, and it attracts all sorts of people. Mercs, bounty hunters, justice hunters, freelancers."

"Justice hunter?" asked Dr. Snowden.

"They're similar to bounty hunters but only take contracts that they deem morally good and exact justice. The contracts tend to be high-value and often difficult."

Dr. Snowden nodded. "I'm guessing what's considered good is up for interpretation."

"Yeah, and justice hunters are generally tough too, mostly ex-military types," said Jake. "I remember one of the Seceltor shippers I delivered to had a justice contract on her. Turned out she had a bad habit of killing human slaves and eating them *without* paying. Sad part was that the crime was she didn't pay, not that she killed slaves, so she got collected on."

Emily grimaced. "Hopefully we don't run into anyone."

"I concur," said Evaran.

The Torvatta entered the planet's atmosphere and, after twenty minutes, flew above Killikin.

Emily watched the communication signals that appeared everywhere as dotted lines. Killikin was a busy place, and it had an old feel to her, but the signs of an advanced city were present as well. Concrete buildings mixed with sleek advanced ones while stone tile meshed with areas of metallic pathway. Aliens bustled on the streets while ships cruised overhead. She flinched a few times when ships flew by the Torvatta. They would have no idea the Torvatta was there.

Jake pointed at a blue door on the side of a dusty road. A robot stood outside. "There's a broker booth there."

Emily studied the data label that hung off the door. The building was one story and one of many. It reminded her of a strip mall, except with advanced aliens walking around everywhere and one or two pillars that had some high-tech gadgetry on them.

"There's a weird mix of technology here," she said.

Jake nodded. "Yeah, the Drakas were pushed into the world of technology when they weren't ready. They're now sorta known as the power brokers of the criminal world."

Jelton pointed at an alien. "That appears to be a Draka. They have an unusual shape."

Emily agreed with Jelton's assessment. They looked like a walking gumdrop.

"One thing you'll see is there are a lot of strange-looking aliens here, relative to us of course," said Jake.

The Torvatta hovered behind the building and in an alleyway.

"The Torvatta can hover here, and we can drop behind the building, then walk around to the front," said Evaran, standing. "Is everyone ready to go?"

"I need to get my suit on," said Emily.

Evaran nodded. "Okay. Let us meet on the ramp in five minutes."

Emily hopped up and flew to her living quarters. She was used to always having her suit on, but this morning she had it off due to Jelton being around. The Torvatta was the only place she considered safe enough to be without her suit. If she had not had it on when Ziekah had attacked, the trip to the past would have been much worse.

After a few minutes, she had her suit on and helmet up. When she reached the ramp, she noted that everyone else except Evaran was suited up. She poked V in his robot form.

"I haven't seen you use this mode in a while," she said.

"Analysis. It is my sturdiest form and would be more beneficial in an altercation."

She chuckled. "Defensive mode, I remember. Now we just need to apply a holographic form over it."

V swiveled his head toward her, then Evaran. "Acknowledged."

"I am aware that it is on your list of enhancements," said Evaran.

V's chest lights glowed brighter.

Emily wondered how long V's enhancement list was. It seemed extensive based on V mentioning adding items to the list in the past whenever he saw something he liked.

The group dropped off the ramp.

Emily found it surprising how effortlessly Dr. Snowden jumped down about fifteen feet. Everyone else she expected to with no issue, but Dr. Snowden was not known for his agility.

Evaran looked around before motioning forward. "To the front of this building."

The group followed Evaran as he took off.

When they reached the front, the robot scanned them. "The chamber is available for use. Please secure your weapons and stand at least two feet away from the walls at all times."

Evaran nodded at the robot. "It is done."

The door slid open and they entered.

Emily remembered visiting a booth before, and this one seemed similar. The room was octagonal in shape, and a platform resided in the center with seating on the edges.

Everyone took a seat.

A holographic male human appeared above the platform. "State your business."

Evaran extended his hand and projected a hologram from his ring. "I am Evaran and am looking for someone with this energy signature."

"Your payment method?" asked the male.

Evaran nodded. "We are personal friends of Sandas, but in another timeline. We offer videos of him from the original timeline, as well as information on Maxilogoraxifintocolosta, or Max the matter mage, as we call him. To prove for now that we know Sandas, I offer this: He is a Rogorian and was uplifted by Max. At the point of uplifting, Sandas tried to figure out why it was hotter as his planet heated up. For the videos and information of Max that we offer, it would be best to meet in person."

The male paused for a moment. "Please head to the following coordinates."

Emily studied the set of numbers and letters that appeared. Her helmet translated it to a location on a planet several systems away.

"Thank you. We look forward to meeting you," said Evaran.

"We'll see," said the hologram before dissipating.

Emily figured Sandas was listening, and the information Evaran shared about the uplifting was something Sandas had discussed when he had traveled with the group. It was very specific, and she suspected not many would know that. That had to pique Sandas's interest.

The door slid open and they exited.

Emily's eyes narrowed at the six or so aliens standing in a half circle. She sensed there was another nearby on a roof. Their weapons, which reminded her of assault rifles, were drawn and aimed forward. Whatever intent they had, it did not seem friendly. It was time to fight.

Jake recognized some of the partial-helmet-wearing aliens. They consisted of one Xibian, two Drodalians, two Unherals, and one Lazaram. They were all humanoid but with some differences. Xibians had dreadlock-like hair with one big eye versus two. The reptilian Drodalians were rivals of Fredoria. The insect-like Unherals' buggy eyes stood out while Lazarams, a larger reptilian race, reminded him of what a humanoid alligator would look like.

When groups contained strange combinations like that, they were either a merc crew or a bounty hunter pack. Jake had run into similar groups when delivering and sometimes watched them take down marks. If the mark proved tough or was in a group themselves, the hunter pack would collaborate for efficiency reasons and then split the bounty. It could also just be a merc crew looking for easy pickings.

The speed at which Evaran and the others moved surprised Jake. Before the Xibian pulled the trigger on his weapon, Evaran had his energy shield out. It reached to the ground and covered about a five-foot-by-eight-foot wide space. Emily got the left side and formed her own energy shield, which stood at a thirty-degree angle to Evaran's shield. Dr. Snowden did the same on the right. That allowed V to charge off to the other side. Jelton slipped behind Emily with weapon drawn.

Jake barely got his blaster out before the weapon fire started. By the time he moved behind Dr. Snowden, a mist beam from Emily and Dr. Snowden bathed the mercs while Evaran lit the mist up with a stun beam. The mercs' kinetic shielding sparked, and some fell to the ground. V dashed in and picked up the Lazaram and body slammed it and the Drodalian into a wall. Jelton shot twice and hit the two Unherals. Another burst at the nearby roofs suggested he got the ones there too.

Evaran dashed into the middle and with a stun from his utility handle turned staff, two Drodalian fell to the ground and struggled to get up. He then moved over to the Xibian, who lay on the ground next to an unconscious Lazaram.

It reminded Jake that he did not have cosmic energy in him like the others. He had had a similar feeling of not being able to fully contribute when he had traveled with Evaran and the gang to deal with Caltorus on Earth. Evaran and the others most likely viewed everything as moving in slow motion. Only the Xibian remained conscious.

"Why did you attack us?" asked Evaran with his staff inches away from the Xibian on the ground.

The Xibian wheezed. "We thought you were easy pickings."

"For what reason?"

"You have no weapons on you and…your group is a boy, a girl, an old man, and maybe two who could fight."

Dr. Snowden harrumphed.

Jake stood next to Evaran. "Ambushes around broker booths aren't unheard of."

"What…what are you?" asked the Xibian, staring at Evaran.

"I am a hard picking. When you wake up, you will forget you ever saw us and tell the others the same, unless you wish for a second altercation," said Evaran.

The Xibian nodded vigorously. "No problem."

Evaran stunned the Xibian, who passed out. "I now wonder if there are bounties on us. It seems these mercs did not know of any if they existed."

Jake chuckled. "Yeah. Ziekah might have put them out just in case and didn't expect the bounty to ever be picked up, or there could be no bounties. However…if this group identifies us and it gets to Ziekah…"

Evaran eyed Jake. "We will not kill these mercs."

"Of course not. I'm just saying that would be the only way she doesn't learn of our presence," said Jake.

"I understand, and I am giving these mercs a chance. They know who we are and will not risk a second encounter," said Evaran.

"This is a rough city," said Jelton.

"I'll say," said Dr. Snowden.

Evaran waved forward. "Let us go to the Torvatta."

After a few minutes, they assembled in the command center.

"V, take us to the coordinates given to us by the broker hologram," said Evaran.

"Acknowledged."

The Torvatta ascended.

"Are we going to stop her in this timeline, even though it will go away?" asked Emily. "Like Salazar?"

Evaran nodded. "We are. However, I have an idea in that regard. She can be stopped in this timeline in this time period, while we remove her from her original entry into the timeline."

Jelton chuckled. "So she would be stopped in the past and present."

"That is the goal. The denizens of this alternate timeline still have their future rendered regardless of what we do with Ziekah."

Dr. Snowden shook his head. "It took me a while to wrap my head around the idea that a timeline is rendered until the end of time."

"It is not something someone would know unless they had a Torvatta."

Jake enjoyed these types of conversations. They provided a glimpse into Evaran's world and the type of adventures he went on. Jake understood how rare it was to be one of the select few to interact with Evaran. Jake would have laughed if someone had told him back when he had lived at Jell's space station that he would travel through space and time in the future. Now, he just enjoyed the moment whatever came his way.

He chuckled. "That was one of the quickest fights I think I've ever seen, and that didn't look like an easy group. If it had been me, I'd probably have lost a shipment and gotten bruised."

"It's a lot easier when they're all moving in slow motion," said Emily with a grin.

Jake laughed. "All I saw was a blur of energy shields and weapon fire. Oh, and V charging off like a bull."

"Analysis. My shielding is strong."

Jake nodded. "Those mercs picked a good ambush spot, and if it had been anyone but us, they might've succeeded. They were probably as surprised as I was."

The group chuckled.

The Torvatta reached low orbit, then opened a portal and flew through.

Jake studied the data labels of the planet that appeared before them. They were in uncharted space, relative to what he remembered from growing up, but the planet had a harsh atmosphere. The barren world had an average temperature below freezing, although very little snow or ice appeared.

"You sure this is where we're supposed to go?" he asked.

Evaran nodded. "Sandas likes to build bases in inhospitable areas."

Jake shrugged. "I'm looking forward to meeting him, assuming it's a him."

"He's a Rogorian, a squirrel-like species," said Emily.

"Cool," said Jake.

"It will be my first time meeting Sandas as well," said Jelton.

Dr. Snowden smiled. "Sandas's personality is…different."

"In what way?"

"Oh, you'll see," said Dr. Snowden, glancing at Emily, who grinned big.

Jake tried to imagine a squirrel-like species, and his pulse beat faster to think that he would finally meet Sandas, the information broker. While Jake had grown up on the edge of Seceltor space, he had heard many stories of the broker and the various speculations on who it was.

The Torvatta descended through the planet's atmosphere and, after thirty minutes, hovered over a large circular dusty metallic seal on the ground.

"V, establish communications."

"Acknowledged." After a moment, V said, "Communication protocols accepted. Relaying."

Jake noted that only audio came through.

"We are here," said Evaran.

"I don't see you out there," said a high-pitched voice.

Evaran nodded at V.

A data window showed the Torvatta leaving scan profile one mode and then decloaking.

"Ohh…quite the fancy ship you got there!" said Sandas.

Emily laughed.

"And quite the group from that recent fight."

"You saw that?" asked Evaran.

"Of course. I'm the information broker!"

"I am aware of that."

"But you didn't come all this way to discuss that. I'll open the seal, and you can fly in and dock. I've set the atmosphere to something humans can breathe, so…no helmets need to be up," said Sandas.

Jake figured that Sandas wanted to scan everyone's faces, although Jake thought Sandas would have seen that at the booth.

The seal slid back revealing a vertical tunnel.

"V, take us in," said Evaran.

"Acknowledged."

The Torvatta descended vertically thorough the tunnel for a while until it reached a small hangar. After landing, the group exited the Torvatta with helmets down.

Jake looked around. The small hangar had several other ships around. Metallic panels covered the walls, floor, and ceiling, and he suspected it had taken some effort to build.

A humanoid male in light tactical armor walked out. "Hello, hello, I'm the information broker!"

Emily and Dr. Snowden laughed.

The broker focused on them. "I am!"

Evaran half smiled. "This is a robot with a holographic shell. Sandas is a Rogorian, but I understand you taking this precaution."

The robot sighed. "Well, then."

Jake stared at the small squirrel-like humanoid that came out of a hallway in the distance. That had to be Sandas. Jake found it interesting that Sandas used a decoy, but given the base's secrecy, Jake understood the security measure. He looked forward to meeting Sandas.

20

Dr. Snowden smiled as he watched Sandas with his brown fur saunter up with a small weapon in his hand. Sandas wore light clothing but had a utility belt packed with gadgets. A pair of goggles rested on his head, and he was as Dr. Snowden had remembered. He wondered how close the timeline versions were to each other.

Evaran bowed as Sandas stood next to the robot. "It is good to see you again, Sandas, in any timeline."

"You know my name," said Sandas. He waved his small weapon around. "If deception is in your eyes, I can be quite dangerous!"

Emily giggled.

Sandas smiled big. "I guess that's not quite as fierce as it was in my mind."

"I understand your caution," said Evaran. "We are strangers to you in this timeline, but are close friends with another timeline version of you."

Sandas put his weapon away and eyed Evaran. "You keep mentioning timelines, and that has caught my interest. That's one area I have little knowledge of, and information is always nice to have, yes, very nice. You also have knowledge that I've never told anyone."

"You told us about your moment of sentience when you traveled with us. There is more, including videos of your other timeline version as well as Max," said Evaran. "All we ask in exchange is for some help in finding something."

"Well, you came to the right place if it's information you desire!" said Sandas, wagging a finger at Evaran. He studied the rest of the group. "Who do you travel with?"

Evaran pointed around in sequence. "I have with me Dr. Albert Snowden, Emily Snowden, V, Jake Melkins, and Jelton Stallryn."

"Interesting," said Sandas. "Humans, an AI of some sort I'm guessing, and…whatever Jelton is."

"A Rift Guardian from another timeline," said Jelton.

Sandas smiled big. "I think there's a lot of information we can trade." He spun around and raised a finger in the air. "Follow me!" He bounced away.

Dr. Snowden chuckled as the group followed Sandas. So far, his mannerisms were as Dr. Snowden remembered them.

They walked through several hallways until they reached a circular room with couches lining the walls.

Sandas gestured for everyone to sit while he sat opposite them.

Everyone complied.

Dr. Snowden's muscles relaxed as the comfortable couch absorbed him. There was an unusual odor in the air that he could not trace the source of. It reminded him of an earthy smell. Several rods from the ceiling ended in bulbs that lit up the room. The place was cozy, which seemed odd for a secret base.

Sandas studied Dr. Snowden. "Surveying the room, are we?"

"I didn't expect a room like this in a secret base is all," said Dr. Snowden.

Sandas smiled. "Sometimes I need to hide people or groups away, so every base has an area for that. This is a communal room for that scenario, and also serves as a place to meet others, such as yourselves."

Evaran nodded. "And we appreciate you meeting with us. I assume by allowing this, you agree to an exchange of information."

"You assume correctly."

"How do you wish to proceed?"

Sandas chuckled. "If I didn't know better, I'd say you were an android, but you don't read as one." He looked around the group. "I'd first like to understand more of the situation, especially in regard to the timeline thing you mentioned."

"I understand," said Evaran. He surveyed the others before he focused on Sandas. "In the original timeline, you worked with us on several occasions. We became good friends, and that bond strengthened when we rescued you from a time eddy. You would have died had we not intervened."

Sandas raised a clawed finger. "Dying is never good, no, not good."

Emily chuckled.

Sandas eyed her for a moment. He looked at Evaran. "I get that in this other timeline, we were friends. You're suggesting this is an alternate timeline."

Evaran nodded. "Unfortunately so. A being known as Ziekah came into the original timeline and changed it in the past. Everything is not as it should be."

"Hmm. So in this new timeline, we never met. I'm guessing that Ziekah is not the rightful ruler of humans."

Dr. Snowden shook his head. "Definitely not."

Jake chuckled. "Yeah, what he said."

"I see," said Sandas. "So what's your plan? I assume you want to remove Ziekah, but it sounds like you need to travel to the past for that."

"My ship, the Torvatta, can do that," said Evaran. "However, due to the way timelines work, when we remove Ziekah, this timeline is still rendered until the end of time, and Ziekah needs to be dealt with. To that end, that is something Max could deal with."

Sandas wiggled his whiskers. "I see. So what information did you need? You seem to know more than I do, as preposterous as that sounds!"

"Ziekah's history, and more importantly, where she came from. That will allow us to prevent her crossing into this reality, and by extension, to reset the timeline back to its original state."

Sandas eyed Evaran. "I love it! I'd like to understand timelines more as part of our deal. You mentioned rules...so I'd like to look at the rulebook as well. In regard to Ziekah's history, I can probably get that, but it will take some time. My network is decentralized, but I have an informant in the region with her first known appearance. I've kept track of Ziekah because of how powerful and ancient she is."

"I have no problem with sharing timeline rules with you," said Evaran. "Normally I would not, but this is a unique situation, and when we talk with Max, those rules will need to be explained as it is."

"Max…what do you know of him?"

Evaran half smiled. "Quite a bit."

Sandas grinned. "Well played. You have my curiosity, which is hard to get, yes, very hard." He stroked his snout. "Okay. I'll go put in the call to my informant and afterward we can discuss those videos you mentioned in the booth and Max." He hopped up and dashed out of the room.

"Looks like we're in business," said Dr. Snowden.

"It does," said Evaran.

"Sandas seems like the original one," said Emily.

"Analysis. There was a 91.4 percent chance he would be."

Emily wrinkled her brow. "Why not one hundred percent?"

"There was an 8.6 percent chance he would have been dead and someone else fulfilled the role."

"Oh."

Jake grinned. "I like him and definitely didn't expect him to look like a large squirrel."

Jelton nodded. "We share the same thought, my friend."

After a few minutes of light conversation, Sandas popped back into the room. "Okay, my informant is looking into Ziekah's history." He plopped down on the couch. "Now… about Max and videos…"

"Which do you prefer to start with?" asked Evaran.

"Max."

"Very well. V, show our meeting with Max."

"Acknowledged." V flew to the middle of the room and displayed a holographic projection of the event.

Dr. Snowden remembered meeting Max and learning about matter mages. They were getting decimated by the

Hoxscarus, humanity's final evolutionary form from what Dr. Snowden understood. Pozarra, the Hoxscarus near Max's planet, kept Max prisoner there per Evaran's decree. That had to do with a time loop since when Evaran had talked with Max in the original timeline, he had been set free by Evaran.

Sandas gazed with rapture at the projection. Once it ended twenty minutes later, he said, "Hah! That's Max all right. The deathlights he talks about were still there the last time I tried to visit him."

"Hoxscarus is what they are called," said Evaran. "If there is one there, I can talk to it and inform it that Max is not to be guarded. However, as we are past the time index of when this event occurred in the original timeline, there should be no Hoxscarus present. I am hoping that Max will assist in Ziekah's removal in this time period while we handle her removal in the past."

Sandas tilted his head. "As powerful as you and this Hoxscarus seem to be, why aren't either of you dealing with Ziekah now?"

"I always prefer a timeline denizen solution if possible," said Evaran. "We will have to attend to it if Max is unwilling."

"Mm-hmm," said Sandas. He stroked his snout. "Max handling her would free you up to get Ziekah at her entry point. Interesting, very interesting. It appears I could go see Max now without being chased away."

Evaran nodded. "Yes. Perhaps we could both arrive at the same time and talk to him, and I can bring the Hoxscarus down, assuming it is there, to show that Max has nothing to fear. In the original timeline, I took him to a colony. However, it may be beneficial for him to reside with you so he can deal with Ziekah."

Sandas eased back into his seat. "Ziekah would stand no chance against a matter mage."

"She is powerful, but not that powerful. I can relay her tactics to you and Max and you two can deal with the situation. Ziekah is a threat that must be contained, and Max satisfies that criteria."

"And you think he would help with her?"

Evaran half smiled. "I do. Although he believes in natural evolution, he had come to understand that his mere presence could be a part of that. I am hoping that he will reach the same conclusion."

Sandas chuckled. "All right. Now about those videos…"

Emily had enjoyed the last two hours of Evaran showing videos for Sandas. Although not all were shown, her heart melted when she saw some of them. The one where Sandas had said goodbye at his secret base made her eyes mist a little. She had caught him eying her a few times throughout, and she wondered if he understood the deep connection they had with the original timeline's version. Perhaps it would change his perception of the group, even.

The first video had shown the group's initial encounter with Sandas. He had cracked up at scaring her, but that had been his reaction in the original timeline as well when he had traveled with them to deal with Salazar. The other videos showed his time aboard the Torvatta. She chuckled each time he stroked his snout and said, "Interesting."

After the last video finished, Sandas puffed his cheeks. "That…was great!"

"I am glad you think so," said Evaran.

"It's obvious my timeline counterpart and I are very similar. He made a lot of the same decisions and comments I would have."

Evaran nodded. "That has been my observation as well to this point. On another topic, I am curious about Ziekah's rise to power."

Sandas sighed. "Ziekah. She's long-lived. From the history I have on Earth, they've been an advanced technological society for over a thousand years, rivaling even the Kreagan Star Empire. She is ruthless and crafty, and seems to be looking for someone called Seeros. Oh, and she had put a bounty recently on you, Jake, and Jelton."

Jake chuckled. "Probably in case we somehow survived our last encounter, which we did. She thought she killed Dr. Snowden, Emily, and V in the past, so no need for a bounty on them."

"Deception *was* in your eyes." Sandas shook a clawed finger at Jake. "I didn't see you in the videos. Are you from Earth in the original timeline too?"

"Sorta. I actually was abducted, then raised by a Crustican until I was of breeding age for the Seceltor Empire."

"The Seceltor Empire...now that's a name I haven't heard in a long time. Ziekah absorbed them around three hundred years ago."

Jake wrinkled his brow. "What about the Crusticans?"

"They were swallowed up too, although they did rebel, just unsuccessfully."

Jake nodded.

"Although you were not in the video, I sense this is not your first trip with Evaran."

"Yeah. I've traveled with him before."

"I see." Sandas pointed at Jelton. "You weren't in any videos either."

Jelton grinned. "I'm from another timeline, my friend."

"So we're both timeline outsiders!"

They shared a laugh.

It warmed Emily's heart for Sandas to be kind to Jake and Jelton.

Evaran rubbed his chin. "When did Ziekah leave Earth?"

"My records show around AD 1500. I'm not sure if that translated to you right," said Sandas.

"It did. So she has had roughly five hundred years to build an empire."

Sandas sighed. "And she has grown it. I stay far away from her, yes, very far. Ziekah also avoids Max's planet, no doubt due to the deathlight—well, Hoxscarus."

Emily smiled. "It sounds like that's our next place to visit."

"Is there a room for me on your ship?" asked Sandas with hopeful eyes.

Evaran cleared his throat. "Unfortunately, you would be temporally shielded if you were to board the Torvatta. You do not want to be in that state when the timeline changes. However, we can meet you in orbit around Max's planet. I will ensure the Hoxscarus, if it is there, does not destroy you."

Sandas eyed Evaran, who half smiled.

"You joke, but I like it! All right, I guess we'll meet in three days," said Sandas. He paused. "Actually, you'll probably just jump forward three days, and for you, it will be a few minutes."

Evaran raised a finger. "A few seconds."

"Oh! You're taking the fast lane while I get the slow one."

Emily liked watching Sandas and Evaran play around. It made her want to visit the original Sandas when they got back. That was one aspect that bothered her at times, that she did not get to interact more with some of the people the group met.

Sandas gestured at Evaran. "I'll have some time on my ship so…it would be nice to have some videos to watch, or watch again."

Evaran interacted with his ARI. "They have been transferred, and I also sent you the location to meet us at."

Sandas checked his forearm device. "How…how did you know to put it in secure storage? It accepted your credentials as mine!"

"It seems some things do not change," said Evaran.

"Hah! So true. Okay, we'll meet soon."

The group assembled back on the Torvatta, and after a bit, they ascended through the atmosphere.

"He's quite a colorful character," said Jelton.

Jake laughed. "Yeah, he is. I'd never have guessed he looked or acted like that. I always thought it would be some sinister-looking alien or something."

"Then it was a pleasant surprise. Those are usually the best."

Emily nodded. "Sandas didn't seem to be too impacted by Ziekah's disruption. Then again, he is the information broker and would have hidden in the shadows."

"That is my conclusion as well," said Evaran.

The Torvatta reached orbit.

"V, take us to the coordinates given to Sandas," said Evaran.

"Acknowledged."

The Torvatta opened a portal and flew through.

Emily studied the planet before them. She recalled seeing it for the first time when visiting Max. It had been her and Dr. Snowden's first voluntary trip with Evaran. So much had changed since then. An image of Andia Kiggs flashed briefly in Emily's mind. She missed Andia and hoped she was doing okay. Rakar Ho Jador, a Kreagan, and Sandas were the other two from that trip, and she wanted to visit them after dealing with Ziekah.

"Whoa, a rogue planet!" said Jake.

"Yeah. I had no idea what that was until we traveled to one," said Emily. "Planets with no star still seem strange to me."

Jelton gestured at the planet. "That means we should expect an inhospitable environment."

Dr. Snowden chuckled. "You're gonna be surprised, then. Think...jungles."

Jake smiled. "That must be Max's doing, then."

"Yep."

"Analysis. There is a communication request from Sandas."

"Put it up," said Evaran.

Sandas appeared in a window on the front wall. "Hello, hello! I'm here, and in one piece."

"Analysis. A Hoxscarus approaches."

"Oh...it waited until I contacted you!" said Sandas.

"Do not worry," said Evaran. He stood. "To the roof."

Everyone assembled on the roof.

Emily remembered first seeing the Hoxscarus as a large ball of light with tendrils.

Sandas pulled his ship alongside the Torvatta.

Evaran interacted with his ARI, and a hologram of Sandas appeared on the roof.

"This works!" said Sandas. He looked around. "To stand on a ship's roof in space is never a good idea, yes, never, unless it's your ship, I guess."

Evaran half smiled. "Your holographic projection is secure."

Jake pointed out at the rapidly approaching Hoxscarus. "Wow. Look how fast it's coming."

After a moment, the Hoxscarus reached the Torvatta.

Evaran tapped at his ARI, causing a part of the roof's guardrail to drop.

The Hoxscarus flew through, and as it did, it changed into a pale woman that wore a white robe with silver segmented lines and dark gray straps crisscrossing the outfit. She had fair skin and long blond hair, and her yellow eyes slightly glowed.

"Pozarra!" said Emily.

"It is I." Pozarra raised an arm, palm forward toward Evaran.

He joined palms with her. "It is good to see you again. I understand this encounter must seem unusual at this point in an alternate timeline."

Pozarra smiled. "Not at all. I knew to be here."

Dr. Snowden wagged a finger at Pozarra. "Oh…future Evaran will tell you in a future event about this. Out-of-sync thing."

Pozarra nodded.

"That means you're aware of our meeting outside the plane," said Emily.

"I am, and I'm here to give assurance to this timeline version of Max that I will not destroy him," said Pozarra. She eyed Jelton. "Jelton! I was not expecting you to be here."

Jelton tilted his head. "I…don't believe we've met."

"Oh…"

Emily found it interesting that Pozarra knew Jelton. That meant she had met him again at some point in the future. Maybe he was part of that future event that she had learned about early on when traveling with Evaran.

"If you're a friend of Evaran, you're a friend of mine," said Jelton.

"Of course," said Pozarra. She smiled at Jake. "Jake Melkins. I've heard so much about you."

Jake drew his head back. "You have?"

"Yes. Your fierce loyalty to Evaran and friends is commendable, regardless of Evaran's version."

"Huh."

Pozarra studied Sandas. "And little Sandas, one of the most curious beings I've ever met."

"And most charming too, I bet!" said Sandas.

Everyone shared a laugh.

The group relaxing around Pozarra made Emily remember how special it was to be able to be where she was. Not many could claim to have met a Hoxscarus, or even to have been teased by one.

"It's so strange," said Emily.

"What is?" asked Jake.

Emily pointed at Pozarra. "We met her when looking into Evaran's origin." Emily gestured at Jake. "After that adventure, we dealt with Caltorus, and Jake was with us."

Jake nodded. "I remember."

Emily motioned at Sandas. "He joined us when handling Salazar on the next adventure."

"My counterpart seemed to do well!" said Sandas.

Emily nodded and then pointed at Jelton. "And he grouped up with us on the adventure dealing with the Mortani."

Dr. Snowden wrinkled his brow. "That is interesting. It all kinda blurs together sometimes."

"Yeah," said Emily. "And now we're going to visit Max, who we met on our second trip, well, first voluntary one, with Evaran. If we had Jane Trellis, Dr. Bryson, or Kess with us, it would be someone from every single adventure in one spot."

Evaran rubbed his chin. "That is an astute observation. However, it is time we meet Max."

21

Jelton enjoyed listening to the group talk as they descended toward the planet. Sandas's ship kept up with the Torvatta and his hologram showed him seated in a chair. Although the first part of the trip with Evaran dealt with Earth, it seemed this part was outside of it. At some point, they would have to go to the nightmare lands, or the connections to the junction dimension as Evaran called them.

Jelton sensed that Pozarra had great power, even more than Evaran, at least while inside the plane. Evaran was much more powerful outside as Jelton understood it. How Pozarra knew him was a mystery, but one he suspected he would learn more about in time.

Several times during the descent, Emily had walked over and leaned into him. He had learned to slip his arm around her waist in social encounters similar to this. Dr. Snowden and Sandas were enthusiastically talking to Pozarra, while Jake appeared to be trying to absorb the moment. Jelton understood that sensation. With so many elements of Evaran's travels in one place, it would be difficult for anyone to understand it all, except for Evaran of course.

The Torvatta broke cloud cover and approached a massive jungle.

"Just like I remember it," said Dr. Snowden, peering over the edge.

"Let's hope we don't have to fight statues this time," said Emily.

Sandas shook his head. "I already communicated with Max, and he's going to meet us outside a temple."

"Much better there than inside," said Emily.

"What happened last time?" asked Jake.

"We had to fight statues, slide down tunnels into the mountain, and finally we were able to meet Max," said Emily.

"Sounds wild."

Emily chuckled. "Yeah, it was. This time, though, we get to meet outside and avoid all that."

Jelton made a note to search for any video of the previous encounter. He enjoyed watching videos from Emily's previous trips.

After another ten minutes, the Torvatta landed outside a massive stone stairway that started in a small open area between a jungle and a mountain and ended up at a landing area with large pillars in front of a huge entrance. Ant-like humanoid statues stood on the stairway's sides and were spread out evenly.

Jelton was not sure how the environment could exist, but it was right in front of him. Most rogue planets he had seen were not places with any sign of civilization.

The group assembled outside and met up with Sandas.

Sandas interacted with his forearm device. "Max is coming."

"Excellent," said Evaran.

Jake looked around. "This is the last place I'd expect to see a jungle, or carved statues."

"I had the same thought, my friend," said Jelton.

Pozarra smiled. "I think it's beautiful."

"Me too," said Emily. "I remember being here. Well, in the original timeline."

Dr. Snowden chuckled. "Yeah, but remember, those statues' eyes moved when we scanned them."

Emily nodded. "Oh yeah."

A humanoid man with fair skin, black hair, and glowing golden eyes appeared before the group in a flash. He wore a featureless gray suit that conformed to his body. After bowing, he said, "I am Maxilogoraxifintocolosta. You can call me Max for short."

Sandas rushed toward Max.

Max's eyes glowed brighter. "Sandas!"

Max picked Sandas up when he arrived and they spun around as they hugged.

When Sandas was back on the ground, he said, "We're back together! Sandas and Max!"

"It has been a very long time, but you're looking good!" said Max.

Sandas raised his head a bit. "I always look good!"

They shared a laugh.

Max focused on Evaran. "I suspect your new friends have something to do with our little reunion."

Evaran slightly bowed with his left arm across his stomach. "I am Evaran." He pointed to the others in sequence. "With me are Dr. Albert Snowden, Emily Snowden, Jake Melkins, V, Jelton Stallryn, and Pozarra."

Max moved a hand slowly across the group. "Hmm. Interesting. You all have some form of unique energy, except for Jake. He's like Sandas."

Jake shrugged. "I'm the normal person here. Well, and I guess Sandas is too."

"I can't sense your molecules," said Max, studying the others.

"Understandable," said Evaran. "You are detecting exotic energy, which is beyond your control as a matter mage."

"I see you're aware of my limitations."

Evaran gestured at Pozarra. "We do, and with me is what you call a deathlight, although she is referred to as a Hoxscarus."

Max took a step back. "What's she doing here?"

"I'm not here to hurt you," said Pozarra. "I was only to keep you from leaving the planet, which is no longer required."

"And why's that?" asked Max.

"Evaran has arrived."

Max scrutinized Evaran. "Why was she guarding me until you arrived?"

Evaran nodded. "It was part of a time loop. Nothing malicious was intended."

Max snorted. "Other than my fellow matter mages being wiped out of existence by these Hoxscarus!"

"That was also a part of the loop, but you were spared."

Max shook his head. "How nice."

Pozarra lowered her head toward Evaran. "Perhaps I should go so you can continue your discussion."

"That may be best," said Evaran. He raised his arm, palm forward.

Pozarra placed her palm in his. "Until we meet again." She hugged Dr. Snowden and Emily and high-fived V, and when she got to Jelton, she laid a hand on his shoulder. "I look forward to you meeting me again."

Jelton smiled. "It will be interesting, I am sure."

She nodded and moved over to Jake, shaking his hand while smiling big. "Watch over Evaran. All versions. You're a good anchor."

Jake returned her handshake with a wrinkled brow. "Okay...I'll try."

"I know you will, and I'm honored to have known you," said Pozarra.

"Same. Well, I mean, known you, not me."

They chuckled.

She stepped away from the group.

Jelton watched as she transformed into a being of light and then into a bright glowing golden ball. She burst into the sky and disappeared. He noticed her transformation into a sphere caused Max to take several steps back.

"You have her word and mine that you will not be a focus for the Hoxscarus," said Evaran.

"Your word's value, and hers, is unknown to me," said Max.

Sandas piped up. "I think you can trust Evaran."

Max eyed Sandas. "Why?"

"He has videos of meeting you, and me, and at least for me, it's definitely me in there from the other timeline."

Max gestured at Evaran. "May I see the videos?"

"Of course," said Evaran. "V, display our encounter with Max, and subsequent travel to the matter mage colony."

"Acknowledged," said V as he flew in the center of the group.

"Wait, you said matter mage colony?" asked Max with narrowed eyes. "There are some still alive?"

Evaran nodded. "Yes, and this video will show you not only our meeting, but their location. It should still be the same."

V displayed the encounter from the original timeline.

Jelton smiled as Max's defensive posture changed. His eyes were glued to the projection, and Jelton thought he saw a smile form at some of the things said.

After the video played, Max studied Evaran. "It seems we got along well in your timeline."

"We did," said Evaran. "I understand your anger with the Hoxscarus and me for an event in another timeline that currently does not exist."

Max chuckled. "I wasn't even aware there were other timelines, although I always postulated they existed. I also think that you didn't come here only to tell me I'm free."

"You are correct. We plan to discover where Ziekah first came into the timeline and prevent that event from occurring. However, she needs to be dealt with in this time period. We were looking to you for assistance."

Max gestured at Jelton. "Ziekah has something unique, similar to what he has."

"Rift energy," said Jelton.

"I see," said Max. "She needs her arms in order to do the circle motion that activates her portal abilities. I have crossed paths with her when I was the broker, but I let her go, and she avoided any confrontation with me."

Emily drew her head back. "You escaped her portals?"

Max laughed. "I'm a matter mage. You have to be pushed through her portal for it to be effective. She couldn't force me to go through, and I simply wrapped her up with stone, except for her head."

"Yeah, that sounds like it would work."

"As powerful as you seem, and with the Hoxscarus, you could easily deal with her," said Max.

Evaran raised a finger. "We are temporally shielded. The better solution is for a timeline denizen to handle it."

"You mean me," said Max.

Evaran nodded. "If you do this, then we can meet in the future and I can give you knowledge on how to reach the matter mage colony instantly and anytime you wish."

Dr. Snowden wrinkled his brow. "Would the colony creation event still have occurred?"

Evaran nodded. "Yes, as it was before I came to the Milky Way galaxy, so Ziekah's changes here would not affect it."

Max slapped Sandas on the back. "What if I want to stick around? This little guy probably needs my help."

"Hah!" said Sandas.

"It is your choice. You could stay in this region and visit the colony whenever you want," said Evaran.

Max smiled big. "All that...to remove Ziekah from power?"

"Yes. As Sandas would say, information for an action."

Sandas pointed at Evaran. "I would say that!"

Max looked at Sandas and then Evaran. "When you change the timeline, won't all this go away?"

Evaran shook his head. "This timeline has been rendered to the end of time, so you will experience it as is."

"End of time...relative to life?"

Emily's eyes narrowed. "What do you mean by relative to life?"

Max chuckled.

Evaran extended his hand, palm up, and shot a projection from his ring of a black cylinder. A small blue ring resided near the bottom. "Imagine this is a timeline with the bottom being the start, and the top, the end. The tiny blue ring at the bottom represents the window of time in which life exists. Everything else is devoid of life, minus a few spots."

Emily's eyes widened. "You mean life is only a small blip in the timeline?"

"Yes. Max was asking if the rendering went to the end of the blue line, or the timeline." Evaran pointed at the top of the cylinder.

"Wow...I didn't realize life had such a short time frame."

Dr. Snowden raised a finger. "It may seem small overall, but that is a *long* time from our perspective."

"That is correct," said Evaran.

"How do you know about that?" asked Emily, glancing at Max.

"I'm a matter mage and understand what happens to matter in the long run," said Max.

"Being truly immortal must suck, then," said Jake.

Emily nodded. "Yeah. What would they do after life is gone? Float around?"

Evaran raised a finger. "Most immortals leave the timeline by then, either to a dimension or another reality."

"Like I will," said Max. "Nonetheless...let's meet here, five years from this exact moment. I'll even have Ziekah with me—subdued, of course, but she will be out of power."

Evaran studied Max. "That is acceptable." He extended a hand.

Max eyed Evaran's hand before shaking it.

Sandas laughed. "They're going to pop in their ship, travel five years forward, and come right back here!"

"You are very perceptive," said Evaran.

Jelton chuckled. He liked Sandas's ability to lighten a somewhat tense mood. Jelton followed Evaran and the others to the Torvatta. When Jelton peered back, he saw Sandas and Max talking animatedly with their hands. They had a lot to catch up on. Since Sandas had the videos, they would probably go over them. Jumping forward in time for an appointment was something Jelton had done before, so this was not new. He was curious, though, to learn what happened to Ziekah when they came back.

Jake eased into his chair on the Torvatta. The group had left the rogue planet, entered orbit, and jumped forward five years, and now they were on their way back. He had been fascinated at being able to listen to such powerful beings talk.

Max had been angry at Pozarra, but Jake understood why. He wished he had more time to talk with her, and for that matter, Sandas and Max. Although these were the alternate timeline versions, they were not far off from the original ones per Dr. Snowden and Emily.

The Torvatta approached the landing area after twenty minutes. Sandas's ship sat to the side, and the front window highlighted Max and what appeared to be a stone cone.

Jake scrutinized the data label that displayed Ziekah's name. Apparently, most of her body was encased in stone.

"Looks like Max was true to his word," said Dr. Snowden.

Jelton perused the data highlighting on the front wall. "This Max is quite powerful."

Emily chuckled. "Yeah, not against a Hoxscarus, though."

"That gives me an idea of Pozarra's power."

The Torvatta landed next to Sandas's ship and the group disembarked.

Jake grinned at seeing Ziekah's head popping out of a stone mound. Max and Sandas stood out front, and Jake noted that they wore matching formfitting black-and-gray outfits.

"Hello, hello!" said Sandas.

Max bowed. "Welcome back. You came, just as you said you would."

Evaran returned the bow. "As Sandas mentioned, it has only been the time it took us to get to orbit, jump forward, and come back down, roughly forty minutes."

"I told you!" said Sandas.

Max chuckled. "Yeah, you did, multiple times. He wouldn't stop chattering away about it!"

Jake noticed a big difference in Max's personality. Perhaps five years was long enough to calm down about the Hoxscarus situation.

"You!" said Ziekah as her head moved around. "You caused this!"

Evaran stood in front of Ziekah. "It appears you need arm movement to generate your portals, and this stone encasement prevents that."

"So you got it all figured out. How about you show me mercy, and I'll leave this timeline."

Evaran shook his head. "Your actions show that you did not extend that same courtesy to me or my friends. You were content to have them killed."

"That was then. I can change."

"I do not believe so."

Jake felt a chill run up his spine. Evaran seemed colder than usual, but then again, Ziekah had tried to kill him and everyone else.

Max focused on Evaran. "I will keep her nearby on an inhospitable moon for the rest of her natural life. A livable area to exist in shall be provided, but should she escape, she would have a quick death due to the environment. The moon's past is violent, so if she tries to flee that way, it would not end well for her. A virtual simulation in her mind will be provided to her so she can be mentally free there, and animated servants will tend to her basic food, drink, and bodily needs."

"A good plan," said Evaran. "We can continue our discussion without her presence."

Max nodded and then waved a hand at Ziekah.

Her stone encasement lifted off the ground and flew inside the temple.

"There. We have privacy," said Max.

Jake swallowed hard. Max had brushed Ziekah away like she was a paperweight. It was hard to fathom how much power Max had and all the things he could do with it.

"Then, as agreed, I will give you the information on the matter mage colony," said Evaran. He shot up a projection of the colony's location in another galaxy. "It is there."

Max studied the projection. "And how would I get there? It would take a long time to travel that far."

"There are two rift doors on Earth. When I was there, I did not see any information on them, meaning they were hidden away before Ziekah could use them. That was always a contingency plan from the original timeline—if they were in danger, they would be hidden. One of those can be placed here, and the other at the colony. That will allow instantaneous travel between the two locations."

Max grinned. "So I need to go to Earth and find them."

"They will be easy to locate if you use this rift energy signature," said Evaran. His ring projected a series of vertical lines of varying colors.

Max examined the projection. "If they're on Earth, then I should locate them fairly quick with that signature."

"That is correct. My guess is that the elementals guard them. I can give you a video to show them that will tell them that you are to be given the rift doors."

Max grinned at Sandas. "We got some work to do." He looked back at Evaran. "Let's meet here again in another five years."

"We can do that," said Evaran. "I am curious. You do not seem to be in a hurry."

Max shrugged. "I've enjoyed being the broker along with Sandas. Everything has changed and I'm enjoying the diversity of life again. While I would like to visit the colony, it is not a pressing concern."

"What happened to Ziekah's empire?" asked Emily.

"Janzia Kiggs, who led a powerful resistance, is now in power. She is focused on undoing Ziekah's impact on history, it seems."

Sandas wiggled his shoulders. "She is quite feisty, yes, feisty!"

"Ahh," said Emily.

Evaran looked around at the group. "Board the Torvatta while I record a video for anyone who may have the rift doors on Earth."

The rest of the group complied, and after Evaran made his video, he entered the Torvatta.

Jake found it fascinating that they were time hopping around one sequence of events. He wondered if Evaran had ever done that with someone, seeing them when they were a child, all the way to their death. It might be less than a day to Evaran, but a lifetime to the person he interacted with.

The Torvatta ascended into low orbit, jumped five more years into the future, and then descended back to the same spot where they had been.

Jake spotted two rift doors and their associated control podiums sitting outside Sandas's ship. Ziekah was nowhere to be seen, and Max and Sandas stood next to the podiums. Jake wondered how Max retrieved the doors and where they had been, but he figured with everything going on with Ziekah, there were other important topics to cover when they landed.

The Torvatta parked next to Sandas's ship, and the group disembarked.

Sandas grinned big. "So one point five hours for your group, and ten years for us."

Evaran nodded. "It is good to see you both again."

Max gestured at the four control rods and two podiums. "You were right that the elementals had the rift doors. They weren't sure how they worked, so I'm hoping you do."

"I do," said Evaran with a half smile.

"Earth has become a better place under Janzia Kiggs's rule," said Sandas. "She got rid of retirement camps and instituted a new government there."

"I wish we could visit it," said Jake.

"Unfortunately, we have some other issues to deal with," said Evaran.

"I know. Still, it'd be cool."

Sandas popped over to his ship and returned with a small box. "This is a data cube that has everything known about Earth and this region since Ziekah left power. Oh, and it also has all the information on Ziekah herself, gathered from across our network." He raised a clawed finger. "I usually charge for this!"

"Sandas…," said Max, eying Sandas.

"I know, I know," said Sandas. He walked up to Emily. "Here you go."

Emily accepted the box and smiled at Sandas. "Thanks."

"You're very welcome, Emily Snowden," he said with a big grin.

She laughed.

Evaran walked up to one of the rift door podiums. "I will leave you with information on how they work and take the other one to the colony. V, load two control rods and a podium to the Torvatta."

"Acknowledged," said V.

He flew into the Torvatta and came back out in robot mode with a hover slab after a few minutes.

Jake watched as V effortlessly lifted the rods and podium onto the narrow slab. The slab was wide enough for the rods, and with the podium on its side, it all fit on top. In the original timeline, one was stored at facility maintained by the ancient vampires, and with the Earth Ward's cooperation, expeditions were sent out through the rift doors.

Evaran shot a projection from his ring that flashed information in a blur.

Max nodded. "Got it. Seems straightforward. I'll set it up here and wait for you to open it."

"Very well," said Evaran. He looked around at the gang. "Let us go."

Over the next two hours, Jake observed as they traveled to the matter mage colony and set up the rift door. Once it had been activated, Max and Sandas came through. Jake realized how rare it was to visit a matter mage colony. The matter mages appeared to walk out of the rock wall on the side of a mountain. Max's reunion with them was a happy one, and it caught Jake by surprise to see Max shed a tear. He was glad that Max had found his own people.

Per Max, he and Sandas would stick around for a while, then Sandas would travel back to handle business, with Max spending some additional time at the colony. It was no surprise that when they had landed, the matter mages hugged Evaran and greeted him with a lot of enthusiasm. He seemed to have that effect no matter where he visited.

The mages had faded back into the mountain wall, leaving just Sandas, Max, and the rest of the group.

Evaran extended a hand toward Sandas. "As always, it is a pleasure to work with you."

"A handshake?" asked Sandas. He bounded over and hugged Evaran's waist. "You get a hug, free of charge!"

Emily chuckled as Sandas hugged her next.

"I can see why we were close," said Sandas.

Emily tilted her head.

"Your reactions from the video, and the way you look at me. I admit I'm hard not to look at."

They shared a laugh.

Sandas eyed Jake. "Out of everyone, you seemed the most keen on studying me."

Jake smiled. "Yeah, probably. I grew up hearing so much about you, well, your other version. I've never met him, so it was cool to meet you."

"Cool...yes," said Sandas. He grinned big. "I am...cool, to use Earthborn slang."

Jake laughed. He loved Sandas's unique personality and envisioned that him traveling with the group would have been fun.

Sandas shook Dr. Snowden's hand. "Like Emily, it seems we had a deep bond. You took a shot for me that would have killed my other timeline version."

"And I would do it for you too," said Dr. Snowden.

Sandas nodded. "I suspect you would." He moved on to Jelton. "You are hard to read."

"I suspect I would be, my friend."

"Friend...yes, I believe we are at this point."

Jelton bowed slightly.

Sandas stood in front of V in projected mode. "I liked my other timeline's interaction with you. I would have loved to continue doing humor with you."

"Analysis. You were a good teacher."

V high-fived Sandas, much to his delight.

Sandas moved on to Evaran. "I have to say...I'm sorta used to meeting powerful beings, but you are something else."

Evaran half smiled. "I have heard that before."

"Hah! You joke, but I'm serious. I think no matter the timeline, we're always friends."

"I like to think so."

"I already hugged you, but a handshake is in order as well," said Sandas.

They shook hands.

Max extended a hand toward Evaran. "Sandas has been a ball of energy, but I can't blame him. These are exciting times."

Evaran returned the handshake. "I hope that you find some peace after the current events."

"I have, and it seems the colony has their own tales about the Hoxscarus, but you helped them too."

Evaran nodded. "Life should be much less dangerous for you now."

"Indeed," said Max. He visited each member of the group and shook their hands.

"There is a large volume of information to sift through, and Ziekah still to deal with at the point of her entry to the timeline," said Evaran.

Max nodded. "You know how to stop her, now it's a matter of finding her."

"And we shall," said Evaran.

The group boarded the Torvatta.

Jake's muscles relaxed. They had come a long way since Ziekah's first appearance and were finally homing in on putting a stop to her timeline meddling. He wondered if Evaran would mention any of the timeline changes to the original versions of Sandas or Max. Either way, it was time for the group to go over all the data they had and determine the next steps.

22

Dr. Snowden eased back into his conference room chair. It was 8:30 a.m., and he was the first to arrive for a 9:00 a.m. meeting. After Sandas and Max had been dropped off, Evaran wanted time to go through all the information Sandas had provided. Everyone else had taken the rest of the day off. Dr. Snowden had enjoyed a leisurely read of Lord Noskov's book, and after a long and restful sleep, he was ready for the day.

Although events in this timeline were different from the original one, it made him wonder about his own doppelganger in other timelines. From his research, there were, at a minimum, tens of millions of parallel timelines similar to the original one he came from. He chuckled at the thought of having a conference of variations of himself, and what that would be like.

His mind briefly wandered to Kess. He missed her and wondered what her take on things would be. Ziekah could potentially have wiped her from existence with the new timeline. He sighed.

Jake popped into the room and went to the matter replicator. "Morning."

"Hey. Sleep well?" asked Dr. Snowden.

"Oh yeah," said Jake. After a moment, he sat across from Dr. Snowden with a plate of bacon and scrambled eggs and some orange juice. "Yesterday was kinda wild."

Dr. Snowden chuckled. "Yeah, it was."

Jake chowed down a strip of bacon, then wagged another at Dr. Snowden. "That must have been kinda weird for you to see another version of Sandas, Max, and Pozarra."

"Sandas and Max, yeah, but it was the same Pozarra. It makes me want to visit Sandas. Max is already at the colony, and I have no idea where Pozarra is."

Jake took a swig of his orange juice. "She seemed pretty powerful."

"To say the least. As powerful as she is, it's nothing compared to Evaran's main form."

"Have you seen it before?"

Dr. Snowden shook his head.

"I hope to see it sometime," said Jake, burrowing into his scrambled eggs.

Dr. Snowden took a sip of his coffee as he studied Jake.

Jake looked up with a mouth full of eggs. After swallowing, he said, "What's up?"

"Something Pozarra said. She mentioned you were to watch over Evaran, for all versions. Oh, and you were an anchor."

"Oh, yeah."

Dr. Snowden rubbed his chin. "You've already met another version of Evaran. What if…every version of Evaran checks in with you? You would be a gauge of sorts."

Jake chuckled. "A gauge of what?"

"I don't know. Maybe his character, or how he is perceived, relative to his other forms. You know this version, so you have a baseline. In essence, you would be an anchor for Evaran."

Jake sighed. "I…can't really speak to that."

Dr. Snowden nodded. "I understand."

It made him wonder what the other future versions of Evaran were like. One thing that seemed obvious to Dr. Snowden was that he and Emily did not travel with the future versions. He hoped the cause was not them dying off. Perhaps every incarnation of Evaran had different companions, a sort of unwritten rule.

After Jake cleared his plate, he pushed it back. "I will say I have a special bond with this version, and with you and Emily and this version of V."

Dr. Snowden nodded. He thought he saw sorrow in Jake's eyes for a moment, as if he remembered something painful. There was a future event Pozarra had mentioned a long while back that involved the Hoxscarus. Perhaps he and Emily did not survive, or neither Evaran nor V. Perhaps that could be what Jake was remembering, or Dr. Snowden might be reading into things.

He smiled. "We're a good group."

"Yep!" said Jake. "Never forget it!"

Dr. Snowden raised his cup of coffee toward Jake, who clinked his orange juice glass on Dr. Snowden's mug.

They laughed.

Dr. Snowden enjoyed being around Jake. He had a friendliness about him that Dr. Snowden appreciated. It was no surprise Evaran had been at Lord Noskov's base with Jake when everything had happened.

Emily and Jelton arrived and visited the matter replicator. After getting some breakfast, they took their seats.

"You're early again," said Emily, eying Dr. Snowden.

"Trying to change things up," he said, smiling.

She shook her head and dug into her ham omelet.

Evaran and V came in several minutes later. Evaran sat at the head of the table while V in projected mode plopped down on the opposite end.

"I hope everyone is rested," said Evaran.

Everyone nodded they were.

"Good. We can start if you all are ready."

Everyone again indicated they were.

Evaran interacted with the table console.

A projection shot up of the galactic region Earth resided in.

"Sandas had a lot of notes on Ziekah. He truly kept detailed records," said Evaran.

The projection zoomed into a planet roughly fifty light-years from Earth.

Evaran gestured at the planet. "Ziekah's first appearance is recorded on March 4, 2012, at 1:30 p.m., roughly a month after Seeros was dealt with in the original timeline. The planet is called Gezelrus, and there is a Kreagan scientific research station there. It seems they logged a report of her visiting and acquiring transport off-world."

"Did she attack the place?" asked Emily.

Evaran shook his head. "It appears, according to the record, that she told them she was lost."

"So you think she arrived in the timeline on Gezelrus?"

"I do," said Evaran. "Observe."

The projection showed an image of Ziekah, with a robe and no technology on her, walking into the station.

"I suspect she crossed into our reality with minimal resources and then built her way up."

"Normally I'd admire her ability to get up and going, but not in this case," said Emily.

Jelton chuckled. "Her passion for finding Seeros must sustain her."

"I concur," said Evaran. "Our next step is to go to this planet and track down where she came from."

"How're we going to do that?" asked Jake.

Evaran nodded. "A good question. We can start at the station and then travel back a few days and verify where she is. The goal is to repeat that until she is no longer detectable. At that point, we can narrow down the time frame, and hopefully observe her entry." He pointed at Jake. "You will introduce her to Guudinka, the ancient Seceltor martial art."

"What?"

Evaran half smiled.

Jake laughed. "Yeah, right."

The group chuckled.

Evaran raised a finger. "Once we determine her entry point, we will need to shut it down. Unfortunately...it requires us to shut the other end as well," said Evaran, looking around. "A quantum beacon is required so the Torvatta knows where to go."

"Can't the Torvatta fly through the connection and shut it down?" asked Jelton.

Evaran shook his head. "From my experience, and the Torvatta being what it is, that causes the connection to split, opening other connections between the junction dimension and the reality it is attached to." His eyes slightly glowed. "I will not repeat the same mistake. The only way to shut down the connection is to pulse the shielding at both ends."

"Understood," said Jelton. "Perhaps we can bring the Ravaw to help traverse the connection."

"It may be more difficult to move a larger group, though. We can do this with our group. V will need to stay behind in the Torvatta, and once we cross over into the junction dimension, he can bring the Torvatta there."

V frowned.

"One of us could hang back to keep V company," said Emily.

Evaran studied the table console before raising his head. "Unfortunately, sometimes a time dilation effect is present between the time of entry and the time of exit. We could go in and be gone for an hour, but a year might have passed in our reality. V can go into low-power mode if needed and activate when the quantum beacon signal is detected. For us…it is better we experience it together if time dilation is involved." He cast a sidelong glance at Emily. "We do not want any of us to be alone in that situation."

Dr. Snowden watched Emily's face get serious for a moment. He remembered looking for her on a previous adventure. Although only three days had passed for him, it had been nine months alone on a prison planet for her. Evaran was not taking that chance, and Emily's facial reaction showed she did not want that to occur either.

"Another thing," said Evaran. "The connection can take on many forms. It is better for a small group to go through than a large one from my experience."

Dr. Snowden noted how Evaran's lips moved down slightly. He must have had a bad experience he was remembering.

Jake cleared his throat. "What about Ziekah?"

Evaran nodded. "We will capture her first and take her to the Rift Guardian's prison planet before dealing with the connection."

"The prison planet is to drain her exotic energy," said Jelton, glancing at Jake.

"Ahh," said Jake.

"Yes," said Evaran. "At that point, I want to learn about her obsession with Seeros. I suspect…there is a lot she is not telling. If another timeline version of Seeros is behind this, that must be dealt with."

Dr. Snowden sighed. "That guy, in any timeline, is a pain."

Emily's eyes narrowed. "Probably more than one…"

"A council of Seeroses. Great."

"One thing at a time," said Evaran. He looked around. "Let us go to Gezelrus shortly before Ziekah's arrival."

Emily studied Gezelrus as the Torvatta broke cloud cover. They had traveled to an hour before Ziekah's appearance at the research station. It had taken twenty minutes to reach the surface, which left another forty to wait around and try to detect her.

Emily had seen the data labels that indicated that Gezelrus was a habitable planet by human standards. The mountainous range in the distance seemed to be where the station was located. The green forest with pockets of blue mesmerized her. If the focus was not on capturing Ziekah and finding her entry point, this was someplace she could take a vacation to.

"This place is cool," said Jake.

Dr. Snowden chuckled. "Good atmosphere, lots of green and…blue. I'm guessing the trees are a little different here."

"Yes, and this research station's focus is learning more about this planet. To that end, they have quite a few experts in various fields," said Evaran.

"They must have good travel options," said Jelton. "This planet is not small."

Evaran nodded. "Per Sandas's notes, there is an attached spaceport, around one hundred personnel, and twenty ships."

"That's a large research station," said Dr. Snowden.

"Given that they are isolated, there is enough defense if needed from minor attacks, and any attack would draw a response from the fleet in this sector."

Jake eyed Dr. Snowden. "I guess we'll have to hold off on our commando raid."

They shared a laugh.

Emily shook her head. "You boys. I don't think we're going to land or dock at the station, right?"

"That is correct," said Evaran. "I do not know which direction she will come from, but we will remain in scan profile one and in stealth mode. Her unique signature will allow for easier detection."

"You don't think she'll detect us, do you?" asked Emily.

"Analysis. We will be high enough that she should not detect us," said V in projected mode.

Jelton grinned. "She couldn't before, so I'd say we were safe there."

Emily stood. "Works for me. I'm going to the roof for this."

"I'll join you," said Jelton.

Evaran rose. "We can all go."

The group assembled on the roof.

V formed a console and attended to it while the others stood near the front guardrail.

The Torvatta arrived at the station and hovered.

Emily peered over the edge. The research station had been built next to a river. Its sleek metallic-domed buildings with connecting tunnels contrasted against the dense forest. A variety of verandas and patios ringed the domes, and various equipment lay about outside the buildings. The spaceport was further inland, and only four ships were parked in a cleared area. There was probably an underground hangar of some sort. Kreagans walked around while a swarm of drones flew overhead.

"Busy place," said Dr. Snowden. "I'd love to take a look at what they're researching or what they've found."

"Sandas has information on this facility if that interests you," said Evaran.

Dr. Snowden nodded. "It's not quite the same as visiting and talking to the people there, though."

"I understand."

Evaran gestured at V. "It is close to Ziekah's arrival. Begin the search pulse."

"Acknowledged."

A light pulse shot out from the Torvatta in all directions.

Emily wondered if the Kreagans would detect it, but from her experience, they probably would not due to the pulse's exotic nature. Even if they did find something, they might attribute it to part of the planet.

"How far does the pulse go out?" asked Jake.

"Roughly fifty miles," said Evaran. "Geography is the limitation."

"Cool. I guess we wait."

"Analysis. Ziekah's signature has been detected," said V.

A blinking red dot highlighted on the interior of the Torvatta's shielding.

"That was quick!" said Emily. She wrinkled her brow. "Looks like it's moving fast."

"She may have been picked up on a ship. Her official appearance date would be when she got to the station. V, take us there," said Evaran.

"Acknowledged."

The Torvatta flew to the red dot.

Emily studied the sleek ship that cruised above the forest. The ship was rectangular in design with a sloped front, and about the size of a semitruck. She figured that would help with carrying equipment around.

"Analysis. Ziekah is on the ship."

Evaran nodded. "Follow behind. Once it lands, we can run a scan and determine what its flight path was."

"Acknowledged."

Dr. Snowden glanced at Jelton. "You said the portal you found was a cliff wall behind a waterfall. Was there any visual sign outside of that?"

"I remember a slight shimmer," said Jelton. "However, it was the energy readings that indicated something was off. That and the Hazgrodah ran into the wall and disappeared."

"So once we find out where the Kreagan ship and Ziekah met, we can scan around the area for that portal signature," said Dr. Snowden.

Jelton nodded. "As advanced as the Torvatta's scanning is, I suspect it will have no problem with that."

After twenty minutes, the Kreagan ship landed.

"1:30 p.m. on the dot," said Dr. Snowden.

Evaran nodded.

Emily's eyes narrowed as Ziekah exited the ship. "So close…"

Jake stood next to her. "I'll help you if you go."

She smiled at him. "I know you would." She figured they all would, but it would cause a timeline change. For the moment, she was content with Evaran's plan. Ziekah would pay for everything she did.

After Ziekah and the accompanying Kreagans had entered a building, Evaran motioned at V. "Begin the scan of that ship."

"Acknowledged."

A light beam shot out from the Torvatta and connected to the Kreagan ship.

Jake chuckled. "I remember when Evaran had to go to the ramp and manually place his UIC to do something like this."

"A beam is much more efficient," said Evaran.

"Yeah. It was odd watching the Torvatta line up with a satellite, then you reach out and place the UIC, but it worked."

"We had the beam on our first voluntary trip with Evaran. Used it on a Kreagan satellite near Kreagus," said Dr. Snowden.

"That's cool," said Jake. He sighed. "I wish I could have joined you both back then."

Evaran laid a hand on Jake's shoulder. "You had other concerns at the time."

"Yeah."

The beam dissipated and data windows appeared on the Torvatta's interior shielding. A map of the area displayed in one window with a red dot.

"According to the ship, she was picked up roughly seventy miles from here. V, take us to that location."

"Acknowledged."

The Torvatta rose and flew to the red dot.

Emily studied the clearing that the Torvatta hovered over. It was near a river with a small campsite nearby. Kreagan equipment and metallic containers lay about, and several Kreagans moved around the area.

"Seems like an active site," said Dr. Snowden. "I bet they're studying the ecosystem."

"How can you tell?" asked Jake.

Dr. Snowden pointed at some boxes with glass tops. "They're taking samples."

"Ahh," said Jake.

"Analysis. No portal signature detected."

"It may be masked," said Evaran. He perused his ARI. "Perform an expanded search. I suspect if we get close enough, it will register."

Jelton shook a finger. "She could have taken a long time to get to this camp. The portal might be very far away."

Evaran rubbed his chin. "That is possible. V, take us up, jump back two hours, and then come back here. That will at least show us the direction she came from."

"Acknowledged."

V completed Evaran's request.

As the Torvatta hovered over the camp, several data windows popped up, one of which had the area they were in.

Emily pointed at a red dot in one of the windows. "Looks like she's coming from the southwest."

Jake peered in that direction. "Big mountain range over there. I bet the portal is around there somewhere."

"I concur," said Evaran. "V, take us to her location, then on to the mountains."

"Acknowledged."

The Torvatta took off. After a moment, it hovered over Ziekah.

Emily noted that Ziekah paused to look around for a moment, but continued on.

Evaran interacted with his ARI and the Torvatta flew toward the mountains.

The Torvatta reached a hilly area before the mountains.

"This terrain makes scanning difficult," said Evaran. "However, we can still do targeted scans, but I believe given the distance she is from the mountain, we can travel back four hours to get a better idea of the portal's origin." He looked over at V.

"Acknowledged."

After the Torvatta had ascended, jumped back, and descended to the area where they had been, several data windows popped up.

Emily scrutinized them. "I don't see a red dot anywhere."

"I suspect when it does appear, we will know where the portal is," said Evaran.

Dr. Snowden chuckled. "I guess it's a good thing the Torvatta can't detect itself. Otherwise, we'd be detecting ourselves all the way out here."

"That is by design," said Evaran.

"I know, but I still find it fascinating."

"Yeah, I do too. We'd still have to do the search, though, to make them appear," said Jake. "I guess we wait, or maybe go forward a bit in time."

"We shall wait," said Evaran. "Given the speed at which she walked, the portal is in this area. We can scan around, but I suspect she will arrive soon."

"Then we wait," said Jelton.

Evaran nodded.

Emily leaned into Jelton, who slid an arm around her waist. Her muscles relaxed. She wished Jelton could come with them on every trip, but he was needed by his own people. The fact that he had come to her aid despite that said a lot. Now she would hopefully watch Ziekah get captured.

23

Jake relaxed for the next twenty minutes. He enjoyed the light conversation and the general feeling that everyone was happy to be where they were. Emily and Jelton made a natural couple. While she could be aggressive, Jelton was calm and collected. Jake liked that Jelton called everybody his friend. Dr. Snowden studied the data windows alongside Evaran, and Jake felt like he had developed a closer bond to Dr. Snowden. V had been silent for the most part, with an occasional comment.

It was strange to have arrived initially at 12:30 p.m., but it was now 8:20 a.m., four hours and ten minutes before. Jake was appreciative that a data window off to the side kept both Earth time and whatever time they were in.

A dot appeared on one of the data windows.

"Analysis. Ziekah detected. Initiating targeted scan."

Another window showed a visual of a portal and Ziekah under it on the ground.

Jake shook his head. "No portal here, it looks like. She came from the future sometime."

"What do we do?" asked Emily.

Evaran raised a finger. "There is enough information to know where she portaled from. We now have multiple points of data to work with."

"We do?" asked Dr. Snowden.

Jake grinned. He knew what was coming. Every time Evaran raised a finger and said he had enough data, that meant there was a well-thought-out analysis about to drop. Jake had seen it through several versions of Evaran, and it always remained the same, despite the personality differences.

Evaran interacted with his ARI.

A full-size holographic replica of Ziekah appeared with the portal above her.

"Note the portal color's intensity," said Evaran.

Everyone did so.

"It is dim, relative to the ones we have seen." Evaran tapped at his ARI, and three other portals appeared next to the current one. "With Emily, it was very dim. V's was brighter, and Dr. Snowden's was the brightest. From this, we can deduce that the darker the portal is, the further back in time it goes."

"Can that relationship be calculated?" asked Dr. Snowden.

Evaran half smiled. "Yes, it can."

Numbers popped up above each portal. "If each year further in the past dims the portal, then you can take the differential between each of your portals, calculate how much it dims by year, then apply that calculation to Ziekah's portal. Based on that, Ziekah is 1448 years in the future relative to this time."

"Impressive," said Jelton. "However, the portals also move in space."

Evaran nodded. "There is another aspect of the feature that correlates to that as well."

Another set of numbers appeared above the portals.

"Note the portal's radius. While each one has a static base number that is wide enough to allow whatever is coming through to do so, there is an additional amount that extends the portal radius." Evaran gestured at Emily's portal. "Hers is the largest, while Dr. Snowden's is the smallest."

Jake chuckled. "So the larger it is, the further you get moved."

"Exactly," said Evaran. "The only limitation appears to be her arm length, and the size of the circles she can make in the air. There is another observation based on her movements. Her left arm is for how far away you go, while the right arm handles how far back. Also, she makes a small movement with her finger on her left hand to indicate direction."

"You got her figured out!" said Emily.

Evaran gestured at Ziekah's portal. "More importantly, we can determine not only when she came from, but where. Based on the portal we saw her come through, she opened it at the Kreagan Station."

"Time to check it out," said Dr. Snowden.

"I concur. V, take us there and five minutes prior to the time index I have entered."

"Acknowledged."

Jake wondered if he would have figured that out on his own. He suspected he might have had he had time to do so. However, with Evaran, there was no need as he could work it out. It made Jake wonder if Evaran had already known this information, since Ziekah's portal would not have been required for that analysis. Perhaps another data point was needed to see if the calculations worked out. Either way, they were one step closer.

The Torvatta ascended to low orbit. When it arrived, it jumped forward to the amount of time to descend plus five minutes before Ziekah opened her portal, then descended to the Kreagan Station.

Jake looked out at the morning sun as it lit up the misty forests. A light haze rested on the treetops, and alien birds flew overhead. He looked at the others. Jelton had slipped his arm around Emily's waist, while Dr. Snowden gripped the guardrail. Evaran was cool as always, with his hands behind his back and sunlight bouncing off his face. V almost looked like he glowed while in projected mode at the console. Jake smiled as his throat constricted. This was one of those moments he knew he would always remember.

After the Torvatta arrived, Jake studied the abandoned station. Vegetation had claimed a lot of it, and parts of the domed structures he had seen before looked like they had been caved in. A red outline of Ziekah appeared on the Torvatta's interior shielding.

"There she is!" said Emily.

Evaran nodded. "I have calculated what her arm movements should be."

A data window popped open with two circles side by side.

"When she opens the portal, her arm movements will be overlaid on these circles."

Dr. Snowden chuckled. "This is one of the wilder applications of math."

"We still need to find where the portal is," said Jake.

"Indeed," said Evaran. "I suspect she had been here for a while, based on her tattered clothing, and found this station abandoned. As advanced as she is, she would be able to determine how far back to go, and we saw the result of her calculations."

After a few minutes, she opened a portal and jumped through.

Jake watched in amazement as her arm movements played out over the two circles on the projection. Even the finger flick was accurate. "Exact match."

Evaran nodded. "V, take us back in increments of two hours and to her furthest location each time."

"Acknowledged."

Jake opened a holo menu and created a chair. It took twenty minutes to reach orbit, then another twenty to come back down, and they would probably need to do it a few times. Hopefully only a few would be needed.

"Jake has the right idea," said Evaran. "This may take a while. If anyone needs to do anything, now is the time to do so. I will alert everyone once we have the portal's location."

Emily and Jelton nodded and went to the elevator along with Dr. Snowden.

Two hours later, Jake almost fell out of his chair when V woke him up from his nap. He had updated his chair to something more comfortable and had settled in. Although he had living quarters, he wanted to be there when the portal was found. He yawned and rubbed his eyes.

"I guess we found it?" he asked.

"We did," said Evaran.

A refreshed Emily, Dr. Snowden, and Jelton exited the elevator to the roof.

Evaran motioned for everyone to focus on a data window. "We are above the portal, roughly forty miles from the station, and it is embedded in the side of a boulder. Observe." He tapped at his ARI.

Jake watched the outline of an irregularly shaped doorway appear on the Torvatta's interior shielding. It looked like a ketchup stain, except much larger.

"When does she come out of it?" asked Dr. Snowden.

"Sometime in the next two hours. The second-to-last check showed her coming from this area. The last one does not show her at all," said Evaran.

"Are we going to hop around until we get the exact moment?" asked Emily.

Evaran shook his head. "I have another idea. V, place us behind the boulder and expand the shields."

"Acknowledged."

Jake peered over the guardrail as the Torvatta landed. He smiled when the shields expanded instantly. "So she'll essentially walk into the Torvatta's shielding area of effect, where her portal powers won't work."

"That is the idea," said Evaran. He pulled off his utility handle. "Everyone will wait here in the Torvatta while it is stealthed. I am going to apprehend her when she appears."

"We can help," said Jelton.

Emily squeezed Jelton's arm. "Evaran is much faster than any of us. She won't be escaping him, especially with her portal abilities."

Jelton nodded at Evaran. "We are here should you need us."

"It is appreciated," said Evaran. "I will be back."

He jumped over the guardrail and hustled over to the boulder. When he got there, he hopped on top and held his utility handle out.

"I guess we wait," said Jake, facing the boulder. "At least she won't see us."

Dr. Snowden chuckled. "Yeah, and Evaran jumping down to subdue you is not something I think anyone plans on or expects."

"Evaran, can you hear us?" asked Emily.

She jumped when a holographic projection of Evaran appeared next to her.

"I am here and can speak to you in this manner."

Jake looked out and saw Evaran perfectly still atop the boulder. "He's doing the creepy ventriloquist thing again."

Emily chuckled. "I think he likes doing that. Anyways, I guess we wait."

V took off and hovered over and in front of the boulder.

A screen appeared in midair on the roof and showed an isometric eye view of the boulder and surrounding area.

"That works," said Jake, grinning.

After an hour and ten minutes, the portal began to shimmer.

"Analysis. The portal appears to have become agitated."

Evaran nodded. "I can sense its state changing." His projection dissipated.

Jake was more tense than he thought he would be. Looking around at the others showed they were as nervous as he was. Although Ziekah was powerful in her own right, and she would be at a disadvantage, there was that fear that she could defy the Torvatta, or even escape. His eyes were glued to the screen.

After a moment, Ziekah stepped through the portal and looked around.

Jake noted that she wore a simple cloth shirt and pants, and also was barefoot. Her hair appeared frazzled, and it looked like she had dirt on her face.

Evaran jumped down behind Ziekah.

She spun around and gasped.

He zipped up to her and tapped her with his baton.

Blue arcs danced around her for a moment before she collapsed.

Evaran picked her up and faced the Torvatta. "It is time to visit the Rift Guardians' prison planet."

Jelton stood on the roof along with the others as the Torvatta flew through a portal to a processing facility on the prison planet that the Rift Guardians maintained. Evaran had gone to the research lab to put Ziekah into something transportable and to lock her arms and hands down so she could not create portals. Although she should not be able to on the Torvatta, Evaran did not want to take the chance. Jelton smiled as the massive facility came into view.

Jake pointed out. "Whoa! That's a big building!"

"Yes, it is, my friend," said Jelton.

"So where are we exactly?"

"A prison planet that we maintain. It is one of the few planets left near the end of time when planets existed in my timeline," said Jelton.

Dr. Snowden chuckled. "Even if the prisoners were to escape, there aren't many places to go. The rift door to get here is in space, and they ferry them down."

Jelton nodded.

"Huh," said Jake. "So are the prisoners in cells or something down there?"

Jelton raised a finger. "Not quite. They get a tract of land to live in that has rift shielding as borders. There is a locked-down matter replicator they can use, and they live out the remainder of their natural life there."

"Awesome," said Jake. "Humane living conditions."

"They're physically by themselves, although they may travel to other prisoners' cells if the other prisoners let them," said Emily. She glanced at Jelton. "From what I recall, you were installing holographic projectors for communication among prisoners instead of only a screen."

Jelton chuckled. "Yes, and we actually have it installed in a few places. But the projector tech is not on the ground. It's a drone per cell that allows that. The prisoners have a rudimentary console they can interact with, but that too is locked down."

"If I ever went to prison, this is where I would want to go," said Jake. He shook a hand at Jelton. "Not that I would ever *want* to go, just to be clear."

Jelton enjoyed observing Jake's curiosity. It reminded him of when Dr. Snowden and Emily had first come to the Rift Guardians' headquarters and the prison planet.

"Analysis. Incoming communication request."

A data window popped up showing the torso of a Rift Guardian with light gold-and-green armor. "Torvatta confirmed and Evaran Protocol established. Jelton Stallryn and Gowldin Khull will be notified."

Jelton smiled. "I'm here, actually. However, let Gowldin know that we are going directly to the siphon tanks."

"Yes, sir," said the Rift Guardian. The data window closed.

"Landing coordinates received," said V.

"So this is where you go when you visit Jelton, Emily?" asked Jake.

She shook her head. "I go to the Rift Guardians' headquarters."

"Ahh."

Jelton studied Jake for a moment. "When this is all done, I will show you around there."

Jake smiled big. "Awesome!"

They shared a laugh.

Ten minutes later, the Torvatta landed on a large square metallic landing pad surrounded by gray dirt.

"Siphon tank time," said Dr. Snowden. "Assuming Evaran is ready to go, that is."

"Let's find out," said Emily as she headed to the elevator.

The group assembled in the research lab a minute later.

Jelton studied Ziekah lying on the slab. Thin metallic strips wrapped around her body and kept her arms close to her sides. Her wrists and ankles were strapped to the slab. It was obvious that if Ziekah were to wake up, she would not be doing much.

Evaran exited a side room with a hovering wheelchair. He surveyed the group. "I assume we have arrived."

"We have," said Jelton. "It appears Ziekah is ready for transport."

Evaran pushed the wheelchair next to Ziekah's slab. He released her from it and placed her into the wheelchair. After securing her, which included a chest and waist strap, Evaran faced the group. "She is ready now. Lead on."

Jelton nodded and exited the Torvatta with the others in tow.

The group walked down a well-maintained concrete-like pathway to the processing facility.

Jake looked around. "It's much bigger out here when you're on the ground."

"That was my thought too when I first came here," said Dr. Snowden.

Jake chuckled. "Not a lot of ships, though. I'm guessing it's only used when dropping off prisoners."

"A good observation," said Jelton.

"How long will Ziekah be out for?" asked Emily.

"Long enough. When she gains consciousness, she will be fully mortal," said Evaran.

Jelton noticed that Evaran had a covered syringe on his belt. That probably had the nanobots that would allow Evaran to interface with Ziekah's mind. Although Jelton did not normally approve of mental manipulation at that level, he understood that for those who had proven dangerous, it was sometimes necessary. That was something Emily seemed to have no issues with, but Dr. Snowden had shared Jelton's concerns in the past.

Evaran's unusual silence reminded Jelton of when the Mortani had been brought to the siphon tanks. Although Evaran was angry, it was difficult to tell. Facial and body cues were limited as always, and Jelton resorted to sensing some fluctuation in Evaran's cosmic energy.

Jelton laid a hand on Evaran's shoulder. "She will face justice, my friend."

"Yes, she will," said Evaran, nodding at Jelton.

They reached a massive open doorway with several Rift Guardian guards in heavy armor standing outside. The guards performed a Rift Guardian salute as the group entered the facility.

Jake surveyed the interior. "I thought it was big outside..."

"This is only the entrance area. We'll take an elevator down to the siphon tank room. It is much smaller by comparison," said Jelton, smiling.

Jake nodded.

After thirty minutes, they reached the siphon tank room.

Jelton remembered the last time that Evaran and the others had come. Over a hundred Mortani had had their cosmic energy stripped, and Evaran had probed every single one of them after they were mortal.

A technician wearing a formfitting light gray mesh suit saluted the group.

Jelton returned the action.

"The siphon tank is ready and Gowldin is on his way," said the technician.

"Very good," said Jelton. He motioned at Ziekah. "Get her strapped in."

"Yes, sir."

"I will assist," said Evaran.

He released Ziekah's slab constraints. With minimal effort, he picked her up and placed her into an open cylindrical capsule. It had metallic plates on the sides with wires and a diamond-shaped rift crystal up top.

The technician got to work securing Ziekah. "She is ready for siphoning."

"Thank you," said Evaran. He looked around the group before interacting with a nearby console.

The rift crystal glowed and extended green tendrils that snaked down over Ziekah. Once they had reached her feet, the tendrils pulsed.

Ziekah began to shake uncontrollably, but the restraints held.

After a moment, the tendrils retreated and the rift crystal dimmed.

"It is done," said Jelton.

Evaran scanned Ziekah. "She is mortal now."

"Wow," said Jake. "This is something the Torvatta could use."

"Perhaps," said Evaran. "However, this process is not something I take pleasure in, and there is a chance it could be misused by others on board. I think the process of visiting Jelton each time to use it is a good one."

"Jelton is a secondary check," said Emily.

Evaran nodded at Jelton. "I trust his judgment, and his counsel is appreciated in these matters."

Jelton smiled. It was rare to get praise from Evaran, and Jelton would take any given.

The technician unstrapped Ziekah and motioned at two nearby guards. "Take her to the holding room."

Evaran pulled his syringe out. "Before she goes, let me place these nanobots in her."

Everyone stood back.

Evaran uncapped the syringe and lightly jabbed Ziekah in the arm. "It is done." He gave one of the guards the hover chair while the other guard got Ziekah in it.

After a moment, the guards exited the room.

"So what now?" asked Jake.

"We wait," said Evaran. "When she awakens, it will be her first moments as a mortal, and that can be disorienting from my observations."

Jelton gestured around at the group. "In the meantime, we have a lounge room with some replicators. We can wait there and get some food and drink, or use the newly installed restrooms I had put in for those who need it."

"In case we came back," said Dr. Snowden. He shook a finger at Jelton. "I like it."

"I used the design Evaran provided. I believe he called it a Krotovore mist room."

"Oh…I remember that," said Emily. She smiled at Jake. "You might want to use it even if you don't have to go."

Jake chuckled. "Sounds like relieving yourself is an adventure."

The group laughed.

Jelton appreciated the lightheartedness of the group. Although the action of stripping a being of what made them unique was something he considered violent, it was warranted in Ziekah's case.

Dr. Snowden eased back into his chair in the holding room. To his right were Emily and Jelton, with Jake and Gowldin to his left in their own chairs. Dr. Snowden enjoyed seeing Gowldin again, and he seemed excited to see everyone as well. Evaran paced around with his hands behind him, while V was in orb mode.

A table sat in front of him, with an unconscious Ziekah fastened to a chair by a waist strap that had a tranquilizing system built into it. A technician stood near a console ready to release the tranquilizer if needed. Evaran had already mind probed Ziekah, and now the group waited for her to wake up.

While relaxing in the lounge room, Dr. Snowden had a burger for dinner. It seemed Jelton had made sure that Earth foods were in the replicator patterns. He must have suspected that they would be back. Thankfully, they only had to wait an hour before coming to the holding room.

Ziekah began to stir.

Although she was now mortal and strapped down, her mere presence made his pulse quicken. She had gone out of her way to try to kill everyone, and it was a sober reminder that he would always have a target on his back. He had only wanted to go home and relax, not get tossed into AD 1842 and potentially killed.

Ziekah grunted and squinted her eyes.

Dr. Snowden sensed her heartbeat increasing. He appreciated that he still had the ability to sense some aspects of beings. Her breathing stood out to him as she slowly opened her eyes and looked around.

"What...where am I?" asked Ziekah.

Evaran focused on her. "You are in a holding cell in a processing facility on a prison planet maintained by the Rift Guardians."

"What?"

Evaran repeated what he had said.

Ziekah took a deep breath and looked around. "And who are you?"

"I am Evaran," he said. He introduced the others.

Ziekah studied everyone's faces, then tried to move.

"You are confined to the chair," said Evaran.

"What is this?"

Evaran nodded. "Your confusion is understandable. You are a Hazgrodah, from a junction dimension. You came into this reality. However, we were there to greet and subdue you."

Ziekah's breathing increased. "Why?"

"Your presence in our timeline caused changes and violated timeline integrity. I cannot allow that."

"I just arrived. I have no idea what you're talking about."

Evaran's eyes slightly glowed. "That is because after you tried to murder my friends and alter the timeline to subjugate civilizations, we used my ship, the Torvatta, to come back to your initial entry point to the timeline. You have been banished from ours."

Ziekah smirked. "That's one possibility. Who's to say that I won't do that since I'm now aware of the consequences?"

"You are to say. I probed your mind and now understand your desire to seek out Seeros. You work for the Seeros League, a multi-timeline society of Seeroses focused on his extraction from every timeline he is in. Your mission would never change, and based on the other timelines you have interfered in, I do not believe you are capable of altering your mission. Once you had discovered we were responsible for Seeros's death, you would come after us as you already did in our past."

Ziekah harrumphed. "And who are you exactly to make that judgment?"

"I am Evaran, and I deem what is acceptable and what is not in the timeline," he said as his eyes and fists glowed bright for a moment.

A chill went up Dr. Snowden's back. The tone with which Evaran had said his last sentence made it seem more strongly worded than what he would have said in the past. Although others might not see it, Dr. Snowden could see that Evaran seemed closer to his main form. Perhaps that was a function of the recent cosmic energy increase. Dr. Snowden cast a sidelong glance at Emily, who had wrinkled her brow. She must have thought the same thing. A quick look at the others showed they had similar reactions.

Ziekah laughed. "You and your friends made a wrong calculation. I know your faces now, and if you truly believe you saw my future, you would understand how bad that is." She waved her arms in circles. "What?"

"Your portal ability is no longer possible. You are mortal now," said Evaran.

"How? That's impossible!"

Evaran gestured at Jelton, then at Gowldin. "They are Rift Guardians, and possess technology to strip away exotic energies. You are under their care now and will get a tract of land on which to live out the rest of your natural life."

"You don't know what you're dealing with!" said Ziekah.

Evaran paced around with his hands behind his back. "I do, actually. The junction dimension connections, both to our timeline and the Seeros League's dimension, will be severed. They will not be able to send any more Hazgrodahs... to *any* timeline."

Ziekah laughed. "You think you can disable the Seeros League's connection, and they'll let you? You're delusional."

"Perhaps. However, I know the entry and exit points of their connection."

"Even with that, they possess defenses I was never told about for this exact scenario."

Evaran nodded. "I am also aware of that. They will not have encountered someone like me, and the last Seeros that did is no longer here."

Ziekah seethed as her brows angled. "So that's it? I come through into your timeline, and now my life is over because of something I haven't done yet? Your sense of justice is warped. Do you even have proof of what I've supposedly done?"

"Of course. V, display Ziekah's encounter with Dr. Snowden."

"Acknowledged." V flew over the table and showed the initial encounter.

"Display Dr. Snowden's death attempt."

V complied.

Evaran eyed Ziekah. "You showed no mercy. V, display Emily's interaction."

"Acknowledged." V displayed Emily's initial encounter and death attempt.

Evaran motioned at the projection. "In both instances, your intent was clear."

Ziekah sighed.

"V, display your encounter."

V complied.

Ziekah scowled. "So three events. Now that I know, I won't interfere, and I'll only focus on retrieving Seeros."

Evaran raised a finger. "I am not done yet showing you your crimes. V, display the holographic Ziekah from the data vault."

"Acknowledged."

After V displayed it, Evaran's eyes narrowed. "At this point, you believed that we were all dead. You had also changed Earth's trajectory into the future, and by extension, humanity. Your recklessness could not stand."

Ziekah smiled big at Evaran. "So you decided to come back to my timeline entry point and stop me there because I was too much for you to handle."

"Your bravado is unwarranted," said Evaran. "You would be stopped. It was only a matter of...time."

Ziekah leaned back in her chair. "I've been sentenced to life imprisonment and stripped of my powers? That's your *judgment*?"

Evaran nodded. "You will be treated humanely."

"If I'm so dangerous, kill me now! I'd prefer that to whatever this is!"

Evaran's eyes and hands glowed for a moment again. "No. You crossed my line, and that is a dangerous place to be. You will experience the consequences of that."

Dr. Snowden breathed a bit heavier. There was no doubt that Evaran seemed more aggressive than before. Dr. Snowden remembered how Levaran, one of Evaran's other plane forms, had not been shy about showcasing her abilities or even emotions. She was tough and could be cold as needed. It seemed Evaran had taken on some of her personality.

Ziekah sighed as she looked down. "I understand. You're right. I messed up, but I can change. What harm could I do as a mortal? Let me go back to where I came from." A tear fell on her cheek.

"Your fate has already been sealed. Your appeal to my empathy will not work."

Ziekah glared at Evaran. Through gritted teeth, she said, "I'll make you all pay!"

Evaran shook his head. "Unlikely. You are now aware of your situation, and who put you in it." He nodded at the technician next to Ziekah.

The technician interacted with a console, which caused the waist restraint to inject Ziekah with a sedative.

She breathed hard and moved her head around haphazardly before slumping over.

Evaran looked around the group. "We can convene in the morning to discuss the junction dimension's connection to our timeline."

Dr. Snowden pondered the moment. Ziekah was done and dealt with, and now they had to deal with closing two connections: one that connected the junction dimension to his reality, and the other that the Seeros League used. His gut told him that neither would be as easy as it sounded.

Evaran's warning about what form the connections took sounded dangerous, and the look on his face indicated he had some bad experiences with them. Dr. Snowden sighed. It had been a long day, and he was looking forward to a good sleep.

24

Jake grinned as he eyed his bacon omelet in the conference room. Although he had only been back on Earth for a year, he had come to enjoy all the new food available to try. Having spent life aboard a space station from age six to twenty-one did not leave a lot of options for Earth food. Although slavers sometimes sold replicator patterns, it was rare, and as he found out, the patterns comically wrong. Pizza was definitely not a pancake with roast beef cubes on top.

As he dug into his omelet, he reflected on the previous night. After Ziekah had been removed from the holding room, she was taken to her new cell. Gowldin had been a fountain of information, and seemed surprised that Jake had been so interested. From his perspective, he had never seen something like the Rift Guardians' setup. Seceltor prisons were tiny and meant to be temporary. If in one for more than a few weeks, you were most likely going to be killed, but the Rift Guardians had an elegant solution.

Jake enjoyed talking with Gowldin and Jelton, and although Jake wanted to visit the Rift Guardians' headquarters, he knew that Evaran wanted everyone in one place for the night, and that was at the processing facility. Evaran, Jelton, and Gowldin had some things to discuss, so Jake joined Dr. Snowden and Emily for a tour of the facility. It was far larger than Jake had expected.

It was almost 9:00 a.m., and Evaran had called for a meeting at 9:30 a.m. He usually arrived early and started if everyone was present. Perhaps that was a psychology thing to tell everyone a time with the expectation they would all arrive fifteen minutes early.

Dr. Snowden entered the room and got a cup of coffee. "Hey, Jake."

"Hey," said Jake.

Dr. Snowden took his seat. "Heck of a day yesterday."

"Yeah. I'm just glad Ziekah is behind us. I'm guessing the timeline is reset by now."

Dr. Snowden nodded. "Yep. Her removal would cause a timeline change that takes about twenty minutes to render. What surprised me was that I always thought that timeline changes were towards the future from where the change occurred. Apparently, if the cause of the event has traveled to the past, the changes ripple from there too."

"I wondered about that," said Jake, shaking a piece of bacon at Dr. Snowden. "She effectively never existed in our timeline."

Emily and Jelton arrived. Emily got breakfast while Jelton sat next to Jake.

"Gowldin said you were extremely curious," said Jelton, glancing at Jake.

Jake grinned. "It's not every day you get to see a Rift Guardian prison planet and facility."

Jelton chuckled. "I suppose not. He enjoyed your company."

"He's cool."

"Yes. I will let him know he is…cool."

They shared a laugh.

Evaran and V, in projected mode, entered the room. Evaran sat at the head of the table while V sat next to Dr. Snowden.

"Everyone has arrived early," said Evaran, glancing at Dr. Snowden.

"Why are you looking at me?" asked Dr. Snowden.

Emily chuckled.

Dr. Snowden eyed her.

Evaran motioned at Dr. Snowden. "I was not implying anything. Nonetheless, we can begin if everyone is ready."

Everyone nodded that they were.

Jake grinned as the pattern for meeting time and Evaran's arrival held true again, although this time it was almost twenty-five minutes before instead of fifteen.

"Very well," said Evaran.

He interacted with the table console.

A holographic projection shot up of a horizontal four-by-four blue grid with a white background and black cylinders that shot up at each point for a total of sixteen cylinders.

"Imagine each cylinder is a timeline."

A green blob was added that touched a few of the cylinders and extended off the grid.

"The green object would then represent a junction dimension. Note that the object is not its true shape, but conceptually, it will do."

Dr. Snowden pointed at one of the timelines. "So where the junction dimension touches a timeline, a connection forms."

"Yes. Observe."

The projection zoomed into the area where the junction dimension was near the timeline. A squiggly line connected the two.

"The line is the connection that allows passage from the junction dimension to another reality," said Evaran. "As I mentioned before, the connection can take on many forms. Sometimes it is a tunnel, other times, a cavernous maze, and sometimes, filled with liquid."

"It sounds like you've seen a few," said Emily.

Evaran looked down. "I have, and I will not underestimate them." He looked back up. "There is sometimes a time dilation effect. The connections are dimensions in their own right. The goal is to enter this connection with a quantum beacon and get to the other side. When we exit, the Torvatta will pick up the beacon."

Jake tilted his head. "The connection can prevent the quantum beacon from being detected?"

"Yes. The connection, by its very nature, is formed from a quantum fluctuation of the junction dimension. Imagine a ball covered in slime, then shake the ball. Every place the flung slime touches forms a connection."

"That's...an interesting image."

"How do junction dimensions form?" asked Dr. Snowden.

Evaran nodded. "When a universe is created, its matter and energy are in a quantum state, meaning it exists in every combination at the same time. During the decoherence phase, a pulse of planar energy sweeps across the universe that collapses the quantum states into a classical one, forming timelines, and sometimes dimensions, such as the junction ones."

"Like the double slit experiment, where the wave acts like a measurement, which then causes state to change," said Dr. Snowden, shaking a finger.

Evaran nodded. "When the wave washes over everything, junction dimensions vibrate before collapsing into a classical state, and in turn, they come into contact with timelines. However, due to what they are, they form a connection, instead of being a part of the timeline."

"Yeah...that was my thought too," said Dr. Snowden, clearing his throat.

"Analysis. I do not believe that was your thought."

Dr. Snowden chuckled. "You're right. I'm a bit rusty on my quantum mechanics. But I understand that somewhat."

"I sorta did," said Emily.

Jake chuckled.

"What precautions can we take when entering the connection?" asked Jelton. "The one we went through was a nightmarish landscape. Our armor protected us, and I think to an extent, the fact that we were of rift origin."

Evaran motioned at Emily and Dr. Snowden. "We can use one of their flying patterns and go in with helmets up. When I was in Ziekah's mind, I saw the connection and the path she took through the environments. There is no solid ground immediately on the other side, and the flying platform will prevent us from falling to our deaths. Some areas will involve the need to walk through."

"What was her form inside the connection?" asked Jake.

"Imagine an ever-changing blob with tendrils."

"Huh, that's crazy."

Evaran raised a finger. "The connection is a hostile environment." He perused his ARI and flicked it at Dr. Snowden and Emily. "I created a flying pattern that will work there."

Dr. Snowden and Emily checked their PSDs.

"That's an interesting design," said Dr. Snowden.

"I like it," said Emily.

"There are also two main creature types to expect," said Evaran.

The projection changed to show a large hoofed quadruped creature with a torso on the front.

The head reminded Jake of a snake, and the body was covered in scales. What stood out was the sheer size as it stood around thirty feet tall.

"What is that?" asked Emily.

"Per Ziekah's memories, it is a Cronik," said Evaran. "A divide splits the level we will be on into two areas. The Croniks inhabit the first area with the portal to our timeline."

Jake shook his head. "They're huge."

Evaran nodded. "Ziekah seems to believe they are hostile, and she ran from them when she came through their area. The divide itself has a wormlike creature known as an Anwark. They created tunnels in the structure that we need to access. They have quills of some sort and Ziekah's route avoided them, although she had to kill a few on her way through. We do not need to go too far before we are on the other side of the divide, but we will need to be careful. To that end, I have sent you a new pattern for your PSD."

Emily checked her PSD. "Huh. Looks like a block of metal...with a grappling beam."

"Yes. I refer to it as a grappling hammer. You can swing it around and clear the area around you."

Dr. Snowden smiled as he studied his PSD. "Sorta like what Thor did. I like it. Based on the design, we can pull the grappling beam in or extend it out, and even raise and lower it like you did in the past except this time we don't need a body on the end."

"That is correct." Evaran gestured at them. "Between your natural strength and your suit, you will have enough power to wield it."

Emily cracked her neck. "I'm ready to use it if need be."

"I suspect you are," said Evaran, studying her for a moment.

"What do we know about the divide other than what populates it?" asked Jelton.

Evaran nodded. "Ziekah's memory showed it is a massive wall."

"Is it a rocky wall?" asked Dr. Snowden.

Evaran shook his head. "It is a somewhat moist material, yet solid enough to stand by itself."

Dr. Snowden rubbed his chin. "You mentioned levels. That sounds like there is more than one."

"Yes. Ziekah explored the connection and found around forty-seven layers. Apparently the divide goes through multiple ones, which allows for traversal. Thankfully for us, the portals are on the same level."

"Place sounds nuts."

Evaran half smiled. "I understand your concern." He looked around. "Are we ready to go?"

"It sounds dangerous, so of course we're ready," said Dr. Snowden.

Emily smiled. "Let's do this!"

"Very well. V, take us to the portal. Everyone else, get in any last-minute snacks or drinks and any bodily functions you need to handle, then assemble on the ramp."

"Acknowledged," said V as he exited the room.

Jake stood and exhaled as the others left. They all had cosmic energy, and he did not, and they would have an advantage if things got rough. Although he figured he should hang back with V, he also understood it could be a long time. Jake was surprised that taking him back to Earth had not been mentioned as an option. Perhaps he had earned Evaran's trust to stay with the group in a potentially dangerous situation.

Evaran eyed Jake.

Jake smiled as he exited the room.

Emily surveyed the boulder where the portal resided. The sounds of alien birds flying around drew her attention and she reflected on how nice it was out. Jelton's presence made everything better, and she smiled when thinking about Ziekah being put away.

The challenge ahead was daunting, but with the current group, Emily had no doubt they would succeed. Evaran's flying platform design intrigued her. It reminded her of her initial attempt, except with a covered top that was transparent.

Everyone but Evaran and V was on the ramp. She suspected that Evaran was giving V some additional instructions. It bothered her that V could not come, but she understood from both a tactical and logical stance, V was the backup. With his ability to go into low-power mode, he could wait indefinitely whereas she knew she would crawl out of her skin if it took a long time for the quantum beacon to signal. Having to endure the effects of time dilation alone was not something she was eager to experience again.

"Now who's thinking?" asked Dr. Snowden as he laid a hand on her arm.

She smiled. "Just happy to be at this point."

Jelton chuckled. "I think we're all glad that Ziekah is gone. Now we can focus on preventing anything like her from ever coming through."

Jake cracked his neck. "We got this."

"We will face it together, my friend," said Jelton.

Jake nodded.

Evaran walked out with a metallic backpack on his back while V followed him.

Evaran crooked a thumb back. "I believe we are ready to go. The quantum beacon is in my backpack and once V receives a signal from it, he will take the Torvatta to it. Any questions before we go?"

Everyone indicated they did not.

"Very well. Dr. Snowden, please form the flying pattern."

Dr. Snowden moved off the ramp and stood in front of the boulder.

"You may wish to step back some," said Evaran.

Dr. Snowden complied. When he was about twenty feet out, he extended his PSD.

Emily observed the PSD form a metal rod to the ground to form the base. She had expected that to occur, and when the sides formed and created a ceiling with the top half of the platform being transparent, it made her wish she had thought of that before. The back part of the rectangular box had a sealed door, and she saw how the PSD essentially manufactured a small ship, albeit a slow one with light protection. It was definitely not made for battle.

Evaran gestured around. "It has minor kinetic shielding but also allows us to see around, while having some physical protection. There are also some minor additions that provide illumination."

"Wow," said Jake. "I still can't believe all that can be created from the PSD."

"Me either, sometimes," said Dr. Snowden, chuckling.

Evaran nodded. "As always, there is a trade-off. Dr. Snowden cannot use his PSD while it is in this form, and the flying platform is focused on hovering with some minor thrust. It would take a redesign to support everything needed to create a true craft."

"Yeah. It worked well when I was in 1842, so no complaints here," said Dr. Snowden.

Emily chuckled. "I love my PSD."

"Wish I had one," said Jake.

Evaran interacted with his ARI after studying Jake for a moment. "I did not know you wanted to use one."

"Well, yeah, who wouldn't?"

V took off into the Torvatta and, a moment later, returned with a PSD.

Evaran motioned for V to give Jake the PSD. "This was used by Dr. Bryson on our last adventure. You can use it while on the Torvatta."

"Whoa! Awesome!" said Jake as he flipped the PSD around.

"It may take some getting used to."

"I already know how to use it," said Jake, grinning. "It's not my first time with it."

"Analysis. A future Evaran allowed you to use it."

Jake licked his lips. "I can't say."

The group chuckled.

Evaran gestured at the flying platform. "Okay. Let us go. V, we will hopefully see you soon."

"Acknowledged."

Emily high-fived V, and the others followed her lead as she boarded. She sighed as V's lights dimmed when the door sealed. It hurt her heart to see V sad, even if this was what needed to happen.

She checked out the interior. Two rows of seats lined the sides with a clear aisle in the middle separating them. One seat at the front was immediately behind the PSD, and Evaran took that seat. Dr. Snowden and Jake sat in the first row, and she sat on the left side of the second row while Jelton plopped down on the other side. As far as transports went, she liked it.

The flying platform hovered before it slowly moved forward into the portal.

Emily's breathing became heavier as the environment around the boulder disappeared. She was glad they were on the platform as the new surrounding came into focus. The platform hovered over a massive chasm, and the portal sat high up on what she figured was a rock wall of some type.

Off in the distance were dark gray cone-shaped structures of various sizes. Dark green spherical crystals jutted out of the structures and provided dim illumination, giving the place an overall dreary appearance. The platform's lighting made shadows dance on the wall behind them.

"This is interesting," said Dr. Snowden. He peered over the edge. "I'm glad we didn't walk through."

"Yeah, me too," said Jake.

"This is a unique environment," said Jelton.

Emily agreed with Jelton's assessment. "How did Ziekah get to the portal across this?"

Evaran pointed off to the side. "There is a point where this wall meets the open area ahead. We are going there now. I am using Ziekah's route through the connection as my guide."

Emily studied the chasm as it began to close the further they flew. It was apparent that Ziekah could run along a vertical wall in the form she used in the connection. Emily noticed something moving on one of the massive cone structures in the distance. They were not alone. She wondered about the walking part they would switch to, but for the moment, it looked like they had a flight path between the cones.

The flying platform reached the intersection of the open area and the wall.

"Ziekah must have some serious rock climbing skills!" said Jake.

Emily laughed. "I was just thinking that. If it was us, we would grapple above the portal and pull ourselves across."

"Yep!"

The flying platform entered the dense cone maze.

Emily got a closer look at the cones. They were made up of something resembling rock with a type of fibrous material that wove in and out of the structure. It reminded her of rope embedded in rock.

The creatures skittering around made her skin crawl. Most were insect-like, but she spotted what seemed like squirrels with fangs and horns. A few creatures flew around that resembled vultures, but much bigger. Small pools of brown liquid lay scattered at the base of the cones, and a thick mat of slick foliage and what looked like red moss or algae covered the floor. This environment did not seem friendly to humans.

Dr. Snowden shook his head. "This place is like a nightmare."

Jelton chuckled. "Nightmare connections to nightmare lands."

"Good point," said Dr. Snowden.

Emily spotted a group of large creatures below. "There's the Croniks."

"Do not worry. We will not interact with them," said Evaran.

"Yeah, let's not tangle with them," said Dr. Snowden.

Jelton laughed as he slapped Dr. Snowden on the back.

Emily always got a kick out of seeing Jelton laugh at Dr. Snowden's comments. The Croniks did not seem like a laughing matter, though.

They continued on for twenty minutes without incident.

Emily flinched when something smashed into the cone they were near. "What was that?" She peered over the edge.

"It appears we have the Croniks' attention. They are throwing some type of rocks at us," said Evaran.

Jake stumbled out of his seat when the platform tilted to the right.

"Brace yourself. This is going to be rough," said Evaran.

Emily planted a foot in the center aisle and the other in front of her while placing a hand on the back of her seat. Several Croniks had gathered below and were pulling clumps of the ground out and tossing it at the platform. Evaran was able to guide the platform around the tossed material, and he used other cones as cover. The Croniks' speed surprised her for something that large. She focused on the massive wall that seemed to stretch from the floor to the ceiling and across the whole area.

"We are approaching the divide," said Evaran. "There is a passageway we will go through, but this platform cannot fit through."

Emily peeked behind and observed the Croniks hustling to catch up to the platform. "Let's get there before the Croniks, then."

"It will be close. Once we are at the passageway, we need to get inside quickly."

Emily gazed at the divide as it got closer. It looked like it had the consistency of meatloaf. Holes covered a decent portion of the surface, which made her wonder if the Anwarks made the holes.

Evaran pulled the flying platform up to one of the holes and turned the platform around so its door was next to the hole. "Ziekah came through this one. When I open the door, go into the hole."

The door slid open.

Emily and Jelton were the first through, with Dr. Snowden and Jake following.

Evaran shot a grappling beam at the ceiling of the hole's entrance. With the press of a button, Dr. Snowden's PSD collapsed back into its pen shape. Evaran reeled himself into the passageway and motioned forward.

"Move!" he said as he handed Dr. Snowden back his PSD.

A massive clump of debris hit the hole's entrance after they moved in some.

"Wow. That was kinda close," said Jake.

Evaran nodded. "They are persistent per Ziekah. However, we are now in the Anwarks' territory. Although we do not need to go too far before we are on the other side of the divide, I suspect the Anwarks will detect us. Be alert. I will take point."

Emily exhaled as she puffed her cheeks. Fighting worm-like aliens in a meatloaf-like divide was not on the top of her list of fun things to do. The tunnel they were in was dark, and the only illumination came from the area they had flown in from. The Croniks continued to toss debris, and some of it landed inside, but the group had moved in far enough to avoid it. She hoped they did not run into any Anwarks and their trip through was without incident, but she knew that would probably not happen.

Jelton squeezed her arm.

She smiled as she nodded and focused on the trip ahead.

25

Jelton reflected on how different the connection experience was for the Ravaw he had ordered through in his timeline versus what he saw before him. They had not even gotten to the junction dimension, and only traveled as far as they could before returning. He grimaced as he remembered only one exiting. So far this trip had gone well, although he knew that if they walked to the tunnel they were in, the Croniks would have been a major threat.

Emily seemed remarkably calm, and even Dr. Snowden was relaxed. Jake's erratic movements showed he was nervous, but given what they had seen so far and how alien the environment was, Jelton understood. Evaran was calm as always and moved with purpose. Like other Rift Guardians, Jelton saw Evaran as a god in mortal form, and walking through an unfamiliar and hostile area with no fear was what Jelton would have expected from Evaran.

The group marched through several tunnels.

Jelton observed that the tunnels enlarged the further they moved in. He also picked up chittering sounds in the distance. There did not seem to be any coherent design to the tunnels, and they seemed to split off or join in a random pattern. Thankfully Evaran had Ziekah's journey to draw on to lead the group through.

The group paused when Evaran raised his hand.

Jelton could sense something in the wall as well.

Evaran motioned at Jake. "Step away from the wall."

Jake did so.

"Everyone, get behind me," said Evaran.

The group complied.

The wall vibrated near where Jake had stood. A moment later, a hole formed and an Anwark popped through.

Jelton grimaced at the brown-and-green Anwark. Chitin plates on segmented rolls covered its wormlike body. Massive pincers resided on the front roll, with multiple black beady eyes surrounding it. The thin, sinewy tendrils on each segment seemed more geared for manipulating the environment than for usage as legs.

The Anwark emitted a piercing shriek as it focused on the group.

"Move!" said Evaran.

He took off with the others in tow.

Jelton pulled out his dual pistols. He did not want to have to fight in a cramped tunnel but would do so if needed.

The group moved with determination as it rushed through several intersections. They eventually burst into a large room.

Jelton did not like the unusual structures near the end of the room. They were covered in holes with Anwarks popping in and out. The Anwarks varied in size, with smaller ones on the structure, and much larger ones, relative to the one from the tunnel, on the ground outside the structures. The larger ones possessed additional spikes on each of their back segments.

"What the heck is all this?" asked Dr. Snowden.

"It is a nursery of some sort," said Evaran. He pointed at a tunnel between two of the structures. "Ziekah came through there. I will use the new pattern for this area, so follow me with shields out and be prepared to fight if need be."

Jelton gripped his pistols as the group stood back.

Evaran moved forward and extended his utility handle. A block of metal was created and then dropped to the ground with the grappling beam attached to it. He raised his arm and began to swing in small circles. The grappling hammer whizzed by in a circle over Evaran. He marched on.

Several Anwarks challenged Evaran and moved toward him.

The first Anwark to reach Evaran was knocked away by the grappling hammer. Another flared its quills out and approached Evaran, then got knocked out.

"Let's go!" said Emily.

The group gave Evaran enough room to clear a path.

Jelton observed Dr. Snowden take the right side with his human-sized energy shield out. Emily took the front, while Jake positioned himself on the left. Everyone had their PSDs in their right hand and ready to fire. Jelton aimed both dual pistols behind the group. He liked the formation, as it provided defense against flanking, and there should be nothing coming from behind if they were cleared out.

The sounds of the Anwarks getting hit by Evaran's grappling hammer filled the air.

Emily, Dr. Snowden, and Jake began to fire repulsion blasts at Anwarks who rushed in behind Evaran.

Jelton focused on the several Anwarks that dashed in from behind. He unloaded a volley on them, causing them to turn away. He peered behind and saw that they were getting close to the tunnel on the other side. Unfortunately, the Anwarks were agitated, and their piercing screams filled the air.

Jake tumbled as six Anwarks rushed him.

Dr. Snowden turned around and fired a repulsion blast, sending the Anwarks back.

Jelton helped Jake up, then shoved him away as a smaller Anwark fell from the ceiling and smashed Jelton into the ground.

The Anwark flexed its quills.

Jelton grimaced as some of the quills penetrated his armor. He tried to roll to the side, but the quills pinned him.

Emily hit the Anwark with a grappling beam and yanked the Anwark off.

Jelton's vision blurred.

"Whoa," said Jake.

Dr. Snowden and Jake pulled out the quills stuck in Jelton, then helped him to his feet.

"Are you okay?" asked Emily, running her hands over the quill wounds.

"I...I think so," said Jelton. "Those quills hurt."

Emily looked up. "Always the ceiling. C'mon!"

Jelton stumbled.

Dr. Snowden put an arm around Jelton on the left, while Jake got the right. They abandoned their shields and wielded their PSDs in their free arm. As they moved, they shot repulsion and stun beams.

Emily fired sticky globules behind them, which trapped several Anwarks creeping up.

Jelton squinted as he grimaced. Fire flared through him. His body tried to absorb whatever poison had been injected into him. He did not like the painful side effect.

Evaran reached the tunnel and then joined the others in firing at the Anwarks, which were beginning to swarm. He fired a mist beam past Dr. Snowden, which Emily lit up.

Anwarks shrieked as they stopped moving.

Evaran scanned Jelton as they pulled him into the tunnel.

Emily laid down a large mass of sticky globules outside the entrance. As each wave of Anwarks got caught on it, she reapplied it until the tunnel entrance was covered.

"You have an unusual poison in you meant to melt the divide material. Your natural healing ability is fighting it. However, we need to get you to the Torvatta soon."

"That sounds like a good idea," said Jelton, grimacing.

"That woulda been me. I wouldn't have survived that," said Jake. "You took the hit for me."

"You are safe, my friend."

Emily scooped up Jelton. "I got you."

Jake laid a hand on Jelton's shoulder.

Evaran motioned forward. "The exit to the divide is ahead. Let us go."

Jelton tried to focus, but he now understood what was in him. The Anwarks spewed the poison to soften or weaken the divide's material to form tunnels. Now that poison was trying to weaken him.

The rift crystals in him fought back, and he suspected he would pull through this, but he understood how in his weakened state, he would have died if left alone. He could see

Emily's look of defiance on the inside of his helmet. Being a liability was not something he had planned for, but he was thankful to be with this group.

Dr. Snowden breathed a sigh of relief when they exited the divide thirty minutes later. The Anwarks had taken a while to chew through the glued ones to break into the tunnel, but by then, the group had reached an exit point. Although the bright environment suggested he could lower his helmet, he kept it up. Red and green grass lay ahead, with rocky outcroppings rising out of the ground at various points.

The exit was embedded in a cliff, so the group grappled down to the grass and moved away from the divide.

The floating boulders in the sky caught Dr. Snowden's attention. He was not sure how that was possible, but then again, he had just fought worms with porcupine-like quills. In the distance, he thought he glimpsed a body of water. Grasslands with the occasional outcropping covered everywhere else.

"This is much different than the first two areas," said Jake.

Evaran nodded. "From here, we can fly to the exit. Dr. Snowden, please form the flying pattern."

Dr. Snowden complied.

After everyone had boarded, the platform hovered and took off.

Dr. Snowden and Jake sat on the left side, while Jelton and Emily were on the other side. Emily knelt next to Jelton as he slumped in his seat. He seemed to be in pain. Having the equivalent of acid in the body would do that. Dr. Snowden figured if the Anwark struck him or Emily, their nanobots would have kicked in, but he was not sure how effective that would have been, and he had no desire to find out.

Dr. Snowden peered over the side and caught a glimpse of the environment from a bird's-eye view. Several herds of strange hoofed animals stomped around. They reminded him of cows, except these had beaks and tails with spikes. Birds, or what he thought were birds, flew above. It puzzled him how such disparate environments coexisted.

He peered back at the divide. It reached all the way up past the point that he could see. He imagined that the two sides had been carved out of the divide. As curious as he was to understand the place, and some of the creatures in it along with the scientific processes at play, he wanted to get back to the Torvatta to help Jelton.

After thirty minutes, the platform reached one of the rocky outcroppings on the ground.

Dr. Snowden studied the outline of a squiggly area on the slanted rock surface. No creatures were around, and it would have been difficult to know a portal existed without looking hard.

It made sense why crossings between realms was not more common. Most would have died if they tried to cross the connection, and they would not know where to go in the first place. Ziekah must have had some ability to detect the portals, and with her unusual form, she moved fast, something highly valuable in a place like this.

The platform landed.

Emily scooped up Jelton as the platform receded into the PSD.

Evaran handed Dr. Snowden his PSD. "Per Ziekah's memory, the portal on the other side is in the side of a tree, but there is ground. We can cross over on foot."

"Let's do this!" said Emily.

Evaran nodded and waved forward.

Dr. Snowden followed everyone through the portal. It seemed strange to fall into a rock surface that was angled, but when he appeared on the other side, he was standing on the ground beside a massive tree. The sounds immediately caught his attention, as did the sight of other large trees with vegetation everywhere. His helmet showed extreme humidity and a high temperature, two conditions that would make sweating useless. He appreciated his suit's air conditioning even more.

Small bug-like creatures scuttled around, and his cosmic senses let him know about the abundant amount of life around. The vines that appeared on some of the trees made him swallow hard, but they were not moving.

Evaran pulled the quantum beacon out of his backpack. "The beacon has activated. V should be here momentarily."

Ten minutes later, V appeared on the inside of Dr. Snowden's helmet. "Analysis. I am coming to you."

"V, it is good to hear you," said Evaran. "I am sending you information for the medical lab. Jelton has been injured and will need the medical nanobots programmed."

"Acknowledged."

A few minutes later, the Torvatta hovered in the large gap between the trees.

Emily hustled to the Torvatta after it landed. The group followed her.

Dr. Snowden's muscles relaxed as he stepped onto the Torvatta's ramp. He lowered his helmet and took a deep breath. Although he appreciated the suit, sometimes it could be claustrophobic if worn for a long time. He sensed Jake had the same sensation from how fast he lowered his helmet.

Emily was a blur as she rushed to the medical lab. Dr. Snowden followed her in. She laid Jelton on the medical slab, and V, in projected mode, jabbed Jelton in the arm with a syringe and accessed the slab's side console.

Holographic body layers appeared above Jelton.

It intrigued Dr. Snowden to see an exotic energy layer.

"Analysis. The medical nanobots have begun working."

Dr. Snowden observed the nanobots circulating through the body. They appeared as blinking red dots in the layers. A solid black layer with affected areas colored dim blue made everything easier to see.

Emily gestured at the exotic energy layer. "That's new."

Evaran nodded. "Due to how many people we get in here that have exotic energy, I decided to add the layer for a better analysis."

"Kreagan nanobot programming could use that," said Jake. "I don't even think most of their medical wards can detect exotic energy."

"That changes in the next thirty years," said Evaran.

"Really? What causes them to be able to detect them?"

"Blake Brown."

Jake nodded.

Dr. Snowden had heard Blake's name several times and figured he was part of some wild event that elevated him to a high status, enough so that the Kreagans took notice.

Jelton grunted. "It hurts, but I'm starting to feel somewhat normal again."

Emily held his hand.

Dr. Snowden focused his gaze on the solid black layer. When the nanobots reached the affected areas, they turned the area black. "So how are they fighting the poison?"

Evaran stood next to the slab and gestured at the exotic energy layer. "The nanobots are carrying small doses of a chemical that will interact with the Anwark poison and neutralize it into something that Jelton's body can naturally process."

"I guess if you know a body's profile and what went into it, the nanobots are the perfect delivery system," said Dr. Snowden.

Jake chuckled. "You'd be surprised at how big the field of medical nanobot programming is. Just getting all the body profiles and understanding what chemicals to use or what operations to performs is a daunting task, and that's not counting whatever quirks an individual has. Thankfully, an AI can handle all that part, assuming you have a medical AI. If not, you rely on a medbot programmer, or at least that's what we called 'em back when I was on Jell's station."

Dr. Snowden nodded. "Medbot programmer. I like that name."

Jelton smiled. "They're working fast." He cracked his neck.

Dr. Snowden checked the black layer, which showed almost all the affected areas cleared. "Wow, they do work fast."

"They are not rebuilding anything," said Evaran. "If you recall, Dr. Bryson had broken bones, which took some time. In this scenario, only a delivery is needed."

After a few minutes, Jelton sat up and stretched. He slid off the slab. "I'm good."

"Excellent," said Evaran. "Let us go to the command center."

The group complied.

Evaran, in his command chair, motioned forward. "V, extend the shields to the portal and pulse them."

"Acknowledged."

The visual outline of the shield extended past the tree and pulsed. The portal, which had appeared as a squiggly outline, dissipated.

"Take us to the entry point on Gezelrus in our timeline," said Evaran.

"Acknowledged."

The Torvatta rose. After ten minutes, it reached a sufficient height to open a portal and fly through. After another twenty minutes, it approached the boulder where the portal resided.

"Repeat the same action on this portal as the last one," said Evaran.

"Acknowledged."

The Torvatta landed and extended its shields before pulsing. Like the last portal, this one faded away.

"It is done," said Evaran. "Connection denizens can no longer come into our timeline via the portal. Now we will do the same for the connection that links the Seeros League to the junction dimension. However, perhaps we should break for lunch and go over the next step."

"Works for me," said Jake.

Dr. Snowden rubbed his chin. It amazed him still how powerful the Torvatta was. The shielding dispelled portals, and he had seen rifts untangle due to shield pulsing. With

Ziekah locked up and the connection shut down, he breathed easier. The next segment of the trip might involve interacting with the Seeros League. The thought of seeing any version of Seeros would be unpleasant, but if that was what needed to be done, it would be done.

26

Emily munched on her beef-and-bean burrito as she relaxed in the conference room. Dr. Snowden and Jake had tacos while Jelton fidgeted with a chicken burrito. Emily did not know if her choice of lunch had inspired anyone else to get similar food, but it had happened without discussion. V was in projected mode and sat on the left side of the table along with her and Jelton, while Dr. Snowden and Jake had the other side. Evaran sat at the head of the table as always. It had been a short twenty-five-minute break, but lunch had invigorated her.

Evaran looked around. "With Jelton better, we can move on to our next step." He interacted with the table console.

A projection shot up of a black rectangular area filled with a pattern of rootlike green branches with spikes on them.

"This is what I sketched from Ziekah's memories of the connection between the Seeros League's reality and the junction dimension. It is populated with branches of some sort that have thorns on them."

A line appeared that stretched from one end of the area to the other.

Evaran motioned at the line. "That is the path Ziekah took. If you notice, there are small silver dots scattered around. Those are automated turrets that fire on anyone not authenticated."

Dr. Snowden's eyes narrowed. "And how do we get authenticated?"

"We will not. With the flying platform, we can use the branches as cover to break line of sight. There are one or two turrets that will need to be disabled, but the others can be avoided," said Evaran.

"Looks like a briar patch," said Emily.

"An apt analogy," said Evaran.

The projection changed to show a room with a circular metallic ring standing vertically.

"Once we exit the connection, we will be in what Ziekah refers to as a dimensional portal room. She seemed to possess little information on the facility overall, and she did not know all of its defenses. I suspect that is by design."

"So we're going in sorta blind," said Jake.

Evaran nodded.

Jelton studied the projection. "We secure the portal room, then, until V arrives."

"That is my thought. However, if it is a planet that this facility resides on, the Torvatta will be popped into orbit upon entry, and its descent may take some time. Twenty minutes at a minimum."

Jelton smiled. "We can hold out that long."

The projection changed to show the portion of the facility layout.

"Perhaps. However, this is Seeros and his alternate timeline versions we are dealing with," said Evaran. He pointed at a room further in. "If need be, we can retreat to here. It has one entry point and seems to have multiple workstations there."

"We got this," said Emily, cracking her neck.

"I appreciate everyone's confidence, but there are a lot of unknown variables. I suspect they kept Ziekah in the dark for these types of situations and potentially others."

Dr. Snowden sighed. "I'm not looking forward to seeing Seeros again."

Evaran nodded. "Although there are alternate versions of him there, Ziekah did note that the guards were robotic."

"Seeros probably didn't trust anyone else but robots," said Emily. "That would definitely be his personality."

"I concur. After you finish your lunch, we can leave in two hours. Assemble on the roof at that time."

"The roof?" asked Jake.

Evaran half smiled. "We will be flying over the junction dimension. The roof offers a good viewing spot."

"Gotcha," said Jake. He gestured at Jelton. "I wanted to say thanks again for pushing me out of the way."

Jelton nodded. "Of course, my friend."

Jake puffed his cheeks. "I'm not sure I woulda handled that poison as well as you."

"We can find out if you wish," said Evaran.

Jake eyed Evaran, who half smiled.

"Yeah, no, thanks!" said Jake.

The group chuckled.

"Okay, meet in two hours," said Evaran.

Resting time whizzed by for Emily. She spent some of it relaxing with Jelton in her living quarters. It seemed his mind was elsewhere, but she understood that he was probably still in fight mode. The discussion on the encounter might have contributed to that. Everyone had assembled on the roof, including V in projected mode. A quick peek outside the shielding showed they were in Gezelrus's orbit.

"V, take us to the junction dimension," said Evaran.

"Acknowledged," said V.

The Torvatta opened a portal and flew through.

Emily hustled over to the guardrail and peered out. She was not sure what she was seeing. It looked like someone had cut strips of land and haphazardly connected them. The strips extended as far as she could see. Outside of them, it was dark and misty.

"I wasn't expecting this," she said.

"Yeah, no kidding," said Dr. Snowden, adjusting his glasses.

Evaran pointed at the nearest strip. "This junction dimension seems to be made up of these strips, like a ribbon of sorts."

"How far does it extend?" asked Jelton.

"Per the Torvatta's reading on entry, about the size of Milkomeda, so it is relatively small compared to our reality."

Dr. Snowden drew his head back. "Really? That's…wow."

Emily wrinkled her brow at Dr. Snowden, then at Evaran. "Milkomeda?"

"An elliptical galaxy formed when the Andromeda and Milky Way galaxies collide in approximately 4.5 billion years," said Evaran.

"That sounds huge, and these strips just exist everywhere here?" asked Emily.

Evaran nodded. "Note that areas nearest a portal take on some of the connection's properties." He pointed at a mountain as they flew over it. "The second area in the connection had grasslands, mountains, and the like. You can view its influences here."

"But...I see clouds, and it looks like daylight, but there's no sun," said Emily.

Evaran half smiled. "Observe."

On the Torvatta's interior shielding, a U-shaped shield appeared over the strips.

"The junction dimension void is what is outside the encapsulated strips. Its interaction with the strips, up to a certain distance, provides light and an atmosphere based on the connection. When we go to the area where Seeros's connection is, you will notice a remarkably different strip area."

"Huh," said Emily.

"Definitely different physics at play here," said Dr. Snowden.

"Not so much different as unknown, relative to human knowledge from your time period," said Evaran.

The Torvatta flew for another forty minutes until it reached the portal to the connection linking where they were to the Seeros League's reality.

Emily studied the stark contrast from what she had seen when they had first arrived. It looked like a massive briar patch on the land strips.

"Whoa," she said.

Jake shook his head. "This seems like a place you never want to get lost in."

"We are in agreement," said Jelton.

"Analysis. We need to burn through to reach the portal. In order to provide room to form the flying platform, I recommend extending the shield's radius."

Evaran nodded at V. "Proceed."

The Torvatta's shields fluctuated as it descended. Its shielding burnt the branches, causing them to turn black, then crumble. After ten minutes, it reached the ground before a massive rootlike structure. A squiggly outline appeared on the trunk.

Evaran looked around. "Get your gear and assemble on the ramp."

Emily hustled to get her gear on, and after getting a quick drink and relieving herself, she assembled on the ramp with the others. Creatures scurrying around outside the shielding caught her eye. Large animals would not survive as the mass of vines, branches, and roots was too thick. The Torvatta, though, had cleared out the surrounding area.

"Dr. Snowden, form the flying platform," said Evaran.

"Acknowledged," said Dr. Snowden with a serious face as he complied.

V tilted his head.

Dr. Snowden grinned. "I'm teasing you."

"It is quite okay," said V.

Everyone high-fived V before boarding.

Emily's heart sagged when V looked down with a frown. She knew he wanted to come, but he was needed on the Torvatta to get them when they came out on the other side. He must have felt left out, and a part of her wanted to stay with him. However, she would be needed in the upcoming fight, if there was one. She sighed as the platform door sealed.

Evaran peered back. "Is everyone ready?"

Everyone indicated they were.

"To the connection, then."

The platform hovered, then moved through the portal.

Emily was glad the portals were large enough for the flying platform. When the platform passed through, she studied the new environment. Massive rootlike branches, similar to the ones outside the connection, weaved and connected everywhere. The land strips were gone, so it seemed like the branches were in space. Large thorns with an odd glow stuck out. Her helmet interior outlined several small life forms.

"This place is creepy," she said.

Jake looked around. "Yeah. I know I said it before, but I think this wins the award for places I would never want to be lost in."

The platform moved forward, dodging branches and avoiding the thorns.

Dr. Snowden shook his head. "So Ziekah traveled through this without a ship or platform?"

"She did," said Evaran. "Her tendrils have sticky ends, so she could move fast and jump around with ease. I am sensing another presence here, but I cannot tell where it is. That is highly unusual."

"Great."

Emily grimaced as she imagined Ziekah hopping around. It boggled her mind how much knowledge and skill would was needed to traverse not only the connections but the junction dimension as well. On top of that, portal detection skills were required.

Although Emily appreciated the skill set Ziekah must have possessed to do what she did, Emily still disliked Ziekah.

Emily gripped her PSD. She sensed something like Evaran did, but she could not pinpoint it. Hopefully it was nothing.

* * *

Jake's skin crawled at the unusual sounds he heard. The connection between the junction dimension and the Seeros League's reality seemed more dangerous than the previous one they had been in. His helmet interior highlighted small bug-like creatures scurrying around the branches, and with the low light, the place appeared to be a death trap. It bothered him that despite the ability to see ahead, every direction showed branches and thorns.

It took ten minutes to reach the first turret.

Jake noticed the uneasy silence of the group. They probably felt what he did. The temperature showed it to be around thirty degrees Fahrenheit, so in addition to the dark, it was cold. Thankfully the platform's kinetic shielding kept the inside of the platform warmer.

The platform hovered behind a massive branch.

Evaran faced the group. "The first turret is around this branch and back a bit. This platform is too slow to fly past, and we cannot take fire. However, I have an idea, but it needs testing. I will be right back."

He exited the platform and jumped onto the branch. After extending his arm off to the right, palm forward, he projected a silver sphere.

Jake's eyes widened when he saw a red beam scan the sphere. Projectiles passed through a moment later. The sound of the turret firing was much louder than he expected. The fact he could hear it at all meant there was a medium for sound to travel through.

Evaran shut off the projection. "It seems the turret performs a scan before shooting, even on a hologram. We can use that to our advantage. I will distract it while the platform moves off to an angle where everyone can shoot stun beams at the turret. Use your shields as well." He gestured at Dr. Snowden. "As your PSD is being used, you can pilot, and you will need to disable the top part of the platform."

"Uhh…okay," said Dr. Snowden.

Evaran looked around. "Everyone understand?"

Everyone indicated they did.

Dr. Snowden took Evaran's seat and grabbed the PSD handle. He accessed the pattern builder and removed the platform's top. The temperature drop was noticeable, but his suit handled it.

Evaran extended his arm and projected the sphere again. This time, it flew around in the air.

The turret fired on the sphere.

"Go!" said Evaran over comms.

Dr. Snowden navigated the platform to the left and up a bit before angling it so that Jake, Emily, and Jelton could fire. They already had their energy shields out and over the platform's guardrails.

Jake gulped when the turret came into view. It had two barrels embedded in a metallic block that sat on a rotating platform. The barrels looked like they could move up and down, and with the swiveling ability of the platform, the turret could hit many angles. Thankfully for the group, it was busy focusing on Evaran's projection.

"Fire!" said Evaran.

Emily fired a stun beam at the turret while Jake and Jelton fired their weapons.

The concentrated salvo overwhelmed the turret, causing its barrels to stop firing.

Dr. Snowden swung the platform back to pick up Evaran.

Once Evaran was on board, they moved out.

"That worked well," said Jelton.

"Yes, but there are seven more to go. Without Ziekah's memories, I suspect these would have been fatal encounters," said Evaran.

Dr. Snowden sighed as he retook his seat. "I get that feeling too. Just trying to move around on these branches without a platform or grappling beam would be a nightmare." He shook his head. "Everything seems like a nightmare out here."

"This will be over soon, I hope," said Emily, squeezing Dr. Snowden's arm.

He nodded.

Over the next two hours, the group handled four more turrets with the same tactic.

"So far, so good," said Emily.

Jake chuckled. "They're not quite as dangerous once you get the hang of them."

Evaran raised a hand.

Everyone went silent.

Evaran stood and looked around. "The presence I sensed earlier is now stronger."

"I saw some bug things scurrying about earlier," said Jake.

"This is something bigger."

Jelton peered over the edge. "I sense it now too." He pointed at a bulge in the nearest branch that pulsed toward them like a wave. "Something there, but I don't see anything other than that bulge coming our way."

Jake did not like the appearance of the bulge that moved through the branches. It reminded him of a snake that had swallowed an egg that traversed the length of the snake's body.

As if on cue, one of the large thorns shot up out of the branch when the bulge hit it. The thorn was connected by a thick musclelike tendril, and sharp armlike appendages splayed out to the side. The thorn dipped so that its sharp point was toward the platform and then thrust itself forward.

The platform flew up and evaded the thorn.

Several other thorns ahead of them began to wiggle.

"It seems that something can travel in the branches and use the thorns," said Evaran. "I am adding the top part of the flying platform back."

Thorns began to burst out from the branches around them and shoot toward the platform. Some hit the kinetic shielding and fell back.

They moved forward until several of the thorns had wrapped around and immobilized the platform.

Jake was glad they had kinetic shielding and the top part back, but they were not going anywhere with the thorns immobilizing them.

Evaran stood and moved to the sealed door. He unsealed it and extended his glowing hand to touch a thorn.

The thorn jerked back and slid off the platform's shielding.

Evaran exited and jumped on the platform's roof. Once there, he ran around touching the other thorns.

Once they had been removed, he said, "Dr. Snowden, move us forward."

Dr. Snowden complied.

Evaran rejoined the group and took his spot back at the front.

Jake observed that the thorns ahead of them did not wiggle. "I think your glowing hands made whatever that was back off."

"I concur," said Evaran. "There is a creature or energy of some sort that seems to be able to move inside the branch structure."

"Ziekah's memories had no recollection of that thing?" asked Emily.

Evaran shook his head. "They did not. The turrets seem to keep the creature or energy away. As we have disabled five turrets, I suspect the creature came to investigate and found us."

Dr. Snowden chuckled. "Vines…and now thorns. Plants love me."

"Now that we are aware of the creature, we will move on immediately after defeating a turret."

"Sounds good," said Dr. Snowden.

Jake wondered how the Seeros League had set up the turrets. They would have run into the creature, and it seemed they understood how to keep it away. He suspected Ziekah might have had a hand in that.

Over the next hour, the group handled the last three turrets.

"We are almost at the portal to the Seeros League's reality," said Evaran.

"Finally," said Emily.

"This connection is well defended," said Jelton. "It had natural defenses, along with turrets. The Seeros League has probably never had someone other than Ziekah or another Seeros come through."

"We're going to be a big surprise," said Jake. "If they have what I know of Seeros defense systems, it's going to be rough."

Dr. Snowden sighed. "And of course, they did not seem to trust Ziekah enough to show her the scope of the defenses. I guess we're going to find out."

Jelton laid a hand on Dr. Snowden's shoulder. "We fight together, just as we did against the Mortani, my friend."

Dr. Snowden nodded.

Jake was reassured to have Jelton along. He always seemed confident, and his fearlessness was admirable. Jake's breathing got heavier as the platform approached the portal, which was now visible in the distance. Evaran had marked the portal's location, so it showed up as a squiggly outline on a massive branch. Jake suspected there was about to be a lot of fighting, and he hoped he would be able to show his improved skills since the last time he had fought alongside Evaran.

"We are almost there," said Evaran. "Prepare yourselves and get your shields out. Dr. Snowden will fly us through, and once we arrive, we will form a defensive circle. Emily, you have the left side, Dr. Snowden, the right. Jelton, you have the rear, and Jake, you take the center. I will handle the front."

Jake's heartbeat accelerated as Emily and Jelton got ready. Jake cracked his neck as he gripped his PSD. He bet that the others could detect his breathing increase and general state of anxiety, but no one said anything about it. That was just how the group was, and he was glad to be a part of it.

27

Jelton's eyes narrowed as the flying platform went through the portal. The first thing he noticed was that they came through a ring-shaped structure. The floor, walls, and ceiling were metallic panels, and a large doorway resided ahead of them. A guardrail encircled the area but left enough space for them to land.

The bright room had turrets, similar to the ones from the connection, along the upper part of the wall near the ceiling. Smaller sealed side doors resided to their left, right, and behind them.

After the platform landed, Dr. Snowden pulled it back into his PSD and the group formed around Jake. Evaran stood with his shield out and utility handle in his right hand. Emily had her shield ready and her PSD formed into a baton on the left side. Dr. Snowden stood to the right, while Jelton focused behind them. Although everyone had their helmets up, they were still able to communicate via comms. He sensed movement outside the room despite the immediate vicinity being clear.

A blue light pulsed from the ring, and the large front door sealed shut. Green gas spewed into the air.

"Stay calm," said Evaran. "The gas is meant to incapacitate an Antigulan, but your suits should be able to handle it."

"Should we switch on camouflage shielding?" asked Emily.

Jelton shook his head. "The gas will show our movement. I also noticed that the gas is cool, which will make us stand out more."

"I concur," said Evaran. "I believe they are curious about us. Nonetheless, the quantum beacon has activated, so V should be here soon."

After a few tense moments, Jelton relaxed as vents on the walls sucked the gas back. He turned around and faced forward along with the rest of the group.

A hologram of a humanoid male in a white robe appeared. A metallic belt segmented the robe, and thin metallic strips outlined various body areas. The male had silver hair and pale skin, and his hands were covered by a thin black mesh. His metallic boots and shoulder pauldrons made him appear bigger than he actually was.

"Seeros!" said Emily.

Jelton sensed Emily and Dr. Snowden's increased heart rates.

"Stay where you are," said Evaran. He strode forward and stood a bit away from Seeros. "You are Seeros."

The humanoid eyed Evaran. "Seeros-1, actually. I'm surprised you know something about me, and you can speak fluently as well..."

Evaran nodded. "I am Evaran, and I am using a translator to speak with you. We have dealt with Seeros before, another version that is, in our timeline. He no longer exists."

"Evaran…I can't say I recognize the name," said Seeros-1. He gestured at the group. "And who are your friends?"

"They do not need to be named."

Seeros-1 paced around with his hands behind his back. "I see. You wish to protect them. Your group's presence here means one of two things. You either ran into one of our extractors, which led you here, or you came here randomly."

"It was an extractor," said Evaran.

"I figured. What did they look like?"

"I cannot tell you that, but the extractor, as you refer to them, has been handled."

Seeros-1 paused to study the group. "Interesting. What is your purpose here, then?"

"To shut down this portal," said Evaran.

Seeros-1 stood straight. "Why?"

"Your extractors corrupt timelines."

Seeros-1 sighed. "So because one of our extractors affected your timeline, you're here for revenge? Is that it?"

Evaran shook his head. "Although I am mainly concerned about our timeline, I do try to stop chaos in general, which is what your extractors create. I have seen what type of timeline damage they can inflict. It must stop."

Seeros-1 chuckled. "Even if you do close the portal, the extractors are from the dimension beyond the one outside this portal. They'll continue to do what they do."

"I suspected they were native denizens of the junction dimension. Thank you for confirming. In regard to them continuing their behavior, they might, but they will do so naturally, and not on orders to extract another version of yourself."

"Interesting viewpoint." Seeros-1 placed his hands behind his back again and smiled. "So you're aware, you were scanned on arrival." He gestured at the group. "They have advanced suits that can't be penetrated, although we got some basic readings. However, you...you're something unique."

"So I have heard."

"Powerful beings stopping in is not new to us," said Seeros-1. He gestured out in an arc. "It's taken into account when we design or do anything. So far, nothing has beaten the collective intelligence of the Seeros League, and I don't think you will be the one to do it either."

Evaran tilted his head. "You are very confident...and you are stalling."

Seeros-1 laughed. "Maybe you are smarter than you appear. Yes, something is coming to greet you." He raised a finger. "They may not be as *friendly* as me. You will be detained for research and then we can revisit whatever timeline you came from."

"You will not have that opportunity."

"And you say *I'm* confident?" asked Seeros-1 with an amused look. "I'm curious...do you even know where you are?"

Evaran looked around, then faced Seeros-1. "On a planet... deep underground."

Jelton watched Seeros-1 move his head back slightly. It was a subtle movement, but it seemed Seeros-1 had been surprised. Jelton had figured they were on a planet but was not sure how Evaran had determined they were underground.

"Impressive," said Seeros-1. "And how did you come to that conclusion?"

"I can feel the planet moving," said Evaran as his eyes slightly glowed. "However, the sensation is dulled somewhat due to being underground."

Jelton focused, but he did not sense movement around him other than the remaining small pockets of gases still being sucked away. It was a reminder of how fine-tuned Evaran's senses were.

Seeros-1 eyed Evaran. "Unlike your companions, you wear no armored suit. I suspect you are much more powerful than you are letting on."

"Was that factored into what is coming to greet us?" asked Evaran.

"Oh yes, of course. Unless you surprise us."

"Perhaps, then, while we wait, you will answer some questions."

Seeros-1 gestured at Evaran. "As you wish."

"How many Seeros versions have been extracted?" asked Evaran.

"Several thousand. I'm the first, and I founded the league."

Evaran nodded. "What is your intent with the league? Is it to only extract versions of yourself?"

Seeros-1 chuckled. "Of course not, but when you realize that you're the most unique individual in a timeline, it makes sense to gather all the versions in one spot to learn from each other. Each timeline version we extract adds to our uniqueness."

"Do you maintain a presence outside of this reality?"

"Of course we do. There is a lot to learn, and we can't do all of it from here."

Evaran paced around with his arms behind his back. "I see. What areas of knowledge do you learn about? I suspect other species do not interest you."

"Not unless they have advanced technology," said Seeros-1.

"So you are essentially centralizing information from across timelines," said Evaran. He waved his arm around in an arc. "That is what allows you to sustain your presence here, and build facilities like this. I do not believe you share your technology with those civilizations that you take it from."

Seeros-1 chuckled. "You're quite perceptive. And, no, we don't share with others. You've earned the information gleaned from this conversation, as it will not be going anywhere once you're detained. Once your usefulness has ended, you will be terminated."

Evaran nodded. "That will not occur, and whatever you have coming has arrived."

"We're impressed," said Seeros-1. "We now have a small betting game as to how long you and your group will last." Seeros-1 pointed at Emily and Jake. "I'm betting they go down first." Seeros-1 then gestured at Dr. Snowden. "He will go next, followed by the other unnamed one, then you will be last."

"You may be surprised."

Seeros-1 laughed. "I love your confidence. You speak to me as an equal, and perhaps you've earned that by just being where you are. However, this conversation is done. We can pick it up again once you've been captured."

Jelton gripped his pistols. Whatever was coming had numbers and was strong enough to send vibrations with each footstep.

Evaran rubbed his chin. "Prepare to be disappointed."

Seeros-1 laughed as his hologram faded.

Evaran faced the group. "There are large robots coming our way. Their configuration remains unknown, but there are many. They are also coming in from the sides and behind us."

"We're going to be surrounded!" said Jake.

"Yes. Our goal is to exit through the main front door ahead and get to the room we discussed earlier. It will provide a better defensive location."

"Where's V?" asked Dr. Snowden.

"I suspect, being where we are, communications have been dampened," said Evaran. He raised a finger. "However, the quantum beacon can still be tracked. That means that although V cannot contact us, he is on his way. It takes time to fly down from orbit, then burn through the ground. If my calculations are correct, it will take him a total of thirty-two minutes, fifteen of which has already been used talking to Seeros-1."

"You were stalling too!" said Emily.

Evaran half smiled. "Yes. We now have seventeen minutes, assuming I am correct and V has not run into anything that would slow him down." He turned his head to the side. "Get into battle formation. The turrets go down first."

The group complied.

Jelton looked around with unease. His battle experience reminded him that they were in a tough-to-defend spot. Dr. Snowden and Emily were weakened relative to the last fight they had had with the Mortani, and Jake, while determined, would not last long in a protracted fight. Evaran would be formidable as always, but Jelton suspected there would be some pain involved for the group. His eyes roamed the rear wall. Whatever it took, he would defend his friends.

Emily's pulse quickened as she focused on the left wall. Something behind the doors created vibrations that she could detect. There had also been an unusual buzz, which she interpreted from experience as robotic. Evaran had said that there would be robots, which made her wonder why it had taken so long for them to arrive.

Although it was harder to detect Dr. Snowden, Jake, and Jelton through their suits, she figured they were as anxious as her. No matter how much training or experience she had, a potential fight always amped her up. Evaran, with his never-moving hair, stood prominently nearby, and she felt confident with him at her side. Jelton's presence made things a little less tense, and she knew Dr. Snowden and Jake would do whatever was needed.

All the doors to the room rose up as the lights went out.

"Oh crap," said Jake over comms.

"Focus and adjust. Emily, disable the left front turret. Jelton, get the left rear one. Dr. Snowden, you are on the right rear one," said Evaran. He fired a stun beam at the right front turret, causing it to swivel a moment before stopping.

The rest of the group fired on their designated turrets.

Emily had not expected to be fighting in the dark, but her helmet adjusted. She was glad the turrets were out of commission as they could have fired a stream of whatever they fired and pinned the group down. Her attention focused on the doors on her side. Silver humanoid robots stormed out. Their smooth metallic skin seemed odd and reminded her of a Kreagan destroyer she had seen in an alternate timeline.

These were about her size, and they moved fast. Similar robots appeared from the rear and other side.

It was what arrived in the front that made her eyes widen. The new robots were different from the other robots she had seen. The new ones had two legs that reminded her of a chicken's legs, with a body on top that resembled a horizontal teardrop. An array of heavy weaponry sat on the sides of the body, with a horde of tendrils that ended in a variety of extensions sprouting out around the body. Her helmet identified the light shimmer around the robots as some type of shielding.

Evaran motioned forward. "I have the heavy defense robots ahead. Handle the light ones on the sides!"

He charged forward and used his shield to deflect projectiles and beams while using his grapple hammer to push back the heavy defense robots.

Emily focused on the light defense robots as they opened fire with some type of beam fired from their arms. She concentrated and angled her shield to reflect the beams back, knocking out some of the robots.

One of the light defense robots reached her and tried to grab her shield.

She fired a repulsion blast point-blank, which only pushed the robot back.

Another robot rushed in.

She tried a stun beam in a sweeping arc that hit both robots, causing them to stumble. Her eyes narrowed when the robots continued to move, but much slower. It seemed even the stun beam would not be enough. She switched to sticky globules and fired a mass in front of her.

The robots got stuck in the globules.

"Use the sticky globules!" she said.

She sprayed another round in front of her, using a similar tactic to the one used against the Anwarks earlier. She peered behind her and saw that Dr. Snowden was also forming a wall of robots that got stuck on each other. Jake fired the sticky globules nonstop behind the group, while Jelton mixed in shooting with his pistol and using his energy dagger to deal with any robots that got close. Evaran had moved far enough away that the gap between the grappling hammer and the group was small.

Dr. Snowden grunted when a robot leaped over the wall of stuck robots.

The robot kicked Dr. Snowden's PSD out of his hand and shoved him to the ground. Another robot jumped over and landed on Dr. Snowden's arm and began to stomp.

He cried out.

Emily spun around and charged forward. She formed a bladed end on her PSD and decapitated the robot before kicking it into the wall of stuck ones. She then chopped off the leg of the other robot while grabbing its arm and tossing it over the wall.

"Jelton! Cover him!" she said.

Jelton rushed over to Dr. Snowden and pulled him to the center.

"Jake, take Uncle Albert's spot," she said.

"On it," said Jake.

Emily moved back to her spot and continued to fire globules.

Any robot that leaped over met a quick end due to Jelton, who had switched to dual daggers.

Emily was impressed at how fast Jelton sliced the robots up. Each one he destroyed was added to the wall, and it did not take long before the wall encircled the group in a dome formation. She could see robots flying in the air in the distance. Sometimes it was just parts of them. She figured that was Evaran trying to clear a path.

The wall on Jake's side exploded as a heavy defense robot barreled through. It pierced Jake with one of its sharp tendrils.

Jake grunted and changed his PSD into a knife that cut off the tendril.

The robot kicked Jake back and then pivoted to fire on the group.

Dr. Snowden used his good arm to shoot a mass of globules on the front of the robot's body.

The robot began to move erratically.

Jelton jumped on top of the robot and spun around, slicing off all the tendrils before taking out the weaponry. He jumped off and took off one of its legs, then kicked it back through the breach.

Emily covered the robot in globules when it was in the breach, fusing it to the other stuck robots.

Jake struggled to stand.

Emily took a moment to pull Jake to the center. "Evaran! I don't know how much longer we can hold here! Uncle Albert and Jake are hurt!"

Evaran opened a tear in the wall of stuck robots in front of the group. He marched to the center. "I have taken out most of the heavy defense robots, but the light defense ones keep on coming. We will be swarmed if we stay. Emily, use Dr. Snowden's PSD to form a hover slab with high guardrails. We can transport Dr. Snowden and Jake in that."

"What's the plan to fight through to the main doorway?" asked Jelton.

"You and Emily will need to hunch over and stay close to me," said Evaran.

Emily grabbed Dr. Snowden's PSD and flipped through the patterns until she found the one Evaran had mentioned. A moment later, the hover slab with high guardrails had formed. She picked up Dr. Snowden and set him inside while Jelton helped Jake.

"We can still help," said Jake, taking a deep breath.

Evaran nodded. "You can fire from the slab. Dr. Snowden, stay down. Emily, take the left side, Jelton, the right. I will pull the slab. Everyone understand?"

Everyone indicated they did.

Evaran grabbed the slab and marched forward. When they were outside the glued robot dome, he swung his grappling hammer around.

Emily stuck close to the hover slab's left side. Once they had exited the circle of stuck robots, she fired globules behind the group as they moved forward. Jelton had switched back to his energy blade and pistol setup, and any robot that tried to sneak under Evaran's grappling hammer got shot. She noticed the broken bodies of the heavy defense robots. Evaran had all but crushed them.

Evaran reduced the radius of his grappling hammer as they neared the door. "Jake, are you okay to push?"

Jake took a deep breath. "Yeah, I think I can." He climbed out and got behind the slab.

When they arrived at the doorway, Evaran changed his grappling hammer into a staff and enlarged his forearm energy shield. He pushed into the hallway leading out of the portal room with the others in tow.

Emily wasted no time in blocking their retreat with a wall of sticky white globules while Jelton fired on any that got too close.

Robots tried to push through but got stuck.

Light defense robots in the hallway ahead were dealt with quickly when they got within range of Evaran.

"The room we need to get to is not far. Be alert!" said Evaran. He took off down a side hallway.

Emily's senses were on fire as she continued to fill the path behind them with a wall of sticky globules. Some robots had taken to trying to burn through the sticky globule wall, but the globules only hardened, making it even stronger. Sticky globules were one of the PSD's lesser-used pieces of functionality, but they had worked well in this scenario.

After thirty minutes, the group reached the designated room. They hustled in.

Emily and the others defended the sole entrance while Evaran ran around the room manually disabling every robot present. The few Seeroses that were present were stunned.

Once the room was cleared, Evaran scanned around and then smashed open a panel and cut several metallic tubes. With great effort, he cranked a manual lever to seal the door.

After the door sealed, Emily pulled Dr. Snowden out of the slab and then retracted the slab into his PSD, which she laid next to him. Jake slumped against the wall next to Dr. Snowden. Jelton stood next to Emily and gave her a quick hug. She enjoyed the momentary lull, although the pounding on the door from the robots in the hallway filled the room.

"Everyone relax," said Evaran. He motioned at some nearby workstations. "I am going to try to gather what I can, and see if I can contact V."

Emily sat next to Dr. Snowden, who cradled his arm. The fight had been far rougher than she had expected, and it angered her that Dr. Snowden appeared to have a broken arm. Jake held his side, and both seemed to be in pain. She had her own bruises and as tough as her suit was, she had taken a few hard hits. Without Evaran, they would have been captured. She shuddered at that thought.

Jelton sat next to her and put his arm around her.

She leaned into him and relaxed. The next step was to hold out until V arrived. She hoped Evaran could contact V soon as she was not sure how long the door would hold.

Dr. Snowden winced as he tried to move his arm. There were definitely some broken bones there, and the pain reverberated throughout his body. Thankfully his suit had helped prevent more damage; without it, he would probably have had his arm torn off. His nanobots were doing their best to heal him, and he was thankful that he could focus and calm himself down.

Evaran knelt next to Dr. Snowden and scanned his arm. "There are several breaks, but your nanobots are already working on healing them."

Dr. Snowden grunted. "Yeah…I can feel that."

Evaran scanned Jake. "You have bruising and a busted rib."

"It coulda been worse," said Jake, grimacing.

"Yes, it could have," said Evaran. He motioned at Emily. "The sticky globules were a good choice."

Emily sighed. "It's times like that where I wish I had my old cosmic energy levels."

Evaran laid a hand on her shoulder. "I understand." He faced Jelton. "You fought well."

Jelton smiled. "Enough to get us here. Now we need to determine where the Torvatta is."

"I concur," said Evaran.

He walked over to a workstation and interacted with it.

"Not going to use your UIC?" asked Emily.

Evaran shook his head. "It will not work here based on my previous scan. However, I can navigate this interface."

A holographic Seeros-1 appeared on the far side of the room.

"You again," said Evaran.

Seeros-1 pointed up. "The projection system is independent of this room's power. You may have stopped our access to this room's specific systems, but the holography system was made for scenarios like this. I never thought it would get used, but here we are."

Evaran continued to access the interface. "What do you want?"

"I'm observing. That was quite a fight your little group put up." Seeros-1 pointed at Dr. Snowden and Jake. "They should have been neutralized."

Dr. Snowden's blood boiled. "Looks like you failed."

Seeros-1 chuckled. "Did we? We've already adjusted to your battle tactics. They were quite interesting. A glue-like material…I wonder how many plan defenses against that. Not only that, but the sheer amount of it was surprising. Those little devices seem to carry more than they should. You've helped us evolve not only our tactics, but also our robots, and oh…don't worry, more are coming."

"Then we'll fight them too!" said Jake, standing.

"Ahh, the small one. Well, the other small one. You're not as resilient as the others," said Seeros-1. He eyed Jelton. "You were impressive, though. It's obvious you have some battle experience. After we capture the others, your skills might be of use."

"I will always stand with my friends," said Jelton, rising.

"For now," said Seeros-1.

"Did you come here to taunt us?" asked Dr. Snowden.

Seeros-1 shook his head. "No. As I said, I'm making observations, and to ask about something that seems to be melting through the ground and coming this way. We can't detect whatever it is, but the effect is obvious." He glanced at Evaran. "Is this your doing?"

Evaran paused to glance at Seeros-1. "It is not." He focused back on the console.

"At the speed it's moving, it will crash into this room and decimate you all."

Evaran studied Seeros-1. "So you plan to destroy us."

"It's not ours. If this is some sort of bomb, our facility would be destroyed as well."

Evaran placed his hands behind his back. "Perhaps, but the portal will be closed."

Seeros-1 laughed. "Ohh…how naive. You think a simple explosion will take down the portal?"

"Possibly. Perhaps there is a faction you are unaware of that has set something in motion."

Seeros-1's eyes narrowed.

Dr. Snowden recalled that Evaran sometimes used disinformation as a tactic. If Seeros-1 thought that the room would be the epicenter of an explosion, he would probably clear the surrounding area. On top of that, Evaran mentioning another faction was meant to sow doubt. Another benefit was the stalling aspect. Dr. Snowden decided to help the masquerade.

"I guess if we're going to go, you're going with us," said Dr. Snowden.

Seeros-1 focused on Dr. Snowden. "Oh, I'm far away, but this is a waste. You should surrender now, and we can get you somewhere safe."

"So is that your plan? To scare us into submission? How do we know there is anything even coming? You're probably lying."

"And you're choosing to die. What a waste."

Evaran's icon activated inside Dr. Snowden's helmet.

"Move to the wall nearest the door," said Evaran over comms.

Dr. Snowden stood with assistance from Emily and joined the others as they moved.

"What are you doing?" asked Seeros-1. "Whatever is coming will destroy everything in the room regardless of where you are. I would have expected you to understand such basics."

"We have no confirmation of how fast this object is approaching, or what it is. However, I am more attuned to the environment than the others, and whatever is coming is near, and will arrive over there," said Evaran, stepping back to join the others while pointing at the opposite wall.

After a tense minute, Dr. Snowden flinched when the Torvatta melted through the wall. He rushed with the others to board. V's icon appeared on Dr. Snowden's helmet interior.

Everyone assembled on the ramp inside the shielding.

"What is this?" asked Seeros-1.

Evaran waved his arm out in an arc. "My ship."

"You *did* know what it was! Unfortunately for you, it will be captured too!"

The door burst open and light defense robots entered the room. They fired on the Torvatta's shielding with no effect.

"I do not believe so," said Evaran. "It is time to go. I am now aware of where this location is. You do not want me to come back."

Seeros-1 scrutinized Evaran. "You lied, but at least we know of you now. This will not be our last encounter."

Evaran and Seeros-1 locked gazes. Evaran motioned for everyone to go inside the Torvatta.

After a moment, they assembled in the command center.

"V, it is good to see you," said Evaran.

"Acknowledged. Dr. Snowden and Jake should go to the medical lab."

"I want to see that portal closed," said Dr. Snowden.

"Same," said Jake.

"Very well," said Evaran. "V, take us to the portal room."

"Acknowledged."

Dr. Snowden stood next to Evaran's chair. Taking a seat was Dr. Snowden's natural instinct when injured, but it would be too painful in his current condition. Jake apparently had the same thought. They could go to the medical lab afterward. Dr. Snowden wanted to see the portal close to put his mind at ease.

The Torvatta rotated. It burned through more rock as it moved forward.

Dr. Snowden enjoyed seeing the rock turn into a lavalike material and flow around the Torvatta's shielding.

After a moment, the Torvatta burst into the portal room.

Dr. Snowden studied the ring and the outline of the portal inside it.

"Extending shields," said V.

Once the shields were extended, a pulse caused the portal to dissipate.

Seeros-1's hologram appeared. "No!"

Heavy defense robots poured into the room and opened fire.

"V, take us out of here," said Evaran.

"Acknowledged."

The Torvatta rose to the ceiling and burned through. As it ascended, melted rock dripped below. Ten minutes later, the Torvatta breached the surface and continued to ascend.

Dr. Snowden was mesmerized by the highly advanced city in the distance. Its white towers sparkled while ships approached.

"Analysis. The rest of the dirt has been cleared from the shielding. We are now in scan profile one and in stealth mode. They can no longer detect us."

Dr. Snowden observed the ships flying around the hole the Torvatta had created. "Where is this planet at exactly?"

"Timeline 492,341," said Evaran. "I have made a note to revisit this location to get more information later."

"Yeah, let's get right on that," said Emily.

Evaran eyed Emily.

She smiled. "Okay. Uncle Albert, Jake, to the med bay, stat!"

"Yes, ma'am," said Dr. Snowden.

Although relieved, the pain from his arm made sure he did not forget it was still broken. A good night's dinner and rest was on his agenda. He followed Jake into the medical room and gingerly rested on a slab.

Evaran and the others assembled in the room.

"I know there are a lot of questions, but we can address them after you all rest," said Evaran. He interacted with Dr. Snowden's and Jake's slab consoles.

V pricked Dr. Snowden and Jake with a syringe.

"That should take care of your healing," said Evaran.

Jake grinned at Dr. Snowden. "I guess racquetball is not an option for tonight."

The group chuckled.

Dr. Snowden stared at the ceiling. The medical nanobots worked with his cosmic ones in repairing his arm and he could feel them swimming around. Although it was painful, it was nowhere near what it had been before.

He smiled when Emily and Jelton laid hands on his shoulder. Evaran and V were over talking to Jake, and for the moment, everything seemed relaxed. Dr. Snowden had some questions now that the junction dimension connections were gone, but he was in no hurry. It was almost 10:00 p.m. Earth time, and it had been a long day. Sleep was in his immediate future.

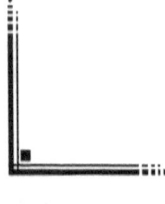

28

Jake scarfed down bacon and eggs. He had slept like a rock through the night as he was healed. Although his injured area no longer hurt, it was tender. As long as he did not plan to fight robots anytime soon, he figured he would be okay. Traveling with Evaran was always risky, but Jake loved every minute of it.

The Torvatta floated in low Earth orbit, and it was 9:10 a.m. the day after Ziekah had initially portaled everyone away. He chugged his carbonated orange drink when Dr. Snowden entered.

"Hey," said Dr. Snowden as he walked over to the matter replicator to get coffee.

Jake nodded. "Hey. What a fight, huh?"

Dr. Snowden sat across from Jake and took a sip of coffee. "Yeah." He grimaced. "Arm still hurts, but it's back to its normal state."

"The wonders of the Torvatta medbay."

They shared a chuckle and winced in unison.

"Yeah, we should probably avoid doing that," said Dr. Snowden.

Jake grinned. He enjoyed hanging out with Dr. Snowden. It pained Jake to know Dr. Snowden's ultimate fate, but Jake understood that was a topic never to be discussed. All he could do was enjoy moments like this as much as possible.

Emily and Jelton entered the room.

Jake noted that they looked refreshed. Both of their suits had been cleaned, and they seemed like they could go another round with the robots if needed. Jake was aware of Emily's ultimate fate as well, but Jelton's demise was unknown. At least Jake had had the chance to meet Jelton.

Emily and Jelton paused to stare at Jake.

"Is something wrong, my friend?" asked Jelton.

Jake cleared his throat and looked away. "Nah, it's nothing."

After a moment, Emily and Jelton took their seats with some food and drink.

Evaran and V, in projected mode, arrived and took their respective seats.

Evaran motioned at Jake and Dr. Snowden. "Your injuries have healed, but it will take some time for them to fully regenerated."

"Oh, we know," said Jake.

Dr. Snowden nodded. "Rest and relaxation for the immediate future."

Evaran nodded and focused on Emily and Jelton. "You both appear refreshed."

Emily smiled. "Nothing a good night's rest wouldn't fix."

"Excellent. If everyone is ready, I can begin."

Everyone nodded at Evaran, who interacted with the table console.

A projection shot up of a vertical line with several dots on it.

"We are going to check various points in time to ensure the timeline has been returned to its original state. Afterward, we will visit Sandas."

"I wondered if we would visit him," said Emily.

"Analysis. We can verify the state of information from after dealing with Salazar."

Emily nodded. "Cool."

Evaran raised a finger. "We will also give him his alternate timeline videos. I suspect he would be interested in those."

"That won't mess anything up timeline-wise, will it?" asked Jake.

"No. Sandas is somewhat unique in his knowledge and can be trusted."

Jake grinned. "Awesome. I get to meet the information broker for real this time."

Evaran nodded. "After meeting with Sandas, we will drop you and Jelton off."

"Jelton has to stay for a cookout!" said Jake.

"I would be honored," said Jelton.

"We can do that." Evaran gestured at V. "After we visit Sandas, take us back here to 7:00 p.m. and notify Lord Noskov and Lord Vygon of our arrival. That should give them twenty minutes to get the grill out."

"Acknowledged."

"Do you think this is the last we will see of the Seeros League?" asked Emily.

"I do not," said Evaran. "One Seeros was difficult enough to deal with. A group from across the timelines bearing a grudge will not sit idly by."

Jelton raised his head a bit. "The Rift Guardians stand ready should you need us."

"It is appreciated. However, I do not think the Seeros League will make its presence known for a long time. If they do, a more permanent solution may be required. They have been warned and given a chance to exist. What they do with that is up to them and they will not be given a second opportunity if they decide to misuse it."

Jake was not sure if the others noticed, but Evaran's tone was a bit colder than what Jake remembered from when he had first met Evaran.

"Sounds fair enough," said Dr. Snowden.

"Any other questions before we check the timeline?" asked Evaran.

"I would like any information on the connections and junction dimension. It will help the Rift Guardians," said Jelton.

"V will get you whatever you need."

Jelton nodded at V.

Evaran looked around. "Okay, let us check the timeline."

The group assembled in the command center.

Jake slid into his seat in the left U-shaped seating area as everything outside the Torvatta faded away and then eased back in.

"Analysis. It is now January 30, AD 1933," said V.

"Hitler again?" asked Jake.

Evaran nodded. "We should not detect Ziekah in the same room. V, take us down."

"Acknowledged."

The Torvatta began to descend. After twenty minutes, they hovered out of visual range of the Chancellery building and an excited crowd watching Hitler from a window.

"Analysis. Ziekah's signature was not detected."

"Excellent," said Evaran. "Let us visit two more timeline checkpoints. V, take us to the Delaware River in AD 1776."

"Acknowledged."

As the Torvatta rose, Dr. Snowden smiled. "George Washington crossing the river."

Evaran nodded.

"Look at Mr. History," said Emily with a grin.

"I've studied some!" said Dr. Snowden.

After twenty minutes to orbit, a jump back in time, and another twenty minutes back down, the Torvatta hovered over a segment of the Delaware River.

"Analysis. It is now December 25, AD 1776," said V.

Jake studied the flatboat ferry that had been outlined. On it were horses, cannons, and troops. The area of river being crossed was approximately three hundred yards per the data label, and it was night out with snow falling. The torches lit up the area surrounding the ferry, and it looked like there were cables of some sort.

Emily walked over to the front wall. She pointed at the outline of a man leaning against a cannon. "There's George Washington!"

"Analysis. This matches the Torvatta's historical record."

Evaran nodded.

Jelton stood next to Emily and slipped a hand around her waist. "Humanity seems to enjoy war."

Emily smiled. "Yeah. I've read about this event so often. This is so cool to see it."

"Thankfully they won't see the Torvatta being outlined by the snow falling," said Dr. Snowden, wagging a finger. "That could've made it into a painting!"

Evaran half smiled. "But it did not. V, take us to the last timeline checkpoint."

"Acknowledged."

The Torvatta went to low orbit, jumped back in time, then descended.

"Analysis. It is August 25, AD 79."

Emily examined the front wall. "This must be the Pompeii explosion!"

Evaran nodded.

Jake studied the ash and pumice in the air. "Wow. That city looks like it's about to have a bad day."

"It did," said Emily, looking around. "Be glad we're in the Torvatta for this event."

"Analysis. Historical records match."

"Very good," said Evaran. "If Ziekah's influence was still present, this city would not exist as she would have detected the unstable nature of Mount Vesuvius. The timeline appears to be stable." He looked around. "Who is ready to visit Sandas?"

Emily smiled big and took her seat along with Jelton.

Jake relaxed as he watched Emily rattle off historical facts to Jelton about Pompeii. Dr. Snowden jumped in with his own facts, and Jake enjoyed the friendly atmosphere and being able to be a part of it.

The mere mention of Sandas seemed to make both Dr. Snowden and Emily happy. Jake's heartbeat shot up as he thought about getting to meet the real Sandas, the mythical information broker. Jake clasped his hands as he smiled and looked around. Despite the dangers of traveling with Evaran, it was moments like this that Jake truly enjoyed.

Emily smiled when labels popped up showing they were in the Gyradack system near a planet called Intara III. Her brow wrinkled when she noted the time. It was roughly one hour after they had dropped Sandas off when dealing with Salazar from a previous adventure. She chuckled thinking of how surprised Sandas would be. Her muscles relaxed as the icy world came into view when they descended from orbit.

"Analysis. It is April 16, 2008, 1:00 p.m., one hour after our last visit," said V.

"Cool," said Emily.

"An interesting location for a base," said Jelton, peering around.

"It's a secret base," said Dr. Snowden. "From Sandas's perspective, we would have just dropped him off from our adventure dealing with Salazar."

Evaran nodded. "Yes, and we arrived at this time because we know where he is."

"Makes sense," said Dr. Snowden.

"I can't wait to meet the real information broker!" said Jake.

Emily laughed. "He's just like the one we met in the alternate timeline."

"Cool."

After twenty minutes, the Torvatta breached a body of water near some massive icy landmasses.

"V, contact Sandas," said Evaran.

"Acknowledged," said V. He interacted with the front console. "Communication protocol accepted. Relaying visual."

"Hello, hello!" said Sandas, appearing in a window that spawned on the front wall. He looked around. "You're back! With some new friends too!"

Evaran half smiled. "It is good to see you again, Sandas, and it has been some time for us since we last met. We determined you would be here at this point in time and wanted to verify some things and also stop in to visit."

"Of course," said Sandas, grinning big. "I'm irresistible even across space and time." He winked at Emily.

Everyone shared a laugh.

"I've unlocked the docking bay. I'm sure you remember how to get to it."

Evaran nodded. "We will meet shortly."

The communication window closed.

"Just like I remembered him," said Emily.

Dr. Snowden chuckled. "I wonder what he'll think of seeing his alternate self."

"He'll love it," said Emily.

"Yeah, probably."

After another ten minutes, the Torvatta had entered and landed inside Sandas's base's docking bay. Once it was pressurized, the group exited the Torvatta.

Emily grinned when Sandas, still wearing a beige suit with gadgets everywhere, walked out. Goggles rested above his eyes. It was the same setup from when he had last traveled in the Torvatta.

Sandas smiled big as he approached. "I wasn't expecting a visit so soon!"

Emily rushed over and gave him a big hug.

"Well, someone's missed me!" said Sandas as he placed a furry paw on her back. After she stood back, Sandas studied her. "You've had a rough experience."

"You're reading me again," she said, eying him.

He laughed. "Of course, I'm the information broker!"

Evaran gestured at Jake and Jelton. "With us are Jake Melkins, and Jelton Stallryn, a Rift Guardian from another timeline and dimension."

"Oh!" said Sandas as he shook hands with Evaran, Dr. Snowden, then Jelton and Jake. "Now that's an interesting pair." He tilted his head at V. "A new mode." Sandas walked around with his furry finger in the air. "Holographic shell. Yes, yes, I like it."

V smiled.

"Hah! And you can show emotion!" said Sandas, pointing at V.

"Analysis. It is called projected mode."

"Excellent!"

"I'm curious if you can read Jake and Jelton," said Emily.

Everyone except Sandas gave her a quizzical look.

She chuckled. "Sandas read everyone last time he was on the Torvatta. It's a freaky skill."

"He did?" asked Dr. Snowden.

She nodded.

"Very well," said Sandas. He walked around Jake, who turned to keep up. "Human. Let's see. As Evaran doesn't just let anyone travel with him, and the only humans I know of that he has were allowed due to being rescued, I suspect Jake was as well." Sandas peered at the PSD in Jake's hand. "He wields the PSD with confidence. This tells me he has traveled with Evaran before."

"Wow," said Jake.

Sandas raised his furry hand. "I'm not done yet! When you walked out of the Torvatta, your face lit up when you looked at Evaran. You have a special bond with him. You also had a recent injury as you touched your stomach several times. For that matter, Dr. Snowden was injured too, on the right arm."

Dr. Snowden's brows rose. "That's impressive."

Sandas grinned big as he walked around Jelton.

"I welcome your assessment, my friend," said Jelton.

"Hmm," said Sandas, rubbing his snout. "You're a fighter. Your loadout indicates proficiency in close to medium-range combat. My scan of you indicated the presence of something unusual, similar to what Dr. Snowden, Emily, Evaran, and V possess. I suspect it's cosmic energy, and there's something else in you…" He smiled. "You also have a close relationship with Emily, perhaps her boyfriend."

"How could you tell?" asked Jelton.

"You slapped her butt on the way down. Your arm would be broken unless she was okay with it," said Sandas.

Jelton laughed. "This is an accurate assessment."

Emily eyed Jelton.

Sandas chuckled. "The marking on your armor indicates you possess some level of power in whatever group you're in. Based on the armor's elaborate detail and the confidence in your walk, I'm going to guess you're a leader. That would be who I expect to travel with Evaran."

"You are very talented," said Jelton.

"Of course I am!" said Sandas. "But I don't think Evaran came all this way for a social visit, although I don't mind that at all!"

"You are correct," said Evaran. "I need to verify the state of information in your systems. We fought an entity from another dimension who hopped around and changed the timeline. She has been dealt with, and I need to ensure that everything is as it should be. I need to check the information image from when we were last here to now."

"Of course, of course, but you could've done that by accessing a satellite or visiting a city. No, no, there's something else!"

Evaran half smiled. "As always, you are quite perceptive. In the altered timeline, your alternate version helped us out."

Sandas paused for a moment as he studied Evaran. "And... do you have any recordings of that encounter?"

"I do, and while we compare information states, we can watch the recordings as a group."

Sandas smiled big. "I figured something along those lines, unless Emily was extra excited to see me."

Emily eyed Sandas.

He chuckled. "How long has it been since we last met from your perspective?"

"Several months," said Evaran. "You will also enjoy seeing Max in the videos."

Sandas's eyes lit up. He moved to the front of the group and did a flourish with his arms. "Then follow me as I show you the wonders of my secret ice base."

Emily laid a hand on Sandas's shoulder. "We're really glad to see you. Lead on."

Sandas looked around. "This last adventure must have been tough."

"It was," said Jake.

"Yeah," said Dr. Snowden. He smiled. "I'm curious to get your thoughts on your alternate self."

"Hah!" said Sandas, clapping his hands. "Ever the scientist. C'mon!" He waved forward.

Emily smiled as Jelton grabbed her hand and they followed Sandas. She took a slow look around the group. This was her family and friends. Her eyes misted. Despite Ziekah's best efforts to break everyone up, the group had held strong. Even Sandas in his alternate timeline version had helped. She caught Evaran studying her. It made her wonder what he thought about at times like this. She was just glad to be near him and where she was.

29

Although Jake was glad to be back on Earth, he had enjoyed spending a few hours at Sandas's base. It surprised Jake that Sandas was almost a clone personality-wise of his alternate version. Jake noted that Emily and Sandas seemed to have a special connection as they passed inside jokes, one after another. When they recreated the scene where Max had spun Sandas around after being reunited, Jake could barely contain himself. He understood why Sandas had such a good standing with Evaran and the others.

As Jake had grown up, he had always imagined the information broker as a mysterious alien with cloaking technology. Sandas was easy to spot in a crowd, though, and his easygoing personality and somewhat fast-talking nature made Jake think most ignored Sandas if they saw him, something that would be very useful as a broker. What caught Jake's attention was the warm and immediate acceptance by Sandas, who treated Jake like they had been friends forever. Definitely a perk of being associated with Evaran.

Jake leaned against a guardrail as he surveyed the rock outcropping outside Lord Noskov's base high up in the Appalachian Mountains. The area had three landing pads that jutted out, and the Torvatta rested on one of them. A warm light breeze wafted through the air, and the smell of burgers and other grilled foods filled his nostrils. Soft music played in the background, and everyone seemed relaxed.

Jake grinned when he watched Robert, his dad, interact with Emily and Jelton off to the side. Lord Noskov, Lord Vygon, Mikhail, Dr. Snowden, and V had cornered Evaran by the open grill and were rapid-firing questions. That was not uncommon. Lord Vygon and Lord Noskov always had a list, ranked by priority, for when Evaran was around.

Emily and Robert joined Evaran and the others while Jelton walked over to Jake.

"Your father is an interesting person," said Jelton.

Jake nodded. "Yeah, he can be."

Jelton looked out over the edge and into the dense forest. "Back to where we began."

"Yep, but I'll always go should Evaran need me."

"Me too, my friend."

Jake grinned at Jelton. "I'd still like to visit your head-quarters at some point."

"Gowldin and I would enjoy that. I've already talked with Evaran and Emily, and the next time Emily comes out, you're more than welcome to come along with her."

"Really?" asked Jake. His heartbeat accelerated.

"Of course."

Jake grinned big. "Awesome. I've only heard stories, and I got to see your prisoner planet."

Jelton nodded. "Our headquarters are a bit more interesting."

"I bet," said Jake. He sighed. "Sometimes this all feels like a dream."

"I can understand that. Evaran's adventures can have that effect."

They shared a laugh.

"What's going on over here?" asked Emily, smiling as she joined them.

"Enjoying the moment," said Jake.

Emily nodded as she leaned in and kissed Jelton on the cheek.

"I guess you'll be off to your next adventure," said Jake, looking out.

"Actually, we still have a few Wild Haven classes to go to with Dr. Bryson and Karen," said Emily.

Jake chuckled. "I meant that you could go on another adventure and be back a few minutes later after leaving, similar to our visit to Sandas."

"Ohh, yeah," said Emily. "In this case, Jelton will portal back and Uncle Albert and I spend a few months here. Evaran says it's for us to not forget our roots." She eyed Jake. "You'll get to fly us out to Wild Haven as always."

Jake smiled. "Of course."

Jelton tilted his head. "I'd like to visit this Wild Haven sometime."

"Whenever you want," said Jake.

He had enjoyed flying Dr. Snowden, Emily, Dr. Bryson, and Karen out to upstate New York to the Wild Haven Institute. The classes they attended were meant to introduce new aliens and nonhumans to the world of humans in a safe environment. Jake had gone to it in the past, but after the Caltorus incident and Earth Ward formation, it had opened its doors wider and expanded.

Evaran motioned at Jake.

"All right, looks like Evaran wants me to come over."

Jelton nodded. "Go, my friend." He crossed his arms in an X pattern across his chest and bowed slightly.

Jake returned the Rift Guardian salute. He found it fascinating that he would be one of the few humans ever to recognize and use it. After giving Emily a light hug, Jake walked over to Evaran, who was surrounded by Lord Noskov, Lord Vygon, and V.

"What's up?" asked Jake.

Evaran half smiled. "I was telling Lord Vygon and Lord Noskov about the events that occurred. They will undoubtedly want to learn more from you, so I wanted to say this in front of them. You can be candid in what you tell them, but only them."

"Got it," said Jake.

Lord Noskov shook his head. "This Ziekah must have really irritated you to banish her from existence."

"Only from our timeline," said Lord Vygon. He bared his fangs. "She is now serving time in Jelton's timeline."

"Analysis. She is on a prison planet."

Lord Vygon nodded.

Lord Noskov gestured at Lord Vygon. "He never tells me about future events or knowledge until an event occurs."

"As it should be," said Evaran. He eyed Jake. "I heard Pozarra refer to you as an anchor."

Lord Vygon raised a finger. "And that is all you should hear…for now."

Evaran studied Lord Vygon and Jake. "I see. I suspect my future forms come here often, and possibly before this moment in time. That would be how Lord Vygon did not know about this event although he has future knowledge. My future self did not tell him about it nor did the Torvatta."

"I can't tell you anything about that," said Lord Vygon.

Jake laughed.

They stared at him.

"Sorry, it's funny how out of sync personal timelines can get. I need to make a chart sometime."

Evaran eyed Jake.

"A mental chart!"

Evaran half smiled. "It is okay."

"We still have some things to talk about," said Lord Vygon.

Jake smiled. "And…that's my cue to exit."

Evaran laid a hand on Jake's shoulder. "Go. We will talk later."

Jake nodded at the others and walked over to Dr. Snowden, Robert, and Mikhail. "Hey."

Robert grinned. "Evaran talking mysterious again?"

"He always does," said Jake, glancing at Dr. Snowden.

Dr. Snowden chuckled. "That's Evaran."

"Yes, it is," said Mikhail.

Jake liked that Robert and Dr. Snowden had become good friends. It could be an age thing, but they seemed to share a similar spirit. Maybe that was why Jake had taken to Dr. Snowden so easily.

"I guess we have a few months of Wild Haven classes ahead of us," said Dr. Snowden.

"Yeah. I actually like them," said Jake.

"Thankfully, I don't need them," said Mikhail.

Jake grinned. "Not all of us are over a hundred years old." The group chuckled.

Robert smiled. "Normally I'd say for Jake to get a degree, but I don't think nonhuman studies is something marketable."

"Unless you work for them," said Jake with a grin.

"Does the Earth Ward give you jobs or anything?" asked Dr. Snowden.

Jake shrugged. "Sorta. I usually fly specific people around. Executives or special contractors and the like. Sometimes it's just delivery of a message or cargo." He gestured at Mikhail. "I drag him along sometimes too."

"That's interesting. I'd be interested in hearing about that at some point." Dr. Snowden studied Jake. "On another note, I envy that you've met Evaran's other plane forms."

Jake swallowed hard. "Yeah. I mean, it's cool, but...I like this form the best, although I like them all in general. It's still Evaran, just...different."

"I met one already—well, one of the eight forms that entered the plane. She was interesting."

Jake smiled. "I wish I got to meet her."

Robert shook his head. "How strange it is that we can have these types of discussions."

"I'm just glad to be able to. Otherwise I'd probably be locked up," said Jake.

Dr. Snowden chuckled. "Speaking of which, is Evaran letting Lord Vygon and Lord Noskov view the alternate timeline videos?"

Jake nodded. "Apparently they already met Sandas, I guess from a previous trip Evaran took them out on." He eyed Mikhail. "Did you meet Sandas as well?"

"I did. He talks *fast*," said Mikhail.

"Huh, I wasn't aware Evaran took them on a trip," said Dr. Snowden.

"Me either. I seem to run into that a lot," said Robert, eying Jake.

Jake sighed. "You know I can't say much about some of the stuff I learn."

"It's okay, son," said Robert, laying a hand on Jake's shoulder. "Burger?"

"You know it!" said Jake.

"Count me in," said Dr. Snowden.

Jake laughed as he watched Robert and Dr. Snowden huddle around the grill. This moment in time was unique and rare, and Jake knew the time was coming when he would never see Dr. Snowden and Emily again. Jake's throat constricted. They shared a unique bond with Evaran like Jake did, and he had formed a bond with Dr. Snowden and Emily. Jake wished the night could go on forever. All he could do was enjoy every day as it came, and make the most of it.

"Jake?" asked Dr. Snowden, handing Jake a plate with a burger on it.

Jake took the plate. "Sorry. Thinking."

"I'm rubbing off on you," said Dr. Snowden, smiling. "Enjoy the burger."

Jake laughed. "On it."

Jelton enjoyed talking with everyone, and with his arm around Emily and looking out over a dense forest, it reminded him that one day the Riven might have a world that allowed for events like this. His mind drifted briefly back to the colony the Riven had tried to establish under Rift Guardian control. The defenses had not been enough to stop a Time Warden assault. Better preparation would be needed.

"Beautiful, isn't it?" asked Emily.

Jelton nodded. "Earth is a beautiful planet, with a lot of defense."

"I guess you could say that," said Emily, chuckling.

"Earth has a strong nonhuman presence and the Earth Ward. Outside of that, there is the Kreagan Star Empire, and if there are any major timeline issues, there is Evaran. It's a layered defense that many places do not have."

"Yeah. It'd be cool for the Rift Guardians to set up something here, or near Earth."

Jelton studied Emily. "An interesting idea."

Evaran joined them. "Jelton, I have a request I would like to run by you and Gowldin."

"Of course," said Jelton.

Evaran nodded. "I wanted to give Lord Vygon and Lord Noskov your portal coordinates, but only them. They can be trusted and would be interested in not only maintaining contact, but also learning about the prison planet. It would also be good to share knowledge with each other."

"I thought Earth was not to receive advanced technology," said Jelton.

"That is correct. However, any knowledge shared with them by the Rift Guardians would be isolated from Earth, and even the Earth Ward. Yes, it would give Lord Noskov and Lord Vygon an edge, but as they are two of the most powerful nonhumans on the planet and have proven themselves to be capable stewards, I do not think it would be an issue."

Jelton laughed. "You don't need to ask. You're Evaran."

"It would be inappropriate of me to share your portal coordinates without asking," said Evaran.

Jelton smiled. "You're a god to the Riven, my friend. Even in your plane form. The fact you did ask and possess the power you have once again shows that you're not corrupt and why you have the status you do. The Rift Guardians have removed the past gods of lore and replaced them with you and Syrilus."

"It is appreciated, but I am not a god."

"Close enough to one. We understand how the plane was formed, and after my resurrection, there is no doubt in their minds," said Jelton. He laid a hand on Evaran's shoulder. "You may not consider yourself a god, but to us, you are, and to serve with you is the highest honor."

Evaran eyed Jelton.

Jelton chuckled. "I can introduce Lord Vygon and Lord Noskov to Gowldin. Perhaps Jake can come and I can give him a tour of our headquarters."

"He would enjoy that," said Evaran, looking at Jake in the distance. Evaran gestured in another direction off in the distance.

Lord Vygon and Lord Noskov joined the group.

"Jelton is in agreement about the portal coordinates," said Evaran. He waved a finger between Lord Vygon and Lord Noskov. "Only you two will be aware of it, and I will put a restriction on the rift door podium that the coordinates can only be activated if it senses either of you."

Lord Vygon and Lord Noskov shook hands with Jelton.

"I'm looking forward to seeing your headquarters," said Lord Vygon.

Jelton tilted his head. "I understand you're out of sync in terms of knowledge, and you know the future to some degree. I sense that you and Lord Noskov will visit a lot."

Lord Noskov crooked a thumb at Lord Vygon. "He never tells me anything until it occurs."

"His rules," said Lord Vygon, gesturing at Evaran.

Jelton nodded. "I understand. You both are welcome, and I will get you the proper credentials and protocols for coming across. I look forward to our many discussions." He crossed his arms in an X pattern across his chest and slightly bowed.

Lord Vygon and Lord Noskov looked at each other for a moment, then returned the Rift Guardian salute.

"You're always welcome here as well," said Lord Noskov.

"We know that you will probably use the Torvatta's portal, but ours is open to you," said Lord Vygon.

Jelton smiled at Emily. "When Evaran is away, I could still visit."

Emily bumped him with her hips. "You better, mister."

The group chuckled.

It was not lost on Jelton at how rare a moment like this was. Two of Earth's most powerful nonhumans, alongside Evaran, and Emily, who he was intimate with, all in one spot. Jelton cherished moments like this. When he reported on any interaction with Evaran, Gowldin hung on every word. Emily's suggestion about having some presence near Earth danced around in his mind. A remote possibility, but much closer with a portal connection.

Lord Vygon motioned at the base's interior. "Care for a tour of our facility? The portal is here as well, so we can visit that too."

"Lead on, my friend," said Jelton. He grabbed Emily's hand and followed Lord Vygon and the others.

As they approached the base, Dr. Snowden, Jake, Robert, and V joined up.

"Tour time?" asked Jake.

"Indeed," said Lord Noskov.

"Awesome."

Jelton smiled as he continued on. He was surrounded by friends on a protected planet. Earth would potentially be a strong ally in the years to come, and he looked forward to helping establish that rapport. Lord Vygon's warm embrace and knowledge of the future made Jelton think they would have a good relationship. The night seemed like it would end on a good note.

Emily squeezed his hand.

He smiled at her as they entered the base.

Dr. Snowden surveyed the Torvatta roof. Jelton had already left via the portal in Lord Noskov's base, and Lord Vygon and the others had retreated into the base for the night. It was 11:00 p.m., and Evaran, V in projected mode, Emily, and Dr. Snowden were on the Torvatta's roof.

Dr. Snowden leaned on the roof's guardrail and looked out. His muscles relaxed. The Appalachian Mountains were beautiful at night, and the shielding allowed the crisp air to gently wash over the roof. A bright moon provided illumination, although the base's dim exterior lighting did pollute it some.

Emily sighed. "I wish the night lasted longer."

"Analysis. You miss Jelton already."

"Yeah…but he has some things to deal with."

Evaran nodded. "You will meet him again soon. Your daily routine here on Earth can resume without Ziekah interrupting it."

Dr. Snowden chuckled. "We hope anyways. I bet the Seeros League is going to come here at some point."

"Perhaps. However, they have been given a warning. The destruction of their portals should be some insight into our capabilities should they decide to violate that warning."

"Analysis. They would get their asses beat."

Everyone stared at V.

"Jake said that is what would happen if they attacked this timeline."

The group laughed.

Emily slapped V on the back. "V, you're getting wild!"

"Acknowledged."

Dr. Snowden rubbed his chin. "When we were leaving the facility where the Seeros League had their portal, I observed an advanced city in the distance. I'm thinking they expanded beyond that planet."

"I concur," said Evaran. "There were thousands of Seeroses listed from the information I obtained, and I do not expect they would stay contained to one planet. They have the technology and drive to expand, but I do not believe they have altruistic intentions."

"That's just great," said Dr. Snowden.

"Did you get any more information from the console in that room we were in?" asked Emily.

Evaran nodded. "The extractors, and the damage they caused, were listed there. The timelines they traveled to remain unknown, but the portals they took are known. I will map them at some point."

"That could take some time," said Emily.

"I will do so while you are playing volleyball and Dr. Snowden is teaching."

Emily eyed Evaran.

He half smiled. "I will only do it in scan profile one and stealth mode and can be back a minute after I leave."

"Well, I'd definitely be interested in seeing what you find," she said.

"Me too," said Dr. Snowden. He furrowed his brow. "I had a question on Jake being called an anchor by Pozarra. What did she mean by that?"

Evaran half smiled. "I suspect she is referring to the fact that my future versions check in with him. As such, he would be an anchor for my forms to compare against from a human perspective."

"Okay, that's what I figured, but I wanted to verify that with you," said Dr. Snowden.

"I guess that means we aren't around to do that," said Emily.

"Perhaps not," said Evaran. "However, I believe there are several anchors. Lord Vygon is one, and I suspect Sandas is as well."

"Sandas?" asked Emily.

Evaran nodded. "If you recall from our first meeting, he mentioned that this form is stiff relative to others, indicating he has seen other forms."

"Oh, yeah, I remember that," said Dr. Snowden. "I guess, then, we should just enjoy what time we have."

"You should always strive to enjoy any time you may have."

"You probably take on other companions, then," said Emily.

Evaran half smiled. "I suspect I would. I appreciate the human perspective on events. It allows me to consider different views of a situation."

"Analysis. I provide the AI perspective."

"Yes, you do," said Evaran.

V smiled.

Evaran eyed Dr. Snowden. "On another topic, how did you like the new PSD patterns?"

"I love them," said Dr. Snowden.

"And you?" asked Evaran, looking at Emily.

"Same. It really helped out with the flying thing," said Emily.

Evaran eyed Emily. "Are you still adjusting to losing cosmic energy from a while back?"

She shrugged. "Yeah, but it's nowhere near what it used to be. I've accepted it, and realize that with the PSD and the ability to slow things down by concentrating, I'll be okay. I had no major problems when I got zapped back in time."

"That is good to hear."

"My big concern was that the timeline would change and I end up stuck underground in rock or something," said Emily.

"Yeah, that wouldn't be fun," said Dr. Snowden. "I'd love to go visit Thereze, but since that never happened, it might be odd."

Emily chuckled. "I'd like to meet Kotys, but yeah, would be odd."

"We can search and determine where they are now and if they are alive," said Evaran.

"That's cool," said Emily.

Dr. Snowden raised a finger. "Speaking about traveling in the past, what should we do if it ever happens again? There has to be a way to contact the Torvatta. A quantum beacon is too big to be carrying around, but there might possibly be another way."

Evaran rubbed his chin. "I am not sure, but it is something that I can research."

"Analysis. Perhaps the dimensional energy powering Dr. Snowden and Emily's suits can be enhanced with a dimensional pocket containing a quantum beacon."

"Hmm, it is worth looking into," said Evaran. He studied their suits for a moment. "It is a good place to start. Another option is to determine if the quantum beacon's form factor can be refactored."

"Sounds good to me," said Dr. Snowden. "In regard to contacting the Torvatta, I'm guessing your future form saw the timeline change, and also our requests."

"Yes, but as mentioned earlier, if it is another form's companions, the Torvatta would refuse the request unless authorized by the plane form on the Torvatta."

"But you would already be aware of the event since it's a future version of you," said Dr. Snowden.

Evaran nodded. "And I would know not to interfere."

"Although that sucks, I understand," said Emily.

Evaran examined Dr. Snowden and Emily. "On another topic, you both now have additional memories of events that no longer exist in the timeline. Does that bother you?"

Emily shrugged. "Getting used to it at this point."

"Yeah, same here," said Dr. Snowden.

Evaran nodded. "Do you find it difficult to determine what is real and what is not?"

Dr. Snowden laughed. "You always ask that. I think we can handle a few false memories."

Evaran half smiled. "It is always good to check. You do not want to wake up screaming like you have in the past."

"What?"

"Analysis. Evaran is teasing you."

Dr. Snowden eyed Evaran.

"I was," said Evaran. "If any symptoms from false memories appear, please let me know."

Dr. Snowden sighed. "Let's hope we never get any."

"Yeah, what he said," said Emily.

Evaran nodded.

Dr. Snowden smiled. "You know, I never came across the junction dimensions in the planar cartography lab. I assume the ones we traveled through are there now. Are there any others like that?"

"They are viewable there," said Evaran.

"Huh. There's so much information there, I can only imagine what I haven't seen. There may be unknown things there because I've never searched for them or even had an idea they existed," said Dr. Snowden.

"You can do a search on dimensions, but make sure to filter it."

"Will do."

Emily wrinkled her brow. "Jelton said that Lord Vygon and Lord Noskov could use their portals to connect to the

Rift Guardian headquarters. Do you think if technology is shared it will be an issue?"

"Perhaps," said Evaran. "However, I trust all involved to do what is right."

Dr. Snowden grinned. "Maybe I'll search for a Rift Guardian presence around Earth in the planar cartography lab."

"They do have some presence in the future, although only for a brief period in time," said Evaran.

"They do?" asked Emily.

Evaran nodded. "This is not the timeline they settle in."

"Huh, I wonder why. It seems like a safe place if they wanted to come."

"There are…factors."

Emily nodded.

"I'll still poke around in the lab," said Dr. Snowden. He looked around. "I guess it's go-home time. We were portaled on a Thursday night, and today is Friday. I'm sure the college is wondering where I was. I'll need to contact them and tell them I took a sick day or something."

"Yeah, me too," said Emily. "Although I guess we could just go back to this morning and do it."

"V, take us to this morning so Dr. Snowden and Emily can call in, then take us to their backyard at our current time."

"Acknowledged."

The Torvatta lifted off the landing pad, then took off flying northwest.

After a few minutes in the air, the Torvatta paused.

Everyone focused on V.

"Analysis. We forgot something."

Dr. Snowden glanced at Emily, then back at V. "What?"

"Everything is as it should be," said V, smiling.

The group laughed as the Torvatta continued on.

THE END

EPILOGUE

Seeros-1 glanced around the empty circular room as he pondered what he would say to the other Seeroses. The speed at which Evaran and his group had arrived and taken away the portal astonished Seeros-1. Even with tough defenses, they had defied the odds. This was a new era for the Seeros League, and he had called a meeting of the council, the first ten Seeroses to be extracted from other timelines.

Seeros-1 waved his hand in the air, and the environment went dark.

One by one, the other Seeroses began to appear as holographic images. As they were on different planets, their appearance took some time.

Seeros-1 waited until the other nine members had appeared. He looked around at each one before speaking. "As you're aware…we've had a setback."

"So we've heard," said Seeros-2. "What happened?"

Seeros-1 sighed. "You should all have the files by now. In short, one of our extractors seems to have provoked a powerful being known as Evaran, who decided to take our portal away."

"That's one of our highest security facilities!" said Seeros-7.

"Yes, it is ...and you should now be able to see what Evaran and his friends did."

Ten minutes passed as the other Seeroses checked out the video.

"He's powerful, but so are his friends," said Seeros-3.

"What's important here is how do we get our portal back?" asked Seeros-5.

Seeros-1 shook his head. "We only knew of the portal since I came through and brought you all through afterward. We can't get it back." He raised a finger. "However...that doesn't mean there aren't other portals. We know what to search for, and we control thousands of planets, each run by a version of us."

"If we do find one...there's no guarantee we won't run into Evaran, or another being like him," said Seeros-10.

Seeros-1 nodded. "We're all aware of that. We can use the interaction to learn how to protect the next portal we find. We've fought powerful beings before, but none with a ship that can apparently melt through the ground. Evaran was also faster than anything we've ever encountered."

"Perhaps we need to put some limitations on our extractors," said Seeros-2. "There are several hundred still out and about, and now they have no way back. If we do find another portal, we'll need to get in touch with the extractors and change their extraction protocol. Their activities are causing too many problems."

Seeros-1 grimaced. "We can discuss that later, but I concur."

Seeros-8 shook his head. "Evaran's friends used devices that should not be possible. They shot out that sticky substance, but where did all of it come from?"

"I suspect dimensional mechanics are at work," said Seeros-1. "Those devices should not function, yet they did. We need to get them so we can study them."

"Or we avoid whatever timeline Evaran is in," said Seeros-6.

The other Seeroses sighed.

"It's a valid point. If Evaran did this and gave us a warning, what would he do if we ignore that?"

"You always take the cautious route," said Seeros-1. "It amazes me that you survived as a Seeros in your timeline."

"I survived by being cautious. It's obvious that whatever extractor provoked Evaran was not, and here we are now, paying the price for that," said Seeros-6.

The other Seeroses jeered.

"All right, all right. Calm down," said Seeros-1. "I propose that we first begin looking for another portal, assuming another exists. While we're doing that, we can determine new policies for the extractors."

"We can also focus on *this* timeline. Maybe we have enough Seeroses," said Seeros-9. "There is a lot of galaxy left to explore and conquer, and even more beyond that."

"We can do both," said Seeros-1. "They're not mutually exclusive. By expanding, we might even find the portal on some new world."

The other Seeroses nodded.

"One last question," said Seeros-4. "Evaran said he handled the extractor. Do you think he killed it?"

"No," said Seeros-1. "Evaran seems like one of those protector types with the power to enforce his will. The fact that he could neutralize an extractor and traverse multiple connections shows his power and means he is probably unique. We got unlucky." He looked around the room. "One thing is clear."

The other Seeroses focused on Seeros-1.

"Evaran must die."

I hope you enjoyed the tenth book in the Evaran Chronicles! This book is a light-hearted journey, similar to *The Unification,* book 9 of the Evaran Chronicles. Dr. Snowden, Emily, and V get to deal with the past, and in particular, Earth's history. Although most books have the gang out and about, I wanted to showcase that historical periods are still visited.

This is a standalone and not part of a series arc, but it does advance the series. Jake Melkins gets to travel once again with Evaran, and their relationship since *The Shadow Connection,* book 6 of the Evaran Chronicles, is expanded on. Jake has a unique take on Evaran and his many forms, which will be touched on in later books. Jelton Stallryn also groups up with Evaran and Jake, and his status after the events of *The Cosmic Parallel,* book 8 of the Evaran Chronicles, is explored.

One thing to note is that since Dr. Snowden and Emily no longer possess the strength and power from books before, they have to rely upon their creativity with the PSD. This book focuses on some of that, with patterns for transportation and sleeping. In terms of cosmology, this book covers junction dimensions, and the concept of multi-timeline societies.

If you liked the book, and have the time and inclination, a review would go a long way in helping out this indie author. If you do submit a review, I'll put in a word to Evaran should you find yourself stuck in the far future and being harassed by Bargaltic entities! Want to be notified about new book releases? If so, you can sign up below.

www.AdairHart.com/MailingList.aspx

I will only send you email about new book releases, major updates, and the occasional newsletter, usually once a month. I dislike getting spammed too, so I will use this sparingly to keep you in the loop.

THE ΛUTHOR

I have been dreaming about fictional worlds since I was a kid. I devoured anything related to fantasy and science fiction. I developed a setting over the last twenty years and struggled to find a medium I could express it in. Several years ago I discovered I enjoyed writing. It is a passion of mine now, and exploring my setting with it has been an awesome journey.

I work in the information technology field and have my bachelor's and master's degrees in it. It has helped me to shape some of the concepts I write about. I also enjoy keeping up on futurology and science in general.

I live in central Ohio and enjoy walking, reading, gaming, learning, listening to music, and trying to keep up on my never-ending list of TV shows and movies to watch. If you want to contact me, you can do so on my website at

www.ΛdairHart.com

YOU CAN ALSO REACH ME ON

Facebook............................fb.com/AdairHart
Goodreads.....www.goodreads.com/AdairHart
Email..............Adair.Hart.Author@gmail.com

DEDICATION

To my grandparents, who continue to inspire me.
They may be gone now, but their life lessons and
legacy lives on with me.

ACKNOWLEDGMENTS

This was a great journey for me, but I wouldn't be here without the help of others. I would like to thank, in no particular order,

My editor, Eliza Dee, for providing an excellent service and helping me make my writing shine!

My cover artist, Tom Edwards (tomedwardsconcepts@gmail.com), for a great cover! It shows an isometric view of a junction dimension.

My family and friends who helped encourage me along the way.

My proofreader, Jade Hemming, for doing a great job in making that final pass to make sure everything looked good.

My formatter and interior designer, Colleen Sheehan (www.ampersandbookinteriors.com/), for once again being the professional she is! She is great to work with and I'm glad she works with me!

BOOKS

You can see all books in the Evaran Chronicles
and the Earthborn at

WWW.ADAIRHART.COM/SERIES/ALLBOOKS.ASPX